The Flower Book

By Catherine Law

The September Garden
The Flower Book

The Flower Book

CATHERINE LAW

Allison & Busby Limited
12 Fitzroy Mews
London W1T 6DW
www.allisonandbusby.com

First published in Great Britain by Allison & Busby in 2013.

A CIP catalogue record for this book is available from
the British Library.

First Edition

ISBN 978-0-7490-1116-1

Typeset in 11/16 pt Sabon by
Allison & Busby Ltd.

The paper used for this Allison & Busby publication
has been produced from trees that have been legally sourced
from well-managed and credibly certified forests.

Printed and bound by
CPI Group (UK) Ltd, Croydon, CR0 4YY

*This book is dedicated to
the memory of my grandparents*

'Here in your book, the buds and blooms you collected
ever since you were a little girl speak to me now.
Our very own language of flowers.'

– Aster Fairling

Part One

Violet
Cornwall, 1914

Chapter One

As many mists in March as there are frosts in May

On certain nights, if the wind was right, you could hear the sea from Old Trellick. So the legend has it, although Violet had never heard the waves and her parents would not try, due to the fact, she decided, that they had no imagination.

As a child she'd stand at the open French windows and implore them to be quiet, to stop what they were doing and to concentrate with her, to catch this magical and elusive sound.

'We're far too far away,' her cynical doctor father would tell her. 'Even if the breeze was coming right off the sea, we'd never hear it from here.'

And her mother would advise her not to be so silly. 'If you want to hear the sea, then go to the cove,' she'd say, not understanding.

But at night, Violet would lie in bed, her ears twitching

to catch the sound, imagining the rhythmic hum echoing from the cove up the steep ferny path, meandering over the hillocky meadow made rough by cattle, blowing up the lane to Old Trellick snug in the crook of the valley, right through her window and into her room. She longed to be rocked to sleep safe in the cradle of its consistent sighs and intangible whispering. But, in the silence of long dark nights, Violet knew that if the sea would not come to her, then indeed, she must go to it.

It was the first time this year that she'd been down to the cove. The tide would be full, the waves heavy. She wondered if the first sea holly might be sheltering in the dunes, the marram grass already robust and vivid. The path to the cove was steep, eroded into a gully, sheltered and silent. But as she walked down, she knew that at some point the pristine air would change in a blink and the sound of the sea would at last reach her, suddenly, forcefully, like the turning on of a tap.

She paused, letting her young cocker spaniel sniff around the roots of the hawthorn, and lifted her head to listen. Her nostrils prickled impatiently as she caught the fragrance of sea spray. But all she heard was the wind in her ears, the rattling of the branches, the song of the birds, and from over the stone hedge, the bawling of a newborn lamb.

'We're not there yet, Claudia,' she called out, 'not quite yet.'

Her friend who was a little way behind her, peering into the bushes, acknowledged her call with a wave and a grimace, to say wait for me.

Violet perched on a mossy pile of stones that had tumbled a long time ago from the wall and pulled the puppy's lead close. The russet spaniel quivered under the impact of the moving, breezy, scented world around him. His snout twitched furiously. She reached down with her finger to smooth his worried little brow.

'All right, Jess, sit. Sit, I say,' she cajoled him. 'Now we must both stay here and wait for Claudia.'

'Just looking for where the best elderflower bushes are. Mother wants to make wine,' her friend called out to her. 'Come autumn we won't be able to move in our kitchen for bottles and demijohns.'

Violet watched Claudia's narrow frame as she walked towards her. Her angular elbows had worn her blouse to threads and her skirt was an old school one she'd first had at fifteen, the hem let down many times. Her father was the farm manager at Charlecote and the family gleaned what they could from the hedgerows to make jam, pickles, preserves and a particularly good elderflower wine which Claudia's mother sold at Looe market.

'And there'll be some good blackberrying here, come August,' Claudia said, her pretty, fair-lashed eyes luminous with the thought of telling her mother so. 'Mother said specifically that I was to look, and note, and remember. Some lovely thick brambles pushing through up there. Jam galore.'

'I will look forward to it.' Violet met her smile, admiring the unchanging fairness of her friend's smooth cheeks, dashed with freckles. Then she nudged her puppy's flank with her toe.

'Not sure this one is up to the cove,' she said. 'Look at him shaking. He will be overwhelmed, will be dive-bombed by seagulls, carried off. Never to be seen again.'

Claudia grimaced in mock horror, then peered past Violet's shoulder. 'Are we nearly there?'

'A few more yards, I think.'

'Let's try it.'

The two girls linked arms, their giggles tight with anticipation. They took long strides, matching each other's pace, the little dog scurrying by their feet. And the moment met them. Was it a turn of a corner, a dip in the hedge, the change of the wind? Whatever happened, and it was different each time, the rushing, blasting voices of the sea suddenly hit them.

With a glance, a nod, a full understanding, together they cried out 'Now!' and ran, hurtling down the path, letting gravity pull them on, their ears now full of the heave and swell of the waves. The damp ferns retreated, and the gorse wore fiery yellow. The rocky ground gave way to short, shining grass and then sandy clefts, shifting dunes. And they ran in unison, their laughs hardly able to break out of their bodies as they hit the beach, the sparkling rocks and shallow cliffs now their cauldron and the sea before them an enormous and generous old friend.

Violet threw herself onto the silvery sand. It shifted, lightly and dryly beneath her, her palms pressing on fragments of shells, tiny crystalline pieces of pebble.

'Jess, where's Jess?' she panted.

'He's here, I have him,' cried Claudia. Her voice seemed far away, snatched by the wind.

They laughed now, heartily, as the sea spray moistened their throats. Claudia thumped down beside her and they rested their heads together. The sea was grey, not yet its summer blue, but it was perfect. Violet wound the lead tight around her wrist as Jess leapt and cowered behind them, offering minute yelps of terror.

'Poor little thing,' said Claudia. 'He doesn't know what's hit him.'

'God above,' said Violet, 'Will you look at the state of your skirt?'

The hem was rent with a huge, ragged rip.

'The gorse got me,' Claudia said, tugging at the fabric. 'This is never going to mend. Oh hell, Mother will kill me.'

Violet glanced down at her own skirt. It was new that season, a fine linen of periwinkle blue.

'Yours is intact, not a mark on it,' said Claudia. 'Thank goodness. You always have such nice clothes.'

'I want you to have it,' said Violet. 'I have three others, identical. I don't see why you should have to walk around in your old school skirt. You're a grown-up lady.'

'We don't behave like ladies, do we,' giggled Claudia. 'Not today, anyway.'

Violet lay back into the bed of sand and watched the pewter clouds bowling above her, across the sky. She felt Jess shuffle around her, inspecting her, pressing little dabs from his wet nose onto her cheek and her ears.

'We might have gone to different schools, but we always stayed friends. So glad we did,' mused Violet. 'I did wonder if we might have drifted apart when they sent me off to Exeter Priory.'

'No, never. That's why I stayed your friend, because you still liked to chat with me, and share with me, and come to the cove with me. Me, the little ragged girl from the farm who went to Chapel Street School in Looe.'

Violet supposed that the local church school didn't do Claudia any harm.

'No, but look, I'm still wearing the blessed uniform! I

used to like your school uniform, that lovely deep green.'

'Ugh, but the boater. Give me strength. I stuck out like a sore thumb whenever I came back on the omnibus for holidays and the odd weekend they let me out. Like being set free from a zoo.'

'And what about all the times you ran away?' Claudia teased her. Sitting up, she drew a wriggling Jess onto her lap, planting kisses on his silky ears.

Violet laughed. 'Not one of my finest moments. We don't like to talk about that.' Even so, the memory of her crawling out of a dorm window as dawn broke and running, running, into a short-lived freedom, still gave her a tingling thrill.

One of the many reasons, she assured Claudia, for running away was the deadly dreary lessons.

'Oh, but you loved nature studies, didn't you,' her friend reminded her. 'You love your wild flowers, your trees. You have your Flower Book.'

'But the teacher made me use the Latin names when all I know is coltsfoot, eyebright and cranesbill. She asked me to bring my Flower Book to the lessons, so that everyone could have a look. How *dare* she? I kept forgetting on purpose and then told her I'd lost it. But I especially loved the time we studied the poisonous plants.'

Claudia laughed, 'Look at you – you enjoyed that!'

'Deadly nightshade, of course, so obvious, plus hemlock and tansy.'

'Do you mean bitter buttons? I know that one,' confided Claudia. 'Those horrid little yellow flowers. My mother swore by it to bring herself on, when she was expecting me. She made a tea with it. Worked a treat. I was late and lazy, she said.'

Violet teased her that some things never change. 'Whereas I'm rebellious and ridiculous, according to my mother.'

She shivered, supposing that it really was a little chilly to be lying around in the sand. And what's more, they were both now eighteen. Weren't they a little too old to be playing on the beach? But Claudia had other things on her mind.

'Well, all things considered, you running away from school might have thoroughly vexed your parents but also would never have best pleased that gentleman over there . . .' Claudia squinted into the low sun, wrinkling her nose. 'Unmistakably him. I can tell by his silhouette. Even though the sun is burning out my eyes. Look at the way he walks. It's definitely him, isn't it. With his dogs. Must have come round the head. The tide's on its way out.'

Violet sat up, registering that Mr Weston Penruth was indeed approaching from the far side of the cove. She pulled impatiently at Claudia's arm.

'And why would it not please Mr Penruth that I may or may not have run away from school on the odd occasion?'

Claudia glanced quickly at her, blushing, giggling, telling her that *everyone* knows.

'Knows what? *Claudia!*'

'Come on, don't be modest. My mother told me years ago. You must realise that we all know . . .' Claudia paused as if relishing the nugget of gossip on the tip of her tongue '. . . that, in his wisdom, Mr Penruth, our very own Lordy, paid your school fees.'

The breeze took away Violet's shout of surprise. 'How did you all know! I only found out by chance when Papa let slip a few years ago, something about a bursary and me not needing one. Heavens, Claudia. You can't *all* know!'

15

She looked over to where Weston Penruth was walking and calling to his dogs, two boisterous black retrievers, who were bounding over the breaking waves. He was squire of Charlecote, the biggest landowner in this corner of Cornwall. Landlord to Claudia's father, and also of Old Trellick and, seemingly, benefactor wherever he picked and chose. Since the elder Mr Penruth died, a few years before, Weston was in charge of the estate and had become more formidable than ever. Violet had not seen him for a while, but reminded herself of what she always thought of when she saw him: aloof, fine-looking and exactly ten years her senior. That is, she thought, absolutely ancient. He walked, she noticed, with a peculiar air, wincing and stiff-backed, as if his jacket was far too tight across his shoulders. He moved gingerly, carefully, as if considering every muscle spasm.

Mr Penruth stopped then, to bellow at his dogs again and Violet watched him as he seemed to release a great sigh, as the wind whipped at his collar, drawing a flask from his greatcoat pocket, taking a nip.

'Still a drinker, I see,' whispered Claudia. 'Good God, he's seen us, and me with this awful ripped skirt.'

Violet commented that he could hardly have missed them here on this otherwise deserted beach. She got to her feet and brushed herself down.

'We better be polite, say good afternoon.'

Weston Penruth approached, taking a slow measured pace across the sand. Violet plucked Jess from the ground and held his quivery form to her bodice, feeling the tick of his heart, fixing a pleasant smile on her face. Claudia was mumbling with trepidation and Violet told her to shush.

'Good afternoon, Mr Penruth,' Violet called. 'How do you do? What a lovely day.'

He nodded, and took off his hat, revealing dark ruffled hair.

'How do you do, ladies? I see you have one of the Churchtown puppies, Miss Prideaux. A good choice, although he will be hard work. How are your parents? How are Dr and Mrs Prideaux?'

'Very well, sir,' Violet replied, wishing immediately that she had called him simply 'Mr Penruth'. She fought the desire to tilt her chin in defiance, to prove to herself and Claudia that she was not intimidated by him. Claudia, she noticed, kept her eyes on the sand.

'And you, Miss Ainsley?' he asked. 'I trust you are well?'

Claudia said she was, and then concentrated on tickling Jess around the snout as he strained to exit Violet's arms.

Weston then gazed around him, his eyes focusing far out to sea where the light broke through the milky clouds to sit in pools on top of the water. Then, as if remembering, looked suddenly at Violet, and spoke quickly, 'How rude, I have not asked you, Miss Prideaux, how you are—'

'Here come the dogs,' Violet cut in.

Weston turned and faced off the brutish onslaught of sopping-wet retrievers with a sharp bark of a command, and they ducked to the sand, panting.

'They're good dogs, Mr Penruth,' Violet said.

'Trained them myself.' He seemed to swell his broad chest out. He planted his hat back on his head. 'Well, I must be getting on.'

'Of course,' said Violet and she was amazed to see Claudia bob as if in curtsey.

They left too, for it would seem very strange to flop themselves back down onto the sand and loll about like schoolgirls while Mr Penruth was still walking on the beach. Hurrying back up the path, letting Jess scoot ahead of them, they panted and sweated under their high collars, their giggling breaking free again once they were inside the quiet seclusion of the path.

'Did you not notice? He has such a soft spot for you,' teased Claudia. 'No wonder he paid your school fees.'

'Well, I wish he hadn't. And I wish he didn't,' she muttered. 'Soft spot? That man is hard as granite. Did you not notice? He couldn't wait to get away from us. He was stiff with embarrassment. We are just silly little girls to him.'

'Oh no, no,' Claudia teased her. 'He likes you. You could do worse.'

Violet reminded her friend that she could also do a lot better.

'Have you ever noticed, he is always alone?' Claudia pondered. 'Somehow, that's quite appealing.'

'Alone with his dogs, yes,' said Violet. 'And I think that tells us a great deal, does it not?'

'Just think.' Claudia was laughing; she linked her arm through Violet's and began to tug her up the slope. 'If it wasn't for that gentleman, *in his wisdom*, and his social conscience, you'd be in rags right now, just like me. Oh, what's that you have there?'

Violet drew a sprig of gorse out of her pocket, intense yellow.

'This shall be duly pressed,' she said, 'and mounted in my Flower Book. It will be entitled, "Ides of March, 1914, first walk to the cove. The gorse that ripped Claudia's skirt."'

Chapter Two

In the language of flowers:
Narcissus, egotism

After three days of sea-blown rain, the forsythia that had brightened the front of the house since February finally wilted away, leaving only the crumpled trumpets of daffodils and shredded petals of crocuses around the quince tree to be coaxed into one last blaze by the spring sunshine. Violet stood at the morning-room window, fascinated by the way raindrops still clung to the tight green buds. Sodden and sopping, the earth was warming up and pressing out its shoots. The season had turned a corner.

She watched her father walk his bicycle over the granite slabs of the front path, bicycle clips clamping his tweed trousers. On fine days, he preferred to cycle, leaving the wagonette in the old barn. It was rather unpredictable, its function sporadic, he said, and he would rather rely on two wheels not four. Once through the gate, he hooked his leg over and rode off down the lane with his doctor's bag stowed in the box on wheels that he pulled behind him. His whistle was faint but tuneful.

Violet's mother, taking coffee by the small fire in the drawing-room grate, shook out her newspaper and said, 'Papa's off to Lansallos. They think little Benjamin Davey has pneumonia. This is the time of year for it. Weather warming up, all the coughing starts. He'll be gone all day, no doubt, and probably half the night. But not a lot he can do for the little lad.'

Violet pondered on her father's dedication, his standing in the community. How people from all walks of life, from the likes of the Daveys, fishermen from the damp cottages behind Lansallos quay, to the families of the big houses, like the Penruths, respected Dr Prideaux and turned to him in their time of need. From Looe to Liskeard, he helped at births, deaths and everything in between, including ironing out disputes and witnessing legal documents, which he performed out of duty and would take no payment for. But, Violet thought, with a pinch of irritation, he had no qualms about accepting money from Penruth for her schooling. The very idea of it, its demeaning nature, stung her. What made matters worse was that, according to Claudia, it was common knowledge all over the neighbourhood.

'You're looking a little cross with the world. Seen something out there you don't like?' her mother observed.

Violet shrugged, sighed and came away from the window.

'Well, my girl,' May Prideaux pressed, 'what are you going to do today?'

What, indeed, Violet thought, was there to do for a gentleman's daughter of rather slender means?

'Thought I'd take Jess out for a walk along the valley and teach him some more ground rules,' she said. 'I will try him off the lead this time.'

20

May commented that Violet was very brave to do so, and wondered where was he, by the way?

'He's padding around the lawn in the back garden. I'll call him in in a minute. He was just paying a visit.'

'I hope he will keep out of my herbaceous border and won't go lifting his leg on the delphiniums. Papa has only just put them in. You know, he will have to learn to stay in the boot room at night. I can't stand his whimpering through the small hours.'

'He will improve, Mother. Allow him, and me, some time,' said Violet, sitting down in the chair opposite her mother and reaching across for *The Times*. As she moved it from the table an envelope fell to the carpet. 'Oh, is this a letter from Auntie Muriel? Is she well?'

'Yes, read it if you like. These days she is spending an awful lot of time at Selfridges. How wonderful for her to have it, all five floors of it, just a stroll away. She says it is heavenly. She could walk there, she says, but takes the brougham instead because of all the inevitable purchases. I am going to send off for the catalogue, see if I can't order some bits and pieces.'

'Surely we can't really afford to buy things from such a fancy shop?' Violet quickly scanned the letter, reading Muriel's gossipy snippets and humorous asides. Her aunt sounded her usual maverick self.

'Oh, you know me, anything Muriel has, I want it too. She tells me they have the most incredible Indiennes fabrics.'

Violet bit her lip on her response, thought about it for a second, then spoke her mind anyway. 'But we don't have the Penruth money any more, do we, and I am not earning my keep.'

Her mother looked sharply at her, almost in admiration. 'We don't expect you to,' she snapped. 'And that money all went on your school fees, as you know. Please don't mention it to your father. He wants it all forgotten about. We are grateful to Mr Penruth but it has always been all rather awkward, and the least said on the matter the better, don't you think?'

'I just hope he doesn't imagine he'll see a return for his money, and assume that I will become a scientist, or something.'

May's laugh was like a clanging bell.

'Oh Violet, you are so amusing sometimes.'

'But, Mother, I do find it rather embarrassing; I didn't even know that Claudia—'

Her mother's face fixed into a startled expression as she stared past Violet's shoulder and out to the gate.

'Don't look now, but we have a visitor. The very man himself.'

'Oh heavens, this will be the second time this week,' said Violet. 'Mother, you receive him, will you? I want to go and fetch Jess.'

'He is obviously here to see you. Look what he is carrying.'

Weston Penruth paused under the sweet chestnut that sheltered the front gate to Old Trellick and shuffled at his neck tie, before swapping a large basket into his left hand and back again. The basket was full of flowers.

'Put another log on that fire, get it going. Take the chill off. I will show him in.'

Violet glanced once more through the window. The man unnerved her, made her tongue-tied. Why does he give our family such attention? she wondered.

She was kneeling on the hearth rug, trying to coax more flames, attacking a wad of ash with the poker when her mother showed Mr Penruth in. Hastily she got to her feet and they greeted each other with more than a degree of discomfort.

Violet indicated that he should sit in the chair her mother had vacated. She glanced at the door to see her mother nodding peculiarly at her and ducking out of the room.

Weston Penruth sat down and planted his boots firmly on the carpet. He tucked a handkerchief deep into his top pocket and fixed a rather alarming smile on Violet.

'And what brings you this way, Mr Penruth?' Violet said, unnecessarily, glancing at the basket that he had set on the side table. It was overflowing with floral abundance: a fancy arrangement of white lilies, long-stem roses, and crimson peonies, their heads held at stiff, unnatural angles.

'I hear how much you love flowers . . .'

'What young lady doesn't?' Violet interjected nervously.

'. . . and so I have brought you some rather glamorous specimens.' He sounded immensely proud. 'This arrangement has come down all the way from Covent Garden on the night train. I thought to myself, I know a young lady who will love some fragrance and bright colour in all this dull, wet weather, and so, here they are.'

Violet inhaled sharply and expressed her surprise that indeed this very feat could have taken place.

'That is so kind,' she said, astonished. 'They are absolutely beautiful. And yes, I do love flowers, so I thank you, very much.'

Violet reached a finger to touch the head of one of the roses which were like tight little rolls of scarlet velvet.

'How incredible to see a rose, and a lily and a peony at this time of year,' she said. 'Really, very incredible.' And, she thought, how utterly wrong.

'Ah, they are from the hothouse. Especially for you.'

She told him that he was very kind and her words drifted into silence, during which Weston regarded her beneath his

23

drawn-down brows with unnerving intensity. He turned his hat over through his hands, crossing and uncrossing his legs.

Wondering at his dreadful lack of social grace and searching wildly for something else to say, Violet peered at the arrangement. 'And how . . . how are they able to stand so erect? You see, for me, lilies always flop, the ones I grow in the garden, that is, the ones that come out in June – ah, I see that they are held together with wires.' Violet stared at the mesh into which the tender stems had been thrust, parts of it twisting cruelly into the flesh of the flowers.

'Now, you must remember not to over-water them,' Weston suggested banally. 'My man advised me.'

Violet flinched at his pride in what was in effect a second-hand understanding of flower arranging. She watched him scan the room, each time allowing his eyes to alight on her for a fraction of a second as if he could not bear it. For a man of such standing, she thought, his art of conversation was rather lacking. She felt a strange pang of sorrow for him.

In desperation, she said, 'Mr Penruth, would you like some coffee, because I think that Mother might be making some?'

'Coffee? Yes, yes, indeed.'

'Excuse me while I go and get it. I have to do this myself, you see,' Violet found herself giggling, 'as our maid does not work on Wednesdays. And we don't have a "man".'

Out in the kitchen, Violet begged her mother to come back through to the drawing room with her and help her to make conversation.

'He professes to know me,' Violet complained, 'because he has brought me flowers.'

'Quite a gesture, I'd say,' said May, lifting the tray and telling her to hold the door for her.

24

Over their cups of coffee and May's home-made saffron buns, Weston remarked at length on the weather, and then turned his attention to Jess the puppy, wondering how he was getting on.

May remarked, 'You were going to take him out before luncheon, weren't you, Violet?'

Weston drew himself up in eagerness and told her he'd be happy to accompany her, as his experience with training dogs was second to none.

'Oh, I don't want to bother you, Mr Penruth,' uttered Violet, directing a fierce glance at her mother. 'He is actually all right for now in the garden. I don't want to overtire him.'

'I thought that is exactly what you should do,' observed May. 'Then at least he will sleep through the night.' Then she laughed. 'Listen to us, Mr Penruth, it's just like we are talking about a child.'

Weston wondered if this was the first dog they'd kept, and Violet confirmed that it was.

'If you ever need some guidance, or a hand with training while you are out walking him, then please don't hesitate to ask me. It will be no trouble at all.'

Violet, relieved that he was not going to pursue the matter, thanked him. But then Weston began to mumble about meaning to ask her something, before trailing off. She glanced at him in alarm, wondering what on earth he was talking about as he drained his coffee cup and cleared his throat.

Finally, he said, 'Would you like to accompany me to the Spring Ball at Looe Assembly Rooms? On Saturday week? It would be a great honour for me.'

May piped up, 'Oh, that sounds wonderful.'

Violet conceded that indeed it did, firing another look at her mother.

Weston turned to the older lady. 'I assure you, Mrs Prideaux, that I will take great care of Violet. My driver will see us there and back in absolute safety.'

How odd it was to hear him use her name. It was rather an intrusion – made her skin prickle.

'You are free that evening, aren't you, my dear?' her mother went on, relentless.

Violet admitted that indeed she was. Half-heartedly, she said, 'So I think my answer is yes. Thank you.'

As if suddenly remembering the right and proper way to do things, Mrs Prideaux piped up, 'And, of course, Claudia Ainsley will come with Violet. A chaperone, you understand, to keep everything decorous, of course. That will be satisfactory.'

Violet thought that 'satisfactory' was an underestimation of her mother's true feelings: she was ecstatic, as betrayed by the redness at the tip of her nose.

'Marvellous,' said Weston, rising to his feet, and the full height of his sturdy frame. 'I will take my leave of you ladies now, but I assure you, Violet, that I will be in touch again nearer the date. And I do hope that afterwards, at some point, in the near future, you will do me the honour of taking tea with me at home.'

Violet tried to hide her dumbfounded expression as she and her mother stood under the stone porch to bid him good morning and watch him leave.

'Did you hear what he said?' whispered May, as she waved delicately to Weston Penruth. 'He's as good as invited you up to Charlecote. The lord of the manor has asked you to visit. *Always* a good sign.'

Chapter Three

In April, rain and sunshine both together

Sitting at the table with her Flower Book before her, in front of the little garret window under the eaves at Old Trellick, Violet watched the sky. Inland, towards the moor, stacks of snowy cumulus had set up camp against the vast blue sky, and south over the sea, beyond the garden and beyond the woods, was sparkling brightness. There was a sweetness, a tenderness from it all that reached Violet in tantalising puffs as she pushed the casement wider. She listened, stretching her nerves to hear the chorus of birdsong, to separate with a pin the voice of robin, of blackbird, and, oh joy, the song thrush. Vitality saturated the air, and she breathed deep on it. *The first warm breath of spring today. Will I hear the first cuckoo?* she wrote at the top of the blank page, and added the date.

Violet turned several pages of her journal backwards to

her record of a much chillier day: the day at the cove when she and Claudia ran shrieking down to the waves. She eased the pressed sprig of gorse from its bed of tissue and, dipping her paintbrush into her pot of gum, carefully painted the back. She was pleased with the colour of the flowers, still such a golden yolky yellow; she was satisfied with the way the petals had kept their plump shape even though they were now in two dimensions. The spines were still sharp and perfectly vicious-looking. She used her tweezers to position the specimen, holding her breath until it rested satisfactorily on the page. *The gorse that ripped Claudia's skirt.*

She glanced at her pocket watch and remembered that her friend was due to arrive very soon. The dress she was lending her for the ball was waiting for her, aired and ironed and hanging on Violet's wardrobe door. She thought also of her own gown that she had chosen to wear tonight. It was the most beautiful of dresses: a pearly shade of shell pink with a particularly flattering neckline. She had tried it on yesterday at her mother's insistence, to check for loose threads and sagging seams. She had stared at herself in the full-length mirror and was shocked at how the colour of the lace enlivened the russet of her hair and the green of her eyes. Her mother's enthusiasm as she tugged at the ruffles and flounces gave Violet's pulse an uncomfortable beat.

'It's as if you are in candlelight, my dear. It makes you utterly glow,' she said. 'Oh, Mr Penruth will adore you.'

And that, Violet thought, was what she was afraid of.

Up in the garret, she went over to the trestle table where her pressing books were stacked. Heaving the hefty *World Atlas* off the top of the pile, she carefully opened it at the pages she'd marked with paper. There, between the layers of tissue and cartridge paper, bearing vivid stains of petal juice, the blood of flowers, lay an impressive peony head that she'd plucked from Weston's bouquet, flattened. It looked stricken and rather undignified, but its colour remained as flamboyant and as false as the day Weston gave it to her. Its artifice had no place in her journal, Violet surmised, but she felt impelled to give it its own page, paste it down. After all, the book was her chronicle and she may as well be honest.

The peony was in place and dated, Violet had no desire to elaborate, when she heard Claudia's cheerful hello below. Her father, who was out in the garden pruning, responded and Violet heard him tell her to go straight up. And soon enough, Claudia came along the landing and bumped the door open with the tea tray. Jess, close on her heels, scampered in around her ankles and made a beeline for Violet, resting his paws on her knees.

Claudia's cheeks were flushed, her eyes glowing. Laughter seemed to bubble out of her. 'Tea, Violet! I've brought you tea. Your mother had just brewed it.'

'And look who's followed you. Down, Jess. That's it. Go and chew a slipper.'

The little dog obediently retreated to the corner to his stash of old shoes and set to gnawing one of Papa's rejected slippers with a concentrated look around his muzzle.

'Oh, your hair is lovely,' Violet told Claudia, taking the tray from her. 'Whatever is the matter? You can't stop smiling, can you?'

'We're going to the Looe Spring Ball! I am beside myself. Look at my hands trembling. Mother spared me some time to do my hair this morning. I thought it has made me look a bit like a china doll, but the ringlets are all right, aren't they?'

Claudia gleefully twitched her shoulders and her corn-coloured hair danced in spirals.

'You look absolutely beautiful.'

'And what are you going to do with your hair?'

'I haven't really thought, I . . .' Violet hesitated, swallowing down unease. 'Perhaps you'll help me later.'

'Later? We'd better start soon, or I will rush and panic and mess it all up. We can't have that, can we. You must look wonderful for Mr Penruth.'

Abruptly, Violet told her she needed to pack away her pressed-flower paraphernalia, and perhaps she'd give her a hand? Violet turned her back on her friend to hide the twist of despair on her face and concentrated on wiping her paintbrush on a piece of old rag.

'And what time is Mr Penruth expected?' Claudia chattered, as she restacked the heavy volumes on the table.

'Far too soon, I fear,' Violet said.

Claudia turned sharply and asked, whatever can she mean?

Violet sat down, weighted by the oily sump of dread in the pit of her stomach. The obligation to go to the ball was overwhelming, the temptation to flee even stronger. 'Claudia, I'm really not feeling very well,' she sighed, ashamed at the pathos in her voice. Her confession was the truth. She may be physically fine, but her spirits lay in tatters.

'Oh no, no. You must rest, then, have some tea.' Claudia's dismay stretched her pretty face wide. 'You'll perk up. Whatever is the matter?'

Violet did as her friend advised. She sat down, sipped her tea. She pondered aloud that the lurching inside her had nothing to do with anything she had eaten, even though Claudia insisted on pressing her to try to remember something, anything, that might have caused her malaise.

'What did you eat for breakfast? Last night's supper? You didn't drink any of last week's milk, did you? Come, now, you can't let me down, not tonight. We have a party to go to,' Claudia said sadly.

Violet revealed gingerly that she thought she'd better go and have a lie down. 'I haven't dared tell Mother yet. She is more excited about tonight than I am.'

'I think I am too,' Claudia muttered, as she followed Violet down the stairs to her bedroom. She sighed when she saw Violet's gown hanging next to hers. 'Oh, and your dress is sublime.'

'Perhaps you should wear it in my place.'

A shadow of delight moved over Claudia's face. But she sighed and took down the dress next to it, the one that was waiting for her. She held it against her, fingering the cream satin. 'Oh no, this is what I shall wear. I am so very grateful that you are able to lend it to me. And,' she said pointedly, 'you shall wear yours.'

Violet, weakened by anxiety running in her blood, said, 'I really don't think I can.'

'You do look very pale. I'll go and fetch your mother.'

'I don't want to bother her. She will be furious.'

But Claudia left her anyway and hurried downstairs. Violet lay on the bed, breathing as deeply as she could, steadying herself for her mother's reaction. Ever since Weston Penruth brought her the flowers and asked her to go to the ball, May Prideaux had gossiped and supposed and surmised many eventualities, including Violet married to the lord of the manor and settled over at Charlecote. And, rightly, Mr

31

Penruth was a fine catch for any young lady. Violet knew she should be flattered, knew she should be obliging, but something about him, and the way he engaged with her, made her feel sour. He stunted her, sapped her spirit. He made her insides shift with a strange sort of sorrow.

Jess ventured in, wondering where she had got to. She reached down and rubbed his puzzled forehead and told him to be good. 'I just don't like him very much,' she whispered to Jess. 'Is that such a bad thing?' Jess ignored her, and settled his little russet body, with a plaintive sigh, onto her hearthside rug.

Violet heard her mother exclaim all the way from her chair in the drawing room, and then the inevitable and immediate footfalls across the stone hallway and up the stairs. In a snatch of silence, as her mother evidently caught her breath on the landing before launching herself at her bedroom door, Violet heard the cheerfully double-beat piping of the cuckoo from across the wood.

The car, so grand, so large, so important, pulled up outside the gate and Mr Penruth's driver leapt out to open the door for him. The fenders gleamed, the lamps were polished, the engine hummed like a snoring beast.

Violet stayed upstairs, her curtains drawn at her bedroom window. She stood to the side, feeling foolish and sad, and peered through a gap in the curtains to watch Weston climb out of the car. He had a bright eagerness about him. He tugged down his fine waistcoat and sniffed the fresh evening air before his driver carefully handed him two corsages which Weston then held aloft and awkward as he walked up the path.

Humbled, her stomach in a hard knot, Violet came away from the window and sat on the bed, pressing her hands over her ears. Even so, she could hear their voices below. She heard the polite murmuring of good evenings and then a mumbling drawn-out explanation from her mother. There was no word from Weston. After a few excruciating moments, Violet heard Claudia's excited voice ring out goodbye and Violet returned to the window to see her friend all but skip up the path beside Weston, one of the corsages pinned to her dress. She hopped in the car and smilingly waved back towards the front door where, Violet presumed, her mother was standing in fuming silence.

The car door closed on Claudia with an abrupt slam and Violet watched, pained, as Weston took himself around the back of the car. He halted, seemingly unobserved, and fished in his pocket to draw out a flask. He took three hasty sips, before throwing back at Old Trellick a grimace of naked disappointment. His face then drooped with boredom as he climbed into the car to sit beside Claudia.

Chapter Four

In the language of flowers:
Foxglove, insincerity

Jess's silky fur was curling over his collar quite preposterously, Violet thought, just like a cavalier's ringlets. She sat on the bottom stair and ran her fingers inside the leather strap.

'You've grown bigger, haven't you, these last few weeks,' she reminded him. 'Let's loosen this up a bit. That's it. Give you a bit more breathing space. It'll be a five-mile walk today, so I hope you had a good breakfast.'

'He did, that's for sure,' said Violet's father, coming out of the morning room with his pipe tucked in his mouth. 'I saw to that. Plenty of scraps in his bowl. Where do you intend to take him?'

Violet thought she'd like to go to the cove, to seek out sea holly in the shelter of the dunes. But the day was so blustery that it might feel rather unpleasant.

Her father agreed. 'It's certainly whipping up, we might

even see a storm. Not good for May, is it?' He tapped the barometer on the wall and adjusted the needle. 'Says "wind and rain". But with any luck it should blow itself out over the sea.'

Violet clipped Jess's lead onto his collar and commanded that he sat still while she buttoned up her coat. She rather hoped the bad feeling that shrouded the house, the sodden stifling cloud, would blow itself out too. Her mother had barely spoken to her since the night of the ball and her snubbing of Mr Penruth. And that was over a month ago. Her father was rather ineffectual at being the go-between. Stony silences greeted her at breakfast, lunch and dinner, and barbed asides when Violet tried for a conversation between asking for her to pass the salt.

'Say goodbye to Mother for me, won't you,' said Violet, with a weary catch in her voice. She put the strap of her canvas bag over her head and shoulder, checking that her scissors, notebook and tissue paper for cradling clippings were deposited inside. 'Tell her I should be back in time for lunch.'

Her father shifted his eyes to the drawing room where his wife sat, in full earshot, noisily snapping the pages of *The Times*.

Violet whistled for Jess and headed up the path, with one hand holding the lead, the other clapped on the top of her hat to keep it on. The breeze was wild and flapping, with great puffs blowing fiercely up from the ground. From the cleft in the hills she could see in the distance that the sea was very lively, the gulls gliding up on bouncing currents of air.

'Come, let's go to the pinewood,' she whispered to Jess.

As she walked along the sheltered track, overarched by the tunnel of trees, she thought of Claudia's account of her evening at the Liskeard ball. Her friend had wasted no time, and visited her the day after, primarily to check how Violet was, whether she was still poorly. And then, once Violet had assured her she was quite well, Claudia broke into a full stream of chattering and giggling at the joyous memory of dancing with each of the Davey twins in turn. They were both in the rudest health, she reported, as their ruddy faces and strong fisherman arms affirmed. They had broken their mourning for Benjamin to dance, and what a merry time they had, reported Claudia. They had only buried their little brother just a month before. She thought it was just the cure they needed.

'I told them it was doing them good. The music, the laughter, all that shuffling round the floor. I had a wonderful time. I have trouble telling them apart at the best of times,' Claudia had laughed, 'and by the end of the evening, I was even more confused. Perhaps I should tell who is who by the way each of them kisses.'

'Claudia!' Violet had chastised her, but had secretly enjoyed hearing about everyone else's amusement, deflecting the attention from herself. Inevitably, Weston Penruth cropped up.

'And what a sour, grumpy gentleman he is,' Claudia complained. 'Wouldn't dance one song, and all those eligible young ladies of the county there trying to catch his eye. Of course, I don't count myself among them. Yes, so I arrived in splendour with him in his motor car, but he dropped me as soon as we went in and headed for the bar. I was pleased, really, couldn't stand the looks people were giving me. As if to say, who does she think she is coming with Lordy? I was perfectly happy with Peter and Eddie.'

And then, Claudia ventured to say that perhaps a night

of dancing might have cured Violet's ills, just as it did for the twins. Violet dismissed the very idea with a forced laugh. Guilty as she was of rather juvenile behaviour – pretending to feel ill – she had certainly felt unwell inside herself. Her struggle now was trying to understand why. And dancing with Weston Penruth would certainly not have alleviated this.

Violet came out of the cover of the bridleway and into the pinewood. Jess was tugging to be let off the lead, so she conceded and he bounded ahead, his ears streaming behind him. Drops of rain peppered the wind and the tops of the pines roared. And yet below, amid the cloister of dark trunks and soft beds of ferns, where beams of foxgloves sprung up, all was soft and silent, the space like the interior of a wide and scented cathedral. As Jess snuffled and pattered around her, she was glad of the wood, for its composed nature, for its solace, which helped her see things clearly. She wanted to put the whole sorry episode behind her.

She stopped at a fork in the path to cut a particularly eye-catching foxglove head, an exquisite curl of tight buds, still blind and unformed. Tucking it into the tissue in her bag, her attention was taken by the prettiest of maidenhair ferns amongst ten thousand: how delicious both plants would look, she thought, pressed and pasted together in her book.

In the background she was aware of the incessant rustling of Jess. He was pressing his nose into the undergrowth and scuffling up the soft earth of the high banks where the white stars of wood anemones were fading away. Despite the rainwashed day, late spring was settling into a delightful rhythm. As she fingered the tender fern frond and tucked it away, abruptly all went quiet.

She whistled, scanning the mounds of fern. She peered

along the descending footpath that hugged the side of the slope. It plunged away, down through thick verdant groves towards the stream in the crook of the valley. She tried again, and called him, his name a hard hiss. But the listening pinewood threw her voice back at her. He was gone.

Violet hurried down the lower path, imagining Jess had smelt a rabbit and was in pursuit. The way soon became steep and treacherous. She usually avoided this track for that very reason. Breathless, she called again, peering to left and right.

'He can't have simply vanished,' she muttered.

Her foot slipped suddenly on loose chunks of flint and she lost her balance, sitting down rather ungracefully, right on the edge of the path. Violet laughed nervously as, unable to stop herself, she began to topple down the bank in a peculiar sitting position. Her heels gouged the rough earth, her toes tripped on roots. Half standing, half squatting, she gripped on to what she could to break her progress. Ferns broke under her weight, and spindly shoots snapped in her hand. She tumbled and stumbled and finally came to a soft rest near the bottom by the stream, where sunlight could hardly penetrate. Under the dank deciduous trees, the trickling water was earthy and sluggish in the gloom. The wood towered above her, no longer so friendly but stretching high, obstructing the sky. She called Jess again with a shriek, cursing him and the soil marks on her skirt and boots. She craned her neck, surprised at how far down the bank she'd come and swallowed her shock to see the figure of Weston Penruth above, striding along the top path just where she'd left it. Thank god, I missed him, she breathed. Oh, where is that damn dog? And look at the state of me.

And then, suddenly, a dreadful sharp yelp from the dense green-black undergrowth, and two retrievers came churning through the water, showing no mercy to their quarry – the little brown struggling figure of Jess. Violet screamed and hurled herself into the stream. But then, pinned by shock, she froze, ankle-deep in water, terrified by the thrashing, the utter mayhem before her.

'Leave him, leave him!' she cried, cold sickness kicking her stomach.

She watched, helpless, as, in one slow, dreadful motion, one of the dogs snapped its long-jawed head up and flung Jess from its mouth and through the air. She dived then, her arms outstretched, sinking to her knees in the water to pluck the little dog up and cradle him close to her face. The retrievers' muscly shoulders barged her, their tails lashed, teeth snapping close to her, their hot wet breath on her neck and her hands. She wanted to yell at them, warn them off with the ferociousness she felt inside, but all she could manage was a trailing moan of fear.

The stream was cold, shockingly so. She held her breath, her bones locked, the water clinging to her clothing, weighing her down. She wondered for one awful moment if this was to be her and Jess's last. Her senses filled with black fur, jaws, bright animal eyes, and snarls so sharp that they pinched the air around her ears. She cried out, helpless.

A warm, strong presence, suddenly, was at her back and two hands gripped her under her armpits and tugged upwards, bearing her out of the water as if she was being born from it. She sensed who it was, this large figure behind her who was bellowing in her ears, splitting her head, carrying her and her limp furry bundle still tucked under her chin to the weed-strewn bank. She knew who he was as his great boots kicked the dogs away, as his great voice continued to order them, and her.

The retrievers circled, cowered and retreated into the bushes, heads and tails low to the ground.

'Oh my good God! Violet!' Weston cried, his voice pinched, his arm heavy around her shoulder. 'Are you all right? Did they bite you? If they did, by God, I'll get my shotgun. Look at me. Are you all right?'

'Never mind me,' she murmured, her head drooping to the twitching form in her arms. 'What about Jess? What have they done to Jess? What have they done to him?'

Weston's fingers eased the grip she had on the little dog and he gently prised him away from her.

'He's injured.'

Bright blood soiled the collar of her coat and Weston's palms; Jess's head was tilted, his eyes closed.

'It's his shoulder.' Weston rummaged in his pocket and drew out a handkerchief. 'Thank God they didn't get his throat.' In a moment he had cradled Jess on his lap and spun the cloth around his body, tightening it. Speechless with terror, Violet stared at the concentration on Weston's face, his blank encompassing concern, the red flower of liquid that immediately stained the handkerchief.

'Another one, another one,' he said.

She gave him her scarf and he used it, expertly binding the little dog's shoulder.

'He needs a veterinary,' said Weston.

'Please help him,' Violet whispered. She stared at the man, at his muddy trousers, sopping boots, bloody hands. His eyes were dark and distressed, sending her arrows of his own pain; his guilt. 'Weston, please help him.'

'I will, I will, but are you all right? Give me your hand, are you hurt?'

'Not at all. Take him.' Impatiently, she shook her hand free of his. 'I am fine. Take him now.'

He placed Jess carefully on the ground and stood over her. He bent down, resting his hands on her shoulders. Their weight conveyed his power, his will. 'You are still shaking. I cannot leave you here.'

'You must,' she spoke faintly. She snapped her head up to look him in the eye. 'I will find my own way. I need you to help Jess. He's hurt more than I am.'

'Come, do as I say.' Weston slipped his arm around her waist and he pulled her up to him, helping her find her feet.

She leant against him, as shock eased its grip on her and left her weak. His body, so fierce and masculine, was surprisingly soft, surprisingly warm. He scooped Jess up and made her walk with him, moving her along the side of the stream, pushing aside the undergrowth, finding a way through. She could not fight him any more. If she did as he said, she thought, then he is bound to help Jess.

At the top of the slope, she sat down on a log. They were both out of breath. Violet's clothes were damp, she was clammy, her muscles burning. She noticed a film of sweat over Weston's face.

'Take him now,' she said. 'I insist. I can get myself home. I am not hurt. I will just slow you down.'

'Violet, really . . .'

She reached her hand and touched Jess's forehead. The dog, lying in Weston's arms, was stunned, his eyes blank and far away. Whimpering bubbled from his mouth.

She glared at Weston with all the strength she could muster. 'Do this for me, please,' she said through her teeth. 'He means everything to me.'

Weston glanced down at the dog and back at her. He seemed to absorb what she said. He nodded succinctly, and then hurried off with Jess. 'I will make that veterinary save him. I will let you know as soon as I have any news,' he called over his shoulder. 'I will be at Old Trellick before sunset.'

Her father opened the front door as she walked shivering and unsteady up the path.

'Good God! Have you had an accident?'

'I need a bath,' she mumbled, barely able to look at him.

'What on earth has happened? You are soaking wet.'

Violet told him she'd fallen in the stream.

'You did what? Good God, Violet. Are you all right? Where is the dog? Is he wet and dirty, too? You know your mother won't have him in the house if he is covered in mud.'

Violet stood in the hall and gingerly lifted her canvas bag over her head. She was dazed and trembling. Slowly she began to unbutton her coat. Her hands were grimy, the bottom of her skirt tide-marked with water. She had lost her hat.

'He's with Mr Penruth.'

Her father let out a yelp of surprise.

There was a clatter of a teacup from the drawing room and the sound of hasty footsteps along the hall. Her mother appeared swiftly at her side.

'What did you say? Weston Penruth has the dog?'

'There's been an accident, May,' her father said. 'Violet fell in the stream.'

'I need a bath,' Violet said, longing for hot, steamy water to melt the deep chill from her bones. She peered inside her bag: the foxglove and maidenhair fern were crushed and useless.

Her father scratched his head and supposed he had better

fire the copper up, considering that it wasn't their usual day for bathing.

'Never mind that,' said May. 'Did you say Mr Penruth was with you? And why has he got the dog?'

Violet's sigh was weary with frustration. She stared at her mother and mused how easily she had broken her sulking silence at the very mention of the landlord's name.

'Jess is injured,' Violet told her, her words cracked and tired. 'He is taking him to the veterinary. If you'll excuse me, I have to go upstairs.'

'But *Mr Penruth* was walking with you?' Her mother could barely contain her excitement.

'He wasn't. I was on my own. I didn't go to the cove, I went to the pinewood.' Oh, if only, she thought, I had gone to the cove. 'His dogs attacked Jess. They nearly killed him. He was nearly ripped to shreds. I think he is going to die.'

Her father stepped closer. 'Oh Violet. How awful.'

'But *Mr Penruth* has taken him to the vet?' May insisted. 'Well, isn't that wonderful.'

Violet's mother made a fuss of pulling the best armchair closer to the fire and demanded that her husband stack the applewood logs high. Violet sat with a blanket around her, a hot-water bottle at her feet and a bowl of broth on her lap, and yet the chill of her shock still battled with her and the shivering inside continued. Her father sat turning the pages of *The Times* at the glossy card table by the French windows, commenting every so often on the activities of the Kaiser who, he thought, had very worrying delusions of grandeur, and also the unprecedented strength of the storm that was closing in on them. Violet's mother, meanwhile, sat in the chair opposite her, chattering and twitching with little glances at the clock. She read out Auntie Muriel's latest letter from London. Violet listened to tales of supper clubs and bridge games, haberdasheries on Bond Street and the new blossom over Regent's Park. May declared that she would write to her sister that very evening and tell her all about the day's events. Or at least, she added, those that have the happiest outcome.

Violet watched through the window as the wind curdled the white lilac bushes, petals scattered like snowflakes. She cocked her ear to the sound of the wind, allowing her mother's voice to fade. She caught only snatches of Muriel's account of a visit to one Lady Welstead of Cumberland Terrace. The evening at Old Trellick was drawing down beneath the swell of the breeze and a lone blackbird was still singing gamely. Sunset, Violet thought, he said he'd be here by sunset. If he doesn't come, that means Jess is dead.

The wind grew louder, rumbling over the chimney top, making its presence felt at the hearth. For Violet, the hard shock of the dog attack was merging from nightmarish flashes into a much cooler reality. Inch by inch her nerve fibres became used to what had happened, her consciousness slowly played over the horror, absorbed it, and accepted it. She remembered the look in Weston's eyes. It came back to her then, as she sat in the familiar safety of her own drawing room with her parents' conversation in the background. His eyes, glazed with shame, had pleaded for her forgiveness as he walked away with her stricken Jess in his arms. Something inside drew her to him, and yet it was something she didn't want, nor understand.

And then, from her cosy armchair, she heard a new sound, deeper than the grumbling wind in the chimney. Her father stood up abruptly, causing a sheet from the newspaper to drift to the floor.

'I hear the motor car,' he said.

Violet turned to the drawing-room door with an excruciating mixture of fear and excitement.

Her mother snatched the soup bowl off her lap, muttering that she did not want Violet to look like an invalid and pulled the blanket from around her shoulders. She folded it quickly and stuffed it behind the sofa.

'How pale you are,' she said, admiringly. She followed her husband quickly out to the hallway.

Left alone, Violet heard an exchange of men's voices, quiet and deep. She gripped the arms of the chair, and screwed up her eyes to listen harder, to catch their inflections. Her mother's words were more discernible, so much more high-pitched. How very grateful and obliged she was.

'Not at all, Mrs Prideaux,' Weston said. 'Now, may I please see your daughter?'

He came into the room, and Violet felt her body slump back against the armchair as if it was emptied, right then, of everything. He was carrying a bundle wrapped in a blanket. She saw a floppy, curly-haired ear, a wet-nosed snout.

'Here he is,' said Weston. He knelt down by the fire and put Jess on the hearthrug. The dog remained still, but rested, snuggling deeper and gratefully into his blanket. 'Veterinary's given him a thorough check-up, and seen to his wounds.'

'Is he going to be all right?' Violet could barely speak.

The man turned to her, his face wide with amazement. A smile broke over his hard features.

'Of course he is.'

Violet felt her eyes sting and she swallowed hard. It took

a while for her words to come. 'Thank you . . . so much. I can't tell you.'

Weston sat by her, drew his chair to her side.

'Try.'

Violet dipped her head, recoiling at his presence, shy at how close he was to her. She realised after a few moments that he had taken her hands in his, and, with this blaze of surprise, the chill and the horror was swept away. Aware, suddenly, of the pleasant feeling of having Mr Penruth hold her hands she smiled rashly, drew them back and got to her feet. Kneeling beside Jess on the hearthrug, she stroked his forehead, and spoke softly to him. He groaned, the noise she knew well when he was sleepy and gratified.

'Give it two weeks,' Weston said, 'and that dog will be giving you trouble again.'

Violet glanced round at her visitor. He sat, poised on the edge of his seat, his whole stance, from the tips of his fingers to the position of his boots on the rug, was friendly enough, but she was conscious of a strangely troubled tension in the set of his jaw, the flick of his eyes. It seemed to her that he was cautious of her, dancing around her, never sure of what she was going to say next. Violet watched him and wondered how a man who had the world at his feet could be so ill at ease with it.

In the quietness, she was aware that they had been left alone. Her parents had gone out of the room as soon as they knew Jess was well and had shut the door behind them. The clock on the mantel ticked its familiar hollow sound, and the fire crackled. An applewood log fell in the grate with a contented thud and the sparks made Jess lift his head briefly before he settled back with a deep, doggy sigh. And Violet felt the weight of Weston's hand, once again, in hers.

Chapter Five

In the language of flowers:
Orchid, luxurious beauty

Weston Penruth was right, as Violet knew he would be. Jess was up and about within a week of the attack, his shoulder healing well and his mischievous spirit soaring to new and rowdy heights. Just a month later, the little dog was as lively as ever. And today he was causing a great deal of trouble by chewing the guy ropes for the pagoda that the farmhands were erecting on the wide, flat lawn of Charlecote for Violet and Weston's engagement soirée. Violet was particularly relieved that the two retrievers were chained up securely and far away in the farmyard.

Charlecote House was not as deep-rooted in the Cornish landscape as Old Trellick, she thought as she gazed up at it from her garden chair set out on the lush turf. A granite Gothic manor, just fifty or so years old, Charlecote's dramatically sullen windows scowled and its chimneys towered. It sat sturdily in the curve of the valley beyond the pinewood. Neat gardens surrounded it and the farm was perched on top of the hill behind. From the servants' windows under the slate roof, Violet had been told, one could see the sea.

Weston's grandfather had made the family money from Devon wool and had endeavoured to display it in finely hewn granite slabs and mortar on this side of the Tamar. Charlecote was certainly built in splendour. It had four storeys, a little-used ballroom, an orangery of steamy tropical temperature and an ice house tucked away in the little copse beyond the lawns. The garden had had just fifty years to mature compared to Old Trellick's near thousand, but, looking around her today, it pleased Violet in a mild and trifling manner.

The warm air was scented with cut grass and the drifting sweetness of the last of the horse chestnut flowers. The fountain bubbled merrily and the standard roses were ablaze with bees. At least, Violet mused, as she settled back in her chair in the shade of the pagoda, and whistled for Jess to behave himself and come and sit at her feet, even in all this magnificence, she would not be far from Old Trellick. Not far away from home.

Her parents were here, and Claudia, too. The day had turned out perfectly, even though her father had warned her, as he tapped his barometer in the hall at Old Trellick earlier, it may still grow cloudy. But at least for now the sun twinkled on the silver and bone china and on the faces of the guests. The table under the pagoda was laid abundantly with tea things and the canvas sides were rolled up to give her a view of the garden on all sides, with sunlight slanting through. She was pleased to see that the rather chewed guy ropes were firmly in the ground. As a breeze came in under her hat and ruffled at her hair, Violet allowed herself a sigh of pleasure.

'Yes, it is wonderful, isn't it,' commented her father, looking up at the sky. 'Such a change from the awful May we had. But all that rain was worth it. Just look at this garden. I want to congratulate Mr Penruth on it. Where is he?'

The weeks had passed quickly in a whirlwind for Violet. The sopping, rain-soaked month of May and the hasty courtship had become a strange blur of happy surprises and demonstrations of parental approval. Her mother, particularly, was beside herself.

'The sun is shining just for you, Violet,' said Claudia, accepting a glass of lemonade from the tray that Willis the butler presented her. 'I can see how happy you are. We both said that, didn't we, Eddie, when we arrived. How happy you look.' She pressed her arms to her sides as if to squeeze out more joy. 'I have always known this place to be grand but my, to be sat here, like this.'

'You are very kind to invite me, Miss Prideaux,' said Eddie Davey, sipping at his lemonade. His eyes were large and watery, a shaving rash on his neck.

Violet assured him that it was her absolute pleasure. Smiling, she remembered Claudia telling her how she would, as a child, tag along with her mother who came down from the farm cottage to clean the Charlecote silver. How large the house was, Claudia had said, and how cool and how empty of voices. All those closed doors, rooms she was not allowed to enter. And, in its serene and profound silence, the stone-paved corridors echoed, Claudia told her, ceilings soared above her. It seemed frozen and unreal, she'd said, and scared her half to death.

'And now, Violet, you have a butler,' Claudia giggled behind her hand.

Mrs Penruth's voice barked at them across the cake stand arranged so precisely on the pressed-linen cloth.

'Now, now, no whispering,' she commanded. 'I know what you girls are like. We're not in school now. If it can't be said to all of us, it shouldn't be said at all.'

Weston's mother's high crown of hair was topped by a stupendous towering millinery creation topped with silk flowers. Due to its weight, Violet surmised, Mrs Penruth could barely move her head above the straight set of her shoulders, stiff in pleated olive-green silk, and her shelf-like bosom. And yet her eyes swivelled, not missing a thing. Beside her, Violet's mother in her starched Sunday best looked startled at the sudden turn in conversation and nodded furiously in agreement with Mrs Penruth. She fixed Violet and Claudia with one of her intensely meaningful stares.

'Yes, of course. I'm so sorry, ma'am,' Claudia cried. 'I was only saying—'

'Oh never mind, dear, and I was *only* joking. Are we having buns, Willis?'

The butler sloped off back to the house with his tray and May Prideaux leant into Mrs Penruth's person as if confiding in an old friend.

'Oh, Mrs Penruth. Such a shame that my sister Muriel was unable to come down from London. She lives in Marylebone, you know. Well, I should say Fitzrovia, really. After all, Marylebone is a railway station, isn't it. Twisted her ankle, unfortunately, but she sends her love and regards. She will be here for the wedding, make no mistake.'

'Yes, yes, quite,' said Mrs Penruth, biting into a raspberry that she had pierced with a tiny silver fork. 'I'm just hoping this one is sweeter than the last. My son does insist on forcing his fruit in that stifling glasshouse of his. I don't believe in raspberries this early. We should really only just be having the first strawberries.'

Dr Prideaux chipped in, 'August at the earliest for raspberries, and they should really be brought down from the Scottish glens. We rarely have them at home. Such a luxury. I can't remember the last time—'

'But how lovely that Mr Penruth has grown them,' May interrupted her husband, drenching her bowl of fruit from the sugar dredger. 'I think home-grown raspberries are a fine way to celebrate our daughter's engagement.'

Violet dragged her eyes away from her mother's exaggerated and fixed smile and glanced towards the house to see Willis emerge from the French windows carrying a silver tray, heavy with a bottle of champagne stuffed into an ice bucket. His gait was efficient and docile. Behind him came Weston, who seemed to be speaking quickly at Willis, urging him on impatiently. He then swept past his butler, and came down the terrace steps, his hair bouncing over his head, his long legs striding across the lawn. His usual stiff gait seemed easier today, although he was holding his shoulders as if he could not bear the cloth of his shirt to touch his skin.

Violet watched him, and reminded herself that he loved her. She set her face into a pleasant welcoming smile, one that she hoped would befit a bride. Weston came straight to her, dipping under the pagoda, his smile beaming. He picked up her left hand and kissed it with a flourish.

She gazed at him openly, realising how her feelings had swooped from agitation to admiration so quickly that she had had no hope of doubting them. His charismatic presence since the incident with the dogs had tugged at her sleeve, until she could ignore it no longer. She smiled up at him, taking in his handsome physique. In fact, all faces around the table were drawn to him.

'Ladies and gentlemen,' he took in everyone with one bright look. 'On this most glorious of days, I wish to extend my welcome to you all to Charlecote. I wish to propose a toast . . .' he motioned to Willis to hurry up with the champagne.

The butler deftly dealt with the cork and, in the subsequent pause, as Violet watched him fill the glasses she felt a door close inside her heart. There it was again, the barrier against Weston's energy and his eagerness and his appetite. Once more, the admiration faded and a strange dead sensation filled her chest. Nerves, she told herself, simple nerves. And what bride doesn't feel them?

The party waited in eager silence as Willis expertly presented the glasses around the table. Violet took her champagne, squinted into the sun and saw the light dazzle for a moment on the gold of her engagement ring. The breeze brought the sweetness of orange blossom over from Weston's herbaceous border and it unexpectedly lifted her spirits like a promise. She smiled, concentrated on the tiny bubbles in her glass, knowing that they were all looking at her.

Weston stood by her chair. He gripped her hand and held it against his chest.

'Ladies and gentleman,' he announced again, his voice elevated with pride. 'A toast to my wife to be. To Violet.'

They all raised their glasses into the sunlight and drank. Pleasantries were muttered and Jess stood up from his spot under Violet's chair, yawned and made to head for the shrubbery.

'If it wasn't for this little fellow,' said Weston, reaching out swiftly and yanking him back by the collar, 'we wouldn't be here now, so . . .'

'Weston, I am not going to drink a toast to a dog,' cut in his mother, her voice withering and cold.

Violet watched as chips of anger momentarily brightened Weston's eyes. Her insides hardened in anticipation of an outburst, but instead he smiled and shrugged, ruffling the dog's curly ears, mumbling that of course his mother was right.

They drank then, exchanging chatter until Mrs Penruth began to pass round the sandwiches, urging everyone to eat up before they started to curl.

Claudia came to sit by Violet, her pretty, oblivious face open and smiling. 'Oh, let me see your ring again. Isn't it beautiful.'

'Was my mother's,' Mrs Penruth informed her across the table. 'A family heirloom. Three garnets and seven pearls. Weston had it reset. One of the stones was loose.'

As her friend examined the ring, her fingertips brushing the luminous pearls, Violet was struck suddenly by the fact that she didn't like it. She'd never been one for garnets and also had no affinity with Mrs Penruth or her departed mother. It dawned on her: the ring was second-hand. Not quite what she had imagined for herself. And, weren't pearls unlucky?

But Mrs Penruth was warning her, 'Take good care of it, young lady.'

'Of course she will,' said Violet's father, sounding rather affronted, his voice coming from inside his collar.

Violet glanced warily at her future mother-in-law and asserted that she would always treasure the ring.

'And I will treasure you,' Weston whispered in her ear, so that no one else could hear, his breath surprisingly hot and sour with brandy fumes.

Violet turned to look at him, like she knew that she should, and willed her despondency to disappear. She concentrated on his dashing symmetrical features, his devotion to her. She sat back in her chair, holding her fiancé's hand and sipping her champagne.

'Well here we all are, then,' said Mrs Penruth, scanning the faces around her and then fixing on Claudia. 'I know about you, Miss Ainsley, you grew up under my nose, up there at the farm. And, of course, Violet. We know all about you, where you live, where you went to school. But what is your background, Mr Davey?'

Eddie, surprised at the sudden interest, spilt a little champagne as he set down his glass. He fumbled with his collar. 'Fishing, ma'am. Our family have been fishing out of Lansallos for centuries.'

'As well you know, Mother,' Weston interjected. 'You surely don't need the lad to spell it out.'

Weston drew out a flask from his pocket and tipped a splash into his champagne glass. Violet watched the pale liquid turn a murky shade of brown.

'I was only making conversation with Mr Davey,' laughed Mrs Penruth. 'Oh, how serious you always are. You'll have to watch that, Violet. Your husband-to-be can't take a joke. But of course we all have to laugh at his own.'

Weston was silent, his grip on Violet's hand grew tight again and Violet shifted her fingers tactfully to stop them being crushed.

Willis stepped in with a freshly opened bottle of champagne and Violet's father asked him if *The Times* was handy.

'Oh, not today,' complained her mother. 'Can't you leave it all just for one day?'

'I just wanted to know what the Kaiser is up to. I don't like what's going on in Germany at the moment, to be frank. "Aggressive fool" isn't the word.'

'Well, what is, then? And that's two words. Really, George, Violet doesn't want to hear all that on her engagement day. We should talk about flowers, dates. A September wedding. What do you say, my dear? Bride's prerogative to name the date.'

Weston agreed, making encouraging sounds. 'Yes, my dear, we need to set a date.'

But Violet supposed that they had plenty of time to make arrangements.

Her mother didn't think so. 'It's never too early to start.'

'They'll get married in the chapel here, of course,' said Mrs Penruth.

Violet winced, staggered by the assumption. She had imagined the church at Lansallos. But, then, this was barely the place to dispute it.

Weston asked his mother if she'd like more champagne.

'Yes, but I think you had better stop with the brandy. I've seen you totting up. Lethal mixture, Weston.'

He stood up abruptly and waved for Willis to fill the glasses.

'I shall stop drinking, Mother, to please you.'

Mrs Penruth laughed so raucously that Violet thought that she surely hadn't seen anger clouding her son's face.

'In the meantime,' said Weston, clearing his throat and changing the subject, 'would you, Miss Ainsley and Mr Davey, like a tour of the house? Violet and I will show you round. It would be a great pleasure.'

Eddie Davey tentatively assured him that the pleasure, and honour, would be all theirs.

Violet agreed that it was a lovely idea, and felt relief dripping through her blood as the four of them walked back across the lawn towards the terrace.

'I do apologise if my mother sometimes appears rather overbearing,' Weston told Eddie, standing aside to let the younger man walk through the French windows in front of him. 'It's just her way. You know what elderly ladies are like. I'm afraid I'm used to it, so I let it pass me by.'

Eddie, ever the gentleman, begged him not to mention it. Claudia linked Violet's arm and drew her back.

'Isn't he a lovely man?' she whispered. 'I made my choice. The right twin.'

'Eddie is coping very well with visiting Charlecote,' replied Violet. 'I don't think I am.'

Claudia told her not to be so silly. 'Of course you are. And you're not *visiting*. This will be your home. And I can tell – you love Mr Penruth. I always knew you did. You always hid it, circled round it. It will take you a while to realise. This often happens, my mother told me. Once you are married, everything will be fine.'

Violet stepped through the French windows into the cool drawing room, and could still hear Mrs Penruth's voice inside her head, dictating where she would be married. The dark-oak panelling was restful after the bright sunshine, and the gleaming ornaments were now familiar to Violet, but she regarded it all with new and alarmed eyes. This was Mrs Penruth's home, she reminded herself. And always would be.

Claudia was admiring everything: the fine needlework of the curtains, the woven rug, the tassels on the chairs. All of it, she informed Eddie, was the height of fashion. And look how wonderful the silver is, Claudia laughed.

'I am happy to say I had a hand in that,' she said, reminding everyone that she had only ever seen the inside of the scullery. There she was, she said, six years old, bent over an ocean of silver and being told to give it some elbow grease.

'Come on, Claudia,' Eddie urged her. 'Mr Penruth is about to open up the ballroom.'

It took Weston and Eddie some five minutes to open every shutter in the wide majestic room. Violet and Claudia stood in the centre of the polished parquet floor and, little by little, shafts of sunlight blazed in to light up the duck-egg blue walls, scrolling plasterwork and the enormous chandeliers suspended from the lofty ceiling.

Claudia clapped her hands. 'I often used to dream of this place, wonder what was behind the double doors when I was a child. And this is it, it's perfect. Violet, this is where we will dance at your wedding.'

Weston's smile was warm and broad as he walked over to Violet and put his hand on her shoulder.

'What a wonderful idea,' he said. 'My dear, we will fill it with lilies, we will fill it with roses. We will fill it with violets. And orchids. Absolutely stupendous orchids.'

'Ah, but, Weston,' Violet said, 'not all of those plants will be at their best come September. And, really . . . orchids . . . ? The violets particularly—'

'You and your flowers. What nonsense. I will see to it that they are at their best.' Weston dismissed her and turned quickly before Violet could explain why she would not want those plants to decorate her wedding ball. She wanted the dahlias of September, and chrysthanthemums and the hips of wild guelder rose, and everything that filled the autumn hedgerows with gilded gold and burning red.

But Weston had already walked back over to Eddie.

'Next stop, Mr Davey, will be my orangery. There you will see some, dare I say, unseasonal wonders.'

'Thank you, sir,' Eddie said, 'but I'm not sure I will have time for that. I do actually have to leave now. I am going out on the night boat.'

The group left the ballroom by the far doors and paused in the stone-flagged corridor outside the glass doors of the orangery. Inside, through the perspiring window panes, Violet glimpsed a jungle of giant ferns, monstrous palms and potted greenery – the stuff of fantasy from the other side of the world.

'Another time, then, Mr Davey.' Weston shook his hand. 'And you too, Miss Ainsley.'

'Thank you for inviting us.' Claudia hugged Violet. 'We'll pop out and pay our respects to your mother, Mr Weston, and say goodbye. It's been such a charming afternoon.'

'Do you know the way?' Violet asked. 'We've come a different way round. I'll walk with you.'

'No, dear. No, stay with me,' Weston said. 'I want to

show you the orangery. You haven't seen it yet, have you?'

Violet watched Claudia and Eddie leave, their cheerful, playful voices teasing each other, their laughter receding down the corridor, their footsteps fading to silence. She turned to Weston.

'I better get out and see if Jess is all right. He might be bothering your mother.'

Weston took her hand, smiling persistently. 'Oh, she will have to get used to him, won't she, once we are married. Come on, I have a new orchid I want to show you. It is exquisite. And the strawberries. Did I tell you about my strawberries? There are melons too. My dear, once we are married, you will have every fruit and flower you will ever dream of. Everything you could possibly want. Come with me.'

Chapter Six

In the language of flowers:
Clover, be mine

Weston opened the glass door to the orangery and ushered her in, telling her to be quick as he did not want to waste the heat. As soon as the door was closed, Violet took two shallow breaths and coughed.

'Goodness, how stifling it is in here.'

The atmosphere was hot, saturated. Within a moment, Violet's skin glistened. The moist heat seemed to come from inside her body, radiating outwards.

'I had the furnace specially built to cope with the size of this space. It's underneath us. Had a basement dug out especially.' He stamped on the terracotta-tiled floor and then pointed upwards. 'See those pipes, painted white? There's a whole network of them, churning out the heat. You will get used to it, I promise you. Now the best thing to do is walk slowly, and don't talk. I'll do all the talking,' he chuckled and placed a finger over her lips. 'There, that's it.'

The pipes travelled upwards and sideways and turned sharp corners through a tangle of glossy foliage that displayed itself in all manner of whorls and undulations, intertwined with stupendously robust, rubbery-looking flowers. Violet craned her neck to follow a pipe that soared through the verdant mass right to the lofty glass roof above her, two storeys high. Wrought-iron pillars were draped with rampant creepers that reached curling tendrils out to strangle the plants around them and, indeed, themselves.

'I hope to have some limes this year. Perfect in a gin and tonic, what do you say?'

She nodded and said that it would be nice to have some lime cordial. A weight compressed her chest as she struggled with the heat. Weston told her to follow him and she made her way slowly along one of the paved walkways, her skirt brushing dewy ferns that bulged out of raised beds. They certainly weren't her delicate, beloved harts-tongue from the pinewood but sturdy primitive specimens. She reached a finger to touch one, marvelling briefly at the luminosity of the green.

'The seeds came all the way from New Zealand,' Weston told her. 'They're a tough one to propagate but well worth the effort, don't you think?'

The English sunlight shone merrily through the glass roof and through the hundreds of metal Gothic-arched window panes onto Antipodean plants. Weston took her hand, which she was conscious was rather clammy, and led her through, reeling off Latin names as he pointed out one sultry specimen after another.

When they reached his orchid bed, he stood proudly to

one side while Violet stared at the serenely white flowers. They were impossibly curved and stiff, splashed with blood-red and a rather rude pink inside their throats.

'They don't look real,' she said, feeling moisture settle on her top lip.

'Oh, they're real enough, and worth a fortune,' said Weston. 'I hope to start selling soon to the discerning county people. Perhaps send them up to Selfridges. Terribly delicate, though. One mistake with watering, or feeding or heat or shade and they die on me. Have to treat them with great care.' He paused and then pulled her hand up to his lips and kissed it. 'Look, see how your hair sticks to your neck. Allow me.'

She felt his fingertips brush over her collar, and then inside her collar.

'Thank you, Weston.' She stopped him with a smile. 'That feels better.'

She took out her handkerchief and dabbed it discreetly under her nose.

'I don't know how you can spend so long in here,' she observed.

'Ah, but I haven't shown you the melons, or the limes. You'll love the limes. This way.'

He led her towards the far side where the tropical greenery subsided and into a separate glass-walled anteroom where the air felt less dense and a little more comfortable. It was furnished with a wrought-iron chaise longue with linen cushions, a coffee table and a cabinet of mahogany. The sun sent shards of light flickering through the foliage, making dappled patterns on the floor and the chaise longue and on Violet's hands.

'This is my temperate area,' Weston informed her as he reached up to a series of cords at the windows around the chaise longue and let down the blinds. Violet had lost her bearings and guessed that they were on the west side of the house, facing the little side garden. The lawns, the terrace and the party, she decided, must be around the corner.

'Take a seat, my dear, and I will mix you a drink.'

'Oh, that's lovely but shouldn't we be getting back outside? Your mother will be wondering . . .'

'Let her wonder,' he said. 'I have everything I need here.' He opened the cabinet door and took out a bottle of gin. 'Why don't you pick your own lime for your drink?' He laughed and pointed to the group of miniature fruit trees in terracotta pots. 'I have a knife here, some cocktail sticks. Everything.'

Violet reminded him that she didn't really like gin.

'I suppose I should ring for some ice, and for some tonic water. But then we don't really want to bother anyone, do we? Sit, Violet. Take a seat. You must be parched.'

Suppressing a strong desire to get out into fresh air, she politely perched on the end of the chaise longue, wiping her hands with her handkerchief.

'This little room is more pleasant,' she ventured, politely.

'Good old Willis,' cried Weston. 'He filled the ice bucket. Still got some cubes, not all turned to water. And look, some lemonade. This will have to do.'

'Lemonade would be lovely,' she said.

He sighed, 'No gin for Violet.'

She watched patiently as if she was indulging a little boy who was desperate to show her his latest toy, while Weston took out two tumblers and tinkled ice into them.

Her stomach twisted in sorrow, the sorrow she always felt for Weston. The sorrow she hoped had drained away. There was no love there, she realised with a horrifying, blinding flash. She rubbed her sweating palms together.

'And here,' he said, presenting her with an orchid, 'is the phalaenopsis I promised you. We can have it in our bedroom, once we are married. Will look beautiful on the mantel. As beautiful as you.'

The flower offended her. It was nothing like her. It was stiff and rather vulgar. It looked like a fake. She thanked him all the same, while her heart dropped like a stone.

'How well you know the Latin names,' she said, as brightly as she could.

'Would you move up a little, my dear,' he said, placing the tray on the table and sitting rather closely next to her. 'That's better, isn't it.'

'I'm afraid I always have to look up the Latin names.' Violet strained to make light conversation as she settled herself against the chaise. 'When I am adding to my flower journal, I like to use the common names. More memorable and so beautifully descriptive. They seem to have a story to tell, don't they? A little bit of country lore.'

'But this rare orchid isn't a plain old marsh mallow, Violet.' Exasperation blazed in his voice. 'You did Latin at school, didn't you?'

'My worst subject,' she admitted, remembering how she sometimes used to miss that lesson, scoot out of school and end up reading Jane Austen on Whitesands beach.

'Surely not,' Weston turned to her and Violet saw a familiar glint of anger in his forced smile. 'After all, your education was the best that money could buy.'

Violet shifted in her seat. A fist of discomfort sat deep in her stomach.

'I just wasn't very good at it,' she told him. She felt a blush burn from her cheeks to her ears.

She realised with a start how acquainted she was with Weston's bottled-up fury.

'Well, well, there's still time to learn. I will teach you, even if those damned overpaid teachers at your school couldn't.' Weston sat closer, his voice a little softer, his arm moving around her back, around her waist. It felt heavy and damp on the hip of her skirt.

'I think I should like to go back outside,' she said. 'It really is rather stifling, even in here.'

'But you said it was cooler. More pleasant, you said. Sip your lemonade, that's it.' Weston moved closer to her until she was conscious of the weight of his body next to her. He sighed, his voice lightening another degree. 'How agreeable this is. We don't have a lot of time to talk alone together, do we? Your parents always seem to be there, or my mother . . .' He trailed off, saying the last word as if it was as bitter as the lime in Violet's drink. 'My mother. You will get along with her, won't you?'

'Of course I will.' She was startled that he asked. She opened her mouth to continue, and managed to utter, rather feebly, 'She's good company.'

Weston's arm was still around her waist. She was conscious of his fingertips plucking softly at the pleats of her dress.

'I'd like you to start a logbook for me,' he said. 'Recording all of my plants here in the orangery, all the correct names. Recording the germination, the setting of seed. Flowering times, number of leaves.'

Violet tried to laugh, horrified at the idea. It was the exact opposite of her real love: roaming the lanes and the fields, observing and gathering at her own pace, at her own volition. Discovering the true heart of nature, discovering its peace and its purpose and putting it all together in her Flower Book. 'That sounds like a life's work.'

'It will be.'

His grip tightened. He pulled her, suddenly, to face him. His features were so close to her that, startled, she cried out. He stared into her face, his eyes momentarily softening.

'How you glow and glisten in here,' he told her. 'You come alive in all this heat.'

'I'm not sure that I do,' she said to his ungallant compliment. 'I'm finding it rather overbearing.'

'What nonsense.' He bent to kiss her full on the lips. His strength forced her against him, pressing her to his chest.

She was winded and surprised, unable to stop him as he grabbed her hands and forced them up and around his neck.

'You've got to hold me too, Violet,' he murmured, trying to sound playful. 'Hold me too.'

'Weston, I don't think . . .' She turned her face, tilted her chin, instinctively straining her shoulders to move herself out of his grasp. It was too soon, too fast, too frightening and not at all right.

He gripped the tops of her arms.

'I said hold me.'

'Please don't.'

The heat from the orangery seemed to coagulate again and intensify. Weston leant back and dextrously peeled off his jacket, dropping it on the floor. Straining to be polite, to be deferential, to salvage an intensely embarrassing situation, Violet tried to ease herself away from him. But he closed in on her, swiftly, his palms on her shoulders. She heard a sharp rip as her collar tore in his hands.

'I'm sorry, so sorry,' said Weston, breathing hard. He gathered her up, preventing her from going. He lifted her and set her back against the chaise. Violet felt a drop of his sweat land on her neck. 'You will forgive me, Violet, you will.'

His hands worked at the front of her bodice, his hands found a way beneath the hem of her skirt, touching her ankles, her knees. Her petticoats were tangled, a useless barrier. His knee was forcing its way between the folds of the fabric. Astounded by the audacity of what he was doing, her bones froze. Her struggles were inconsequential.

'I have loved you since you were a little girl,' he spoke deep into her ear. 'Don't you know that? You must know that. Just a little girl. We're meant to be together. That's why you're here. You're here now with me.'

'Not now.' She tried to speak, her words muffled and pathetic against the great weight of his shoulder. 'Not this way.'

'It is this way,' he said. 'I will not listen to the others. I will not listen to my mother.'

In dreadful and preposterous silence she heard the popping of his buttons. And then, beneath all her linen and petticoats, he found her. He was sharp. It was agonising. Incredulous and terrified, she found herself staring up into his eyes.

His face was limp and twisted as he spoke. 'Just this once. We'll get this over with, and then we'll be happy.' His words grated against her. He was hurting her, tearing her skin. 'You will love me back.'

'Love you?' she seethed, as his whiskers savaged her cheeks and her throat. She found his eyes, stared into them, locked them. 'I can't *bear* you.'

He stopped abruptly. He bent to pick up his jacket from the floor, hunched like a defeated old man. She leapt up from the chaise. She didn't look back. She plunged out of the anteroom, through the heat of orangery and into the chill of the corridor. The sweat that encased her body was suddenly cold, like a dead woman's shroud. She blundered along, not knowing which way she was going. All the while, a scream bubbled inside her, compressing her throat. She chanced upon an open door, a little courtyard by the back kitchens. Here, the sun was bright, was warming a pot of geraniums, kicking up the astringent scent of their leaves.

Violet stood still in the pool of sunlight, her head filled to bursting with a rushing noise. A storm of horror, of outrage, deafened her. Her body stiffened as the fibres of her bones suddenly believed what had just happened. A padding of footsteps was approaching along the stone corridor behind her. They were light and fast, but she could barely make them out. Was he coming after her?

She turned swiftly to the door to see Jess trot out, and she crouched to him, clutching at his silky ears with cold, trembling hands.

'You came to find me, did you?' she whispered into the dog's coat as tears squeezed in her eyes. 'You found me.'

She looked up with a start to see Willis in the doorway, his uniform like a shield, grave and formal in the sunshine. His face was a mask of mute questions.

'Oh, there you are,' said Violet, straightening up, amazed at the breeze in her voice. 'I wondered, Willis, could you please let my parents and Mrs Penruth know that I am going home. I am rather unwell.'

'Yes, madam, of course.' Willis's eye dropped to her ripped collar and flicked straight back up again politely to her face. 'Would you like me to call for the car? It won't take a moment.'

'No, thank you. A walk will do me good.'

'Very well.' He held out the dog's lead. 'You'll be needing this, madam.'

She took it from him, unable to look him in the face.

'I can't thank you enough,' she whispered and knelt to latch the lead to Jess's collar.

She walked quickly along the drive, aware of the great house looming behind her, resisting the urge to look back at its glowering face. She turned into the lane, hurrying along. The breeze had picked up, bringing with it a vague scent of the sea, and dried the tears onto her cheeks. Beyond the hedge, they were harvesting a clover field. The farmhands were concentrated on their work, deep in the rhythm of their song and their cutting machines. Even so, she dipped her head and hurried. It would not do for them to see her, Mr Penruth's fiancée, dashing away from her own party.

The lanes were ripe with cow parsley, the air perfumed. Soon, within days, scarlet poppy, pure-blue veronica and dusky cranesbill would show their fragile faces along the verges. But the thought of it gave her no pleasure as it usually would. For now, all of this was ruined.

She dived into the pinewood, letting it swallow her whole. Under its silent shelter she ran with Jess pacing beside her. Here in the dappled twilight the woodland floor was soft beneath her feet. The towering pines cloistered her, offered their comfort, but she could not take it. The deafening roar in her head stayed with her, had altered her. She stopped in her tracks, dropped the dog's lead, shook her head hard and pressed her hands over her ears. She did not feel safe here, even in this deep and forgiving peace. Weston had taken it away from her, taken peace from everything.

When she finally got to the ford she knelt on the stony slope, breathing hard, leant forward and placed her hands in the shallows. She dipped her face into the cold water. Thrilled by the shock of it, she drew herself out, her hair sopping, soaking her dress. And then she plunged her face in again. And then again. Yet, when she emerged cold and dripping, nothing had changed. She was still soiled and ruined.

How long would it take them to have the conversation? How long before tea on the lawn was finally over, and Willis began to clear away? How long before her parents decided they ought to get back to Old Trellick and see how she was?

Violet opened the front door and rushed up to the garret. Pulling a cupboard door wide open, she hauled out her suitcase. She stopped then, utterly breathless, hit abruptly by the reality. Her legs began to shake. She was exhausted, her blood as weak as water.

'I can't face them,' she muttered, groping for the chair to sit down. 'Because they won't listen. Because they won't believe me. Because they'll *make* me . . .'

She rested her head on the table. She could hear her mother's voice urging her to not be so silly, that sometimes the groom cannot wait. *Men will have their way*, May Prideaux was saying in her head. *After all, it's Weston Penruth. Think about that for a moment. You are going to be Mrs Weston Penruth!* Her father was a mere shadow, unaware, or acting in feigned ignorance. *Chin up, Violet dear*, Dr Prideaux will say eventually, weeks, days, years later: *It's not the worst thing in the world. He's a very eligible man.*

Squeezing her eyes tightly shut, she kept her cheek pressed to the table and listened hard to the silence of her home. A tap was dripping somewhere below, and a loose shutter knocked gently in the breeze. Jess sighed and sat at her feet. She could hear the occasional twittering of the birds in the garden. And then, she heard the cuckoo, except this time, he sounded different. *Cuc-cuckoo.* The weeks and months had rolled on since she'd first heard it on the day of the Looe ball. The same day she snubbed Weston Penruth. And now, so much had altered. It was all so much worse. The cuckoo had changed its tune. It was only a summer visitor and would soon fly away.

On the table, just by her hand, lay her Flower Book. With a cry of pleasure, as if renewing a friendship, she reached for it and jealously held it close. Breathing deeply on the smell of the paper, running her fingertips over the edges of the pages and the deep-green jacket, she felt herself surface back into her own world again. She was Violet again. She dragged Mrs Penruth's ring off her finger and left it on the table.

Chapter Seven

In June, all day and no night

The train laboured sideways over the wide tracks, an endless puzzle of chevrons, on its approach to Paddington. Violet watched from her dirty carriage window as the wheels pounded, the brakes strained and the engine sighed like a massive defeated beast. She shifted in the spot where she'd sat for so many hours, longing to disembark, stretch her legs and ease the tenderness in her back. She glimpsed scruffy, mean backs of terraced houses alongside the line. Blank windows were lifeless and grim and, above, the summer evening sky was a dense blue, just this side of dark – a sullen backdrop to smoking chimneys and slate roofs. She wondered about all the souls who lived behind the murky windows, who slept there beneath the cracked and slipping tiled roofs, until, in a moment, her view was blocked by a metal lid arching over her – the immense ironwork station roof.

All through her journey, Violet had immersed herself in the glorious summer landscape peeling away beside her. The hours melted in a daze of trees and farmhouses and cornfields and her confidence flourished the further the train took her from home. But, an hour after Reading, the haphazard medley of towns and streets invaded, and she drew herself up straight, held herself to attention, to face the encroaching city that would be filled with strangers and filled with questions. She stepped off the train into cold reality.

The platform was chaotic and crowded. Porters hurried through shouting 'mind yer backs', wheeling their carts stacked with trunks. Passengers knocked past her, congregating at ticket barriers. Why did they have to talk so loudly, so fast? She trailed along, drawing her shoulders up, holding her suitcase in one hand, her ticket in the other. She was battered and tired, parched and hungry, and ready to drop. But she lifted her chin, forced herself on and headed outside to the rank where taxis waited, headlamps gleaming, engines rumbling.

Through the din, Violet heard a driver call out to her through his open window as he pulled his taxi forward. It was her turn and she didn't quite know what to do. As she stepped forward, she felt a man nearby make a grab for her suitcase. Startled, she shrank from him, as a scream of shock broke from her throat. Tears scorched her eyes. The man was close to her, his bulky body straining his porter's uniform. She flinched, remembering Weston. She wanted to be sick.

'S'all right, miss. This one's kosher.' The porter's voice was high-pitched and cheery as he threw her suitcase in the back of the cab and gestured that she should follow it. 'He's done the Knowledge. Jus' tell 'im where you're going and remember the tip.'

Knees shaking, Violet ducked into the taxi. The door was slammed unceremoniously behind her and she sat back in the seat and asked for Montagu Square.

'Just off the Plymouth train, are yer, miss?' the driver threw back over his shoulder as he engaged his gears and the taxi chugged forward.

Dry-mouthed with fatigue, Violet muttered 'yes'. The driver, in the time it took him to negotiate the congested station approach, proceeded to reel off his annoyance at the traffic, the lateness of the hour and the price of tobacco.

The cab was fuggy with fumes from his pipe and the air coming through the opened window was warm and thick with diesel and manure. She tried not to breathe deeply, remembering in a painful flash the purity and sweetness of the pinewood. Ahead and all around her, clattering horse-drawn carriages hustled for space and, as the taxi lurched out onto the street, an open-top omnibus rattled past, brutally close. Either side, illuminated by sporadic gas lamps, towered dark terraces. The gloomy sky had been lost to the night and Violet was a tiny speck in the city. She held onto the seat with both hands as the driver overtook a coal cart, smothering her desire to squeal in fear. And then she spotted the Praed Street sign and smiled tearfully. Within the mayhem of Paddington, this Cornish name was a lullaby.

They passed a horse-drawn taxi and, buoyed up and feeling a little braver, she leant forward and asked the driver if he had ever driven one.

He laughed, told her not on her nelly, but that, in hindsight, he was a mug not to.

'You know, when they test 'em, miss, 'orse taxis only have to turn their vehicle in a circle. I had to reverse this blinking motor cab round a corner to pass mine.'

He told her the nags were going, though, and too right too. Won't see many more of them on these roads. Good job. They get right in the way.

'Won't take long, miss,' he said, once he had finished ruminating gleefully on the demise of the horse. 'Won't touch the Marylebone Road. Just down Edgware and left onto George Street.'

This meant nothing to Violet. She wondered, blandly, if he knew all the streets.

'Bless yer, darling. 'Course I do. And you know what else I know? All the clubs, hotels, railways, tube stations, theatres, music 'alls, 'ospitals, police stations . . . let me think, what else . . . prisons, docks, wharves, banks, museums, mortuaries, cemeteries. Everything in this blessed town. Everything.'

Violet squinted through the window, peering at just one segment of the teeming city in which every part of a person's life was tended to and taken care of, one way or another.

And then the cab turned sharp left and, abruptly, the racket from the traffic fell away.

Violet was taken through a grid of silent Georgian streets lined with ghostly white terraces three or four storeys high. The houses had flat facades, smooth bays and iron railings. The cab tyres trundled blithely over cobbles instead of sticky asphalt as they entered a grand, sweeping square. All was elegance and serenity.

They pulled up by railings enclosing the square's garden.

It was peaceful and deep in night shadow, canopied by plane trees that were dropping their flowers over the pavement. Violet looked out of the window at the house she had the address for, peering up at the front, pale in the darkness, a lamp burning at the wide first-floor window.

'Very nice too,' the driver said.

She paid him, tipped him royally, heedless of her meagre allowance. As the taxi chugged away, she walked across the silent street.

Either side of the great black front door stood two Palladian columns, and to her right, the dark steps leading down to the tradesman's door. She realised then, as she rang the bell and it sounded somewhere remote inside the house, how far she had travelled. How far she was from home.

A housemaid, crisp in white apron over a stiff dark dress, opened the door and Violet stepped into a cool dim hallway. The corridor, paved with black and white tesserae, faded into the gloom of closed doorways, while the staircase rose before her up into the yellow lantern glow of the landing above. She followed the maid mutely up the stairs, her slow and tired footsteps muffled by deep maroon carpet. Climbing, she glanced numbly at oil paintings, framed watercolours, the fine scrolled paper covering the walls, noting the hollow ticking of a long-case clock. The delectable peace inside the house made the long stretching ordeal of her journey trickle away.

The maid opened the polished oak door on to the first-floor drawing room and Violet's insides melted in relief. She walked into a room she had not been in since she was a child. The delicate elegance of the Georgian interior was stuffed with black walnut bookcases, with knick-knacks, statuary and endless books gleaming in lamplight, every door and every window muffled with extravagant velvet drapes. The grandeur and glory was as familiar and as frightening as before. Even so, Violet felt she had been released. She was at ease. She could breathe. At last, she was here, inside Aunt Muriel's home.

'Madam is in bed with her ankle,' announced the maid, who had clearly been expecting her. 'Would you like some refreshment?'

Violet, painfully aware of her train-crumpled coat, of the smuts of dirt that must be marring her cheeks and how late in the evening it was, suddenly felt like an interloper and stupidly shy. She simply told her she'd like some tea.

The housemaid took her hat and coat. 'Madam would like you to go straight up to see her.'

Violet hesitated. 'May I please use the facilities?'

Mutely, the maid led her to a water closet near the backstairs. Violet peered at her reflection in her auntie's bathroom mirror. She patted down her hair and washed away the grime of her journey. Her face was pale and her eyes, flickering with exhaustion, were haunted.

She found her auntie sitting up in bed in her boudoir on the second floor, beaming at her. Her salt-and-pepper hair was in pins, covered neatly in a queenly nightcap. A scarlet eiderdown smothered her leg, which was delicately propped up on pillows, and the salmon-pink ruffles of her bed jacket shimmered in the lamplight as she gestured impatiently for Violet to come in.

'My, my, what a journey you've had. You look all in, my dear. Sit, sit here and let me look at you.'

Violet pulled the dressing chair close to the bed, feeling Muriel's sharp eyes scrutinising her.

'Nothing that a hot bath and a good night's rest can't

put right. And soup. Cook made some mulligatawny this morning.' Muriel leant over and rang her handbell. 'I will get Smithson to bring you soup.'

Thanking her, Violet discovered what an effort it was to speak. She hoped she could go straight to bed without too much conversation or explanation but knew her auntie, because of her unprecedented and unseemly trip to London, would most certainly want to talk.

While Muriel was ordering up her food for her, Violet thought about the life she led, up here in Fitzrovia's fashionable quarter. Muriel had married well, to Mr Jeff Strachen, and, as she might often quip herself, had been widowed well too. Uncle Jeff, who had made it big in the City, had died when Violet was young and she did not remember him. Muriel, childless, supremely confident and forthright, shook off her widow's weeds quickly and carved a life of sociability and amusement, determined to seek out people and things to enjoy within the tight confines of her blessed, polite world. Her life, in vast contrast to her sister May's, as well as being the subject of entertainment in the Prideaux household, engendered sibling envy, too.

'Your mother will be worried and not happy that you travelled without a chaperone,' Muriel said gravely, lowering her forehead to gaze at Violet. 'I frankly didn't see the need for such a rush. When I got your telegram, around noon, I wondered if you were desperate to come up to town to shop for your trousseau. I thought, what fun! But from that look on your face . . . ah, Smithson.'

The maid brought the soup and tea on a tray, set it down on the bedside table, and was dismissed for the night.

Muriel gestured to it and encouraged Violet to eat.

78

Violet's shoulders sagged with the effort but she took the napkin and spread it carefully over her lap.

'This is something desperate, I'll wager,' said Muriel. 'Something far more serious than a bride's empty bottom drawer. You don't have to tell me now, my dear. You look shattered. Maybe tomorrow. Have some soup. Sip your tea and ask me how I am.'

Violet looked up at Muriel's kind, expectant face and felt a stinging tremor around her nostrils. Her defensive shield had shut itself around her from the moment she had dragged herself off the chaise in the orangery and she raced back to Old Trellick. And then, during her flight at dawn the next morning, as she left the scribbled note for her parents and patted Jess farewell, her body had been numb and mechanical, her mind disengaged. She barely remembered thumbing a lift to Looe on the milk cart, sending the wire to Muriel from the station and finally slumping in her seat in the carriage and closing her eyes. But now the older woman's dissecting stare made this barrier that Violet had built in the face of disaster fade to nothing.

'Oh Auntie,' she blurted, surrendering to tears.

'You've bolted!'

Violet didn't know how or whether to agree. She had no idea, really, what she had done.

Muriel's face paled and then reddened, as a spark of delight seemed to quiver at the corner of her eye. Violet wondered, briefly, if her aunt looked a little excited. Muriel had barely drawn breath to begin to exclaim her surprise and to assure her niece of her confidence in a crisis, when they heard the doorbell ring two floors below.

'Oh heavens, what now?' Muriel muttered and cocked her ear to listen for Smithson, who surely had not gone to bed yet.

Violet's fear slammed right back into her. Her heart dilated in sheer terror. The bell rang again. Had he followed her here?

Both women waited in excruciating silence as the door below was opened, and an exchange was made. Footsteps eventually approached up the stairs and the boudoir door was knocked upon.

Smithson came in with apologies, carrying a telegram on a tray. 'For Miss Prideaux,' she said and left.

Violet's fingers were weak with relief and trepidation in equal measure as she dealt with the envelope. She heard her auntie's impatient sighing as she fumbled with the chit of paper.

'Well, my dear. Well? Tell me. Has he forgiven you? What is to happen?'

Violet scanned her parents' telegram swiftly, her throat palpitating in confusion. She handed it straight to her aunt, who took it and read aloud, her voice as flat and neutral as the post office clerk at Looe who would have taken it down and then repeated the instruction to her mother, just to make sure.

'Extreme disappointment. We request your swift return. Weston enraged. Shot his dogs.'

He crept around her mind all through the half-dark watches of that summer night. She lay on the bed in her auntie's guest room with her eyes fixed on the pearly light of the premature dawn beyond the curtains. Images exposed themselves against greasy fatigue inside her head: she could not shut them off. She saw the dogs running eagerly and blissfully to their master's whistle. And herself, glimpsed from the steaming orangery rafters, trapped and pinned, unable to fight. The explosion of the shotgun rang out, again and again.

Chapter Eight

In the language of flowers:
Burgundy rose, unconscious beauty

Sitting with Muriel with the newspapers over breakfast in the morning room, Violet drooped with exhaustion. A slice of sunshine bravely found its way through the windows of the first-floor room where Muriel's immemorial drapes and blinds trapped everything in a strange twilight. Nibbling the corner of a slice of toast and sipping Earl Grey tea, Violet's mind was now stagnant and mercifully empty.

Muriel peered at her over the top of *The Times* and stated cheerfully that it was a joy that she was here as she could assist her in getting about a bit more.

'You can help me up and down the stairs, dear, with my blessed ankle. And if you don't mind, to and from the commode. I don't like to bother Smithson too much. She can be rather surly at the best of times.'

Violet assured her that it would be no trouble.

'And you can stay with me as long as you like,' Muriel added cautiously, her sentence ended on a high note, as if in question. 'As long as you feel is necessary.'

When Violet said nothing, her aunt declared, 'He is a madman for slaughtering his dogs. And that's all I wish to say on the matter. Unless, of course, you'd like to tell me all about it.'

Nausea rose through Violet's gullet at violent speed. She shook her head.

'My dear, I won't press you. Listen, you need to get yourself outside. You don't want to be stuck in here around a middle-aged lady all day. Go to the park. It looks like a lovely day out there. It's just a twenty-minute walk. Get some colour in those cheeks.'

Her concern drew sharp tears to Violet's eyes.

'Yes,' Violet muttered. 'I think I must get out, or I feel I might break in two.'

'I've never seen you look so pale.'

They exchanged brief smiles. Something of the warmth and understanding in her aunt's eyes told Violet that she need never enlighten her if she did not want to. For how could she ever explain?

Muriel pressed on her a parasol, as Violet had arrived at Montagu Square ill-prepared for most things, including the bright June sunshine on the London streets, and with only a few shillings of change.

'If you go directly across Gloucester Place and Baker Street, you'll reach Marylebone High Street,' her aunt told her. 'On the corner is my little grocer's. Could you pick up some Robinson's lemonade for me? They missed it out of my delivery last week and I could do with some to go in my gin. Turn left there and you'll eventually get to the park. Now, go quickly. The sunshine will dry your eyes.'

Montagu Square was leafy, shady and quiet. Smartly upholstered nannies were taking their charges for strolls, pushing prams along the pavement. The bread man came and went, doffing his cap and telling her good morning as Violet stepped out. She passed a block of newly built red-brick mansion flats with pristine net curtains in the windows and geraniums spilling from window boxes. But when she reached the main thoroughfare of Baker Street, the tranquillity was curtailed. It melded suddenly into the same hot chaos of taxis, horses and buses that she'd witnessed at Paddington. Violet waited, frozen at the kerb, breathing the fumes and the steaming dung and squinting against the hard sunshine. But this was all part of London life, she told herself, and if she was going to stay with Auntie Muriel for as long as she liked, then she must get used to this madly endearing city.

The grocer on the corner was inviting, with its posters for Bourneville and Pear's soap, but she decided that she'd pay a call on the way back and also treat her auntie to some little confection using her allowance. Perhaps some glacé fruits or ginger in syrup, or a little bit of chocolate? In the shade of the towering shopfronts, she walked busily on, melting into the crowd.

The dense hedges of Regent's Park bulged through the iron railings of its sweeping boundary – a verdant glimmer beyond the grey asphalt. Violet crossed the road and walked over a little bridge that led into the park. Ducks paddled and shook themselves among the lily pads in the water below, and the melee of the streets behind her retreated like a sulking enemy. She breathed deeply on the suddenly balmy green-scented air, and felt the fear that had squatted inside her head since the afternoon of her engagement party gently ease.

Turning a corner under the shade of some willows, she came upon a garden of roses bathing in the sunshine, a cloud of colour under the dazzling light. Row upon row of bourbon, damask and tea roses had been planted in circular patterns and Violet stopped and stared, tearing her eyes away from lemon yellows and dusky lilacs, from the profoundest reds and the snowiest whites. She was drawn across a carpet of daisies towards their tranquil company, and strolling among them, every now and then, she stopped and pressed her nose to open cups and tight buds in turn, drinking in their perfume. In varying degrees of lightness and spiciness, the scents were hypnotic and distracting. She thought of Claudia and how she would love these roses, how she would bury her face in them. Wondering what, if anything, her friend knew about her leaving, Violet's thoughts tightened again into a painful ball. Claudia would be worried and confused, but then surely reassured by Eddie Davey. That night, she decided, or at least tomorrow, she would write to her. But what, on earth, would she say? The comfort of her closest friend was an eternity away.

In a daze, her spirits fading, Violet moved towards a shady bower at the centre of the garden. There was a bench beneath the canopy of trailing open-faced dog roses and she climbed three shallow steps to claim the seat for herself. Sitting with the sun in her eyes and light dappling her cheeks, she shielded her face with Muriel's parasol. The perfect June day seemed to blow kisses around her. She turned her face to catch the breezes as they worked to extract her dark thoughts, break them and scatter them at her feet.

Gentlemen strolled with their ladies among the roses, each one of the couples behaving kindly and courteously towards each other. The female silhouettes were slender with the new fashions, topped by hats of stupendously wide concoction. She watched one man ask his companion to smell a particularly blissfully deep-burgundy rose which he cradled, still attached to its stem, delicately in his hand for her. The tenderness in their exchange brought a thickness to Violet's throat. She thought of Weston and how he had forced her to admire the orchid. She despised him, then, in a white flash of utter rage.

She cursed him, hated him. Greedily she looked around the garden to fill her eyes with the day's beauty again, eager to bring back her momentary happiness. She saw a man, lingering at the corner of her eye. He sat on a stool, sketching, in the lower part of the garden below the steps. Dressed in working-man's blue, a hat protected his eyes and his artist's board was on his lap, his hand moving rapidly over the page. She idly watched him, enjoying the peace that sprang from his stance and his gestures. He looked a little bit older than her; his fair hair clipped short beneath his hat, his shirt open at the neck, a frown of concentration on his brow. His collar was flapping in the breeze but he seemed unaware, such was his rapture with whatever he was creating. The pencil was a mere stub in his fingers and it dashed across the paper, drawing shapes and swirls. And then he looked up at her, straight at her. He was sketching her.

In a flash of outrage, she stood up and swiftly moved away through the mass of roses. How rude! she fumed. How dare he? She stormed on and did not look back.

Once she reached the edge of the park, scooted through the gates and past the pristine white mansions of York Terrace, she broke out suddenly into a laugh. How silly, she thought, and how vain. The artist was drawing the gardens, the roses, the sunlight and the leaves. He wasn't interested in me. I caught his eye because I was fidgeting in my seat.

Feeling a fool now that the still-life magic and peace of the park was broken, she hurried on down the bustling street, suddenly wanting to be safely behind her aunt's front door. She was weary and longed for sleep. Surely, now at last, she would sleep. Abruptly, she stopped, realising she had walked straight past the grocer's by mistake. She turned to go back, to cross the side street and return to the corner. But there he was again. Right there.

He had stopped some hundred yards or more away just outside the grocer's. Clutching his canvas bag, his artist's board under his arm, his gaze was open, almost expectant. She peered as passing pedestrians hid her view and then revealed him again. There was no mistake. He was looking right at her.

She stepped forward and lifted her hand to gesture to him, to perhaps acknowledge him, but at that moment an omnibus came lumbering past, slowing at the junction, blocking out her view. And when it had at last pulled away, leaving behind a plume of exhaust, the artist had gone.

A week later, Violet sat in her aunt's guest bedroom overlooking Montagu Square but, in her head, she was at Old Trellick watching the gathering dusk. There, the garden would be still alive at this late hour with the birds singing, melodious and indistinct, honey around her ears. She

86

imagined the long evening stretching over the south Cornish coast, the long evening in which farmers could bring in their hay and herd their stock; in which cows would plod out to pasture through a lingering, hazy, unreal light. She thought of how much could be seen, all through such a light, brief night-time. Fleetingly, she hungered for home.

But then, in the instance Violet remembered the hostility of her mother's telegram. She looked up from the desk at Aunt Muriel's guest-bedroom window and was relieved to see gas lamps burning around the square and lights glowing in the windows opposite. Out there were scores of strangers, scores of other lives that could so easily distract her from her own. She took out a sheet of her aunt's headed paper and the comforting London twilight wrapped itself around her as she wrote to Claudia.

How are you, my dear friend? She stopped, her mind suddenly blank. *So sorry not to have been in touch until now. As you can imagine, something went horribly wrong, but I am well . . .*

It was a lie. She was far from well. Her body was numb, worryingly so. She felt no pain. There was no evidence of the assault, just a vague and disturbing lightness in her head, a strange tightening of her skin. Then the horror of what he did to her roared up again and she sank her face into her hands, covering her eyes.

She passed many moments like this, tearless and dazed, until Smithson knocked on her door and advised her that her aunt would like her company downstairs.

In the drawing room, the velvet drapes muffled the last of the evening light and the oil lamps were glowing a keen yellow. Muriel was happily settled with her poorly ankle propped on a stool, a glass of deep-brown sherry at her elbow and, on the little table, a china plate of the candied fruits that Violet had bought on her first day in London . . . the day the artist saw her, sketched her, followed her . . . In Muriel's hands her stack of cards gleamed. She sifted them, flicked them over, toyed with them.

'Would you like me to do a reading for you? I'm in the mood. I'm feeling rather lucid tonight.'

Violet sat down and forced out a laugh. 'Really? Then you are doing far better than I am. I don't think I have a choice, do I?'

With an odd mixture of fascination and disbelief, Violet humoured her. She settled back, relishing the distraction of her aunt and her little superstitions and watched her shuffle, choose and lay out the cards. Smithson brought Violet a small sherry and she sipped at the smart, heady liqueur as Muriel ruminated over the spread before her. The lady sighed and flinched as she ceremoniously turned over each new card.

'Goodness, Violet, so many Cups. Look at them, all over the place.' Muriel whispered the names of the cards in awe, tapping with her fingernail over the crude pictures that depicted age-old qualities, ancient archetypes. If there was one thing Violet knew about the Tarot, it was that Cups and their element of water indicated emotion and love. And, apparently, her reading was full of them. 'Goodness me, my dear,' went on Muriel in a rather vague trance. 'Look at the way this one crosses the Ten of Cups. This tells me you will certainly marry this year.'

A sick shiver ran up Violet's spine. 'Impossible,' she retorted, irritated by the audacity of the silly old card game.

Another memory of Weston made her draw her breath. 'Utter rubbish, Auntie, really!'

'Well, I agree,' huffed Muriel, annoyed with herself. 'The way things have been going on for you lately, this is ridiculous. I must be losing my touch. Perhaps we'll do it again later.'

'Later, next week, next month. Can we not talk about marriage, please.'

Violet drew a quick glance of admiration from her aunt, who tidied away her cards and refilled both their glasses.

'Understood,' said Muriel. 'I'm sorry. Rather insensitive of me, isn't it. I'm just so damn bored.'

She flinched as she moved her bandaged foot and asked Violet to slip another cushion under it.

'Doctor's visiting tomorrow to have another look at my ankle. I wonder if it's broken? Should have been healed by now, don't you think?'

Violet wondered about it but suggested that she would be in a lot more pain if it was worse than a sprain. Perhaps she'd be up and about again soon, in any case, if only to relieve her frustration.

'Yes, yes. I'm sure he will have a prod about and want to dismiss me as a fussy lady of a certain age, but then prescribe some tonic or other to perk me up. Well, that's what I pay him for, isn't it? I'll tell him I have all the tonic I need in this little glass of sherry. How are you, anyway, dear? No more telegrams from your mother? You'll be getting a letter soon, no doubt. She is probably still incensed, if I know her. All tied up in knots so far that she cannot pick up a pen and put it to paper.'

'I can only guess at what such a letter might say, going by

the telegram that very nearly beat me here. I've just written a letter to Claudia, though. I thought that would make me feel better but it actually didn't.'

As her aunt began to surmise that Claudia would be ecstatic to hear from her, Violet's mind began to drift. How she missed her friend, and hoped she was happy with Eddie. Who knows, perhaps the cards were for her, and she would become Mrs Davey before the year was out?

'I miss *talking* with her, Auntie,' Violet confessed. 'We would walk for hours with the dog, down to the cove, along by the sea, through the pinewoods and scarcely draw breath!'

'She's missing you, of course she is,' Muriel assured her.

'She *knows* me, do you understand?' Violet felt tears prick her eyes.

Muriel nodded sagely and sipped her sherry while Violet recalled their chattering, their blunt exchanges, proclaiming about everything from Claudia's wine-making skills and insubstantial wardrobe to Violet's spoiling of Jess and her precious Flower Book.

'She's the only person I will allow to tease me about my journal,' Violet reminisced out loud. 'She always laughed about the fact that the one lesson I was interested in at school was nature studies, even though I was enjoying an expensive, private education. And the time we did poisonous plants was the only thing that stopped me running away again. Oh, those plants, what were their names . . . ?'

Muriel's head was nodding, her eyes drooping closed, so Violet sat back and mused to herself: oh yes, hemlock, deadly nightshade and tansy, those horrid little yellow button flowers that Claudia's mother had once used.

Chapter Nine

In the language of flowers:
Red pimpernel, change

'Shall I not order the brougham around for you, miss?' Smithson asked her as she pulled out a particularly large umbrella from the stand in the hallway and handed it to her. 'William is always ready with the carriage. It shouldn't take many minutes and it is such filthy weather.'

Violet told her no, but thank you. She didn't mind the rain.

Her aunt had already berated her on her plan to leave the house that morning.

'You will catch your death and then what will I tell your mother and father? They are already not speaking to me.'

Violet reminded Muriel how much time she spent out of doors back in Cornwall. She was hardly going to shrink away from getting a little wet. At any rate, the umbrella offered to her by Smithson was enormous.

'I suppose I shall have to adjust to your ways,' sighed her

aunt. 'I don't know. Is it the same with all you girls these days? Travelling all the way on the Plymouth train on your own like that. Unthinkable in my day.'

Violet assured her that she would take care, and she wouldn't be more than two hours or so. Aunt Muriel offered her cheek for her to kiss and reiterated that she would be keeping time.

'Nice weather for ducks,' commented the grocery man, coming up outside steps from the basement as Violet left the house. 'Typical June weather, isn't it? I suppose it's all we deserve.'

Violet bade him good morning. She lifted the brolly over her head, wishing to hide her face and settle down into her own privacy.

The clouds over London were saturated grey, the trees dripped and the pavements sparkled. The air smelt fresh and earthy. As she hurried along, crossing the square, she heard the downpipes rushing with water and was acutely aware that there was something missing by her side. Her long walks through the pinewoods of Old Trellick and down to the cove were accompanied by Jess, and invariably Claudia. Now under the slaty city sky, she felt both their absences keenly.

She took a different route, avoiding the park and sticking to the wet and busy road north that skirted it. Through the mesh of her veil, the hectic streets and the parades of buildings looked soft and docile, receding into a murky blend. The houses here along the western edge of the park remained reasonably grand, if a little shabbier than Montagu Square. And then they became smaller, the windows dirtier. These canal-side houses were, in her auntie's world, she surmised, rather undesirable. Aunt Muriel's perplexed imagined voice was badgering her, asking her why on earth she would be in such a place, as she took the steep steps down the side of the bridge over the waterway and found herself on the towpath.

Below the level of the road, shielded by buildings clustered tight to its course, the Regent's Canal eased its way quietly east to west through the city. Backs of sheds, and small factories and coal yards shadowed the dark, oily water pitted with raindrops. Behind her she heard the piping shriek of a Midland Railway train as it crossed over the water and slowed itself down for Marylebone station. Two or three barges were afloat within this section, exhaling smoke from their chugging engine stacks, the bargemen at the helm, hunched and sullen under workmen's caps.

The humid, gritty air around her smelt of industry, of tar. Unsurprisingly, the towpath was empty, as most sensible and respectable people who didn't have to go out – again, she heard Aunt Muriel's voice – were cosy by their parlour hearthsides. Most sensible and respectable people would not be here at all.

Violet began to walk, scanning the shrubby verge where unruly weeds twisted and tangled among long grass bent under the weight of the rain. In her head, she named them all, enjoying the chant she struck up as she went: nettles, dandelions, creeping buttercup, woundwort and red pimpernel like little drops of blood; the Latin names were lost to her, meaningless. She had no need for them. The brick walls lining the waterway, some mended, some crumbling hopelessly, were host to all manner of moss colonies. They clung like parasites, sparkling with tiny raindrop pearls.

At last, there it was. The plant she was searching for blazed out a bright yellow from among the ivy that encrusted a discarded pile of bricks. The tansy was like a beacon amid the mizzle of rain, Violet thought, as she folded away her umbrella and opened her canvas bag. She squatted down and snipped away at the flower heads, filling her bag.

The chug of a narrow boat came closer, pressing on Violet's ears with a humming pressure and filling her nostrils with the chemical scent of exhaust. She stood up and watched as it drew closer. At the wheel stood the bargeman wearing a heavy cape of sackcloth over his shoulders as a shield from the deluge. By his knee stood a young boy whose jacket was tied on to him with a piece of rope around his middle, his head tilted down beneath his cap. Next to the bargeman, his wife was holding a baby, wrapped up in a mess of shawls. Violet found herself staring at her face. The woman was pale, her eyes deep-set, haunted by fatigue, and yet her sopping hat was adorned with a ruby-red flower like a defiant badge.

The baby in her arms suddenly squawked and a little white fist found the drizzly air. The woman tenderly tucked it away and dipped her mouth to kiss its hidden forehead. Mesmerised, Violet sensed a mysterious emotion stirring in her chest. But the reason for her quest for the elusive little weed shone as brightly in her mind as the acid yellow of the flowers amid the rain. She turned her back on the passing barge and its mute occupants, and stuffed yet another handful of tansy into her bag.

She decided to quit the towpath before she reached the Zoological Gardens and walk back through the park. It was, predictably, deserted. Violet passed a few dishevelled gardeners hoeing a herbaceous border and spotted a handful of horse-drawn hansom carriages trundling around the outer circle, all battened down, conveying neatly dressed occupants to afternoons of bezique or bridge at the mansions in the Nash crescents on the eastern side. By the time she reached the rose garden, she was tired, the dampness of the day creeping into her bones and making her spirits droop. The rain had stopped but it was far too wet to sit down under the bower. Water continued to drip from leaves and branches, mimicking its own little rain shower, and the roses were forlorn, hanging their heads like the little boy on the barge. Crumpled petals littered the grass, their colour diluted.

The sun will shine again tomorrow, Violet silently assured them, and surprised herself by reaching up behind her veil with her handkerchief and wiping off a tear. With a wince of foolish disappointment, she realised that the artist was not here. Of course he wasn't, because who in their right mind, as Aunt Muriel would say, would come out on a day like today?

Upstairs in her bedroom, Violet took off her soaked coat and hung it up. Even the shoulders of her blouse were damp. She unbuttoned her boots, peeled off her stockings and unfastened her skirt, its drenched hem making her remember rescuing Jess from the stream. She shivered in her chemise and was thankful that Smithson had thought of building a small fire for her in the grate. Wrapping herself in her dressing gown, she lit the lamp and sat at the desk in front of the window. Beyond her aunt's festooned curtains the dull afternoon was as wet and as sullen as ever.

She laid out her tansy clippings on a sheet of yesterday's newspaper – with headlines that reported suffragette action in London and political issues in the Balkan states – and selected the best one for pressing. Then she opened the Flower Book and turned to the next blank page and prepared it for the tansy which, once pressed between the pages of her aunt's encyclopaedia, would be ready for mounting in a week or two. She wrote:

20th June 1914. Found by the Regent's Canal, London.

Tansy flower (also known as bitter buttons, or cow buttons).

She added its usual habitat, its growing season, its medicinal uses, the fact she got soaked to the skin trying to find it, and the way the rose garden had looked after the deluge.

And then she rang the bell.

'Please could you take my wet clothes away to the laundry. My boots will need reshaping, I'm afraid, and may have to go to the cobbler. Oh, and I'd like some tea with lemon,' she told Smithson.

Smithson pursed her lips, bobbed and returned shortly with the small copper kettle of water and a little blue glazed teapot on a tray.

'Shall I light the flame, miss?'

'Oh no, I shall do it.'

Once alone, Violet knelt by the table to strike a match and ignite the lamp under the kettle. She scooped one teaspoon of leaves from the caddy into the pot and then gathered a handful of tansy flowers. She plucked the little yellow buttons off the stems and threw them in with the tea. She peeled off some of the feathery leaves for good measure.

'Milk or lemon?' she pondered out loud as she sat and waited for the kettle to whistle.

At last steam forced its way upwards from the spout with a rather impolite little shriek.

She made the tea, waited for it to infuse and poured herself a cup through the strainer. After one delicate sip she winced. The flavour was green and pungent, and rather revolting.

'Lemon . . .' she picked up a thin disc with her aunt's silver tongs and plopped it into her cup '. . . and perhaps some sugar will improve this little brew. Either way, it should do the trick.'

Chapter Ten

In July, dog days bright and clear indicate a happy year

Aunt Muriel's single-pony brougham pulled up outside the grand portico of Lady Welstead's town house on Cumberland Terrace at around four on that airless, sultry afternoon. It was the proper and perfect time to call, Muriel advised Violet, who was squeezed in next to her in the stifling confines of the little carriage.

'The visiting card should be left between the hours of three and six,' Muriel advised. 'Any other time and we'd be denounced as socially inept.'

The leather seat was sweating against Violet's back. She pulled her window down and peered up at the exquisitely precise, gleaming-white facade of the Welstead mansion as it loomed imperiously over the park from the eastern side.

'It's all rather magnificent, isn't it?' she commented, craning her neck to take in its, all things considered, discreet Regency splendour. She mentally counted the floors.

'Ah, yes, she runs a very smart household. Sir Giles and Lady Welstead moved up here from Fitzrovia soon after he was knighted for his services to banking,' Muriel informed her. 'I often wonder where I would be now if Jeffrey had lived.' She drifted off into a bleary-eyed reverie which lasted a good number of seconds before she snapped back with, 'But don't be intimidated by their titles, my dear. He's only a life peer. We're all nouveau, you know. I'd heard Jeffrey speak of him when he was simply Mr Welstead, the foreign exchange clerk.'

Muriel opened her handbag and drew out her little tortoiseshell card case. Violet admired the modest style of her auntie's visiting cards: plain cream, no decoration, just *Mrs Jeffrey Strachen* printed in deep-brown ink in the centre and her address neatly on the bottom right.

'We must have some of these printed for you,' Muriel commented as she took two cards out.

Violet said nothing. She did not relish the idea of having her own calling cards printed up. Whatever would Claudia say? She'd laugh, most certainly, wondering how well they would go down in the polite society of Looe and Lansallos. Violet touched her forehead with her gloved finger to trap a drop of sweat. How close it was. How stifling hot. The long hours of the afternoon had stretched and smouldered; the sky simmered overhead, the coagulated clouds thick and milky.

They waited patiently while a footman from the Welstead household walked stiffly down the stone steps between towering Grecian-style columns and offered a silver tray on which Muriel was encouraged to place her cards: one for

Lady Welstead, the other for Sir Giles. Muriel was informed that her ladyship was not at home.

Muriel reached back for the cards and pinched down the top-left corner of each one.

'That's to let Lady Welstead know I've called in person,' she asided to Violet as the footman retreated. 'My, he's a fellow, isn't he. I've heard that Lady Welstead insists her footmen are all six foot two. We'll keep our fingers crossed that her own card will be delivered to us tomorrow or the day after. And then, perhaps we shall have a morning call from Her Ladyship. Then, just imagine, an invitation to dinner, or to the box at the opera. We went when Jeffrey was alive. The Royal Opera. Such a spectacle. You can't imagine, Violet. But I don't want you to miss out on any of this. Well I never, don't look now.'

Violet knew that this meant she should do just that.

The footman held the front door wide as a young man, smart and noble, exited the house and strode down the stairs with cane and an energetic step.

'It's their son, Sebastian. Just down from Oxford for the summer. Ha, who said I'd lost my touch. The Tarot may yet be right. Thank goodness you are with me and not at home pressing flowers.' Muriel laughed teasingly, while Violet cringed, leaning back into the seat as perspiration tingled down her spine. Muriel pushed the window down and called, 'Good afternoon, sir.'

'Ah, madam. How do you do? Blasting hot, isn't it?' Sebastian Welstead stopped and lifted his hat, standing at a courteous distance from the carriage. His nose was large, set in a kind, bland face with not much of a chin. It was obvious to Violet that he had forgotten Muriel's name.

'May I introduce my niece, Miss Violet Prideaux?' she ventured.

'So pleased to meet you.' Sebastian Welstead bowed towards her, squinting through the glass in the glare of the sun. He did not meet Violet's eye. 'What stinking weather this is. Dog days they call it, don't they? My mother is not at home, I'm afraid.' He switched back to Muriel.

'Not to worry, I've left my card,' Muriel assured him.

He said good day to them both and on he marched in all his fine elegance in the direction of the Euston Road.

'Last time I saw him,' confided Muriel, slipping her card case back into her handbag, 'I was at his mother's At-Home two weeks ago. He talked with me for a while about the assassination last month. He was earnest and terribly sad. Terribly worried for peace in Europe. But he seems a lot more chipper today. Perhaps, like me, he has decided that there isn't going to be a war.'

'But it is all very worrying, isn't it?' Violet said. 'The newspapers are full of it.'

'Oh, I think it's all a lot of hot air being blown over Europe like this blessed weather. The Kaiser's the King's cousin, for goodness' sake. Anyway, enough of all that. Mr Welstead. What do you think? You can do no better.' She snared Violet with one of her outrageous glances, laughed and tapped the side of the carriage and called, 'Right, on we go.'

William the driver snapped his whip and the pony walked on, his hooves ringing brightly over the cobbles. Muriel continued to chatter about what a fine young man Sebastian Welstead was and that she was so pleased that Violet could accompany her on their little diversions. Violet half listened, sinking under the heat, and gazed out of the window. Through the towering haze of monumental horse chestnuts, she glimpsed the park, blushing in the sunlight. How she longed to be out of the carriage and somewhere in the shade. The great stretches of grass looked like they'd quench her thirst.

'I'd like a walk, Auntie,' she said.

'Oh, for goodness' sake, now you're playing truant. We can't possibly stop here. Whatever will Mr Welstead think – that I've turfed you out of the brougham? You girls these days. Next thing I know, Violet, you'll be marching on Downing Street with a placard, or chaining yourself to railings.' Muriel sighed, and relented. 'We'll drop you further down, where no one will see you.'

Violet bit on her retort that perhaps Mr Welstead had other things on his mind that precise moment, and anyway he had disappeared off around the corner. The social customs that Muriel followed to the letter subdued Violet with their peculiar weight, and the glimpse of the park seemed almost too superb to bear. She felt an almighty yearning for the liberty that she had relished at Old Trellick: something that she had not really appreciated until now. But how could she ever return? The realisation that her life – with her freedom to walk the lanes, the woods and the cove with Jess by her side – could never be the same rose like a large hand to smother her.

'You know you're going to miss the At-Home at Mrs Emsworthy's on Dorset Street,' chided her aunt as Violet stepped down from the carriage at a suitably unobtrusive spot near the Outer Circle.

'I just need some air, Auntie,' she spoke up at her, folding her veil tightly over her face. 'I will be home for supper.'

'Take this.' Muriel handed out her parasol and crisply wished her good afternoon. 'That sun is a demon.'

Violet lifted the parasol over her head and watched the little covered carriage bowl off down the street, smiling at her auntie's taste for the quaint and old-fashioned. Just like the robust furniture with which she filled her house, Muriel kept herself firmly in the era of when she was a young lady who was newly married and had an exciting life to look forward to. Muriel would not be persuaded to exchange her brougham for a motor car 'even though the Queen has one', and argued that she preferred the soothing sound of the pony's hooves over cobbles to the rattle and smell of exhaust. But surely not, Violet wondered as she walked through the park gates, when the little carriage was being harassed for space by coal carts, omnibuses and great big Morris saloons along Baker Street.

Now, keeping to the shaded walks under the grand chestnuts, where filtered sunlight turned the warm air into powdered gold, Violet relished the moments to herself. The rolling grass ahead of her ushered in cooling breezes and the heat was not so molten here. She was met with another memory of walking Jess in her pinewood and was weary of trying to cope with missing him, missing everything.

Strolling on, she saw the rose garden ahead. It gleamed like a fallen rainbow, the blooms, she was happy to see, emerging in a second flush. As she drew closer, she recognised the reason for this abundance: the care and attention that the two gardeners were giving them, meticulously dead-heading to give the new buds a good chance to flourish. And between them, watching them, and making them both chuckle while they worked, stood the artist.

Violet immediately slowed her pace. He had rolled up the sleeves of his plain white shirt. One tail of it had come loose from his trousers, which were belted tightly around his waist. He had a slender frame, Violet noted, but his shoulders had the mesmerising combination of being both broad and lean. His hair was fair and rather sandy; he'd left his hat on his canvas stool in front of his easel. Violet felt curiously drawn. The artist had walked away from his work to banter with the gardeners, rather carelessly leaving his painting for all and sundry to gawp at.

The sun was dazzling. Twisted tubes of paint littered the glittering blades of grass. A rag and a flask of water had found a patch of shade under the stool, while brushes dried off in an old jam jar. Violet's eyes flicked over these details as she approached, trying to appear casual, but feeling rather embarrassed, swinging her parasol down to cover her face.

She stopped an arm's length away and stared at the painting. A blush instantly singed her cheeks and her eyes rounded in intense astonishment. For there, in the painting, was Violet walking over a carpet of daisies and through the roses. Her parasol – the very parasol she was carrying – was lowered and an unearthly green light, like water, reflected on the flesh of her face and her hands and her throat. Her mouth was a ruddy smudge, her eyes deep pools of an uncertain shade. Her expression was ponderous and sad; the curve of her shoulder and the lightness of her hand were exactly what she saw each morning in her toilette mirror. They were perfect. Violet stood still, trembling.

His shadow fell across the painting, and yet she did not withdraw, or flinch, or dare to look at him.

'Madam,' he said in a mellow and unbelievably soft voice,

a voice that lacked all trace of surprise. He was expecting her. 'I'm Jack Fairling.'

She saw his hand move gently into view before her, offering to shake hers, and her mind crashed with the protest: *but we have not been formally introduced.* She stared at his hand, keeping her own firmly clasped on her parasol and on her purse. And then she looked up to his face as a slurry of phrases to convey her offence thickened inside her mouth. *How dare you paint me. How dare you do this!*

He was beaming at her, thoughtfully celebrating her. His eyes charming in the bright sun. She thought he was extremely presumptuous, but then wanted to laugh, for she had a sudden hilarious thought: *we have not yet exchanged visiting cards. And how could we? For I do not have any.*

'I'm sorry,' he offered, when it was evident that she was lost for words. 'This is not how this was meant to happen. I have been working on the painting for weeks, and have brought it out today to finish it. I meant to warn you . . .'

'Warn?' Violet exclaimed in a flash of fury.

'I mean . . . ask your permission, but, you see, I lost you that day. The day I first saw you. You left so quickly. I did not stand a chance.'

She placed one finger just below her collarbone, where her heart was shuddering. She stared at him, at his crinkled eyes that looked like dancing periwinkles, and his stubbly trimmed beard which seemed to be formed into a permanent smiling shape.

'Why didn't you ask me . . . before you even started . . . I was only there for a few moments . . . I sat just for a minute . . . how could you have painted all of this?'

She gestured wildly towards the painting, too alarmed to look at it.

The man laughed lightly and tapped the side of his temple. 'I keep it all up in here. You see, as Degas says, "imagination collaborates with memory".'

'Well, I refuse. This is preposterous.' Violet lifted her chin. 'I refuse to give permission.'

'I'm very sorry to hear that.' The artist bowed. He stepped away and moved as if to take down the painting. 'I have been experimenting,' he continued, introspectively, as if to explain it to himself, 'taking my idea of Impressionism a little further. When I spotted you the other week, walking there among the roses, and then you sat, briefly, and it was all so fleeting, and spellbinding, I just had to capture it. The light was incredible. It was a moment I could not let go of. Your face—'

'But you've made me look sad.' Violet was outraged. 'It's . . .' She wanted to insult him, tell him it wasn't very good. After all, how could he have got her so precisely in those simple minutes that she had lingered here in Queen Mary's Rose Garden? Her memory of Weston had blighted her and changed the shape of her face. And the artist had captured it – and the blaze of light around her – like a butterfly in amber. And, despite her sadness, the painting was good. She dragged her eyes back to the easel. It was incredible.

Jack Fairling busied himself with the clips that held the artwork in place.

'I will destroy it, of course. I had no right. But then I did not expect to see you again.' He laughed at himself in a radiant outburst. 'You were my evanescent, mysterious stranger. But here you are. You have caught me out. And who wouldn't be drawn back to such a place. It's an oasis here. It's heaven.'

Violet watched him squat down to collect up his tubes of paint. He was quick and agile, scooping his possessions together. He opened a large bag and began to throw in his equipment, winding his brushes in rags and stuffing them in a pocket.

'You will destroy it?'

'Of course, madam, you have my word. In fact, let me do it now, right here.'

Her hand whipped out and tugged at his sleeve.

He stopped and looked down at her fingertips as they plucked at the fabric and then back into her face. 'I think you have surprised yourself, madam.'

She lowered her chin and whispered reluctantly, 'I just can't see something so beautiful destroyed.'

As she withdrew her hand from his arm, the heat of the sun seemed to crack the air. Beneath her parasol she noticed that the skin on her forearms was covered in the same watery light that the artist had captured in the painting. The heat was almost unbearable.

'I will give it to you,' said Jack Fairling.

'It's not finished,' she retorted. 'You must finish it.'

His face grew round with his smile. 'I will, then. I must.'

He took down the painting and rested it carefully on the grass. He folded up his easel.

She knew that she should leave then, for that was the right and proper thing to do. What would Auntie Muriel say, what would her *mother* say, if they knew she had been talking to a complete stranger, a *man*, in the middle of the park, for everyone to see? It did not matter any more whether he might finish the painting or not, for it was no longer going to be her business. What did matter was that he had taken a liberty and rudely snatched part of her. Had *seen* her. But she was struggling to find the fault, to pinpoint the offence that he had committed. Her mind tussled even as she turned to walk away.

'Would you like to get out of the heat, madam?' he asked her, his voice so modest and so agreeable that it made her pause and turn. His presence felt like a cooling breath on her throat. 'Would you like some tea?'

The Pavilion by the boating lake was shaded by pendulous branches of a weeping willow. Their table by the open window was laid with a gingham cloth and delightfully mismatched china. Violet removed her hat, welcoming cooler air around her hairline. She glanced around her at other couples and groups of ladies taking tea. The service was languid and discreet. There was a gentle tinkling of silver spoon against teacup. *Other* couples, she repeated the thought silently. But *we* are not a *couple*.

'Everybody's melting,' she commented but barely glanced at Jack Fairling while they waited for the tray to be brought over. The tea was good and strong and she drank a great draught of it.

The artist thoughtfully stirred his own cup three times, lifted the spoon and tapped it twice on the rim. A funny little habit, thought Violet. It made her smile. He watched her for some moments, tilting his head back a little as if to get her in focus.

She thought that he might lift the teaspoon and use it to check the size and perspective of her head.

He said, 'Didn't Gladstone say, "if you are cold, tea will warm you; if you are too heated, it will cool you"?'

'I believe he did,' said Violet, primly. 'How right he was. I'm afraid I don't have any quotes up my sleeve to throw back at you.'

He drank his tea, watching her over the rim. She found herself smiling. Her instinct to be irritated and affronted vanishing like a forgotten snatch of a song.

'Do you realise you have yet to tell me your name?'

Talking about herself brought with it the same uncomfortable feeling she'd had when she saw herself in his painting. She told him sketchily that she was staying with her Aunt Muriel in Montagu Square, and that her home was in Cornwall, near Looe.

He told her that he had once been to St Ives to paint, and that the light there on the tip of the peninsula was beyond belief.

'It's a long way down,' she said. 'It takes forever to get there.'

'I can tell by the way you are talking that you miss your home. You're going back soon?'

His question was light and breezy, but stung Violet as if she had just brushed past a nettle.

'I don't think so,' she said, her voice faltered. 'I don't feel that I ever can.'

She steadied herself by pouring some more tea for them both. He gave her the courtesy of not wondering why. She took a breath and asked, was he from London?

'I was brought up in Kent, went to school in Canterbury,' he told her. 'My father still lives there in a little village to the east of the city.'

He talked of the village and beyond, where hop gardens patchwork the countryside and the land flattens out to marshes, where the still water is like a hundred mirrors reflecting the sky. He spoke of the beauty of always being close to the sea. And the light at Margate, the stupendous sunsets.

'Which you've painted, of course,' Violet observed.

'I studied art, much to my father's disappointment. And came to London to make my fortune.' He shrugged, laughing at himself.

Violet joined in, relaxing.

'Now I live in Camden Town, just a short stroll that way.' He hooked his thumb over his left shoulder. 'I rent rooms over a pharmacy. I have had the honour of sitting in with a local group of artists. And what venerable men they are. I'm learning a great deal from them.'

'I can see that . . .' Violet's eyes drifted to the easel that was propped neatly at the end of the table. 'They teach you well?'

'They've let me in to their salon, that's enough for me,' he said, dismissing the idea of Violet perceiving his talent. 'They're doing what I want to do, taking urban scenes and making them beautiful, but always with an edge of realism. It could be St James's Park, the Holloway Road, inside the Café Royal.'

Violet expressed a genuine delight and interest, and wanted desperately, in return, to tell him more about herself, to tell him what she loved to do. She wanted to tell him about Jess and the Flower Book. Instead, she asked, was his art school in Canterbury?

'Yes, I had a scholarship, lucky me. Yourself? Where did you go?'

She told him about her boarding school in Exeter. She

warmed her story by recounting one of the ludicrous incidences of her climbing out of the window and running away. His laughter was delighted and cheerful. But the memory of school darkened her face, and dragged her spirit down. Weston returned to her, with his grimace of expectation that she should have done so much better. The question of why he paid for her education had never been discussed, had been battered down by her parents. But now it was unpleasantly very real and it hammered for attention.

'My goodness,' she glanced at her watch, in a rush of panic. 'I really should go. Aunt Muriel will be wondering.'

She spoke in complete opposition to what she really desired. For what she wanted was to sit here, drink tea and discover so much more about Jack Fairling. His growing up in the countryside was not dissimilar to her own young life, and yet how free and motivated he now was drew a hard comparison. Of course, he was a man, so he was different. And yet speaking with him opened a doorway. She felt she could break away from the world built around her. A world where her auntie wanted to convey her to the drawing rooms of those of a totally different class to her; in which money was exchanged in clandestine fashion between Weston Penruth and her parents; in which her mother was eternally livid with her for not complying with her wishes; where her closest friend had chosen to ignore her letter; where her former fiancé brutalised her and she could not tell a soul.

Jack Fairling appeared worried. 'There's that look again, the one I saw when I dreamt up the painting. You look troubled. Oh, I'm sorry, are you quite all right?'

She put down her cup, slipped on her gloves and set her hat firmly on her head.

'I must go.'

He stood as she did, and hurried round to move her chair away for her.

With another glance at his face, she shuddered with the momentous realisation that she trusted him, absolutely. She trusted this stranger who suddenly, somehow, seemed more familiar than anyone she had ever known.

'It has been a pleasure,' Jack Fairling plucked a card out of his top pocket and handed it to her. 'This is my lodgings and my studio. If you ever want to buy a painting . . .'

She laughed then, heartily, thinking that he really ought to have turned the corner of the card down.

'*Buy* a painting . . . ?' she asked, her giggles continuing as she took her veil in her fingertips and covered her face.

'You know I don't mean that,' he said. His expression was now indistinct through the netting. 'When this painting is finished, Miss Prideaux, I shall give it to you, most certainly. My gift to you.'

Chapter Eleven

In the language of flowers:
Wild tansy, I declare against you

The sun slipped behind the chimneys of the houses on the western side of the square yet the white facades remained luminous, glowing with remembered daylight. It was the sort of evening, Violet thought, so illuminated and peaceful, that she would watch the swallows peeping and diving over the meadow behind Old Trellick. She'd tilt back her head to catch the little black sickles against a colourless sky between day and night.

It had been another warm day in London but she had felt compelled to stay home, confined with Aunt Muriel, who was feeling a little under the weather. Her ankle was giving her gyp again. Violet had commiserated with her, agreeing that perhaps she had been out on it too much too soon. Perhaps her sorties out in the brougham to At-Homes and afternoon tea had proved too wearing.

As the long hours passed, Violet felt a peculiar frustration. She remembered her encounter with the artist and wondered at her own boldness in agreeing to take tea with him. Being in London, amid the teeming streets and chattering people, opened new windows to her. Although her mother and father would be horrified by her walking, talking and taking tea with a stranger, the whole episode gave her a thrill of courage. Indeed, she could emulate the women chaining themselves to Buckingham Palace railings, protesting, desiring liberation. Anything seemed possible.

She closed her Flower Book, shutting away the newly pasted pages where the bright yellow tansy now lay, flattened into two dimensions, and with a sigh of aching relief sat down by her bedroom window. The lamplighter had set a flame in the far corner of Montagu Square and would, as was his habit, steadily make his way around. Violet glanced at her watch: ten minutes to nine. Perhaps some warm milk to go to bed with, she pondered, thinking she'd ring for Smithson. She looked up again with a start. A taxi cab pulled up outside her aunt's house and disgorged her mother onto the still-warm, dusty pavement.

During the next few moments, the doorbell was rung and hurried footfalls came up the kitchen steps. There was a sharp call of surprise from her Aunt Muriel below in her parlour. Violet waited, her breathing shallow, as she composed herself behind the door of her bedroom.

She heard her mother say good evening to Smithson and complain how tired she was. There was a silence as hat and wrap were removed, and then a call from Muriel to her sister for her to hurry up and come up the stairs to her parlour, for she could barely move with her ankle.

Violet waited some minutes, trying to quell her pitching emotions of surprise and dread, before she took a deep breath, made her way down to the first floor and walked into her aunt's parlour.

'Oh, my poor love.' Her mother turned at the sound of the door and rose to her feet, travel-worn and a little dishevelled.

Violet stopped in shock as her mother went to her, her arms outstretched in unprecedented fashion, a mask of concern over her face.

'Hello. What a surprise,' Violet muttered as her mother kissed the air by her cheek.

'Oh, my poor Violet, come and sit with me. Come on.'

Violet glanced in question at her aunt, whose face was round and nonplussed.

'May, it's not like you to travel so far, on your own, and spring this sort of visit on us. You usually spend months planning,' Muriel said. 'What on earth has happened?'

Violet's mother sat on the sofa and patted the seat next to her, indicating that Violet should join her.

'I simply came to see how my incapacitated sister was,' she announced, 'and I've also come to take poor Violet home.'

'Mother, I'm perfectly happy here . . .'

Smithson came in with a tray of tea and spent some moments arranging the small walnut table, during which time Violet was able to catch Muriel's eye with a questioning look. At last, the housemaid shut the door behind her.

Muriel leant forward. 'Why *poor* Violet?' she asked her sister.

'Ah now, let me drink some tea.' May sipped at the

114

steaming cup while Violet twisted her fingers together, uncomfortable in her mother's sudden and rather unwelcome presence.

'What's happened? Is Father ill?' Violet blurted.

Her mother shook her head vehemently, and set her cup back in its saucer.

'It's Claudia.'

Violet exclaimed in horror.

'Oh, no nothing like that. She's well, I believe. Perfectly well. In clover, I should say.'

Muriel said blandly from her throne-like armchair, her leg propped on a stool, 'Do get on with it, May, we are on tenterhooks.'

'Claudia has thrown over Eddie Davey,' May's face was a picture of excitement and glee, relishing her snippet of news, 'and, you'll never guess, is now stepping out with Weston Penruth.'

Both sisters turned to Violet, who swallowed hard, trying to disguise her dismay at the news. My dearest friend, no wonder she has not replied to my letter, she thought. Why would she do this? With that man? A cold memory from the Charlecote conservatory compressed her scalp.

'Poor Eddie,' she muttered.

'I was thinking more of you, my dear,' her mother said. 'That's why I rushed up here to tell you, and so I would be able to comfort you. Whatever happened between you and Weston, to break off your engagement, your father and I thought that you would make steps to amend it, and get over your little spat. That's why we wanted you to come home. You can't mend anything when you are hundreds of miles apart. But seems like you are too late, and your chance

115

has gone. And what sort of friend pulls such a trick? Steps into your shoes, like that. It's not fitting, really. It's just not acceptable.'

'There must be more to it.' Violet's voice broke as she tried to swallow her shock. 'There must be some explanation. Oh, good God.' She smiled then, as she did not wish her mother or aunt to know the full extent of her dismay. Claudia could not know the sort of man he is. No one did.

'I think this calls for something stronger,' said Muriel. 'Violet, please pour us some sherry.'

With jiggling fingers, Violet managed to pour out three schoonerfuls and hand them round.

'From the look on your face, my dear,' said her mother, sipping greedily at her drink, 'I think you cared for Weston Penruth more than you are happy to admit.'

Violet shook her head and whispered, 'It's Claudia. I thought she was so happy with Eddie. What can have happened?'

Muriel shifted in her chair, holding her glass aloft so that the lamplight turned the sherry to the colour of embers.

'I think this child should stay here. You can't make her go back to Old Trellick with all this going on. The humiliation, May. It will be unbearable.'

Violet looked at her aunt gratefully.

May bristled. 'I think she should face it, and show them how she can rise above it all. Give them something to think about. Show little Miss Ainsley and that Penruth fellow that this is not the done thing.'

'He's the squire, Mother,' Violet said bitterly, 'and he does exactly what he likes.'

116

Chapter Twelve

In the language of flowers:
Sunflower, admiration

The next day over luncheon, her mother and aunt talked excitedly of a trip to Selfridges.

'I will risk it with my ankle. I will sit while you shop,' Muriel said. 'They have lovely waiting areas in the ladies' department. They'll bring me plenty of tea.'

'You too, Violet,' said May. 'Perhaps a new costume will cheer you up.'

'No thank you, Mother,' Violet was calm and precise, 'I'm heading off to search for specimens. I've seen some delightful wild flowers growing along walls and pavements. Lots of them will be at their best right now.'

'Weeds, you mean.'

Violet ignored her. 'I have rather neglected my Flower Book this last month or so.'

Muriel chipped in, 'It's what makes her happy, May.

We're better off just the two of us, anyway. We can really go to town and behave like respectable ladies of a certain age replenishing our wardrobes and drinking tea in the finest salons.'

May gave Violet a dull look, scrutinising her face, but said nothing.

'I need to have some time alone,' Violet said as plainly as she could. 'I need to get over the shock.'

Her mother settled back in her chair, agreeing and triumphant. 'Of course, my dear. Make the most of your time here, for I've bought our train tickets. We leave for home next week.'

Beyond the white mansions of the Outer Circle, the street turned a sharp corner to the right and narrowed abruptly. Towering chestnuts thinned out to be replaced by scrubby bushes behind railings and unkempt verges. The peace of the park fell away as the road took Violet over the railway lines. The change in the air was immediate. She found herself in busy Parkway, crowded with pulsing noise: chattering women in shop doorways, the clang of light industry from somewhere near the tracks and a low buzz of languid poverty. Men pushed carts of coal and scrap. Women in rolled-up sleeves swept steps or gossiped. Children scattered themselves among the crowd, running errands or playing on the cobbles, their faces pinched and grubby. Violet caught the whiff of straw and dung, raw meat and tobacco and the sewer. She had walked into a distinct enclave and, even though she clutched her handbag tightly, a peculiar exhilaration coursed down her spine. How far away she was from the niceties of tea and shopping with her aunt and mother, calling cards and envelopes left expectantly on the hall table. How far away she was from the great forbidding mansions belonging to the likes of Lady Welstead, and she had only walked a few hundred yards.

Faces turned her way and eyes peered under the brims of hats. A self-conscious prickling inched over Violet's scalp. But she beamed and nodded good afternoon. Some faces ducked away while others cracked opened with a surprised and wide smile.

She found the pharmacy on the corner of Albert Street. A tinkling of a bell announced her as she walked in amid the pleasant scents of soap, camphor and charcoal. All was calm and serene as she closed the door on the street. Dark wood cabinets reached to the ceiling stacked with row upon rows of bottles neatly labelled and corked. The counter was pristine, the scales polished. The pharmacist, with crisp apron and large spectacles, said good afternoon. She asked for directions and he courteously set her straight.

The door was in a niche around the corner from the pharmacy. It needed a good coat of paint, the wood was warped but the entrance way was clean and swept. Violet stood for a moment, composed and quiet, there on the steps of a stranger's home. Confidence surged through her blood and made her smile; she knew what she was doing was right. She rapped gently on the door.

It was opened by a woman with a pile of dark hair pinned around her head and sharp eyes in a smooth handsome face. Her sleeves were rolled up and she had on a rather worse-for-wear apron. She did not speak. Instead she stared at Violet, her cheeks ruddy with a sudden blush. Violet, for a brief moment wanted to step back, suddenly doubtful, her resolve caving in. The woman wiped her hands on her apron, and then across her forehead to smooth her hair.

'It's you,' she said, her voice pitched with astonishment, and she held the door wide open. 'The girl in the painting.'

Violet walked in to a cloistering panelled hallway with a faint smell of chemicals and bacon.

The door was closed behind her, shutting out the light so that the place was suddenly dim, the interior indistinct as if in a dream. She turned to the woman, holding out her hand. 'Good afternoon, I'm Miss Prideaux,' she said. 'I've come to buy a painting.'

Jack Fairling had his back to the door. His easel was set up in front of a huge window that overlooked the back garden of the building. In the sky beyond the chimney pots was a curious cloud formation of stripes against cool blue. Pure daylight bathed him and his work as if in exaltation. Around him were his paints emitting their mineral scent and the same ephemera of his art that Violet had witnessed in the park: brushes, rags, palettes and jars, balled-up newspaper and blunt pencils. He remained still, his palm hooked over his chin, as he concentrated on the painting before him. His feet were planted firmly apart and his slender back was steady and poised. Violet was drawn to the way the light through the window played over the hairs on his arms, sending out colours of bronze and gold.

The woman beside her coughed and spoke up. 'Mr Fairling, you have a visitor.'

He turned and was startled. His eyes grew large and his head jerked back for a split second. Such was his surprise that he seemed unable to move and Violet knew it was up to her to walk towards him, extending her hand.

'Sorry for the intrusion . . .' she began.

'How are you? Are you well?' he asked as he shook her hand in astonishment.

'I'm very well. I just had to get out . . . take a walk. I had to . . .' She wasn't at all sure what she had meant to do by coming here.

Jack Fairling strode across to the other side of the room where a chaise was positioned in front of the other window overlooking the street. He began to gather up the messy array of folded shirts, books and newspapers. He quickly hid an odd sock in his pocket, kicked a pair of boots under the chaise and then plumped the large brocaded cushion.

'Here, sit here, please,' he said.

Jack's landlady slipped away and quietly shut the door. They were alone. Violet sat primly on the edge of the chaise with her hands folded in her lap and glanced across the mellow floorboards covered with a patchwork of beautifully worn Turkish rugs. The scrolled wallpaper was faded to a soft gold and two scuffed Louis-style armchairs were set facing the hearth. Folding doors halfway along the wall were pushed right back to increase the full glory of the room. Paint was a little chipped and furniture and fittings were well past their heyday but, for Violet, this increased the apartment's deep warmth and charm. On the table was a vase of long-spent big-faced sunflowers, their stems dried, their heads bowed and petals wrinkled, littering the dusty woodwork with gold and ruddy flakes.

'What a lovely studio, Mr Fairling,' she said, noticing a sketch of the sunflowers pinned to an easel. It must have been completed days ago for in it the blooms were smiling, upright and perky. Next to it was another, perhaps dashed off that morning, of the now desiccated flowers. This was so much more fascinating, and she told him so.

Jack Fairling looked at her, clearly delighted, and said, 'I thought we agreed in the park. First names?'

Violet laughed and dipped her head, blushing. What am I doing here? her thoughts thundered. I am sitting on a man's sofa, in his own home, and my mother doesn't know where I am.

Jack was telling her that he had this double room as his studio and sitting room, with a bedroom across the hall. Mrs Ellis was a fine landlady. Firm and fair, he asserted.

'She looks after me, sees me as a project, I think. She loves us artists, has always had us as lodgers,' he said. 'There's often a plate of food left outside my door if she knows I'll be painting all night. Sometimes a carafe of wine.'

He asked if Violet wanted tea or coffee, stooping by the grate to shuffle at the embers.

'I don't have gas here,' he told her. 'Have to boil the kettle the old-fashioned way.'

'That's nice,' said Violet. 'I like the smell of the fire.'

She laughed briefly at her easy confession. Through the open sash she could hear the din from the street below: a tuneful whistle from a delivery man, the sudden bursting of a woman's light and happy laugh. As she listened, the noise became restful and pleasant. Absorbed by it, Violet settled confidently back into the chaise, lifting her knees a little so that one foot came off the floor.

'It's a warm day, so seems unnatural to have a fire going, but I need my tea,' he said, gesturing with teapot in hand, acknowledging his own absurdity with a playful grimace. 'Or something stronger, perhaps?'

Violet looked at him and experienced a tremor of rebellion. And her face told him so.

He brought over two glasses of wine the colour of rubies and as he handed her one, she sensed his peculiar energy, just as she had done in the park.

She took a delicate sip. 'Thank you. That's good.'

As he sat at the other end of the chaise, she caught the scent of fresh linen. His shirt was baggy and well-worn; his elbow had eased a hole in the right sleeve. He wore a waistcoat of peacock blue and his eyes, as he smiled hesitantly at her, reflected its colour.

'Well,' he said in a businesslike manner, 'it's lucky you have called in today for I finished the painting last week and it should be thoroughly dry now.'

He placed his wine glass on the floor and leapt up, striding across to the opposite corner of the room to pick up a canvas which had been facing the wall.

'I've called it *Violet in the Daytime*,' he said, approaching, holding the painting like an offering. 'If that's not too *preposterous*. I think that was one of the words you threw at me.'

He looked nervous as he stopped five paces from her so that she could view it properly.

As she gazed at the work, Violet was aware of a comforting tingling in her blood. The painting was truly beautiful – a fleeting moment of light and shadow and colour and tone. She, the subject, was radiant despite her latent distress. She saw that the artist had captured her mood, had looked into her eyes – although so briefly – and she saw that what she actually had been feeling was a blinding burst of anger. It made her powerful and potent and not a victim. He had snatched at her true self,

123

the real Violet beyond the veneer of sorrow and the shame that she had carried with her since the day of her engagement party. By identifying it and depicting it in this way, Jack forced her to challenge it, to look it in the eye.

She glanced up at him. 'Thank you for what you've done. Thank you so very, very . . .'

Her sadness boiled up from nowhere and she pressed a hand to her chest in a futile attempt to stop it spilling out. Tears sprung from her eyes, hot on her cheeks.

Jack leant forward, rummaging in his pocket for a handkerchief. She grasped it and covered her face. It smelt of astringent lavender. She inhaled and felt him take her hand, not in the polite manner of earlier, but tenderly cradling her fingers, his thumb moving over her palm in a circling motion. She had seen herself so clearly in the painting and it had enabled her to grieve suddenly, violently, for her loss of innocence.

Violet pulled her hand away and Jack waited, uttering his concern. Was she all right now? Was there anything he could fetch for her? Shall he call for Mrs Ellis? Violet shook her head, smiling now with relief through clouds of sorrow.

'At least have some more wine,' he said and held up her glass with a soft and generous smile.

That was a very good idea, she told him.

'I feel that I have done a brave and unconventional thing to come here like this,' she said eventually, after a number of sips. 'I barely know you. This is your home and I have invaded it. Terribly rude of me, to come unannounced. So against everything I have ever been taught. If my mother and aunt knew where I was . . .' She laughed briefly and shrugged. 'But I don't think it was a foolish thing to do, because despite getting upset just now, I feel so *rested*, so *right*.'

Jack was watching her closely, a look of worry and of delight flickering over his face.

'You are most welcome,' he said. 'So very welcome.'

'Can I just sit here? Would it be such an odd thing to ask you if I could just sit here and watch you? It's so peaceful. I love the sound of the streets outside, all of Camden out there. And in here, it feels like . . .'

He completed her sentence with 'home'.

Violet dozed as the wine seeped through her blood and the soothing lullaby of the street drifted through the window. Curled up in the corner of the chaise, she observed Jack Fairling continue with his work in progress. The painting was a scene of Camden Lock. The still, fathomless water of the canal filled the foreground, while ramshackle stables, red chimney pots and tiled roofs formed a backdrop against a stormy battleship-grey sky. His sketches were pinned all around the easel to guide him as he worked. His strokes came in quick surges of vigour, the very energy that Violet was acutely aware of, as he applied the oil paint in blobs and daubs. He stood back, suddenly, contemplating in hushed and tense stillness before beginning again.

The afternoon grew cloudy and the light began to fade. Jack stopped his work. He methodically cleaned his brushes and tidied his paints away. And Violet, assured and contented and with a smile on her face, drifted into a swaying, dreamy sleep. She woke with a start to see that the lamps were lit in the studio and the fire had been stoked and reignited.

'Oh good God,' she uttered, sitting up and rubbing her face. 'What on earth is the time? They'll have the police looking for me.'

'It's only six, but it's grown cloudy,' said Jack from his armchair by the hearth. On his knee was a sketchbook and on the small table next to him, a scattering of pencils. 'Would you like some supper? Some tea? I was going to smoke my pipe but thought the smell might wake you.'

'Please, smoke your pipe if you want. I have to go.'

'Mrs Ellis can get you a hansom, if you like.' Jack seemed subdued as he dropped his sketchbook down on the floor and shoved it beneath his chair. 'I really must introduce you properly to her. Earlier, I'm afraid, I was a little lost for words. She is a gem, as I said before. She will find you the best cab in Camden to speed you home.'

'I really must go,' Violet said, barely listening, such was her panic. But then she looked at Jack's peaceful face and found a sureness stirring inside her. She stood up, stretched and walked to him across the shadowy lamplit room, where the ceiling was still highlighted by subdued daylight. 'What's that you have there?'

Reluctantly, with a blush of colour on his cheeks, Jack reached under his chair for the sketchbook, bringing it out along with a rogue ball of dust. He smiled broadly. 'I don't know why I feel so shy about this. After all, you have invaded my home and spent the last hour snoring on my sofa.'

Violet laughed with delight. 'I do apologise. I'm so sorry. And I drank your wine. But what have you done there?'

'It's *Violet in the Evening*,' he told her and handed her the sketchbook.

There, in charcoal on the thick textured paper, was a sublimely accurate sketch of herself slumbering on the chaise in front of the window, with the lamp lit in the corner. The crook of her elbow was divine, the tilt of her chin exquisitely accurate. She held the pad for many moments, incredulous and speechless.

He stood then and took a step towards her, removing the sketchbook from her hands and tossing it to the floor. Taking her hand, he raised it swiftly to his lips. She took a breath, letting the moment flood over her, knowing she was safe, trusting him with her life. There came a sudden pulsing, a heaviness in her belly that she'd never felt before. Her lips trembled into a glorious smile.

Jack beamed down on her. He was confident, now, and looked supremely happy.

'Wait a moment while I wrap *Violet in the Daytime* ... your painting,' he said.

'Oh, of course,' she said, struggling to break herself out of the spell. 'And you must tell me the price. How much do I owe you?'

He glanced around at her, laughing. 'Oh Violet, you know you don't have to keep pretending. I told you before, in the park. It is my gift to you.'

She gathered her handbag and shawl and watched patiently as he meticulously wrapped the canvas in brown paper. His quick and deft fingers tied it securely with string, making for her a little handle to hold.

'Perfect,' he said, as he handed it to her.

As she took the painting from Jack, she was intensely aware of his appeal: his scent and his presence. A bond suddenly linked the space between them in a sharp and decisive instant. It was a promise made physical and Violet did not want to leave his side. Perhaps he felt the same too? She saw a look of recognition flash over his features.

'Yes,' she said. 'It's perfect.'

* * *

Violet was home within half an hour. The hansom that Mrs Ellis so efficiently hailed for her had inched its way through the bustling traffic of Parkway, then squeezed itself over the railway bridge next to a hefty coal cart before bowling speedily along the Outer Circle. Soon she was back amid the avenues and squares of Fitzrovia and walking up the steps to her aunt's house under the cloudy, bird-singing twilight.

She wasn't long upstairs in her room when her mother knocked on her door.

'Where on earth have you been 'til this time? It's getting dark. I said to Muriel, thank goodness you had the sense to take a cab.'

'I have been to Camden. I have been buying art,' Violet blurted, feeling brave and rather proud.

'Have you indeed? *Camden?*'

'Yes, Mother, and I know how easy it will be for you to say that that little town is the wrong side of the tracks.'

'I don't know where it is and it sounds like I shouldn't want to. Been spending up all your allowance, have you? You might just have to hide it away in your room when we get back home.' May barely glanced at the painting propped up against a table leg in its neat brown paper covering. 'You know how particular your father is about art.'

As her mother's typical and unsurprising attitude washed over her, Violet turned to her mirror and began to unpin her hair. Her cheeks were still rosy from Jack's wine, and there was a secret glimmer around her eyes. Her expression was dazed. She was still in shock. After all, not an hour ago, she had been in Jack's company, alone with him in his studio. She felt herself fill up with a warm and delightful confidence at the memory of him. It was as if he was still with her, talking

128

with her, listening to her. Still dazed from her sortie into Jack's world, she exchanged a naughty smile with her reflection.

She glanced up as her mother broke the silence, 'Well, hurry along. Stop daydreaming. You must dress for dinner,' May Prideaux went on. 'This is a special occasion. Since I arrived, your aunt has wanted to show off Cook's skills. And tonight, even though we are dining just the three of us, we're going to have a banquet, so it seems. We're having roasted quail after the fish. And a perfectly exquisite consommé, says Muriel. And Cook loves to make her jellies, so expect a plate or two of those, too.'

Violet's mother stopped and squinted through the low lamplight, as if seeing her daughter for the first time that evening.

'I must say,' she said. 'You do look a little flushed and confused. Have you seen the evening paper too?'

Violet assured her that she hadn't. How could she have done? She far was too busy immersing herself in a whole new world. She had been too busy enjoying the soothing freedom of the company of Jack Fairling, lifting her away from the horror of two months ago, to have bought herself the *Evening Mail*.

'It is grave news, I'm afraid. Your father predicted it, so he will be pleased with himself when he gets *The Times* tomorrow morning. But I know what he would say – let the French slug it out.'

'What on earth do you mean, Mother?' Violet asked.

'The Germans are mobilising their troops.' She sounded rather exultant. 'Just as your father said they would.'

Chapter Thirteen

In the language of flowers:
Blush rose, if you love me, you will find it out

In the sunny parlour, May and Muriel stood side by side, cocked their heads and took a step back in unison to view the painting. Violet's fingers trembled as she busied herself with balling up the string and unravelling the knots that Jack had tied so neatly. When she folded up the brown paper, it crashed and clapped like thunder in the expectant quiet of the room. Her eyes locked on to the two ladies as she waited for their verdict.

Amid the urgent flurry of news and rumour, of reports of France moving its troops and of the Germans heading for the Belgian border, May suddenly remembered the painting that Violet had come home with. She had a keen desire, it turned out, to assess what her daughter had been spending her money on. Now, as Violet removed the paper she felt as if she was peeling away a layer of her own skin and exposing herself, raw and vulnerable. This is momentous, she thought. They have to accept him, as I do. They have to like him, love him. Jack's smile filled her mind and fortified her. This will be different, she told herself. This man will be different. This time, she wanted them to know the truth.

Muriel exclaimed, 'My goodness, how lovely!'

May, with roving, guarded eyes, said, 'Well, it's a good likeness, but you're not standing still and why is it all blotchy?'

Violet began to explain that it was the artist's technique, developing Impressionism with more realism but was interrupted by Muriel laughing mischievously.

'You didn't sit for him in his studio, did you? There you are in Queen Mary's Garden. I recognise all the roses. How wonderful, and that's fine, isn't it, May? It means she was in a public place and nothing untoward could have possibly happened.'

May stepped forward and peered down at the corner. 'Who is the artist, then – anyone I would know?'

Violet wanted so desperately to say, No, Mother, because like Father you know nothing of art and like to put pictures from chocolate boxes on your walls.

'Jack Fairling,' she said, pride swelling her voice. 'He hopes to be accepted into the Camden Group soon.'

'Is that so,' her mother muttered, clearly not going to admit she didn't know who the Camden Group was.

'And, what's more, I'd very much like to invite him here for tea.'

Violet looked at her mother and braced herself. It was a daring leap. But then the foundation of her relationship with Jack so far had been built on a little cheekiness and a lot of bravery.

May bristled, set her jaw and spluttered, 'Well, really . . .'

But Muriel beamed, delighted, for she welcomed any excuse for a social occasion.

'Of course I'd like to have him visit one afternoon,' she said. 'I've never met a proper artist before. We can praise him on his enchanting work, can't we, May?'

Violet's mother forced a smile.

Muriel went on, clearly excited, 'I say, Violet, do you have his card?'

Of course she did, Violet beamed back.

'Then I will send Smithson over with mine straight away.'

Two days later, with her thoughts fragmenting into nonsense, Violet followed Smithson to the hallway in answer to the knock on the door. The housemaid took Jack's hat and set it on the coat hook, while Violet waited, her stoppered apprehension about to break into a flood of pleasure.

Smithson gave her one of her old-fashioned looks and slipped away down the backstairs, and Jack stepped forward to her, his hand offered in greeting. Violet clutched it with both her own, feeling greedy and childish, and Jack raised her hands to his mouth, a flash of jubilation in his eyes. In the cool light of the hallway, with its formal black and white tiled floor and pots of aspidistras and ferns giving off a staid green gloom, they barely spoke. And yet they exchanged a moment of understanding so exquisite and so fleeting that it was gone in a blink.

'This way,' Violet said.

An unexpected tremor of shyness caught her as she led him up the stairs, across Muriel's back drawing room and out through the French windows.

Tea had been laid on the little ironwork table on the pleasant patch of lawn surrounded by high, sun-warmed red-brick walls. Behind her mother and aunt, who sat pretending to chat but with their eyes slanting towards the house, was a pretty bank of roses, the colour of Violet's blushes, giving off suitably pleasing scents and the vibrating sounds of bees. It struck Violet how alike the sisters looked: both sat there in high-necked blouses with leg o' mutton sleeves and towering hats suitable for afternoon tea. Both had the same bearing, hands folded on laps, with a tilt of the chin. Each of them tapping a finger or two. But, then again, thought Violet, how perplexingly different they were.

Muriel stood up with a wide smile and exclaimed warmly, 'So this is the famous Jack Fairling.'

'Hardly, madam,' Jack laughed and shook her hand as Violet introduced her aunt and her mother.

'Lovely day,' observed May, tilting her head to glance at the pale London sky. Violet watched her look back at Jack and cast her eyes up and down. 'How did you get here, Mr Fairling?'

'Oh, I walked,' he told her. 'Fighting my way through crowds of people. So many Union Jacks out, brass bands, the lot. It was the Royal Fusiliers causing all the mayhem, marching along from St Pancras.'

'They've all gone a bit mad, a bit jubilant in the face of such bad news,' said Violet lifting the teapot. 'It's become a celebration.'

'A chance for the Empire to flex its muscles again,' Jack observed. 'It's been a good few years since the African war.'

'Are the King and Queen going to appear on the balcony, I wonder?' mused Muriel. 'Sugar, Mr Fairling?'

Violet assisted her aunt with the teacups, pleased to be busy with something while the conversation span around quickly in search of a comfortable level.

'And what will you do?' Violet's mother asked Jack.

'You mean in reference to taking the King's shilling, madam? I'm not sure yet. They are sending the BEF to France. They're the professional soldiers. I think we should leave it to them.'

'Is that what you think? Oh, of course you're an artist. And what can an artist do?'

Violet gasped and tried to disguise it as a cough. She was horrified, but Jack's face was as open and peaceful as ever. He smiled warmly as he stirred his tea.

'I read an article in the *Daily Mirror* this morning, saying that the army needed medics, tradesmen and motorcyclists and I thought, why not artists too?'

Jack's implication that he might join up made Violet jump in alarm.

Her mother asked him, aghast, 'You read the *Daily Mirror*?'

Jack responded quietly that it was his landlady's copy, but no bother.

'It's all talk,' Muriel broke in. 'Something and nothing. I'll do the cards later, see what they have in store for us. But I must say, I did them last week and I didn't see this coming.'

Everyone laughed then and sat back in their chairs, pursing their lips over steaming cups, while Violet handed out saffron buns, telling Jack that she'd made them especially.

'A little taste of Cornwall,' she told him. 'A local delicacy.'

'This one's perfect,' he said as he bit into it and licked the end of his finger. She was certain she'd seen the ghost of a wink there. 'Your own recipe?'

Violet nodded, her joy returning to a simmer. She struggled to draw her eyes away from him and engage with her mother and aunt.

May put her cup down and persisted. 'Perhaps, Mr Fairling, you'll go back to your home in Kent if you're going to join up? Join a local regiment? Of course, Violet's father will probably make noises about joining up.'

'Oh Mother,' Violet said vehemently. 'He's far too old.'

'But they might need his services. He's a doctor, you know, Violet's father,' May directed at Jack with pride.

Jack nodded. 'So Violet tells me. She has told me a great deal about her home in Cornwall. In a way, our upbringings have not been dissimilar.'

May leant forward. 'So you also went to private school?'

'Indeed I did, madam. In Canterbury.'

This seemed to satisfy Violet's mother who stopped looking like she had a nasty taste in her mouth, for a moment at least.

Their conversation tinkled around schooling and the comparative joys of the Kent and the Cornish countryside and those counties' closeness to the sea.

'Well, my dear,' May said to Violet. 'I can see you are missing the cove and the pinewoods. Missing home.' She fished out her pocket watch. 'We should really start packing our trunks this evening, for the train leaves quite early tomorrow.'

'But, Mother, I have decided. I want to stay here, if Auntie Muriel doesn't mind. I do miss home but—'

Muriel clapped her hands in delight. 'Oh joy. Violet, you are most welcome.' Her eyes flicked cheekily towards Jack. 'Most welcome indeed. You are a delight to have around. If you can spare her, May, I'd love her to stay.'

May looked from her sister to her daughter and then back again. 'What your father will say is another matter.'

Violet stood up. 'Papa won't mind,' she said breezily, and excused herself for a moment to go indoors. Upstairs, she paused at the landing window and treated herself to a secret glimpse of the garden. Jack was pouring more tea for Muriel, who appeared thoroughly delighted with him, insisting on him having another bun. Her mother had settled herself back, her face more reposed and less grumpy, but her scrutinising stare lingered.

On the landing, Violet folded her arms around her middle to contain the elation sparkling inside her. That man, she told herself, I love him. I don't want to go anywhere without him.

Having freshened herself in the bathroom, she returned to the garden with a spring in her step but as she approached, she caught the end of her mother's sentence, '. . . broken love affair with Mr Penruth. An important local landowner, you know. All very sad.'

Jack's face was impassive. He continued to stir his tea.

Violet opened her mouth in fury but Muriel glanced a warning at her and stepped in.

'Really, May. That's in the past now.' She forced a bright laugh. 'What young lady doesn't have a frisson like that at an early age? I must say, I can barely remember my first flush.'

'I'm sure Mr Fairling appreciates knowing a little more about Violet,' May ventured, ignoring Violet's outrage.

Jack cleared his throat, 'Indeed. I look forward to learning more of what Violet wishes to tell me.'

Violet glanced at him with increasing admiration. He was

enduringly courteous and calm in the face of May's deliberate rudeness. Perhaps it's no matter, her frantic thoughts told her. Perhaps he won't mind. And if he does, then I will soon know. Realisation embraced her then. What Weston Penruth did to her that afternoon during those brutal moments in his conservatory not only affected her then, but would continue to have consequences for her for the rest of her life. It would shape her and disturb her for ever.

'Goodness, can you hear the band?' Muriel cried out. 'The wind must be coming from the north. They're in the park bandstand.'

They all fell quiet and strained to listen. Segments of a bass oompah reached them like distant retorts blown on the air as the regimental brass band continued in full and festive flow.

'How everything can change in the space of a few weeks,' Jack said, planting his cup back on its saucer and catching Violet's eye. His smile was a caress that quenched her fear. She sat back and listened as the band played on.

The park was speckled with people flocking to see the soldiers on parade, their uniforms bright, their buttons and colours brighter. The City of London Regiment was the local militia and a source of pride for the residents of Marylebone, St Pancras and Camden. Families picnicked on blankets and groups of men drank beer from brown bottles. Couples in carriages trotted by and Union Jacks fluttered in children's hands. Cheers rose up in the air followed by ripples of applause as the band finished 'Land of Hope and Glory'.

'Here we are,' said Jack, as they strolled around the boating lake to avoid the heaviest of the crowds. 'Feeling the full effect of imperialist propaganda.'

Violet said, 'Thank you for coming to tea, and enduring the ordeal. I'm sorry my mother was so . . .' She wanted to say 'impertinent', but that would show an unattractive lack of respect. 'Sorry she was so forthright.'

Jack laughed. 'She cares, that's what it is. Deep down, she wants the best for you, and wants to make sure that I . . .' he paused and adjusted his smile '. . . that I possibly am the best for you.'

Violet linked her arm through his. He closed his hand over hers, pressing it to his sleeve, and they continued to stroll perfectly at ease, falling naturally in step. The busy and chattering surroundings of the park became a blur as she briefly savoured the contentment of walking arm in arm with Jack, but then a dark memory returned to spoil the moment and her spirits faded.

'Jack, I want to say that I would have told you about Mr Penruth. I wanted to tell you myself. It was a mistake. I was coerced into a relationship I did not want. We were wholly unsuitable. I realise, now, that I didn't like him very much. You can see how forceful my mother is . . .'

'Again,' he said, and pulled her to a stop in the middle of the path, 'your mother.'

He looked into her face, his eyes flicking over her features as if following a familiar map.

'I was angry that she blurted it out like that,' he told her. 'I may not be as brilliantly educated as she might have expected or from the right background, but I know how to pursue polite conversation around a tea table. Thank God for Auntie Muriel.'

'Yes, thank God,' Violet uttered and watched Jack's hopeful, trusting expression. But he did not know the half of it, she thought. He does not know what he did to me. I am not the sweet pure girl he thinks he sees standing here. I am not that girl.

'You look awfully sad,' Jack said.

'I think it's the news today. War declared and all this jubilation.' She gestured to the people, the regimental band who were having a rest and a well-earned cup of tea. 'It's very unsettling. Come, let's walk.'

They reached the newspaper boy who had ventured into the park to take advantage of the crowds. The headline on his sandwich board read *Reservists & Territorials galvanised for action*, and the second, *German advance on Paris*.

Jack bought a copy, rolled it up and tucked it under his arm. They walked on to Queen Mary's Garden and Violet found herself among the blousy, overblown August roses. Stopping to admire the open face of a velvety scarlet bloom, she stooped to drink in its scent.

'Here I am again,' she smiled now, her mood lifted by the waves of flowers. '*Violet in the Daytime.*'

'This time, you have a different expression on your face. That's better.' Jack reached out a careful finger and touched her face. 'And you have pollen on your nose.'

Violet wondered if her expression was at last happier?

'You're not angry, like the first time I saw you. You don't have that gorgeous trapped inferno that I saw as you got up from the seat and blazed off through the roses. You're smiling now, but you still look troubled. I want you to know, that I never want to see that look on your face again. I want to erase it. Paint it out . . .'

He grasped both of her hands and pressed them tenderly to his lips. Violet knew from that moment that this gesture would always be the one that would knock at her heart. She whispered his name, and then cried out in shock as he sank before her onto his knees.

'Violet Prideaux, I have known you such a short time, but I think we both know, don't we? I think we do.'

She nodded. A hot wave of joy rose over her throat. Her tongue twitched with a fountain of words that she wanted to say to him.

'Violet, will you do me the greatest honour . . . will you?'

His face was wide open, serious and determined. He reached his fingertips up to her chin and her cheek, her elbow, her shoulder, caressing her gently, thoughtfully. 'Will you marry me?'

When she got back to Montagu Square, her mother's trunk was packed, labelled and sitting in the hall. She walked past it and up the staircase in a state of euphoria, her body gliding in a cloud of joy. In her hand she clasped the red rose that Jack had plucked for her. As she cradled it the petals began to loosen and fall from its overripe heart. Within moments it would be safely stowed between the pages of the heaviest book she could find in her room. Nothing can stop us, she decided. This is my happiness. She held the rose close. This is where my life begins.

On the first landing, she hurried past her aunt's front drawing room on her way up the stairs but was arrested by her mother's shrill call from inside the room. Violet stopped and poked her head around the doorway. The two ladies were sitting by the fireplace sipping sherry.

'You were a long time, just to walk Mr Fairling to the edge of Regent's Park,' observed her mother pointedly.

'We stopped to listen to the band, they were still playing. There's lots of people about. Quite an atmosphere.'

'I think,' said May, 'that with all this war talk going on, and soldiers filling the streets and the parks, you really should come home with me. As you know, I have booked your ticket. And I didn't appreciate you telling me that you wouldn't come with me like that, in front of a guest we've only just met.'

'Jack understood,' Violet said.

'Jack did, did he?'

Violet threw a silent appeal at her aunt.

Muriel set down her sherry glass. 'I think, May, the way things are going, that those soldiers will disappear in a matter of days. London will be perfectly safe. In any case, Violet and I will use the brougham.'

May shuffled in her chair, flexing her shoulders. She lifted the decanter and added a splash of sherry to her half-full glass.

Violet took a step forward, spurred on by her aunt's support. Her mother eyed her warily, taking tiny sips, her mouth not leaving the rim of the glass.

'Mother, Aunt, I have something I have to tell you.' Violet sat on the fireside stool, her head suitably lower than their level, hands clasped nervously on her knees, her fingertips caressing the bruised petals of the rose. 'The truth of the matter is that Jack and I wish to be married.'

May cried out sharply. She hastily applied a handkerchief to her chin to catch a dribble of sherry.

'What in heaven's name!' she bellowed. 'You hardly know him!'

'Mother, please, I hardly knew Weston Penruth but that didn't seem to bother you.'

'We knew the *family*. Have known them for decades.

That match had pretty much been ordained for years. This man is a complete stranger.'

'But Jack is so very different.' Thinking of Weston in the same moment as Jack turned her stomach. 'It has all been very quick, yes, but we have reached the stage where—'

'*Quick?* I'd say. So you've been flattered and seduced by him painting your portrait. He is a nice enough man, but he is totally unsuitable for you. He hasn't a bean. Your father will be furious. Now cut out all this nonsense, throw that dead flower away and go upstairs and pack.'

'Oh May, really.' Muriel's calm, deep voice rose up beneath the shrill pitch of her sister's. 'Look at the girl. Look how happy she is . . . well, how happy she was when she walked into the room. Are you all right, dear? Did he propose in the park? Oh, wonderful.'

'Not wonderful,' May snapped back. 'Not wonderful in any shape or form. I give up. Is this just a ruse to get back at Weston now that he's with your best friend?'

Violet swallowed hard on her anger. 'That has nothing to do with it. I don't wish to speak of him ever again. As for Claudia, I will make my peace with her.' Tears stung her eyes, and her mouth twisted with sorrow. 'I miss her. I wish her well. I wish I could see her.' Violet wanted to say, and *warn* her. Her voice trailed into a whisper. 'I wish I could see her.'

'You can, as soon as you come home with me. Just put all this silliness aside. This is simply a romance, a passing fancy. Coming to the city has turned your head, as well it might. Come back home with me and all will be well. Think how long it's been since you saw your father, and Jess?'

Violet twisted her hands together. Of *course* Jess – she'd

have to make arrangements for him to travel. She lifted her shoulders and looked her mother full in the face.

'I wish to stay here, and marry the man I love. We want to marry quite soon. We don't see the point in waiting.'

'What, and live in *Camden*?'

Violet's head was a mess of ideas. 'We haven't decided on that yet. One thing at a time.'

'Well, I am going home tomorrow, whether you come with me or not,' May warned her. 'So, of course, I will miss your wedding. Don't expect a telegram.'

Muriel turned on her sister and told her that she was saying things that she didn't mean. She'd regret it and feel bad later, so should stop it now.

Tears soaked Violet's cheeks. Her fingertips shook as she tried to wipe her face.

'Please listen to me. I love him.' Her cheeks burnt. 'That is the easiest, most simplest thing I have ever said.'

Her mother's lip curled and her features drooped.

'What about Weston? We never did get to the bottom of it.'

'Come now, May,' Muriel interjected. 'That is between the two of them.'

'I didn't love him,' Violet glanced at her aunt and back to her mother. 'The word doesn't even come into it. And he clearly did not love me.'

May said, 'Well, if it wasn't for Claudia . . .'

'She has nothing to do with it.'

'But you had such a *chance*. Such a chance that any girl would dream of. You had the chance of a *life*.'

Violet fought the sob rising like a scream in her throat to say, 'But the only life I want is my own.'

Chapter Fourteen

'. . . the bee has quit the clover,
And your English summer's done'
Rudyard Kipling

St Marylebone Parish Church was enormous. Raised up on wide stone steps, it presided with majesty over Marylebone Road facing the wide mansion-lined avenue that led to the park. It didn't resemble the churches that Violet was used to – stocky little granite structures tucked away in Cornish villages – it looked like a temple, squared off and imposing, radiating grandeur. She stepped out of the brougham, driven through the traffic and parked with care and expertise by William, and took her aunt's arm. The air was glorious – bright and breezy and sparkling with gold: perfect weather for a September wedding. Violet remembered, suddenly, the tenuous plans that had been made for a similar event in the ballroom of Charlecote. His shadow reached her, even then, as she stood beneath the London plane tree by the entrance to the church. She glanced through the doorway to see the vicar waiting for her with calm benevolence. Reading the unease on her face as hesitation, he gestured, encouraged her. She snuffed the memory of Weston out with a nod of her head. It was only a matter of months before, but a lifetime ago.

Suddenly a taxi drew up, and a well-dressed couple emerged. For one bright moment Violet thought that her parents had arrived, fresh from Paddington, to join her and Jack on their wedding day. But the lady and gentleman were strangers. They linked arms and hurried off together. Her spark of delight dissolved.

A small group of passers-by had gathered around the steps to watch the arrival of the bride. They didn't pause for long, as weddings had become frequent and hasty in the last month or so. She gave them a cautious little wave, held on to Muriel's arm, and headed into the church.

Her auntie was chattering, rather nervous. 'I'd wanted to invite Sir and Lady Welstead,' she said, 'among many of my other friends, but it was such short notice. They're at sixes and sevens anyway. Their son – remember him? – has just enlisted. Not the society wedding I would have dreamt for you.'

Violet whispered, 'I can't tell you how relieved I am that it is not.'

Muriel squeezed her arm. 'I know, dear, I know.'

The scent of her bouquet became stronger as she stepped into the cool vast space of the church. The flowers were a motley assortment, gathered from Muriel's back garden that morning. Tight cream roses interlaced with a tangle of honeysuckle and a snatch of leggy poppies. Poor things, thought Violet, looking down at the open blood-red faces: they'll be dead before the day is over.

She felt the grand pillared space of the church drawing

her in. There was an intense hush, as if the dead in the vaults were listening. Feeling very small under the achingly high painted and panelled ceiling, she moved forward as the organist struck up. The space around her was too immense to absorb, but her eyes hooked on to the end of the long aisle where Jack stood before a towering altar, waiting for her, his face expectant.

Beside him stood his father, Bertie, who had travelled up from Canterbury the night before. The soft, friendly face of the older man was a replica of what Jack's would become in later years and Violet, in that moment, felt her whole life opening up before her like a great long road she longed to travel. He nodded a welcome, the spark in his eye matching Jack's. Otherwise, the congregation was pitifully scarce, made up of some of Muriel's friends, including the Emsworthys of Dorset Street, Smithson and Mrs Ellis, who were acting as witnesses.

Claudia should be here, Violet thought with sudden vehemence. My best friend should be here, and he's taken her away.

A gleam of sunlight cast itself through the towering windows behind the altar, illuminating the little gathering and sending sparks of delight through her blood as she walked up to Jack and took his hand. They turned together to face the altar as the organ music subsided. Briefly and solemnly, amid the perfume of roses and honeysuckle clutched in her shaking hands, the vicar married them.

The pageboy in neat navy jacket put their suitcases down and Jack tipped him handsomely.

Once he'd gone and the door to the room was shut,

the chamber music drifting up from the lobby below was muffled. The fine notes had followed them up the stupendously snaking staircase of the St Pancras Midland Grand Hotel, lifting them as they walked on deep carpet and marvelled at the lofty Gothic architecture. Terracotta-brick pillars colonised with flowers and leaves stretched up to heady ecclesiastical ceilings and every inch of the panelled walls was papered with ordered and gilded patterns.

'Do you think Aunt Muriel laid on the quartet for us too?' laughed Jack as he loosened off his tie and snapped the catches on his suitcase.

'Not sure she would have the wherewithal for that,' Violet replied, lighting a lamp near the window, relishing the moment now that they were alone, at last. The evening darkness outside was velvety, lit with a haze of gaslights. 'This hotel is incredibly beautiful. So generous of Auntie to treat us to our wedding breakfast here, and the room too. I can never thank her enough. What a lovely surprise.'

Jack went to the window and pulled aside the heavy tapestry curtains to check the view. 'Ah, we're on the railway side. It's late and the last trains will be leaving soon. Should be quieter during the night than if we were facing the main road.' He glanced at Violet. 'You're quite overwhelmed, aren't you?'

'I think I'm entitled to be,' she smiled.

She sat beside him on the window seat. At last, alone, she thought again. And married. A solid calm filled her as she reached a hand to touch his face. But then she grew cold and a trickle of fear went down her throat as she looked beyond him to the bed, all pillows and bolsters and high carved headboard. Later, she thought. Later he will know the truth of me.

'I expect you'd like to sketch the staircase,' she said. 'I've never seen anything like it.'

Jack admitted that he would like to, if there was time. 'But first things first,' he said gently and leant forward to kiss her.

A tremor of desire shot through her body but then, by strange instinct, she pulled away from him. Momentarily confused, he smiled kindly, held her gently, whispering that it was all right.

'Let's have champagne,' he said and went over to the dressing table where a bottle was perspiring in a deep bucket of ice. 'Now, this treat is from my father.'

Violet brightened up and confessed what a pleasure it was to meet him.

Jack twisted the cork out of the bottle and poured two flutes. 'He's staying at my studio tonight. I do hope he's comfortable there. Perhaps we can have lunch with him tomorrow? Would you mind?'

Violet assured him she would not. 'I hope Mrs Ellis takes care of him and gives him breakfast.'

'I'm sure she will.' Jack was laughing as he handed her a glass. 'I think she was giving him the glad eye over the table downstairs. Poor Father. He won't know what's hit him.'

'Funny you should say that, but I thought Auntie Muriel took quite a shine to him.'

Jack wondered if that was the peril of being an eligible widower. They laughed, chinked glasses and sipped.

Violet's happiness brimmed as she looked at Jack but then a sodden sadness returned just as quickly. She picked up her bouquet from on the dressing table, leaving behind a scattering of crinkled poppy petals on the glossy surface.

Pensively, she scooped them up and held them in the palm of her hand.

'I must choose the best flower heads for pressing,' she told him, trying to keep her voice light. 'I think today of all days must command a double page in the Flower Book.'

She dropped the dead petals into the waste-paper bin.

'Are you quite all right?' Jack asked her. 'Are you thinking of your parents?'

Violet admitted, 'It makes me very sad that they're not here. I'm sorry, I will shake it off. Everything else has been so wonderful.'

Jack agreed that it was a harsh thing to do, to not attend their only daughter's wedding. 'Don't take it to heart,' he urged her. 'Don't let it spoil the day for you.'

'Is it spite on my mother's part?' Violet asked, bewildered. 'I just don't understand.'

Jack wondered if he had simply not come up to their expectations.

'But you mean the world to me. Everything,' Violet felt her eyes singe with tears. 'Oh dash it. I don't want to cry.'

'Some might say we have swept each other off our feet. I'm still in shock, I suppose,' he laughed. 'But this could not feel more real to me. Being here with you. Come here, Mrs Fairling.'

Violet stepped into his arms and let herself be held by him. He gently rocked her and spoke softly into her hair. 'I will work out a way to have your parents like me and respect me, accept me. There must be a way. But in the meantime, sketching that staircase is the last thing on my mind.' He pulled back from her and gently brushed her cheeks with his thumb. He took her hand and led her back to the window seat. 'Because now I want to sketch you.'

149

The soft lamplight and the tickle of champagne, the beauty of the room and the sight before her – Jack at work sitting cross-legged on the bed, his face transformed with concentration – made her sadness unravel and float away.

'When have I ever known you not to have your sketchbook and pencil with you?' she mused playfully, settling back into the luxurious cushions, the intricate curtain forming a fantastical backdrop behind her. 'Even on our wedding night.'

'Hush now, I'm doing your mouth.'

Violet smiled, lifting her feet in her soft shoes and curling her knees under. She touched the exquisite fabric of her wedding dress: a delicate grey crêpe, pleated over the bodice and neat at her waist, and inwardly thanked Auntie Muriel again. She turned her hand so that her ring – that once belonged to Jack's mother – shone in the light.

Jack stopped and put his sketchbook down. He stood before her, looking down to admire her, his eyes opaque with devotion. He bent over, laying a sweet kiss on her lips. He touched the shoulder of her dress, his fingertips tracing the seam of it up to her throat and then found their way round the back. Brushing her hairline, he touched the tiny buttons under the collar and deftly undid them. On reflex, longing to touch him, Violet breathed deeply and ran her hands up his arms, feeling their strength beneath his shirt. She wanted him to kiss her again, to hold her and let her show him how she loved him. Jack gently eased her straps over her shoulders so that the fine fabric landed in a pool in her lap. He kissed the edge of her chemise over her collar bones.

He murmured that she should stay still.

'How can I?' she whispered.

He retreated to the bed, picked up his pencil and began again to dash it lightly over the page.

Violet felt a yearning that began to express itself in tiny physical shocks throughout her body.

'Jack,' she appealed to him.

He moved towards her again and knelt in front of her. He tugged the chemise straps down and pressed his face into her naked shoulder.

'I will have to finish the sketch in the morning,' he said.

Fear that her spoilt body would soon be discovered evaporated as desire pounded her bones. In one clarifying second as she cried out for Jack, she knew that her body wouldn't betray the truth. For how could it when she was pulsing and natural, when she was alive and powerful, when she was a thousand years away from the brutal moment in the hothouse?

She dug her hands into his hair as he lifted her and took her to the bed.

Chapter Fifteen

In the language of flowers:
Chrysanthemum, cheerfulness under adversity

The dining room at the hotel was busy and jovial. At their table by the window overlooking the expanse of the St Pancras platforms, Jack read the menu, keeping hold of her hand on the cloth, absent-mindedly running his thumb over her palm.

Violet enjoyed watching the trains pull in and seeing the passengers spill out. She noted the numbers of soldiers, all khaki and kitbags, who seemed to disgorge from every carriage and muster under the barking orders of sergeant majors who held handfuls of lists. She lost count of them and turned back to her husband, gazing at him with confidence. All fear had gone, for last night, it seemed, had transformed them both.

The room was filled with conversation. Sunlight found its way through high-arched dusty windows to illuminate the polished oak tables and the posy of flowers in a vase on each one: a little gathering of scarlet dahlias, purple zinnia and golden chrysanthemums: perfect end-of-summer flowers.

'What will you have?' Jack asked her.

'Oh, the soup I suppose,' Violet said, hugging her joy close.

'Soup it is, then,' Jack smiled. 'Same for me. I'm too full for anything else.'

She reached over to touch his face. 'You silly old romantic fool,' she teased.

'Speaking of old, ha ha, here's Father, just in time.' Jack winked at her. 'Don't tell him I said that.' He stood to greet Mr Fairling.

She wondered if he'd had a good night's rest and he assured her that he had, along with a stupendous breakfast and a lovely walk across Regent's Park.

'And now, I suppose,' teased Jack, 'you are ready for a stupendous lunch?'

'Oh no,' Mr Fairling laughed, 'I don't think anything can top Mrs Ellis's breakfast.'

Jack and Violet exchanged glances of mirth.

'I'm not even going to ask how you two are,' said the older man, settling into his seat. 'It's written all over your faces. Such young, fresh happiness. I want you to know – Violet, that is – I don't think I had the chance to tell you yesterday, what with everything going on, but I have never seen my son look so happy.'

Violet felt a blush heat her cheeks and she assured him that his son also made her very happy too.

'His mother would have been very proud. I'm sure he's told you, she died tragically young. But now we have a new chapter. A new start. Let's have champagne.'

'*More* champagne!' Jack laughed. 'Is this wise? I, at least, need to keep a clear head.'

'Whatever for?' asked Mr Fairling. 'This is your honeymoon,

boy. Are you going to head for the coast for a few days? You ought to go to Ramsgate, you know. Lovely at this time of year.'

The waiter interrupted to take their orders.

'Let's just have the house rosé and table water,' said Jack, his face falling with a serious look. 'I want to suggest something to you both.'

He glanced up then as a pair of army officers, buttons and colours blazing against pristine khaki, were shown to a table and proffered a menu. Resting one high-booted foot on a knee with brazen confidence, they made the room fall into stuttering silence.

'I mentioned to you, Father, that relations between Violet and her parents have become frosty, and that it is purely down to me.'

Violet protested, 'Oh really, Jack, you can't take it all on yourself. There are reasons – my mother . . .'

Jack glanced at her kindly, but continued, 'And the only way I can see through it, is to do something that will make them proud.'

'Son, you shouldn't have to prove yourself . . .' uttered Mr Fairling.

'I do, Father, because Violet is worthy of it. Something her mother said to me, the way she looked at me when I first met her at Montagu Square, has stayed with me. I should elevate myself to Violet's level, I should—'

Violet began, 'Jack, really, I—'

'I am going to volunteer,' he said, bluntly. 'I'm going to head to the London Regiment barracks this afternoon and enlist. That's why I don't want champagne. I need to do this thoughtfully and soberly. I want to do it for Violet.'

'For this skirmish here?' Mr Fairling glanced over at the

two officers who were now partaking of whisky. 'It seems hardly worth it. This lot will go and come back before we can say Jack Robinson.'

'Exactly.'

A violent terror rose up from Violet's stomach. He can't go, she won't let him. He simply can't go.

She stood up, her chair scraping the floor tiles with an ugly sound.

'For me?' she cried. 'Don't do it for me!'

Mr Fairling placed his hand on her arm, soothed her and drew her gently back down into her seat.

Jack got up and pulled his chair to sit beside her, encircling his arm around her shoulders.

'Stop shaking, darling, stop now. Oh God, you're trembling.' He pressed his lips into her hair and held her for many moments. The waiter came and laid the dishes of soup and opened the bottle of wine, offering to Mr Fairling to taste. Minutes passed and the soup was in danger of going cold.

She thought that he must have changed his mind; of course he would now that he had seen what his silly idea did to her. She began to smile, felt her heart ease itself back to normal.

'A few months in France, that's all,' he said, quietly, cautiously, 'and then we can start our life. Move back to Cornwall. I want to paint the light there. I want to be with you there. Our life can begin.'

In dismayed silence she shook her head.

'Until then, stay here in London with your aunt.'

Amid a slow-burning surge of anger, Violet slowly and deliberately extracted herself from his embrace and indicated that she wanted to eat her soup. Mr Fairling poured her a glass of rosé.

'Your mother would have been proud,' he told Jack, gravely,

'but you know what else she would have said: keep your feet dry. Those army boots have a dreadful reputation.'

Jack did not answer his father. Instead, he stared at Violet, his eyes sorry and pleading.

She lifted her face to him. 'You're leaving me already? We've not been married five minutes.' She let out a loud laugh and reached for her glass of wine.

'Just think, Christmas in Cornwall. That's what they're saying. It's something and nothing. Be all over by then. You ask your Auntie Muriel.'

Violet sipped her wine and it tasted sweet and sickly, sticking in her throat to choke her.

'What does she know?' she muttered. 'She gets it wrong more often than not.'

The next few days passed Violet in a haze of arrangements and officialdom. The might of the army, the efficiency of the London Regiment, enveloped Jack in a straitjacket of procedures and checks. They grasped him with open arms. He was to embark for training in Wiltshire within a week, so his commanding officer had stated. He passed his medical, he was issued his uniform. To her shame, Violet cried the first time she saw him in it. He seemed smaller, vulnerable and so very honourable.

She hugged him to try to convey how proud she was even though her pain was preventing it, feeling the scratch of the serge on her cheek, the unfamiliar epaulettes and buttons and buckles under the palms of her hands. Quietly, one evening by herself, Violet tested the rigid inflexibility of his army-issue boots with her own hands and felt repulsed.

Jack left his studio at Camden and moved into Montagu Square. Muriel was only too pleased to take the newly-weds under her wing. There were tears from Mrs Ellis, who vowed that he would always have first refusal on her rooms in the future, that he would always be welcome. His paintings, his sketches, his equipment and paints were all stowed in Muriel's back bedroom on the third floor, but there was no time to set them out, to use them. Within days, Jack received his orders.

They travelled at dawn by hansom cab to Paddington station. Violet curled herself into Jack's scratchy uniform as they jolted over cobbles and he whispered in her ear, again and again, that he wouldn't be long.

'Plan our Christmas at Old Trellick,' he said. 'Send my regards to your parents. And don't forget that my pay will come to you. Think of the difference that will make. I am a poor artist, remember. This will be a windfall like no other.'

'The war is a windfall, I had not thought of that.' She hated the bitter trace in her words. She held his hand tightly in both of hers to try to stop them trembling and dipped her head to kiss his fingers, hiding her tears. 'Do you have your sketchbook? And pencils? And the pressed rose from my bouquet?'

He affirmed that he did, patting one of his vast pockets.

'Not sure I can bear this,' he uttered as the cab turned into the concourse in front of the station. The place was heaving with crowds. Jack's face was ghostly.

'But look at all those other soldiers,' Violet cried, trying for encouragement. 'Within minutes, they'll be your pals. Look at them all. It must be half the London Regiment. Good God, there's Sebastian Welstead.'

Jack wondered who she meant and she quickly told him about Aunt Muriel's social calls to his mother's mansion overlooking Regent's Park.

'Very nice too. Looks like he's joined as an officer. Good

for him,' said Jack, sounding weary, not wishing to waste time talking about a stranger.

The cab came to a standstill and they both got out, Jack throwing his kitbag with a slam onto the pavement.

'A quick goodbye, it has to be. I can't stand it,' Jack muttered into her hair as they embraced. He ran his hands over her back, pressing her to his body. 'You know this is not me heading off to battle. I shall be on Salisbury Plain for months of training. They're not going to send me off completely green.'

Stop trying to fool me, she thought as a sob blossomed in her chest. The mob of soldiers was moving around them, buffeting them. The chaos, shouting and whistling heightened Violet's misery.

The cabbie called down, 'I can't hold the horses here much longer in this crowd. Madam will have to jump back in, or I will have to go.'

Jack grasped her waist and propelled her back up the steps into the cab.

She leant out of the door, precariously, stretching as far as she could to keep hold of his hand. 'Come home safe,' she whispered.

He gripped her fingertips, his face wide open with honesty and pain. 'You are the only woman I have ever known, who I have ever loved. Do you understand, Violet?'

She looked up into his face, understanding, her mouth stretching and trembling with misery. Her terrible secret had not been found out, for Jack knew no better.

'And you . . .' she said, 'you are the only man . . .'

The cabby brandished his whip, the cab rolled on and Violet was torn brutally away from him, whispering, '*You are the only man I have ever loved.*' Jack disappeared into the mass of khaki bodies.

Chapter Sixteen

If there's ice in November that will bear a duck,
there'll be nothing after but sludge and muck

Auntie Muriel, of course, always travelled first class. The velvet maroon seats in the small reserved carriage, with their high backs and cushiony arm rests, were a far cry from Violet's mode of transport when she arrived in London five months before, rattling along on posterior-numbing wooden seats in third class. They sipped on Chablis and nibbled smoked-salmon sandwiches from Muriel's hamper. By the time they pulled out of Reading, Muriel was dozing with *The Times* on her lap while Violet watched the sodden countryside slip by. The fields were saturated, slumped under a hazy mist of damp. Trees were stripped naked and stark against a dull sky while sheep huddled for shelter in the corners of fields. The green of summer was diluted now by rain and wind and turning slowly to dirty brown.

As soon as Muriel had heard rumours that the Germans

would launch Zeppelin air raids, she'd frantically grabbed all of her precious Meissen plates and cups and made Smithson box them up in the cellar. But weeks passed, Jack was still training somewhere in deepest Wiltshire and the sky over London remained calm. Reports came in from the front. The news of retreat and stalemate was harsh and depressing. Remembering the flag-waving and brass bands at the end of summer, Violet thought how foolish, how short-sighted we were.

Lord Kitchener's piercing eyes followed Violet wherever she went. The posters pasted in the grocer's shop window and on the noticeboard in the park were menacing, yet strangely inciting. What man could ignore them, what man could walk past? They were answering the call-up in their thousands. Rumour had it that there was a massive backlog of recruits and Jack was now part of this 'Kitchener's Army'. He had been promoted to corporal already.

Muriel told her that, while having tea the other afternoon with Mrs Emsworthy in Dorset Street, the daughter of the house had come home, her cheeks glowing with triumph, having bestowed a white feather on at least five able-bodied men she had seen walking in the park. The talk of it all being over quickly – a flash in the pan, as Muriel had once said – began to spiral away to empty and jittery unease. A dark storm was gathering, Violet thought helplessly, thundering away across the Channel.

But she found comfort in her aunt's company; Muriel's warm chatter was peppered with support, gently counteracting her mother's cold indifference. So when Violet cried over the letters Jack sent from his training camp which, instead of cheering her, pinned her misery to her like a badge, Muriel had the sense to leave her to herself and let her tears dry before proffering cake with champagne to wash it down.

'We might as well drink the stuff,' she said. 'It could be under a ton of rubble tomorrow, courtesy of the Kaiser's Zeppelins.'

And Muriel sat by her, calm and poised, issuing serene advice when Violet told her, in a voice cracking with both joy and terror, that she was expecting a baby.

'A wedding-night baby,' Muriel had whispered to her. 'How delightful.'

Violet wrote to her parents, a sadly stilted letter, updating them on her status as the expectant Mrs Jack Fairling. She anticipated silence and was prepared for a terse dismissive reply at least, but was amazed that within days a telegram arrived from her father, ignoring the animosity most wholeheartedly, with the plea: *Dearest Violet, please just come home where you belong.*

'Your father is right. It's time to build bridges,' Muriel said, reading the telegram. 'This can't go on forever. Sounds like he has put his foot down with your mother, which will be a first. And I simply won't allow it to continue. Let's both leave London, and bury ourselves at Old Trellick. I could do with a change, a breath of fresh air. Get away from all this dull war talk.'

And I won't be much further away from Jack in Wiltshire, Violet thought with a glimmer of a smile, for the time being at least.

She was relieved that her aunt was to accompany her. In any case, all events at Montagu Square seemed to be culminating towards that very decision. A week or so before, Smithson answered the call for women to work in munitions and handed in her notice. And William had hinted that he would like to do war work too, and asked to be let go. And the pony, Muriel decided, would be sold to the milkman.

'Something tells me,' Muriel said as the last of her Meissen and champagne was secured in the cellar, 'it's time to abandon ship and shut up the house for the duration.'

Violet sat in the swaying railway carriage, watching white steam billow past her window, and then glanced at her luggage stacked in the corner. She'd packed up Jack's sketches and his artist's paraphernalia in a crate to be forwarded down to Old Trellick. Inside that crate, carefully wrapped in fleece and tied securely, was *Violet in the Daytime*. Alongside it was the work that followed – the one he painted in his Camden room when she first visited him: *Violet in the Evening*. But she had left behind the last painting. She felt a dart of pleasure singe her body and a huge smile break her face open when she thought of it, concealed in a dark corner of Muriel's cellar. *Violet in the Night-time* was sketched on their wedding night and showed her as flesh, luminous in white and pink, dappled with lamplight shadows, her limbs languid, stretched out on the window seat at the St Pancras hotel. She adored the painting but could not risk anyone, *anyone* chancing upon it. It was theirs – hers and Jack's – to hold secret, to treasure. Their own private joy.

Smiling surreptitiously at Muriel's drooping, sleeping face she reached over for the newspaper. The memory of their wedding night, and the painting that celebrated it, gave her the strength to turn back to the reality of the day. A first-page report told her that the trenches now stretched from the sea to the Swiss border. There was a dispatch

162

from the town of Ypres by a correspondent who could only pussy-foot around the matter with the meaningless empty headline: *British repulse fierce attack: a brilliant charge by two battalions*. How does he know? Violet thought angrily. How does any of us *know*? As she read, places began to burn with alarming significance into her imagination: Menin Road and Sanctuary Hill. At least, she thought, glancing across the columns, the Germans never made it to Paris.

And then she turned the page as she knew she must, with agonising reluctance, to the casualty lists. She cast her eyes down the lines of type. This dreadful routine had become a habit, Muriel had said, as if they were reading the weather report. As the weeks passed, hundreds became thousands, the type smaller and smaller to accommodate them all. How futile the flag-waving had been, Violet told herself bitterly. How the cheering has quietened now.

And then she glanced upwards and saw him: Pte E.A. Davey, 1st Cornish Yeomen, dead.

She jolted, cried out.

Muriel stirred, opened her eyes. 'Dash it,' she murmured, glancing around, 'I thought we might have at least made it to Exeter. Whatever is the matter, dear?'

'Sorry to wake you,' said Violet, 'but I've just seen Claudia's fiancé – sorry, ex-fiancé – in the casualty lists.'

Muriel sighed, her shoulders slumping. 'Let's have a tot more wine to cheer us up,' she suggested, 'and have a look at the births, or the marriages, at least. Come on. We must keep our spirits up and I don't like to miss out on any news.'

Violet took her glass and set it carefully on the little table in front of her where it juddered and shook. She passed the newspaper back to Muriel. After all, she was more likely to know who was who amid her friends from the Regent's Park and Fitzrovia set who danced around each other in regimented courtship.

As Muriel scanned the column, and announced every so often engagements and christenings of people Violet did not know, she sat back and thought about Eddie. His modest smile came to her. What a polite, innocent gentleman he had been, joining up as soon as war was declared in a fit of heartbreak over losing Claudia. He'd not trained as a soldier, Violet had heard through her mother, but had worked as a stretcher-bearer with the Medical Corps. Sadness merged into anger and she clenched her fists on her lap. Weston Penruth, she decided in a flash of hatred, is responsible. He stole Claudia from Eddie. How could the fisherman compete with the lord of the manor? And what of Claudia? How must she feel? Did she believe she sent her former love off to war? Oh Claudia, Violet felt tears wet her lashes, concentrating hard on the view from the window.

'Well, I'll be blowed,' hissed out Muriel, snapping the newspaper wider and staring hard at the small ads. She glanced at Violet with darkened eyes. 'Oh dear, listen to this: "The first of November 1914. Pleased to announce the marriage of Miss C. Ainsley late of Lansallos, and Mr W. Penruth of Charlecote, Cornwall, at the Chapel, Charlecote."'

Violet fell back against her seat. 'Good God,' she uttered. 'Oh, what has she done . . . ?'

Unable to face Muriel's probing look, she stared down at her trembling hands and turned her wedding ring over and over on her finger. The simple pale-gold band gleamed in the dull light through the carriage window. It had belonged to Jack's long-dead mother and she marvelled at how much she treasured it and wore it with such pride. She thought of Mrs

Penruth's engagement ring – guessing that Claudia would have also been presented with it before her marriage – and unspeakable panic choked her. She wondered, then, how well did that ring fit Claudia?

They arrived at Looe station late in the afternoon and Violet noticed with relief that the lights were still on in the post office across the street. It was nearly closing time.

'Would you hire a taxi, Auntie, while I pop across to post this letter?' Violet said as she hurried off, leaving her aunt to summon the porter.

There was only one other customer at the counter, a fishing wife she recognised from Lansallos. She was one of Eddie Davey's neighbours, also from a long line of fishing folk and destined to live and die within her own realm of about five miles. Her lilting voice was dark and ominous: '. . . they're rounding them up, and sending them off without a by your leave. No sentiment, no explanation . . .'

'It's a crying shame,' the postmaster said, handing the woman her letters across the counter. 'Good old carthorses and farm mares are all going. Army comes into town and within a few hours the stables are empty. But, what can we expect now it's war?'

'All the men, and all the horses,' muttered the woman, her mouth a wretched line. 'You heard about young Eddie?'

The postmaster sympathised. Shook his head. 'I heard even Penruth gave up his stallion for a guinea . . .'

Violet flinched, her fingers tightening around the envelope in her hands. It was addressed, rather messily and with ink blots from the rocking of the train, to Mrs Weston Penruth.

* * *

165

It was very nearly dark when their taxi pulled up at Old Trellick. They had driven past Claudia's old school, over the river Looe that swept through the town and down to the estuary, and then back up the hill and into the wintry evening. Violet looked back to see that the tide was out, revealing silted mud, where seabirds left footprints in the smooth mire. The wooded valleys around Old Trellick were sleeping now under the deepening chill, trailed by ghostly plumes of mist.

Her father was standing under the lighted porch to greet them. He was animated, fussing over the length of their journey, and the coldness of the weather, urging them to hurry indoors.

'Oh, you've brought the damp in with you,' he said. 'Come on, both of you, get to the fire.'

In the hallway, stood Violet's mother, very still, her face inscrutable.

'Are you well?' May asked, giving her a cold little hug. She was, Violet noticed, unable to resist glancing down towards her stomach.

'A rather long journey,' Violet said. 'Caught the earliest train we could. It was dark when we left, dark when we arrive...' She trailed off. 'But in first class with Auntie... very pleasant, really.'

There was a sudden yap and a scurrying of paws as Jess flashed out from the kitchen, leaping up to pummel Violet's knees, his claws dashing her through her coat and dress.

Joy broke over her as she knelt to grab him, bring him to her, his nose wet on her neck. Her face was wide with her smile. 'You scamp. Look how you've grown.'

'Naughty dog, always jumping up,' snapped May.

'*He* must have missed you, Violet,' commented Muriel, heading for the drawing room. 'I do hope the kettle's on, May.'

'Well, she's been baking all afternoon,' said Violet's father. 'Made saffron buns for you. Your favourite, aren't they?'

Violet looked up from Jess's spirited little face and exchanged a private smile with Muriel.

The drawing room, with the card table, thick curtains pulled against the night and glowing chunks of applewood in the grate, was familiar and homely. But Violet had expected to feel more comforted. She sat back into an armchair, numb with fatigue. The journey had taken it out of her. She and her baby needed to rest. Jess sat by her chair and rested his chin on her knee. His velvet eyes searched her face. She barely had the strength to lift her hand to stroke his long nose.

'We've just seen Eddie Davey's name in the paper,' Muriel said as May poured tea.

Her father's voice was troubled. 'There are so many leaving. The trains are full, coming up from Truro and Penzance, sending them on to Bodmin Moor for medicals, training, and then on up to London. Of course, Violet, I don't need to spell it all out to you.'

'Jack's on Salisbury Plain,' she said, her voice a shadow.

Muriel reached out to pat her hand. 'Eat your bun, dear,' she said. 'You look done in.'

But she could barely manage a mouthful and supposed that she was better off in bed. She said her goodnights, and left the room with Jess. Out in the chilly hall, she had her foot on the first stair when her mother left the drawing room and swooped up behind her.

'You know they're married now.' The words fell out of her mouth, rattling around Violet's head. 'We still can't get over the shame of the broken engagement. The utter embarrassment. To think I found Mrs Penruth's ring on the table in the garret where you left it. Gave it back, of course, was the right thing to do. And now all this.'

'Mother, I am as surprised as you are, I—'

'Never mind that. Just tell me why. Why you bolted.'

She was crushed by her mother's intensity. She was so very tired. 'I can't explain, Mother, I can't.'

May seized this. '*Won't*, more like. I can hardly hold my head up around the county.'

I *can't* tell you, then, Violet thought wildly. She gripped the banister, longing to be let go, longing for Jack.

Muriel was suddenly at her side and butted in. 'Leave her alone, May. It's in the past. She has a new life now with Jack. And with a baby on the way . . .'

Violet mumbled, 'I just want him home.'

Muriel tugged her sister on the arm and Violet was released to make her way upstairs.

Lying in bed, with Jess heavy on her feet, she heard a storm rising. The wind was surging in the trees, rattling her window pane. She turned over, cradling her stomach with her arms. She began to pray – ridiculous with fatigue – for Jack's smile to keep him safe.

Chapter Seventeen

When wind takes flail, let no ship sail

Violet took the basket from the back seat of her father's car and headed towards the huddled row of fishermen's cottages. Her father took it from her: it was heavy with her mother's buns, home-made jam and one of Muriel's bottles of Chianti. A fine, soaking mizzle was coming in from the sea, harried by a surging wind, blowing straight through Violet's coat and wrenching dangerously at her hat. Moisture clung to the dirty thatched roof of the Davey cottage and glistened on the bead-like berries on the constantly heaving scrubby bushes around its slate porch. Violet shivered as the damp seeped up from the rutted path. Not nine months ago, this family lost its youngest to pneumonia, and now, one of its fine men to an unseen, violent and incomprehensible end. Her father stood on the doorstep and rapped the knocker, shifting his hat off his head the moment Mrs Davey answered the door.

They walked into a dank, whitewashed room where a black range smoked under the mantel, the wind moaned in the chimney and the air hung with the smell of old fish. Mrs Davey's hands fluttered about her apron top as she muttered that they should please mind the mess and step this way. Her features were blank and bewildered; her cheeks looked like they'd been slapped. She gestured to a wooden settle next to the hearth, where a young girl and boy, two of Eddie's younger siblings, were sitting bewildered by misery.

'Go on, you two, make some space for the gentleman and lady. Get yourselves outside. Go on. Peter's out on the boat with his Da. Though shouldn't be. Not in this weather,' Mrs Davey offered as the children sloped off out into the wind and rain, coat and hatless. 'It's what keeps them going. Lord knows, I try.'

'Sorry to intrude, Mrs Davey,' said George Prideaux. 'We thought we'd stop by to see how the family was. You remember my daughter Violet?'

The woman's eyes flicked blindly to Violet. 'I'd let you through to the parlour to sit,' she said, 'but we've just had him back and I don't rightly know what to do with him.'

Violet's father wondered what she meant but even as he asked, Mrs Davey mutely opened a door at the rear of the room and stood aside. Dr Prideaux politely nodded to her and slipped past her. Violet waited a moment, placed the basket on the settle and then followed.

The room was unaired and dim, although Mrs Davey had lit a lamp and let the precious oil burn on in the empty room. There was one piece of case furniture, possibly for linens, Violet guessed. A drop-leaf table was folded against the wall. The small window, unlike the front room, had lace curtains and the grate was laid with the best applewood. A rattle of rain was thrown against the window, making Violet jump. Blinking in the gloom, she looked around her and then, with a jolt of breath, down. Lying on the knotted hearth rug was Eddie Davey's uniform, stretched out as if clothing an invisible corpse. A cold fist crept up the back of her neck as she stared at it. She knew it to be a uniform by the stuff it was made of, by the fact it had lapels, buttons, front pockets. But not by its colour, nor its condition, for it was soiled, saturated with viscid, foul mud that was not of the earth, not of freshly ploughed fields or tilled soil that Eddie would have known from his beloved Cornwall. The cloth was excreting a story of violence, of weeks of despair, of chaos. And the smell, as Violet took a step closer, was rotten.

She placed her hand over her mouth in slow horror, hearing Mrs Davey speaking behind her.

'They sent it back to us, with bits of his kit and all. It's all we will have of him. They say there's no body. But there must be. How can he not have a body? He was wearing this.'

Violet noticed that the collar of the jacket was shredded and half of the shoulder missing. She looked at her father and saw his ashen face in the badly lit room.

'We must do something with this, Mrs Davey,' he said, his voice tight and decisive. 'We must speak with the vicar and have a proper service. Give Eddie some sort of service. Have the children seen it? Good God, perhaps they shouldn't.'

Mrs Davey shook her head, pressed her hand to her side and dipped out of the room. Violet and her father followed and quietly shut the door.

'I hope our hamper will be welcome,' Violet said uselessly. 'You must all keep eating, keep your strength up.'

Mrs Davey squinted across at her, dashing something from her eye with her sleeve.

'You're Miss Claudia's friend, aren't you?' she demanded. She lowered her forehead and looked up at Violet as if she'd only just noticed her. 'Aren't you the one who left all of a sudden?'

'Yes, Mrs Davey.'

Silence pressed, an unforgiving presence.

Mrs Davey's eyes were scrutinising her, their dead expression suddenly fired with anger. 'One thing leads to another, don't it? I see you're married, heard you were in the family way. Well, bully for you. Don't care what havoc you leave behind, do you?'

Her father broke in. 'We should be going, madam. We will call again.'

'*You* can, Doctor,' she replied. 'Though it might be to give me the last rites, way I'm going.'

'Mrs Davey,' Violet started, 'Really, I . . .' and was silenced by her father's look.

They said good day and as they stepped back onto the path, he told her to walk up the street away from the cottages and he'd go and fetch the wagonette.

Violet waited around the corner, sheltering from the wind, leaning against a slate wall at the junction of the main road. Beyond her lay sodden fields lined with stone fences. Along the line of the hill, the naked, cold trees were buffeted and bent. The damp drizzle settled on her hair and on her gloves and the utter desolation of the day descended hard. She missed Jack, she needed him with her to reassure her and tell her she did nothing wrong. But then how could he help her, when he did not know half of the truth?

She thought about the look in Mrs Davey's eye, her willingness to lash out with blame. She hoped to understand her and then dared not. She never wanted to understand, to experience, what that woman was going through. She thought of Eddie's filthy uniform laid out, the shroud he would never have, while his broken body lay elsewhere, lost and swallowed into the war. Under the sound of the wind, she heard her father's car turning over, choking and spluttering, and then remembered how unreliable it was. And then the sound of another engine, coming along the main road. This car was speeding, splashing up puddles, the chauffer wiping the windscreen with a white handkerchief as he drove. This caught Violet's eye and she stared as the car went past. She saw Weston's face glaring at her through the back window. Her toes screwed up inside her boots. He was glaring at her, his features sharpened in surprise. Beside him, her chin lifted and her pale profile turned deliberately away, sat Claudia. Violet pressed herself back against the wall, her heart squeezing into her throat, her mouth filling with exhaust fumes as the car thundered on its way, and the slate wall digging sharply into her back.

Chapter Eighteen

In the language of flowers:
Lily of the valley, return of happiness

Spring came to Old Trellick in 1915 in the middle of March with yellow forsythia bright against gunmetal skies and cold little primroses huddling on the earthy banks. The throats of thrushes opened wide and their song peeled away like bells to announce the baby born amid a squally day of spitting rain.

The child slipped out of Violet like a wet fish. She was fragile and raw and as delicate as a kitten. Dr Prideaux could not help his granddaughter. In all his experience, her prematurity flummoxed him and he had to call on a consultant from Exeter who suggested the child be taken into hospital at once. But Violet would not agree. On the edge of her own child-bed fever, and without Jack by her side – he was in Wiltshire, unable to get leave – she pleaded for the baby to stay with her, tucked in the crook of her arm, sharing her scent and warmth and milk. This, she knew instinctively but rationally, was the only way the little girl would survive. The doctors relented and sat back to observe, knowing not what else to do.

Three weeks later, silver clouds banked over the house and ghost-like lily of the valley sprang in the moss under the trees. And Violet watched, still desperately weak, from the bed as Jack held his daughter at the window, her tiny head in his hand. A watery light came through the glass and glowed around her husband and the child like an aura. Violet knew then that her daughter had chosen to live and that the world could spin again.

Violet had not cared if she, herself, survived. As long as her daughter was thriving, she could sink back and fade, for nothing else mattered. But Jack stayed by her pillow day and night. Inside, her body gathered its strength, her fever faded from churning red and black to a soft balmy grey and a light sweetness returned to her mind. Her body stopped fooling her, convincing her that she had enormous hands and gigantic feet, and that she could travel the globe in six huge strides. Her mind raced less feverishly and her pulse slowed and was almost back to normal when Jack told her that he had to leave again.

She lay against her pillows, newly changed by her Auntie Muriel, and heard a blackbird outside. That song, she thought, was like a memory of spring. She watched her mother arrange some daffodils by her window and bring her trays of tea. Both her mother and auntie remained as silent angels to Violet, ministering to her and caring so fondly. May's frosty barrier was broken down a little with every careful gesture.

Violet could see through the window that spring was burgeoning, it would be moving forward at its usual steady marching pace, progressing eastwards from the West Country, just as Jack would have to soon.

'How light she is,' he said, cradling the baby by the window. 'She's as light as a feather,' he said. 'What shall we call her? We must christen her.'

Jack was in his civilian clothes. She could not bear to see a uniform. He was home for a week. Just seven short, tenuous days. And then, he had to be gone.

'She's not going to die, Jack,' Violet said. 'She is full of hope. Full of our hope.'

He came back from the window and sat on the bed. 'I was just showing her the sunlight. She could see it. She turned her head towards it. Her little eyes followed it. And her tongue is going. Look she is hungry.'

Jack placed the baby in Violet's arms.

'Your mother has suggested Elizabeth,' he said. 'She has even told the vicar.'

'Aster,' Violet replied, beginning to nurse the baby.

'The flower? Of course.'

'It translates as "star", which means hope,' Violet said. She gazed down at the scrap of a child in her arms and her life was complete. 'Mother can call her what she likes. But she is Aster to us.'

Chapter Nineteen

In the language of flowers:
Bluebell, consistency

The morning, some fourteen months later, was full and lively, the weather spinning round Violet as she walked with Jack down to the sea. She caught the honeyed traces of spring blown from the moors to sweeten the air. She watched the sun sparkling on new leaf and the pale shy flowers in the verges. Little birds soared triumphant against the blue sky. They were lucky, she thought, for the lilac time had come early this May, like Aster had the year before – and Jack was here to see it.

He walked by her side with his cap pulled down to shield his eyes, blinkering himself to the heaven around him. Squinting ahead, his face was averted from her. He was a solid figure, tense and unyielding. He held up a shield which she could not break through. She wanted to take his arm, but his flesh seemed to stiffen at her touch. But then, suddenly, as the path grew steeper and the hedgerows higher, he allowed himself to link his arm in Violet's and the weight of it was pressing but welcome. She was elated to have him by her side, but her fleeting joy had no foundation. The future rolled out before them, dark with dread. He had returned safely to England from the fighting in Loos six months ago, and was now home on leave from his officer-training camp. She had blossomed with pride when he wrote to say that he was up for a commission. But he also told her the other day that there were big manoeuvres in the offing, there was going to be a big push and that he knew his chances. His words burnt into her mind and branded her.

But still, they had some precious days. Violet watched him with an uncertain smile as he carried his little girl over his shoulder down the path to the sea. Aster circled her arms tightly around his neck, happily bouncing along, gazing backwards up the way they had come. Jess trotted ahead down the ferny path to the cove. He was obedient and serene but still as quiveringly spellbound by the world as he had been as a puppy. But there was no need to put him on the lead, for, on Violet's command, he walked at heel. What a pleasant little family we make, thought Violet. If only we all had the conviction we will stay this way.

Any minute now, she thought, we'll reach the place where the sound of the waves will suddenly hit us and fill our ears. Where the ferns fade back and the gorse and dunes advance. In an instant, the sea. She glanced at Jack, wanting to tell him about it, to ask him to listen for it, for the moment, but his face was closed, his eyes brooding. How could she share it, anyway, how could she ever explain?

The sea was calm, a benign green-blue. The sand was

empty, the tide out, hissing backwards over the glistening pebbles at the water mark. Violet spread out the rug in a dip in a dune and they settled down, to any onlooker a complete little family. She drew out a flask and some sandwiches. Aster was momentarily entranced by the sea and the calling gulls, but then shook herself out of it and began to shuffle busily across the rug to make her escape.

'Watch her, she'll be off,' said Violet.

Jack reached forward, picked his daughter up and settled her on his knee, bouncing her, enlightening her to the reasons why she should not go far. He fished shells out of the sand and showed them to her in the centre of his palm. His hands trembled, Violet noticed, sometimes more than ever. Aster plucked at the shells eagerly, put them in her mouth and then grimaced theatrically as sand stuck to her tongue and lips.

Jack sorted her out with his handkerchief. 'There you go, Aster,' he said, and then to Violet, 'Perhaps she can have a sandwich.'

Violet assured him that Aster would only chew the bread into a soggy wad in her mouth. In any case, she had some stewed fruit for her.

'Some tea, then. Does she drink tea? Have you tried her with tea?'

'Not yet. But let's try,' said Violet. 'Although babies her age don't normally drink tea.'

'How should I know? I don't know anything about her. Has she got teeth? I didn't even know she could crawl . . .' He watched sadly as his daughter made la-la noises over the shell booty still cradled in the palm of his hand. His sigh was long, drawn from the depths. 'All of this continues without me. You both carry on without me. I even find it astonishing that spring has come again. Isn't that raving mad? There'll be bluebells in the woods now, won't there? I want to sketch them before I go. Thing is, I'm surprised they're there. Surprised that life is normal, that everything is normal here. While all of that . . .' he tossed his head towards the sea, 'while all of that . . .'

Violet glanced at him, alarmed but eager for him to keep talking for this was the first time he'd alluded to what was going on in France. But he fell into silence; his face, closed down, was once again bland. Then, suddenly, as if fingertips had brushed his cheek, Violet saw a brief shadow of torment cross his face. She was terrified.

Reaching out to touch his trembling hand, she said, quietly, 'I just want you to be home again.'

He would not meet her eye, so she gazed out at the gentle sea, feeling the swing of the breeze, sensing her joy fading. A stillness settled between them, punctuated by Aster's gurgling.

Jack recoiled at a sudden thought, all at once more animated, alive. 'I can't paint any more, Violet. I've lost it. My hands shake badly, you see. Only rough sketches in the trench, that's all. Things I can just dash off. And I can't possibly show anyone.'

Violet wondered why ever not.

He looked at her, his mouth agape. 'They're not for anyone's eyes. For we are no longer human.'

'Please talk to me,' she whispered, tears smarting her eyes. 'For who else can help you? I'm here. I'm always here. We're both here.' She plucked Aster from the rug and held her protesting little body close. She looked at her husband, feeling a broad and sudden estrangement between them. 'Is it that you're missing us? Missing all the little stages of Aster's life? That it's all broken up like this? That you've see her only a handful of times in her life? I try to write it all down, in the Flower Book, every little milestone. The news, the little things. I try to convey it to you in my letters. Perhaps I fail.' She paused as the gulf widened. 'But this is hell.'

He gave a short hard sigh. 'Hell, you say.'

'Jack, I'm sorry. I have no idea. Because you won't tell me. What I'm imagining is . . .'

'Indescribable.'

A breeze picked up and ruffled the sandwich papers. Violet's tea grew cold. Aster shivered and Violet dressed her quickly in the knitted jacket Muriel had made.

Eventually Jack said, 'You remember Sebastian Welstead?'

Violet nodded. She told him of course she did. She suddenly thought of the intense heat of that July day in London, the glare of the sun on the white Regency terraces, the melting green park. Mr Welstead descending the stairs of his family mansion, his impeccable suit, his tailored shirt and his elegant and courteous departure. Within half an hour, she remembered, smiling briefly, she would be taking tea with Jack in the Pavilion.

'He's gone,' Jack said, bluntly. 'Couldn't take it.'

'What do you mean . . . ?'

Jack's eyes were opaque with the memory. 'Our troop is preparing for stand-to,' he said. 'Fixed bayonets. Gas masks on because our boys are sending it over. In the trench, we're all poised on the fire steps, on the ladders. I look to the left and to the right to see my men hunched and stiff with terror.

Welstead is our captain and has his head up first. Leads from the front, always. The whistle blows somewhere down the line and I scramble up into the storm. Bullets and shells on us. Blasting chaos. Welstead is ahead, ducking and flinching, his revolver held in front of him like a poker. Useless. I glance behind me at our line of men. His men, my men. Scattered like pins along the top of the trench, some writhing, others crumpled, completely still. *"Orders are to move forward. If in doubt, move forward!"* Welstead pulls his mask up and screams, *"Get up, you cowards!"* *"They can't sir,"* I scream back, although he can't hear me. *"They're dead."* They're all fucking dead.'

A tide of anger moved in Violet's blood. She kept her eyes locked on Jack. She could not flinch from what he was telling her, for she had to absorb it for him, let him know she was hearing him, *trying* to understand.

'We didn't get very far,' he continued. 'Our own gas was blown back in our faces. The new order was to retreat back to our stinking hole. To crouch like animals in our hovel. We cease being human.'

Violet reached for his hand, but he pulled it away.

'Everything slows down out there. Or speeds up at a ferocious rate. Half an hour later, two hours later, I have no idea, Welstead calmly went out of the bunker and put his revolver in his mouth.'

Aster, perched on her father's knee, ponderously reached a finger and traced the stiff line from his nose to his mouth. Violet's vision blurred with tears, her mouth crumpled.

'I can't look at you crying,' Jack said. 'I can't tell you any more,' and he passed Aster to her, dumping her in her lap.

He got up and walked briskly away across the beach,

followed by an oblivious, bounding Jess. They disappeared together up the path.

Violet tipped away her tea and scattered the sandwiches for the seagulls. She took Aster's plump little hand and walked a tottering zigzag line to the sea. Her daughter's inquisitive innocence found miniature crabs washed up on the shoreline, sparkling pebbles, fragments of sea glass, muted and smooth now that the waves had pounded away their shine. The little girl lifted a stem of seaweed, dripping, limp and luminous green and held it out to her mother. Violet took it gratefully, thinking of the next blank page in the Flower Book.

'Did you have your moment?' There was someone standing beside her. She had crept across the sand in silence and was there, suddenly, gently, by her side. Violet turned to stare at Claudia's face.

In her arms she held her child, a little boy some four months younger than Aster, chubby and milk-fed, his grey eyes round with innate humour, perfectly balanced on her hip. Claudia's smile was as beautiful as Violet remembered.

'Pardon?' she blurted, distracted by Aster who had made a break for the waves.

Claudia, with reflexes quicker than Violet's, darted for the little girl, expertly guiding her back to her mother, simultaneously shifting her baby to her other hip. Violet grabbed hold of Aster tightly and lifted her up and the two women stood facing one another as the spent waves hissed towards their shoes.

Sunlight dappled through Claudia's straw hat, sending bright flecks over her cheeks as pale as butter. Her fair hair was coiled in a great gilded plait at the nape of her neck and her baby proceeded to dig his fingers into it. Her dress was of the finest linen, beautifully stitched over the bodice. She wore lace gloves high enough to cover her delicate wrists. Long gone was the let-down school dress, the ripped seams. She looked as pure and as bright as ever. And Violet, still mute with surprise, suffered a peculiar mix of grief and happiness.

'Did you do it, when you came down the path?' Claudia asked again. 'Did you have the moment?'

Violet conceded quietly that she had indeed.

'Look at us two,' Claudia went on, excitedly and oblivious. 'You have a little girl and I have a little boy.'

'This is my daughter Aster,' Violet mumbled.

Claudia introduced her to placid little Harry.

'I know who he is,' Violet replied tersely and turned to walk back to the blanket, the corners of which were being lifted by the wind. She sat Aster on the sand and struggled to grab hold of it. Claudia followed, set Harry down next to the little girl and helped Violet, spreading the blanket out and sitting on it to keep it down, laughing at how the breeze had taken them by surprise.

Violet shifted in discomfort, glancing over her shoulder. 'I really should hurry back. I need to . . . did you see my husband, on the path? With Jess. Of course, you'd recognise Jess.'

Claudia conceded that she had done. 'Your husband? Of course. Although he did not say good morning. He had his head down, his collar pulled up . . . Home on leave?'

Violet looked at her friend with incredible sadness. Two years had passed since they'd last been together on this beach. And there she was, smiling artlessly and laughing, as if they were chattering about schooldays again and looking after the puppy. Just as they had been before Weston Penruth and his two black dogs had walked towards them across the sand.

'This is ridiculous,' Violet was petulant as her fury ignited. She folded her arms tightly. 'We can't just pick up like this after all this time. We can't just pretend.'

Her friend dismissed the idea with a wave her hand. 'Oh, but we can, Violet. We can.' She was as spirited as ever Violet remembered. 'I was so glad to hear you got married. You beat me to it.'

Exasperated, Violet cried, 'Claudia, what happened?'

Claudia stopped talking and stared, her pretty mouth open in surprise. 'Surely, you have to tell *me* what happened. You left Old Trellick. You ran away. We couldn't imagine why. You were so happy. You'd just got engaged to Weston. It didn't make any sense to us. My mother said, no sense at all. And of course, Weston is a gentleman, so won't speak of it.'

Violet watched her friend pick up her baby son and blow a raspberry into his chest to make him laugh. In Harry's smooth little face, she saw something of Weston, something around the eyes.

'I can't tell you why,' Violet uttered, ice returning to her core. She added quickly, 'But I didn't want any of it to affect us. To come between us. I wanted to explain. I wrote to you.'

'Yes, from Montagu Square. I'm so sorry I did not reply.' Claudia dipped her head, looked away. 'With Weston, you see, I couldn't help myself. It all happened in such a giddy haze. I couldn't tell you. At first, I wanted to look after him for you. Do you understand? He was a broken man.'

'*Broken?* Oh Claudia.'

'And then I didn't hear from you,' Claudia hurried on, fixing Violet with her eyes, soft with tears. 'Even when you came back home. I was so happy to find out that you'd returned to Old Trellick. We were both married. You were expecting. I do wish we'd kept in touch. I thought that you hated me and I accepted that. My guilt didn't help. What I did. To you and to Eddie.'

Violet blurted, 'But I wrote to you on the train on the way down from London. I posted it from Looe even before I got in the taxi.'

Claudia frowned, shook her head. 'I didn't get it.'

She thought for a moment and then realisation flickered over her face.

Violet leapt on this, nodding hard. 'He intercepted it.'

'But, it's not what you think,' Claudia paused. 'He is a good man. Deep down, such a good man.'

Violet suddenly wanted to snatch up Aster and get away so she could no longer hear Claudia, her greatest friend, speak like this.

Claudia gripped her arm with pale, fine fingers. Tears glistened in her eyes.

'Weston is misunderstood by so many people,' she said. 'And, I expect from the way you bolted, by you. But I saw through it.'

'What is there to see through?' mumbled Violet.

Claudia ignored her argument. 'I was there at home, at Charlecote farm, the day after you left,' she said. 'I saw him shoot his dogs. I saw him stand in the middle of the yard and take aim. His face was black with pain.' She shuddered, pressed a hand over her chest. 'Believe me, when the elder Mrs Penruth moved away at the beginning of the war, he changed. That's when he opened up to me. He was so much happier.'

'Mrs Penruth moved away?' Violet asked.

'To stay with her brother in Scotland. Perthshire somewhere. She was obsessed with getting away from the war, thinking we'd be invaded here in Cornwall. She was frightened of the U-boats.' Claudia lowered her voice. 'But she is a very *difficult* woman. It's uncharitable of me to say so, but Weston's and my relationship is better when she is not around. Weston is a better man. I heard below-stairs gossip that she could not stand Weston marrying beneath him, and going for such an ordinary girl "for the second time".' Claudia stared at Violet to emphasise the meaning. 'Really, Violet, there are things I could tell you . . .'

Claudia broke off and began to fiddle with Harry's shoes. Violet gazed down the beach, unable to imagine anyone, least of all her closest friend, having a relationship of any sort with Weston Penruth.

She thought of the time, when Jess was a puppy, that blustery spring day when she had planned to come here to the sands to look for sea holly, but headed into the woods instead for Jess to be nearly mauled to death by the dogs. That was the day she had been manipulated by Weston's apparent goodness and her parents' strange and obsessive ambition. But then, she decided, if she had not gone to the woods that day, had not agreed to marry Weston amid her shy fog of gratitude, then she would never have gone to London. And would have never met Jack.

And how I love him, she thought, as she watched Aster on her lap blithely reach her hand out to Harry, tugging at his sleeve in a questioning manner while he sat oblivious. But how difficult it is to find Jack's love when he shuts himself from me. I must dig deep for it, bring it to the surface, for he needs me. How he needs me.

Claudia interrupted her thoughts. 'When you broke off your engagement, and left for London, Weston was so furious. He was going to evict your parents, make them leave Old Trellick,' she said. 'But I persuaded him otherwise.'

Violet's mouth gaped open. 'He was going to throw them out of their home?'

'I am a good influence on him in so many ways,' Claudia said.

Violet rested her face in her hand. 'I can't believe it. I really can't forgive him for that.'

'You don't have to, I will do it for you.' Claudia peered at Violet. 'I'm sorry, I will never understand everything that happened. That's between you and Weston. But you look so troubled.'

Violet sighed, weary and shattered. She said simply, 'Blame the war.'

Claudia agreed. 'It reaches everywhere, touches everything, doesn't it? But I am happy. Oh Violet, now I have my precious Harry. And here,' she placed a hand on her stomach, her smile brightening, 'another one is on the way, God willing.'

But suddenly Claudia's face broke and she began to cry.

Violet quickly moved over and put her arm around her friend's slender shoulders. She watched as tears fell silently from her friend's eyes onto her lacy gloves. Between the sobs and sighs, and the wiping of tears, she heard a faint mumbling.

'Hush, what is it?' Violet asked, placing everything from the past apart from their true, dear friendship to one side. To gather her own strength, she breathed deeply on the sweet salt air of the cove. 'Remember, I'm here. I am always your friend. Why the tears? Another child? Oh Claudia, you will be even happier.'

Claudia looked up at her, from beneath the brim of her hat. Her eyes were wide and wet, the fair lashes dark with tears. Her pretty mouth was shapeless, trembling. She said just one word, *Eddie*.

The family sat in the drawing room at Old Trellick with a small fire flickering in the grate. Violet got up to draw the curtains on the cool spring evening and saw, beneath the trees at the bottom of the garden, a swathe of pristine bluebells nodding in the deepening violet of nightfall. She longed to point them out to Jack, but bit her tongue.

He was playing crib with her father at the card table, Muriel contentedly knitting and her mother reading the paper. Jess lay with his snout on his paws in front of hearth and Aster was upstairs tucked up in bed. So gentle, it seemed, so quiet and natural was the atmosphere in the drawing room that Violet could hardly bear it. She watched Jack. His smile was false, she knew, his laughter a strain. Her father was teasing him as he slapped down the cards. Muriel hummed to herself, counting stitches, and May occasionally opened the broadsheet to its full stretch. No one would talk about it: the fact that her husband was to leave for France tomorrow.

'For God's sake, I've lost again,' cried Jack, throwing down his cards.

'All you need to do,' said her father, 'is count to fifteen.'

'My brain's addled. Can't think straight.'

Muriel wondered if he fancied a whisky.

'Might do you some good,' ventured May, folding the paper. 'Well, I'm through with reading any more of that. Terrible news. What's going on in the world?'

Violet's scalp prickled with irritability. Even when her mother was being kind, she was still extremely tactless.

'No whisky, thank you. I'd better go up. Early start tomorrow.' Jack glanced at Violet and she saw, once more on his face stiff with affability, a brief flash of torment.

'I'll come up with you,' she told him, and they said goodnight to the three elder faces that were blank with relief.

On the stairs, Jack paused, wondering why he had only just remembered that it had been her friend Claudia who he had seen the other day on the path to the beach. 'It must have been her, from the way you have described her,' he said.

Violet told him that Claudia had mentioned it. After all, she said, Claudia had remembered the dog. Jack fell silent and made his way up to their bedroom.

'I'm pleased that you have made things up with her,' he said, loosening his tie by the mirror as Violet lit the lamp. He fumbled with his cufflinks and Violet stepped forward to help him. She unbuttoned her skirt, tugging her blouse out and starting on the fastenings. Her insides relaxed at the light tone of his voice. When she had the real Jack back, when he spoke to her like he used to, when their intimacy was revived, even for a few moments, her happiness was whole again.

'I do like your new moustache,' she said playfully, sitting on the edge of the bed. 'Shame you had to shave off your beard, though, when you joined up. I thought it was rather dashing, and very artistic. I always did. From the moment we met.'

Her husband bent down and looked at his pale reflection in the mirror. 'Now I'm a lieutenant, I can have my facial hair back, just part of it, anyway.' He smoothed his whiskers down. 'Welstead cops it, I get promoted.'

Violet was horrified.

Jack's laugh was hollow. 'Gallows humour. It's how we get through.'

To her relief, his warm smile returned as he sat by her.

'Before I forget, I found this among the dunes the other day.' He fished in his pocket and drew out a delicate stem of sea holly, apologising that it was a bit battered. 'Not the best specimen ever, but you must press it anyway and put it in the Flower Book, along with that ropey bit of seaweed that Aster brought home.'

They laughed and he placed the plant delicately on the dressing table. They lay back together on the bed and he wrapped his fingers around hers, caressing her tenderly. His trembling had subsided, she noticed, for now. Slowly, it seemed, he got better. It took him the full length of his leave to return to being Jack. And by the time it was over, by the time he had to go back to the front, he was with her again. Truly with her on this, their last night for many, many months.

'So,' Jack said later, 'she married the Penruth fellow.'

Beside him, in the lamplight, Violet stiffened. 'That she did.'

'How do you feel about that?' Jack held her and rolled her towards him. He was close to her, his eyes darting over her features, as if to search the truth from her. His face was in shadow and she could not make him out, and yet she knew her expression was lit by the steady glow of the lamp. 'After all, you were once engaged to him.'

How could she tell him how she felt? Her shame, her undignified escape from the orangery, from Cornwall, from her home. She swallowed hard and told him, their faces

191

close on the pillows. 'Really, Jack it was a flash in the pan,' Violet whispered her lie. 'More in my mother's eyes than in mine. I was young and silly and soon saw the error of it. I couldn't care less for Weston.'

She thought of their wedding night and her body's tainted legacy, the terror that Jack would discover everything about her. And then her poignant relief that her new husband, as worldly and as confident as he appeared, was not so at all. She was, after all, the only woman he'd ever experienced. Yet the reprieve and her concealment turned her sour.

'So why is it always such a problem to talk about?' Jack's expression in the twilight was indistinct. 'Is there more to this than I realise? Are you jealous of Claudia?'

'No, my love. Nothing more than a little bit of foolish pride. I was young, flattered by him. It wasn't meant to be.'

Content with her answer, he moved close to her, telling her he was sorry for questioning her. His fingertips tracing her shoulder and across her collarbone. They began to kiss. At last, thought Violet, finding herself locked in his embrace, my Jack has returned.

But tomorrow he would put on his uniform and become a different man. Tomorrow, he would leave Old Trellick as Lieutenant Fairling, of the London Regiment, and head back to France. And how on earth could she tell him that it was so much more? How could she tell him of her degradation and the hatred that festered there? And that her staying quiet and compliant would ensure her family home is not broken apart by the very man who violated her. She could not allow him to carry that with him into battle.

Chapter Twenty

January: the blackest month of all the year

The hammering on the front door woke up the house and set Jess yapping in the kitchen below. In the darkness, Violet sat upright. Her mind, jolted from its sleep, spiralled with bad news and telegrams. A pool of dread slopped in her stomach. She got out of bed and fumbled with her lamp as she heard her father's footsteps go past her bedroom door and down the stairs. Wrapping herself in her dressing gown, she stepped onto the landing and peered into the gloom of the staircase, seeing the sickening sway of her father's lantern shadows over the walls.

The blast of icy night air through the open doorway was murderous. Violet became aware of a strange crackling silence outside under the high midnight sky. But it wasn't the quiet of a peaceful sleeping countryside; the stricken woods, lanes and hedgerows were holding a collective breath under a deep, hard freeze. She glimpsed cold clouds of stars in the sweeping infinite blackness above and felt a chill like death sweep into the hallway as the boy from Charlecote farm panted on the doorstep, begging for Dr Prideaux. Violet's father took hold of his collar and hauled him inside.

'What now, what now?' he asked, shivering in slippered feet.

The boy stuttered, breathless, his nose running, his cheeks looking like they'd been slapped. He'd run all the way.

'Master says you got to come quick. It's Missus. The baby's coming.'

Violet's father muttered about all the unnecessary commotion, and where was the midwife? After all, it was her second child.

'It's backwards, sir. Someone said to tell you, it's backwards.'

Without a word, Dr Prideaux thrust the lantern at Violet and raced up the stairs to dress, calling back for her to fetch his doctor's bag from the cupboard.

Violet did as she was asked and stayed mutely by the door, holding it ready. Was there something she could do for her friend, apart from just stand there? Was there nothing to be done but wait? By her side, the little boy began to cry, snuffling into his sleeve.

'Pray the wagonette starts first time,' her father muttered. He was in his hat and coat and out of the door in no time, the boy shuffling after him. Violet closed it behind him, shutting out the silent frozen January night. She wandered in a daze to sit by the warm kitchen range, occasionally ruffling Jess under his chin, feeling a little heat ebb from the fire box. But the cold stayed with her, remained inside her, stiffening her body, chasing away sleep until all she could do was wait in the middle of an unreal, unbearable world.

They had revived their friendship with walks to the cove throughout the balmy early summer that followed Jack's departure, enjoying the 'moment' on the path to the sea while Claudia still had it in her to break into a run. And then, as her pregnancy progressed and the summer unfolded, they settled in the garden chairs at Old Trellick, drank tea and watched Jess bound around the lawn, while their children slept in their prams or played on the rug. The days lengthened and the sky widened into pearly blue as appalling waves of news began to reach them from Picardy.

'My mother reads them like the weather report,' said Violet into the drowsy quiet of the summer's day. From a nearby flowerbed came the intimate sound of a bee caught inside a foxglove flower. 'The casualty lists.'

'Call-up papers arrived at the farm this morning,' said Claudia. She was lounging in her deckchair, her hat casting pretty shadows on her nose, her stomach a firm and gentle mound under her skirt. 'We're to lose another lad to it. He's to go to Bodmin for a medical.'

'You'd think he'd be exempt, being a land worker,' said Violet. 'But maybe it's gone beyond that now.'

'The awful thing is, Weston can spare him,' Claudia reached for her teacup.

Violet halted, as was usual, on hearing his name. Apparently Weston had benevolently given his blessing for Claudia to maintain her friendship with Violet, which she found distasteful but decided the least said about it all the better. The subject of Claudia's husband was unavoidable within their daily discourse, but they both tried to steer any such conversation whenever possible. This, their unspoken rule of deep and abiding friendship. Violet decided that if she could ignore Weston and still have her dear friend close by, then she would overcome the worst of it.

Claudia sighed. 'The lad's never been further than Liskeard, his mother tells me. The trains are always packed with them, aren't they, heading east. Jack writes?'

'He does,' said Violet. 'Of course he does.'

She and Claudia looked at each other, knowing something of the other's agony. Eddie's name was never mentioned, but every so often, one or the other would comment about the state of affairs: about how the dead don't come home, that the war simply swallows them. And Violet had told her, briefly, about her visit to the Davey cottage at Lansallos before Aster was born. She had watched Claudia's face stiffen, but felt that her friend should know.

'It's hard to believe, when you don't see them,' Claudia whispered as she poured more tea for them that sunny summer afternoon. 'See a body, I mean. There's no funeral. There's no goodbye.' Violet watched a pulse throb at her friend's throat. 'Why should his life be reduced to a chit of paper? Why is his life worth less than mine?'

Claudia clamped her hand over her mouth and scurried off to a corner of the garden to be sick. When she came back, pale and fragile, they agreed mutually and wholeheartedly never to speak of it again.

And yet, Violet longed to talk. When she saw the casualty lists, vetted each morning by her father, she wanted to voice her ignorance. *Missing, presumed dead* she understood. But

Missing, presumed drowned? Her mind could not work itself around this fate for the country's youth, for how could she imagine the unimaginable? And then she remembered the putrid sludge stiffening Eddie's uniform. They were drowning in the mud. And Jack was out there. She told herself, if he can cope, then so can I. But the strain was unbearable. How she was desperate with longing, right at that moment in the cold Old Trellick kitchen, to talk to Claudia.

Violet didn't realise that she'd fallen asleep, awkward and cramped in the fireside chair, until she jumped awake at the sound of the front door. The watery light of the January dawn had crept its way into the house. Jess was fretful and hungry, her toes were cold and the fire in the range needed stoking. She moved to get up as the kitchen door opened but the look on her father's face pinned her to her chair.

He did not glance at her but made for the scullery out the back, balling up a shirt in his hands but too late: Violet saw that thick blood stained the linen in clotted spreading layers.

She heard him lift the lid of the laundry basket and then he must have changed his mind. He came back in to the kitchen, wandering in a daze to the range, opened the fire door and swiftly stuffed the shirt into the meagre embers.

He stood, his face blank and grey, staring at the wall. The kitchen clock ticked on, its mechanics hard in Violet's head. She waited for him to speak, realising that she had stopped breathing.

'I tried,' her father said, his voice cracking the silence. He turned blank eyes to her. 'I tried the hardest I ever have. I don't think a man could have tried any more.'

Violet stared up at him, the fluid in her body emptying to her feet.

Dr Prideaux said, 'And she gave it all she could.'

Violet felt as if he had just punched her.

She opened her dry, caked mouth to ask, 'The baby?'

'Girl.'

She screamed suddenly, 'Alive or dead?'

Her father took a step back in horror, his face ashen. He informed her that baby Kate was very much alive.

'I left that poor soul Penruth standing mute with shock in the corner of the room, with the newborn screaming in the crib and Mrs Ainsley mindlessly rocking it. The poor cow. What more could I do? Was there anything I could do?'

Violet pressed her hands against her temples.

'And little Harry,' her father blundered on. 'At the front door, I glanced back and he was standing at the top of the stairs, thumb in mouth, hair all messy from sleep, asking where his Mama was.'

Chapter Twenty-One

In the language of flowers:
Rhododendron, be wary

Violet never imagined that she'd come here again. The drive approach to Charlecote was as sweeping and as drawn out as she remembered, curving around grand trees that began to litter their leaves and dense glossy rhododendron bushes ('perfect climate for them,' Weston Penruth had once told her, while she shuddered at their alien gaudiness). And the house itself – at one time incredibly and so briefly the place she expected to live out her married life – brooded in steadfast Gothic monstrosity.

From the outside, nothing had changed. The chimneys still towered above intricate brickwork and the upper-floor windows remained curtained with maroon velvet. But on the ground floor, carpets had been rolled away, curtains pulled down and plain blinds installed in their place. Precious antiques had been carted to disused upper rooms and shrouded in dust sheets. The temperature in the hothouse had been lowered and its spaces given over to growing green vegetables and fruit. And instead of the sleek Penruth car parked outside on the gravel, ambulances pulled up on a regular basis and spilt out their desperate cargoes. For Charlecote was now a Voluntary Aid Detachment hospital and Violet, hurrying up its wide front steps, one of its many nursing auxiliaries.

The once quiet and sedate rooms had been transformed with an air of serious and busy purpose. The elder Mrs Penruth's private parlour, with its floor-to-ceiling windows affording the most natural light, had been stripped and scrubbed and reappointed as the operating theatre. Grand corridors now held court to the scurrying of footsteps, clanking of trolleys and muffled, earthy, sometimes piercing cries of young men. And they came in a steady and hopeless stream, patched up first in dressing stations behind the lines and then processed by the medical corps in Flanders and Picardy. Men with wounds too violent and traumatic to be dealt with on the field were dispatched home with their Blighty, where another army of people waited to receive them in shocked but determined silence.

The old staff of Charlecote had been scattered by the war. They either returned as volunteers at the hospital or they found occupation elsewhere for the cause. Willis the butler made an uncomplaining and unsurprising efficient orderly and the grieving Mrs Ainsley, who was now 'not quite all there' according to Violet's father, was resigned to helping in the kitchens. The staff quarters in the attic, from where Violet had once been told there was a wonderful view of the sea, was still divided into male and female quarters but now played host to medics, nurses and trolley porters.

Weston Penruth quit Charlecote just two weeks after Claudia died in January. Auntie Muriel had told her that there were whispers that he could not bear to be in the house alone with the children. And so, when his mother died suddenly at her brother's home in Perthshire, he took his son Harry and baby Kate up to Scotland to bury her, and then he simply stayed away, leaving instructions to give Charlecote over to the authorities. With the house empty of that man, Violet was willing to cross the threshold once again. But she did it with trembling trepidation each and every time. She longed to bury the past and prove to herself that none of it mattered any more, and working here at Charlecote was a way towards that. That sordid episode had indeed blighted her life but it was over, and from that spring, even though she walked Weston's corridors and opened Weston's drawing-room door on a daily basis, he could not touch or hurt her again. With inhuman strength she suspended her belief for the ten long hours she put in for her shift. She immersed herself in the rounds of towels, sheets, and rough woollen blankets. And it was with the same courage that she faced her patients every morning, the poor souls who were sent to Charlecote. Helping them, she promised herself, would mean that another girl, somewhere, somehow, might be kind to Jack.

With pristine uniform, apron neatly tied and hat and fluttering veil perched precisely on her head, Violet walked under the portico, through the grand front door and turned sharp left into the nurses' quarters to report for duty. Here in the former drawing room with its French windows overlooking the rolling lawn and standard roses, the tapestry cushions and silverware – everything that Claudia had admired as a little girl and everything she had presided over briefly as mistress of the house – had been packed away. The old Charlecote armchairs and occasional tables had been rearranged for the nurses to rest and take their tea. Rings from the cups now marked polished oak surfaces, scuffs appeared on the glowing parquet, the windows were dotted with fingerprints and, Violet noticed with a sniff of a giggle, a saucer from elder Mrs Penruth's favourite tea set was being used as an ashtray.

Two night nurses just off duty chatted and hugged cups of tea by the open French window. They raised sleepy smiles at her and continued their tired conversation. Emily, Charlecote's former parlourmaid, snored gently in her old employer's huge armchair, her folded hands red raw from scrubbing hospital linen. Violet walked over to the register to sign in for her morning's work. It lay open on a George III bureau, which had once been Weston Penruth's pride and joy. Matron took a shine to it and so it remained to 'add a sense of decorum to the nurses' room'. Then, glancing at the clock, Violet hurried off to report to Sister who, mercifully, was from out of the county and knew her only as Nurse Fairling.

'Start in the main ward,' she told her from her desk in the old flower room. 'And begin with bed baths where you can. Leave the worst of the burns patients to Nurse Peters – you are not properly trained for that sort of work.'

'Any losses during the night, Sister?'

She replied in the negative and said she could thank Mr Carter for that, reiterating sharply that he was one of the best surgeons and that she was sorry he was moving on. She opened the admissions and discharge ledger on the desk in front of her and turned to the latest entry.

'This is your new charge: Private Lionel Morgan, aged twenty-two, bullet wound of foot. Bed 42. Came in late yesterday. Large toe destroyed. Second toe can be saved by Mr Carter. I have added him to the list. This patient also has a severe case of trench mouth.'

Sister pulled off her spectacles, breathed on them and cleaned them furiously. 'It's pretty obvious what has happened here,' she said. 'Surprised he made it this far. Thought he would have been court-martialled at the front. Pure case of PBI in my eyes. Go and see to him, Fairling. Book him in and try to make him comfortable.'

Violet assured her that she would do her very best.

She crossed the wide hallway and pushed open the door to the ballroom. The chandelier always caught her eye first, glinting incongruously high up over this bizarrely altered room. Weston's grand shutters had been removed as they had been deemed too cumbersome and bulky to deal with in the efficient workings of a busy ward. In their place, blinds were pulled halfway down the high windows to shield poorly eyes from sunlight. The expanse of parquet where Violet might have danced at her own wedding now played host to two lengthy rows of white metal beds, where figures lay broken, like shadows, weakened facsimiles of the country's youth. Where there was a will and the means to do so, heads turned gingerly and smiles flinched as Violet bustled past. Some raised a hand in greeting, while Cartwright in Bed 36, with his enduringly bleak sense of humour, raised his bandaged stump and waved it at her.

Violet uttered her good mornings, seeing some faces brighten, seeing some faces crumble in a cloud of agony. She noted that the man in Bed 40 had unknowingly spewed up a thick slop of stinking blood down his pyjamas and added it to her mental list of things to attend to. As she passed, she gazed into eyes that were desperate to live, and into eyes that wanted to die. How did they expect her to know how to cope with such people in the extremes of this degradation? Every general should take a turn around this ward, she decreed, instead of sitting behind a polished Louis XV desk in a Picardy château.

Private Morgan lay with his foot propped up and with a festering field bandage still around it. He tried to haul himself up at her approach but shrieked like a child through his teeth as his foot moved briefly against the sheet. He is so young, she thought. He was her age, perhaps younger, his eyes clear and innocent. She asked him if he wanted a cup of tea and told him his neglected teeth and diseased gums would be treated with an hourly gargle of salt water.

'Sounds like a punishment,' he uttered and pointed weakly down the bed. 'But aren't you going to see to that first?'

She assured him of that and began to carefully unbind his foot, watching his face grow pale as agony cracked up his leg. He fought it at first but began to struggle and writhe. Violet froze, her inexperienced hands useless and fumbling. His screams brought Nurse Peters rushing over from the far end. In one seamless movement, she turned him unceremoniously over and, her thin, bony face pinched in concentration, stabbed his buttock with a syringe of morphine. Then she encouraged Violet to help her hold the soldier under the armpits and haul him back up the bed – a grown man being treated like an infant.

'The foot's a mess,' Nurse Peters told her, an earnest glint in her serious eyes, 'but Mr Carter will see to it and will make sure he can rejoin his battalion within the month.' And she turned to respond to a sudden and keening cry from the other end of the ward.

In the slow minutes that it took for the drug to take effect, Private Morgan panted and raged, his fists clenched over his eyes. Violet waited, studying his sparse notes on the clipboard hung over the end of his bed until, minute by minute, the young man returned to a more human shape.

'Thank you, Nurse,' he said, breathless, his face shining with a film of sweat and as pale as sour milk. 'May I have a cigarette? Please pass one from my pocket there.'

Violet was happy to do so. She took one from the packet, lit it for him, placed it in his mouth and returned to the clipboard.

'You look confused,' Private Morgan said as he inhaled deeply, relishing absence of pain and blowing the smoke in a stream towards the intricate plaster carvings on the ceiling.

'Sister mentioned something about PBI to me, in connection with your case,' said Violet. 'You see, I'm quite new and inexperienced and I'm just trying to find out what this was . . .'

The soldier snorted, his young face distorted into a mask of despair by utter derision and a memory of something Violet could not hope to understand.

'PBI? I know what that is,' he muttered, sucking hard on the nicotine. 'That's what we all are. Poor Bloody Infantry.'

Chapter Twenty-Two

In the language of flowers:
Poplar, courage

A week later, Violet pushed a wheelchair containing the grumbling Private Morgan through the grand double door of the ballroom, along the back corridor and out of the house. She negotiated a ramp, crossed the patio in front of the French windows and parked him by a bench with a view of the lawns and the mighty chestnuts at the rear of the grounds that were glorious in ruddy gold. Beyond, as a boundary marker, the spires of Lombardy poplars, planted in a regimented colonnade when the house was built some fifty years ago, hinted at the late elder Mr Penruth's grandiose ideas. How out of place they are, Violet thought dismally, and turned her attention to the more pleasant sight of the rugged native black poplars nestling peacefully nearby.

'Nice 'ere, isn't it?' Morgan joked.

His cheeks were a better colour that morning, Violet

thought, but his eyes retained dull chips of misery and his hands were agitated and constantly twitched at his dressing gown cord.

'Having a nice holiday, I am, in a nice posh house in the country. Except the holiday will soon be over. That doctor, Carter, is pleased with himself. He's too good, isn't he? Should have cut my foot right off. Then I wouldn't have to go back. They say rehabilitation can take months but not from where I'm sitting. My commanding officer's been in touch, did you know? I'll have my orders soon. Back into the thick of it.' He paused, his eyes narrowing. 'I say, Nurse, my big toe's really itchy, could you just . . . Silly me, it's not there any more.'

Violet ignored him, sat down on the bench and gazed at the overgrown, weed-choked beds and lumpy mole-colonised lawn of Charlecote's once pristine gardens. She was to take her break once she'd done a circuit with Morgan around the garden, but her lower back was burning with the strain of lifting patients and bending to tend the wounds and spillages. Her marrow ached, her temples throbbed. Surely, she could take five minutes here in the autumn sunshine? Sister would never find out.

'Don't feel you have to stay,' muttered the soldier. 'I'm not going anywhere. Just going to sit here and rave.'

'I'll push you on in a moment, I just need to sit.' Violet felt in her pocket for Jack's latest letter, thinking that she'd read just a snippet to feel close to him, if, she thought in sudden misery, that was ever to be possible again.

Morgan said, 'That's all I do, sit – ha!'

Violet checked her watch. Just five minutes, that's all I need, she told herself. She closed her eyes and listened to the day. Birds called from the chestnuts to their cousins in the woods beyond. She thought of the soft air around the pines, the haze of ferns now with their golden October coats, the steep stony path to the sea. How she longed to be there now with Jack and Aster. Just the three of them by the sea. She held the dream tightly in her grasp and almost smiled when it began to feel real.

'Do you know what it is that I cannot face again?' Morgan said, breaking brusquely into her thoughts and smashing them to pieces. 'It's the smell. There's this sweetness on the air over there. Rotting bodies. Men and mules. And then there's the pear drop smell, you know, just like when you were a kid in a sweet shop. That's gas. And every time a shell drops, well, you can imagine how it's all stirred up.'

A sudden violent thought paralysed Violet: but he never tells me this. He never tells me *anything*.

'Bullets you think you can take. The wound is clean enough. And we both know how this looks to the officers,' Morgan went on, indicating his foot with resignation. 'But shell shrapnel is another matter. Jagged, deadly. Can rip a man apart. They come over out of the air, sounding like water trickling into a tub. Keep your bloody head down. My pal standing next to me. I think, if he can take the fear then so can I. Talking to me one minute. Blown to pieces before my eyes, the next. And I mean . . . pieces.'

Morgan's bitterness sparked a panic in Violet that drenched her insides. How could she ever understand this war? How could she know what really was happening to Jack? Just a few months before, he'd been back home at Old Trellick on leave. And he barely spoke. His eyes were haunted and always elsewhere. He barely looked at her, barely touched her. He took her, once, in the darkness of their bedroom, silently and swiftly, and then he got out of bed and slept alone in the spare room. He sat and stared at Aster as she chattered and played as if his mind was taking a photograph. And the shaking had returned. His fingertips buzzed and fidgeted; he could barely hold a pen long enough to do the crossword.

Violet pressed him only once and he simply muttered under his breath that only in charcoal and paint was he able to express himself. Otherwise, silence; the husk of the man she fell in love with. She longed for him, for the man she knew to come back to her. To tell her what he saw inside his head.

She shivered and with cold fingers pulled out his latest one-page letter.

Morgan cocked his head. 'Your sweetheart?'

'My husband. He's at Ypres.'

'What rank?'

She told him he was a lieutenant.

'Glad to hear it. Still one of us. Just about. I don't like to say this in polite company, Nurse, but we Tommies hate the red-tabbed staff more than we hate the Boche.'

Violet stared at him. He smiled unapologetically and asked what her husband had to say for himself.

She shrugged to swallow her despair. 'He says he is fine. That his men are holding up. He just talks about the weather. Says that since the beginning of August it has not stopped raining.'

'Like they say, poor bloody infantry.'

A flash of sunlight on metal caught her eye as the postman came cycling up the drive on his delivery round, a bagful of letters, telegrams and newspapers in the front basket. Word came through via this beleaguered soul who, as the consistent bearer of bad news, certainly had to wear a thick skin. Over the years, Violet had grown strangely accustomed to the bulletins: the headlines about pressing on at all cost. Another big push. The revolting, unfathomable lists of casualties. She felt dangerously separated from it, as distinct as the living are from the dead. I am living, she thought, and Jack was amongst the dead.

She watched as the postman, having dispatched his post, hooked his leg back on his bike and wobbled off down the drive, saluting another cyclist who was coming the other way: Auntie Muriel on her own sit-up-and-beg bicycle, on her daily mission to read to the soldiers.

'Ah, that's your aunt, isn't it? What a woman. Such a pleasure. Someone who looks at you like you are a human being.'

In her mind, Violet contrasted her auntie's day's work to her mother's. Today, May Prideaux was going to speak at a rally in Looe, along with other so-called armchair patriots, to garner more support for the war effort. In other words, thought Violet, to persuade more mothers to send off their sons, even if they were in reserved occupation. That morning, she'd found her mother's stash of leaflets in the hallway: a pretty illustration of a mother and children gazing out of a window as khaki-clad soldiers marched on by. The caption beneath it turned Violet's stomach: 'Women of Britain say "Go!"'

She recalled the band playing, the flags waving, the crowds cheering in Regent's Park. And Jack proposing to her near the rose garden. In her mind, the fragrant flowers

210

merged like Jack's mottled daubs of paint – the colours melting from flesh to yellow to white as tears filled her eyes.

But, there was no use in crying. Aster was her priority. Her father was out doing his usual rounds to see his patients, and she hoped that the two elder ladies had coordinated their extremities of war work to ensure that one of them was at home to care for her little girl.

'Busy today, isn't it? Like Piccadilly Circus,' said Morgan as a large car slowly negotiated the drive, chugging around its bends with care and expertise. The driver pulled up near Charlecote's grand portico and killed the engine.

'That'll be one of the prospective surgeons, possibly, with a car like that, coming for an interview with the superintendent,' surmised Violet. 'You know Mr Carter is leaving?'

'Going to spread his infuriating bonhomie elsewhere, no doubt. Oops, here comes Sister down the steps to greet the new one. Look out, she's very keen.'

Violet jumped to her feet and swiftly pushed Morgan off ahead of her. 'Come on, let's get going. If she catches me chatting I'll be for the high jump. Although, she'll have to catch me first.'

'Something tells me, deep down, you're a little bit of a rebel, Nurse Fairling.'

Violet suddenly laughed as the wheels span faster and faster. 'Did I ever tell you about the time I ran away from school?'

With Morgan safely installed back in bed and Aunt Muriel poised to read from *Jane Eyre* to him, Violet headed for the nurses' room to make herself a cup of tea. After all, officially

211

it was now time for her break. But in the hall, Nurse Peters stopped her.

'Fairling, can you fetch the enema equipment from the first-floor bathroom. Cartwright's in trouble again and I need your help.'

'I was just about to—' Violet stopped herself and looked at Peters' pale watery eyes as they rolled with fatigue.

Cartwright was harder work than most of the men because, as well as his stump for an arm, the nurses had to account for his two amputated legs.

'Of course. I won't be long.'

She quickly went up the wide marble-stepped staircase and skirted the carpeted landing. The first floor was generally out of bounds for patients as most of the rooms were shut up, with one or two used as the surgeon's offices. But there was a bathroom just along here, which was handy for the ablutions of the walking wounded.

This corridor was peaceful. Once the heavy door to the landing was shut, the noises from downstairs barely reached her, perhaps drifting vaguely through an open window further along. The passageway looked neglected and bare in the pale sunlight that streamed through its long parade of windows. She remembered that the elder Mrs Penruth had referred to it portentously as The Gallery, and gave a rueful smile. All the paintings had been removed, leaving behind the grubby shadows of their frames and, without its statuary and plant stands thick with specimens cut from the hothouse, this section of such a grand house looked a little apologetic.

But here is that moment I need, Violet thought, away from the constant clamour, voices and tedious agony downstairs.

She inwardly thanked Nurse Peters for sending her on the errand as she paused and looked out towards the gardens. And yes, there it was, that elusive fragment of still, clear-blue sea beyond the fields and the gilded woods. Violet felt herself relax and drift with a stolen portion of pleasure. I expect there is even more of the seascape in view, she thought, reaching for the handle on the bathroom door, from the servants' quarters upstairs.

She stopped, immediately, realising that someone was inside. Opening her mouth to voice her surprise and apology, her blood suddenly changed direction and clotted cold inside her skull. Weston Penruth stood with his back to her, his shirt removed and screwed up in his hand. His back, Violet noted despite her swelling panic, was sweaty and creased with the folds of his shirt, and the skin was torn apart with wide violent scars the colour of butcher's meat that stretched and contorted his flesh. She thought frantically, has he just come back from the front? No, he was in Perthshire. He is supposed to be in Perthshire!

In those moments, in which she took just three ragged breaths, Weston turned and faced her, his dark eyes darting with confusion, his mouth opening to bellow at whoever had stumbled in on him in his own bathroom.

She stepped backwards, knocking her elbow painfully on the door, fumbling for the handle, in an agony of confusion. The sunlight that glinted so ordinarily through the window to highlight the taps and gleam off the porcelain of the capacious bath fell on Weston's shocked and wide-eyed features. He reached out his hand to her.

'Wait!' he cried, his voice urgent. 'Violet, please wait!'

The rape relived itself, unfolding at nauseating speed in

her mind. He used her name, he called her by name. Fear turned her inside out. She was small, trapped, so utterly alone. She faced this man, this dishevelled half-naked man, an enormous figure approaching her, his face quizzical and confused.

Stuttering mixed-up words of regret, Violet's own apology startled her. She turned to the door but his arm reached round her, his palm against the wall.

'Please, Violet. Please.'

'Stay away from me,' she said, tasting fear in her mouth.

'You don't understand.'

'I do understand – you are my nightmare!'

'I never explained to you – you did not give me the chance. You ran. Don't run away again.'

She shook her head in astonishment and assured him that there was no explanation for what he did.

'But Claudia said—'

'Don't you dare . . .' she seethed, her anger spurting like venom.

He suddenly gave up, walked away from her to the window, slumped onto a chair. And his acquiesce alarmed her even more. She should flee, she should run, slam the door behind her and race back down the stairs, back to the reality, the company of her colleagues, her patients. But instead her limbs stiffened, unable to move. She looked on in astonishment as Weston lowered his great head into his hands, bowed forward to his knees and wept.

Into the prickling silence, Violet heard herself ask inanely, 'Shall I fetch someone?'

Without looking up he shook his head and reached his hand towards her.

214

She stayed where she was, her back against the door. His weeping continued, his face smothered by the crumpled shirt, his slumped back jerking with each sob.

A question came to Violet, and stunned her with its simplicity: 'Do you know what you did to me?'

She heard his voice, thin and weak, 'I do.'

Her mouth went slack with rage, 'Then there is no excuse.'

He stood up, his face furrowed and ugly.

'You are right, there is no excuse. But there might be a reason,' he uttered and turned his back to her. 'This.'

Violet again gazed at the lashes that cleaved and meshed his skin. The tightness of the scars seemed to disable him and make him hold himself a certain way. She realised now that his gait was always so erect, that he seemed to concentrate on every move. And now she understood. She questioned him, stepping forward into a stew of curiosity and repulsion, wondering what on earth had happened. Who on earth could do this?

'My mother,' he said.

Violet let out a bark of laughter. 'Your *mother*!'

He sat down again as if suddenly aware of his naked torso and pushed his arms back into the sleeves of his shirt and buttoned it up. He glanced up at her, his eyes like black holes in his face.

Violet refused to look at him, to collaborate with him. 'I came here to fetch some equipment. Ah, there it is.' She darted to the corner to pick up the small metal case she had come to fetch. 'Cartwright will be waiting.' She blundered her way out of the room.

It wasn't until she found herself breathless on the landing, ready to race back down the stairs to continue her duties, that she realised how terrified she had been. But now her pity for Weston surged like it had done once before and rolled around her head in unsteady waves of compassion.

Downstairs in the ward, Nurse Peters took the enema case from her without a word and they both set to work to help Private Cartwright relieve himself. She thought that Peters would comment on how long she had been upstairs but, evidently, she had only been away minutes – such brief moments during which her secret past roared up again to devour her.

'Fairling, your hand is shaking, steady on,' said Peters. 'Does it bother you, Private?'

'Not at all,' Cartwright grunted. 'You two have a light touch compared to some. God help any of us who need to go during the night shift.'

As Peters handed Violet the enamel bowl covered with a towel, she said, 'Did you hear the commotion earlier? The master of the house arrived back, totally unexpected. Sent Sister into a tizzy. She had rushed out to the front door, apparently, thinking it was the new surgeon in his flash car. And now she's in a strop because this Mr Penruth has dumped his two kids on her. Wants to move back in upstairs. Has put her right out. And apparently his loopy mother-in-law has gone stark stinking bats down in the kitchens. Evidently can't bear to look at her dead daughter's children.'

Violet flinched, struggling to keep her face passive. 'Can . . . can Mr Penruth do that?' she asked, her voice remarkably even. 'Move back to Charlecote like that?'

'It's his house. Can do what he likes, I suppose. As long

as the Ministry don't mind.' Peters shrugged and turned back to the matter in hand. 'Now hurry up and get rid of that, it's putting the patients off their supper.'

Violet signed out, tied on her cape and said goodbye to the night-shift girls who were lounging on the sofas having a quick ciggie before beginning work. The evening sky was high and pearly, laced with the scent of woodsmoke and peppered with wide arrows of birds flying south. Air was cold in her nostrils: autumn had settled in again in the space of a few days. As she glanced at the burnished trees in the Charlecote park, grief crept up and clouted Violet. Another season has come and will go, she thought, and yet the war continues regardless.

As she walked down the steps, she flinched. Weston strolled towards her across the lawn littered with fallen leaves. But instead of the disabling terror of earlier, a calm pool formed inside her. She had faced the nightmare that had stalked her for years and found how weak and pitiable it really was. And, that now she had confronted it, she was immensely stronger than she ever imagined.

She stopped and turned to him, her body numb with fatigue and her mind curiously blank.

'Violet, good evening,' he said, stiff with politeness. He had evidently bathed and changed. His solid handsome face was clean-shaven. His stride was as decorous and as commanding as ever now that, fully clothed, his secret was covered. 'Do you have a moment?'

She said nothing but stood and waited, fixing a sardonic expression.

'Perhaps if we . . .' He motioned to the bench where she had sat earlier with Private Morgan. 'You must be tired.'

She assured him she was fine where she was right here, in full view of the front of the house.

'Can I begin?' he said.

Her silence encouraged him, seemed to jolt him. I will give him a minute, she thought, and that is all. His words tumbled out, oozing with pathos, while Violet remained motionless.

Weston told her that when he was a boy, Mrs Penruth had whipped him. It started from an early age, so early he could not remember a time when it did not happen. It became routine, whether he misbehaved or not. The whipping was not about the pain that piggy-backed him day and night, and the disfiguring wounds that he wanted to hide, but about the power and control and cruelty that the woman enjoyed. One flinch of her hand, whether he was coming in to say goodnight to her in her private parlour, or dumbly taking his nursery tea, would set his head on fire with fear. He would cower and stay as still as possible. Perhaps if he never moved again, never spoke again, he said, perhaps she would stop. His father, now dead, of course knew nothing.

'Why are you telling me this?' she asked.

'I need you to know.'

'Do you think I will forgive you now?'

He could not give her an answer but simply fumbled with his cuffs, straightening his necktie like an apprehensive schoolboy. One time, when he was about nine years old, he floundered on, the beating was so bad that the wounds became infected. Mrs Ainsley, who lived at the farm and was to become his mother-in-law ('I *know* who Mrs Ainsley is,' Violet snapped), found him one day, in a fever of pain, his shirt stuck to his back with pus and bleeding scabs.

218

'She took me to your father,' he said.

Violet was about to ask him if he had helped him, but, of course, knew what the answer would be.

'I was so grateful to Dr Prideaux, that even as a young boy I pledged to help him and his family. I promised to do whatever I could. The beatings stopped. Whether she got bored of the game, or whether your father spoke to her, I do not know. My father died, and as I grew up, my mother, even though she still tried to take charge of absolutely everything I did, also seemed to become frightened of me. When I was of age, I told your parents that I would waive their rent, pay for your school fees. Your mother grew warm to the suggestion that I should marry you if you so wished . . .'

Violet grimaced and turned away. 'But instead,' she mouthed, 'you decided to violate me.'

'I was in a dark, angry world. I did not know my mind. None of it was real. I will never know the pain I caused you.'

She looked at him. 'It is real. You will never know. No one does.'

Weston bowed his head, his hands gesturing, beseeching. 'Your forgiveness will heal everything.'

'There is no such thing.'

She turned and walked away, her knees trembling, her core suddenly dangerously weakened with compassion for this pathetic man.

He caught up with her, speaking quickly. 'I wanted to repay your father for his help and his counsel. If it wasn't for him, I'd be dead. Violet, I wanted us to be man and wife. I saw you as my light, my escape into a place so much better for me. I thought it was seduction in the orangery. I thought it was love. I didn't know love . . .'

A surge of anger took Violet's breath away. 'You shot your own dogs.'

'I wanted to show you how angry I was. I tell you, that day, that shotgun could have easily been turned on myself.'

'Do spare me the details.' Violet was furious. 'Your self-pity is becoming tiresome.'

She began to hurry along the drive, wanting to break into a run. Weston kept up with her, not giving up.

'But Claudia . . .' he said.

Violet stopped as a muddy lump of misery dropped to her stomach. She was dizzy, exhausted. She wanted to be home, she wanted to be tucking Aster into bed, to feel safe herself, to feel cherished, to free herself from the crushing loneliness of life without her husband, the life that continued oblivious without him.

But Weston was still talking: 'Claudia saw into my soul. She helped me like I thought you would have done. She persuaded me to see things clearly. She loved me for who I was.'

'My dearest friend was a better person than I,' Violet managed to say, her mind skating over memories of Claudia on the beach, her hair whipped by the breeze, her freckles alive over her skin. The tiny bump of her stomach and the pleasure of anticipation in her eyes. Their reconciliation had been swarming with possible disaster but their enduring friendship beat it away. 'She tried to convince me that you were very much misunderstood.'

'She left me two beautiful children. Could there be any better blessing?'

Violet agreed. Staring at Weston, she remembered Claudia's words, her pleading with Violet to see a good side to her husband. But then, she did not know what he had done to her.

Someone called out from the front door and Violet turned to see Sister trotting down the steps with a young boy, a shade younger than Aster, and a baby who could not be more than nine months old in her arms.

The nurse cried, 'Mr Penruth, I'm glad I caught you. Mr Penruth!'

Weston stared, momentarily confused. 'Oh, the children,' he said. 'It must be their bedtime.'

Violet watched his face loosen with shades of fatherly benevolence as he excused himself and walked to meet Sister. He talked quietly with her for some moments, and she glanced over his shoulder at Violet quizzically, wondering no doubt why the master of the house would be bothering to pass the time of day with a lowly nursing auxiliary.

He thanked her, hoisted his son onto his shoulder, picked up the baby and returned to Violet.

'And so you know,' he pressed on with his story. 'Soon after Claudia died, I then left for Scotland to go and bury my mother.'

'She was a monster,' Violet breathed.

'Yes, but she was my mother.'

Violet could not take her eyes off Claudia's children in Weston's arms and barely listened as he told her that he did not want to keep his son and daughter away from their home for ever. He'd neglected the farm and planned for the biggest and best harvest that Charlecote had ever seen next year. The military could have the main house and he would move into one of the cottages. He would do whatever he could for the war effort.

'It's just these two that need caring for. Where have all the nursery nurses gone? They're all packing munitions. And Claudia's mother is no help. She just caused a huge scene in there, I can tell you. I believe she is rather unwell. Sister just referred to her as a broken-down Annie.'

Violet watched as Harry held tightly on to his father's lapels and looked around him, surveying his home, the garden, with new and appraising eyes. The two-year-old boy was not as chunky as Violet remembered on the beach the year before. His little body was shedding its puppy fat and becoming lean, just like Claudia. Baby Kate looked as if she needed to be tucked up in bed; her cheeks were rosy from teething and stained with tears. Her wispy blond baby hair, sneaking out from under her lace bonnet, was the colour of corn, the exact match of her mother's.

Without thinking Violet said, 'I will take them.'

Weston begged her pardon, asked her to say it again.

'When she's not busy improving her social life among the soldiers here at Charlecote, my Auntie Muriel would be the perfect nanny for the children. My mother and father? Well, they have obviously always thought highly of you, Mr Penruth, so why should they object?' Her sarcasm floated unobserved.

'Violet, do you mean this?' Weston asked.

She scarcely believed her words as they tumbled out. It was not forgiveness, she resolved, for that was unimaginable. But somehow it felt right in light of the innocence of her friend's children, who now stared at her with shattered eyes. She would make this gesture, this sacrifice, in Claudia's memory. And perhaps this truce would ensure that the threat of eviction may no longer hang over Old Trellick; that her and Aster's home would be safe.

'Yes, they can come and stay with us at Old Trellick,' Violet said. What else could she do? She reached out to take a grizzling Kate from Weston's arms. 'And Aster can learn to stop terrorising Jess for she now has someone to play with.'

The evening fell quickly as Weston Penruth drove his car the long way round along the top road, skirting the now dusk-laden woods and valley where the chill of night was already settled. Violet sat in the back seat with the dozing children, a blanket around them so that they formed a little group, a strange little family. Lifting her chin, she watched the rippling inland landscape of harvested fields and stone walls rise out of the gloom, avoiding the view forward and the back of Weston's head. She felt as if she was watching herself in another reality, her own hollowed-out self. She forced herself to suspend belief and attach it to the idea that she was doing the right thing. The bumps and lurches of the vehicle on the stony road went unnoticed. All that remained was the tangible silence inside the car, the tautness of the air, all that was left unspoken.

'Are you a mummy?' Harry asked sleepily in the darkness.

Violet tucked the blanket more around his chin. 'I certainly am,' she told him and he seemed content enough with her answer.

They pulled up at Old Trellick where lamps glowed solidly in the downstairs windows. Her parents and aunt would be having supper, wondering why she was late home from Charlecote and, now, wondering who on earth was parking outside their house.

Amid the fuss of bundling the baby into her shawl and gathering Harry to her side, she saw her father stride down the path in a happy fit of surprise and welcome. While Weston began to hastily explain, Violet glimpsed her mother's stunned face appear at the window as a mask of shock, her mouth working like a bellow.

May Prideaux was soon upon them, hurtling out of the house, calling that Weston must come in for some sustenance. He explained again quickly and succinctly why he had brought his children here, with Violet, and both her parents absorbed this notion, nodding and smiling with barely a glance at her.

Violet stood back and watched how her parents accepted without question this new turn of events. She saw the unwritten obligation that went back so many years being renewed, another link retied. Claudia's children were the unknowing offerings in this archaic barter.

In the lamplit hallway, her mother gathered the children together in an excited rush and began to bundle them up the stairs, commandeering Violet to help her.

'Please keep your voice down, Mother,' she reminded her. 'Aster will be sleeping.'

Before she followed the ragged little group up the stairs, she glanced over her shoulder to see her father lead Weston through to the drawing room for a nightcap and caught sight of Muriel standing on welcome, finding it hard to disguise her flabbergasted expression. Her aunt's eyes flicked from Weston and out to Violet in the hallway, her head jerking with incredulity.

Upstairs May Prideaux swiftly put Harry and Kate into bed in the spare room at the end of the landing and closed the door with an unattractive look of triumph on her face.

'Our little refugees, bless them,' she said with satisfaction.

'It's the least we can do to help that poor man, isn't it? We can make up for so many things.' She paused, then whispered to Violet, 'You look all in. Come down and have a hot toddy. Father's making them.'

Violet told her she might do, but that she wanted to get changed first. Her uniform absorbed the vapours of the hospital so that they travelled home with her and she longed to discard it. She went into her bedroom and lit the lamp. Jess, curled up in his usual spot in the basket at the foot of the bed, lifted his head and blinked contentedly. He soon settled back down with a sigh. There on her bedside table lay her Flower Book and alongside it, she guessed, her usual present from Aster – a single russet-red rose hip – gathered, no doubt, on her daily walk with Muriel.

Violet smiled and tucked it inside the book. Usually, if she hadn't been so late home, she would have turned to a clean page and spent some minutes writing about her day, observing the weather, adding her little countrywoman's sayings. But, today, it would have to wait. Amid a fog of tiredness, her thoughts were in chaos. She undressed and slipped into her nightie and dressing gown, catching now and again the voices below: a rumbling from her father, a quirky observation from her mother, a grateful response from Weston. Above the muffled conversation she could hear that it had started to rain. She opened the window and breathed hard on the fresh, pattering air, longing to clear her mind.

Someone knocked on the door and in walked Muriel, holding a shuffling, almost sleep-walking Aster by the hand.

'Look who I found out of bed,' she said.

Aster opened her eyes and ran to Violet who gathered her

up tight and fast with a wrench of guilt. Despite her concern for Claudia's children, Aster would always be her priority, Aster would always be her world and she was sorry if she had ever let her slip from her mind. Holding the warm, dazed child, she buried her nose in her hair, drawing in her scent, inhaling the little girl's spirit to give herself the will to carry on.

'Rose hip,' the little girl said, wriggling free and pointing towards the Flower Book.

'Yes, my darling, thank you so much. We will press it together tomorrow and you can help me write all about it. Where did you find it?'

'Today. Happened today?'

'Yes, we'll write about today. Now don't forget what you did and where you found it, will you?'

Muriel was waiting. 'Shall I take her back to bed?'

Violet told her not just yet, that she would do it.

Muriel then wondered if she was coming downstairs.

Violet bluntly shook her head. She thought of her parents in the drawing room below sipping a nightcap with Weston Penruth and surely in their element, and shuddered, as she suddenly thought, *What on earth would Jack say?*

Muriel narrowed her shrewd eyes. 'Do you know what you are doing?'

'No, actually,' Violet admitted.

Muriel supposed she'd leave her to it.

Alone now, Violet quietly carried her daughter out of her bedroom, but instead of turning towards the little girl's own room, she walked down the landing to the spare bedroom and gently pushed against the door to reveal the sound of snuffling snores within the dark room.

'This is Harry and baby Kate,' Violet whispered to her bemused daughter. 'They've come to stay with us for a while.'

The lamp on the landing gradually illuminated their faces.

'A boy!' Aster shouted out in hard surprise and Violet shushed her and reminded her that they were sleeping and that she was supposed to be in bed, for it was very late indeed.

Aster struggled to be let down from her mother's arms and tottered over to the side of the bed where Harry was curled, his hand over his face. The little boy stirred and opened his eyes so very briefly with a sleepy smile. Aster crept forward and the boy and girl touched fingertips and exchanged whispered subliminal messages of childhood.

While Violet watched them, a hard gust of air threw raindrops against the windowpane as the autumn rain swelled and changed direction. And yet all is safe and quiet, she thought, here inside Old Trellick.

She walked over to twitch the curtains closed, wondering if it was still raining in Flanders.

Chapter Twenty-Three

In the language of flowers:
Nettle, slander

Violet stood at the open kitchen door at Old Trellick some ten months later with the summer garden waking in front of her. All was immersed in milky light, that moment beyond dawn when the promise of the day was made. She saw that the summer world was waking from the thin dark night, reminding itself, gathering its spirit for the chattering, blazing hours yet to come. Violet noticed how the early light seemed to come from above, leaving shadows to linger in the lower garden until the full mantel of daylight settled. This, she compared to the evening so far ahead of her in time as to be beyond belief, where light was low, long and golden, surrendering dramatically to the soft veil of dusk.

The trees at the end of the garden were thick with green – deep summer green – and the voices of the birds clotted them, adding layers of little chaotic symphonies. Her father's flowerbeds were showing off at their very best, enduring the weight of ragged heads and thick hairy stems for another jubilant day before eventually, so very soon, succumbing to seed.

Upstairs Aster was still tucked in sweet, dewy slumber, and Jess was in his basket. Along the passageway, Harry and Kate were also sleeping. The children would all wake, warm and heavy limbed, ready to be dressed in their oldest clothes and scarper up into the fields, hitching a ride on the wagon, singing along with the workers from the farm and the villages, all congregating to help bring the harvest home.

She glanced over her shoulder at Jack sitting at the kitchen table, sipping tentatively at a cup of tea. She saw his face, his army-cropped fair hair, skin brown from four summers living out in the battlefield, the tan so deep in his flesh that his features became unreadable, his thoughts still unreachable. And yet, during the two short weeks he'd had at home, whenever he stooped to Aster and triumphantly hurled her up into his arms, when he cocked his cigarette to the corner of his mouth and carried her on his shoulder, proudly, concentrating hard, when he talked to her – yes, he talked to her – there was a veneer of happiness over his face like a film of sweat. Violet watched them with childish jealousy. Jack was, she decided firmly, scolding herself, in there somewhere.

As she turned back into the kitchen to face him, the same invisible cord pulled her towards him as it had done in Regent's Park four years before. And a blunt question entered her mind like a flare, only to die and fall to nothing. But she forced herself to note it down, to acknowledge it, even though she'd never dare ask. What were the mornings like out there? What was a dawn like, in the valley of the Somme? How did evening fall along the Menin Road? In what way did the hours of those endless days pass? But he wouldn't say, she knew it, even if she had the guts to ask him. He would never say. And their collective silence crippled her.

She forced a smile to brighten her face and she said out loud, catching Jack's attention as the crystal light and sound of birds singing settled behind her, 'I think it's going to be a beautiful day.'

The standing wheat in Weston Penruth's fields was regimented and cloudy-gold, a hazy thick carpet ripe and ready. It was knee-high to a man, but to a child an immense forest of knife-edge blades and scratchy curling ears of grain, rife with insects, scurrying with mice, darting with birds. They arrived on the back of the swaying wagon, singing the songs that the locals teased them with by starting a few lines and seeing how far they could go. Jack sat holding Aster on his knee, his shirtsleeves rolled up, his smiles extraordinarily warm and long. Violet watched him and their daughter with delight from her perch at the back, clamping her hat on with one hand, holding on tightly with the other.

She spread a blanket at the edge of the field under the shadow of an oak and settled with the three children, and the tea pails and baskets of sandwiches. The morning sun was rising, heating the air and disturbing odours in the earth: tangy roots, pungent soil and the dry, clean scent of the wheat. Cut wheat was already stacked in stooks, leaning heads together like drunken men in the far corner, and the farmhands worked steadily, bending to it, their song voices good and high. Most of the men who had been harvesting the clover that day she bolted from her own engagement party at Charlecote had gone to war. Today, it was a group of old men and boys and women who were toiling to bring the harvest in. And Jack keenly joined them.

She shielded her eyes, peering across the rippling field. She kept finding him, thinking it was him, then losing him again as the harvesters arranged themselves into an even rhythm of work. This would please Jack, would settle him, she decided. Simple, timeless work will help him lose his memories, at least for a few hours.

His two weeks of leave were drawing to a close; early tomorrow a staff car would arrive for him at Old Trellick. The very idea of this cut through Violet like a slash of a knife and the wheat momentarily became a swimming silvery sea. She shook the idea from her head and called for Aster, who was haring along the hedgerow among the long grasses of the field's boundary, her hands filled with wild flowers that would not last the hour.

'Watch out for nettles! There's a great patch over there!' Violet called out to her, realising how cross she sounded. She watched tiny field butterflies bouncing over the surly-green bed of nettles, fascinated by the insects' reliance on the stinging weeds as a safe place to lay their eggs. 'Come and have a drink of water, Aster. It's too hot already for all that running around.'

Harry, always stuck to Aster's side, sloped back too, while little Kate sat more quietly on the blanket, keeping close to Violet, for this field was as big as an ocean to her and was likely to swallow her up.

Violet doled out mugs of water from the cool stone bottles kept in the shade and watched the flush over the children's still baby-skinned cheeks fade a little. They chattered together, the three little ones, pushing their faces close, enquiring of each other's thoughts.

In a letter to Jack last year, soon after Weston's return to Charlecote, Violet told him she and her parents had decided to care for Claudia's children – *temporarily*, she'd added, even underlining it. No mention of Weston, just an oblique reference to difficult circumstances in the Penruth household after Claudia's death, and that the military hospital was no place for little ones. *It may seem a strange little set-up to you*, she wrote, *but I want to do this for my dear friend's children.*

And Jack made no comment. At first Violet wondered if her letter never reached him and was lost at some army station somewhere in France. But over the year, in his succinct letters, he responded to the Cornish news she'd mentioned in that very letter, as well as his usual describing of the weather and the machinations of marching his men to the front and back again. And when he arrived home two weeks before, he barely acknowledged that the Penruth children were installed at Old Trellick. He accepted them, was gracious to them, but his focus was taken up with Aster and her world entirely. His brief spell of leave was intense with everything that circumnavigated his daughter: long, exhausting walks to the cove and into the woods – just the two of them – or complete inactivity, lazing in deckchairs in the garden, a chattering nonsensical conversation ebbing and flowing, while the days slipped far too quickly away.

Claudia's children were peripheral to him, Violet realised with relief. And then, the idea stung her: *as am I*.

'Is Dad going to have a picnic with us?' asked Aster,

scattering the flowers she'd plucked over the grass around her. 'We have enough for him, don't we?'

'Yes, we do. Possibly . . . later. He's very busy at the moment. Look at him out there in the field with all the workers.'

'What is he doing? Where?'

'He's harvesting the wheat, all this wheat.' Violet peered again, shielding her eyes. 'Not sure. Can't tell where he is. The sun's in my eyes. Now show me what flowers you have picked and we'll choose the best ones for pressing. We can write about them in the Flower Book tonight. And then, in a few weeks' time, when they're pressed and ready . . . You'd like that, wouldn't you?'

A long shadow fell over their little group and the usually solemn Harry yelped in surprise, 'Father's here!'

Violet looked up into the sharp sunlight to see Weston standing there in silhouette. He was smart and buttoned up in a good shirt and grey suit, and terribly incongruous among the blustery, dusty field of wheat. On his shoulder was propped a cumbersome tripod, over his shoulder a heavy-looking camera concertinaed neatly into its box, hanging by its strap.

Since they'd taken on the Penruth children a year before, she'd stopped working at the Charlecote hospital, so avoiding him was easy enough. Her mother and auntie chaperoned the children on visits to their father as and when he summoned them. And if he came to Old Trellick, which was rare, she made herself scarce, so their paths rarely crossed. She took Jess out for a long hike along the coastal path. She steered clear of the pinewoods, her old haunt soft with ferns and foxgloves, and even avoided her beloved cove, for Weston knew which places she was drawn to and she knew he would follow and find her there. After each of his visits, both her mother and aunt would scrutinise her silently, watching for a change in her demeanour, a softening of her spirit towards their landlord and benefactor. Their eyes were sharp and searching, with Muriel offering a promise of support; her mother simply keeping her own score.

But now, here he was, standing over her, bidding her a civil good morning and fending off an attack by Harry on his pockets. The boy, Violet thought, overcompensated, worshipped the hero he saw in Weston, longed for his attention.

'What do you have in here, Father?' Harry dipped his hands in. 'Anything for me?' He pulled out some slices of fruit cake and two apples. 'Can I have a go with the camera, Father?'

'Thought I'd record the day for posterity,' Weston offered Violet an explanation, although she had not asked for one. He set the tripod at his feet and began to undo the buckles on the camera case, telling her that photography was his new hobby. 'Got this sent down especially from London.'

Just like those awful peonies, thought Violet.

He began to show Harry the shutter, the precious glass lens, explaining all about sunlight and shade. 'The light's good. Perhaps we can have a photograph later.'

'My husband has thrown off his military hat for today,' Violet said, lightly, indicating the industry behind her. 'Busy with the harvesters.'

She meant this as a warning, to inform Weston that perhaps he should make himself scarce. But he assumed this was an invitation to converse. He sat on the rug, declaring how hot it was already. He loosened his tie, pulled the stopper off a water bottle and drank long and deep.

'How are the children? Or need I ask? They seem very well.' He reached out to clumsily cluck a bemused Kate under the chin. The poor child barely knows who he is, thought Violet, as she saw confusion swim around her little bonneted face.

Aster nudged Violet. 'Mama, the flowers. Which ones?'

Violet turned her back on Weston and her attention to Aster as the little girl arranged the flowers over the lap of her linen dress. The azure blue of the cornflowers was already fading in the heat, gasping their last. And white stars of mayweed were now ragged, the tiny petals falling away between her fingertips. Violet was not surprised that the mint was still robust, giving off its astringent perfume, but the tansy were the most vigorous, the acid yellow ball-flowers luminous in the sunlight.

'The mint we might be able to keep,' she told Aster. 'We can make it into a tea if you like. All you have to do is put a leaf or two in a cup and top it up with water from the kettle. We'll ask Gran and Auntie Muriel later. It'll help you sleep.'

'What about these?' Aster picked up a stem of tansy and watched the tight flower heads bounce. 'Can we drink this one?'

Violet snatched it from her daughter and flung it out into the grass, 'That's poisonous, don't even think of eating it or putting it in a tea or anything like that. It will make you very ill indeed.'

'Why, Mama? Why?'

In two shuddering seconds, Violet relived her quest for this vigorous and ugly weed on the London streets and along the filthy canal through bright soaking rain. She remembered discovering it at last among the broken-down wall of an old factory. And then the quiet ritualistic brewing in Muriel's guest bedroom later that evening.

'It's poison.'

'How do you know, Mama?'

She touched Aster lightly on the cheek. 'That's something a lady can't explain to a little girl of just three and a half. But when you are older . . . perhaps then I will explain and you will understand.'

With those words, suddenly Violet understood her bond with flowers, her unfailing desire to document them. Gazing at her solemn-eyed daughter, she reverted to the girl she had once been in her constant childhood quest for wild flowers: picking over them, keeping some, discarding others, trying to explain herself, to record her young and endless days in her own singular manner. And the flowers would match her mood, whether the first sweet violets of spring, the ox-eye daisies on a summer verge or choking verdant ivy in the depths of winter. The Flower Book was her voice, laced with her secrets, her words coded and secure. And now Aster was watching her, her innocent and steady gaze growing warm with understanding.

With sudden startling assurance, the little girl said, 'Mama, we must throw away the tansy. Let's throw them all away and start again tomorrow.'

At that moment, in the field of wheat, with the work of the harvest going on around them, in that exquisitely private moment, Violet exchanged something of herself with her daughter.

'From now on,' agreed Violet, feeling suddenly breathless with joy, 'we'll share the Flower Book. Starting tonight, we'll go through it together . . . I will show you . . .'

She wished Jack was with her to see his little girl emerging from her swaddling of babyhood. Oh, where is he? She shielded her eyes again to scan the field of wheat.

Behind her, Weston was close, his tall frame making his presence known. Immediately, Violet's brightness vanished like a star being snuffed out by a cloud.

'Nonsense,' Weston announced. 'No need to throw those flowers away. I have the answer right here.'

He produced a neat silver flask from his pocket and offered it to Violet.

'Brandy? No thanks,' she muttered with a curl of disdain, remembering the way he added the spirit to champagne at their engagement party.

She watched aghast as he shrugged and knocked back the contents in two great draughts, then washed the flask out with water, tipping it out on the ground and then filling it again. He spoke to Aster, but was looking at Violet for approval as he gathered up the wilting flowers around them and deftly dropped the stems into the flask.

'A temporary vase. Should keep them nice and fresh.'

Aster, now peculiarly the child again, clapped her hands in excited approval, her eyes wide with gratitude. But for Violet, habitual coldness inched down her middle.

'You didn't rinse it properly,' she sniffed. 'The alcohol will kill them.'

'Probably do them good,' Weston muttered.

She glanced at his sorrowful face and had to look away, wondering how she was able to look at him now and forget what he did to her. Weston's pursuit of her forgiveness and for her to understand him was tangible. And her knowledge of what lay beneath his brash facade, and beneath his fine dress shirt, meant her resolve was harder to bear. Each time she saw Weston, her silent loyalty to her husband died a little and she hated him for it.

She glanced fearfully over the field, unable to make Jack out.

'I hope they're keeping up the pace, we can't have them slacking. We can't fight the Hun if we're hungry,' observed Weston, expecting Violet to laugh. 'Of course, it's not my usual crew. I'm left with elderlies, boys and women. I suppose they can have half an hour.'

He stood up and whistled hard, waving his arms at his team. Violet noticed all over the field heads cocking in their direction. And she saw Jack. This time, he was unmistakable. At first his face was soft and round with curiosity as he stared, wondering who was shouting. And then his features closed in, sharpened and turned to stone.

The red-faced harvesters began to troop wearily in, resting their sickles and pitchforks on their shoulders, rubbing sore arms and hands. They propped their tools by the far hedge and began to settle themselves at a polite distance. The men doffed their caps to Violet and some of the women glanced with curiosity in her direction. This did not surprise Violet as they all knew her as Mr Penruth's former fiancée and had heard she had taken in his children. It was still the talk of Lansallos and Looe even a year later. And there among them was Mrs Davey, Eddie's mother. She must have joined the party somewhere along the way. The older woman stood for a moment and stared at Violet, her mouth twisting into a snicker of scorn. She was with her young son who Violet had seen when she'd paid a visit to the cottage with her father. Mrs Davey glanced at Weston with hatred and then grabbed the boy by the arm and hustled him over to her fellow workers, whispering hard into his ear.

The woman merged herself amongst her peers, beer was poured and sandwiches distributed, and gradually their chatting and gossiping slowed as mouths were filled, and glances ceased to come Violet's way as eyelids drooped for snatched forty winks.

Jack was still dealing with the horse and wagon on the far side of the field. Violet caught sight of him now begin to lead the beast over. As he drew closer, the children became excited to see the enormous animal, with her mane tossing, brasses jangling and hooves stomping.

'Dad!' Aster cried, waving hard, her face luminous with joy. 'Over here! Here I am!'

Weston moved to Violet's side and called out, 'Children, stay close. Be careful of the horse. Don't creep around her back, or you're likely to be kicked.'

Jack halted abruptly, the horse's nose knocking him on the shoulder. Violet realised that in that moment, all her husband could see before him was the happy little tableau of herself and Aster, Weston and the children settled on a picnic rug.

She drew away and whispered hard at Weston, 'Please leave. You must leave. Look what you're doing to him.'

Weston glanced at her, folded his arms and said he was not going anywhere. After all, it was his wheatfield and he was here to check the workers were doing a good job.

Jack resumed his approach, his eyes blazing under his hat. Violet thought suddenly, madly, that it was the most animated she'd seen him in years. All she wanted so desperately was for them to go home: she, Jack and Aster, back to Old Trellick for their last afternoon together. For she had no idea when he would return.

'By the looks of him,' Weston muttered, leaning close to speak in her ear, 'your husband is becoming a little rocky upstairs.'

She hissed at him, 'He's been at the front for years, which is more than can be said for you. Can't you see what it does to a man?'

Violet got up from the rug and darted over to the wagon, waiting while Jack, in drawn-out silence, unhitched the horse and gave the animal a bucket of water. His kindness towards the weary horse was deft and efficient but Violet knew by his jerking, irritated movements that inside his skin he was seething.

She placed her hand gently on his arm, to slow him, to ask him what was the matter.

'What in Christ's name is going on, Violet?' He turned on her, snapping through his teeth and making Violet flinch. He stared at her, his eyes opaque with confusion. 'What is this hold he has over you, and you have over him?'

'It's nothing. Nothing at all,' Violet tried to keep her voice down. 'He just came to see his children and how the harvest was going. This is his land, after all. What do you want me to do?'

She fitted her arm through his and drew him behind the great horse who shielded them somewhat from the others. The midday sun was burning now, the air a furnace. The horse twitched frantically, exasperated by whizzing flies. The scent of leather and horse was pungent and sweet. Jack's frame shuddered with rage, but he was strangely compliant, allowing her to try to comfort him. It was, she thought, as though he had suddenly broken through a wall of numbness and was now feeling pain, a festering deep agony that he'd never noticed before. She wanted to hold him, to know him again, but his arms stiffened on reflex, rejecting her and pushing her away.

She noticed the eyes of the workers slipping their way again but then she heard Weston announce to them that they must have had their fill and should be getting back to work. They began to gather themselves together with nervous glances towards their landlord. They stretched and made bad jokes and went to collect their tools. The chattering resumed as they spread back out over the field.

'Look how he stands there and plays lord of the manor!' Jack whispered, throwing Weston a narrow-eyed stare.

'My darling, that's because he is . . .'

She looked over her shoulder at Weston who, seemingly unaware, was saying to the children, '. . . well at least let me take a photograph of you all together. For the family album. That's right, all of you together. Squeeze in.'

Jack took Violet's chin gently in his trembling hands and drew her attention back to him, uttering, 'Stay away from him. Tell him to stay away from you. I've got to go tomorrow, leave you again . . . and I can't . . .'

'Please, Jack. Let's go home, let's talk properly at home. Please Jack. Come back with me now.'

'Oh, but I can't. Lordy just said we had to get back to work. Your mother was right,' Jack was bitten with paranoia. 'A broken love affair, that's what she said. Looks like he thinks he still has a chance. Does he?'

Weston lifted each of the children and sat them on the back of the wagon. He told Harry to hotch nearer Kate, who sat in the middle, with Aster squashed up on the other side. The children were laughing, oblivious to the storm around them as Weston went back to the camera perched precariously on its tripod amid the stubble. He made a great show of fiddling with the workings, testing the lens and sticking his eye to the hole. He held his finger aloft as some sort of signal and took a photograph.

'I'm going to kill him!' Jack uttered, breaking away from Violet and lurching around the side of the wagon.

Violet cried out as he propelled himself at Weston and made a grab for his lapels, pushing him backwards, his jaw tilting at a menacing angle as he barked into Weston's face. 'These Penruth children are to leave my home – go back to where they came from. I'm not having Aster see these children again. I'm not having it!'

Weston looked down on him in utter amusement and went to brush him aside like a worrisome puppy. 'Take your hands off me, Lieutenant, and mind my camera,' he said. 'It was rather expensive.'

'Oh Jack, please,' Violet ran over, her panic physical, making her feel sick. 'Please Jack, not like this, not in front of the children.'

But Jack was talking with an odd menacing softness, susurrating his words so that Weston rightly understood.

'Penruth,' he seethed, leaning forward to spit the sentence into his ear. 'I want you to stay away from my wife and daughter. I want you to take your children home to Charlecote. They are no longer welcome.'

Weston took a step back, his face infuriatingly calm. He drew out his handkerchief and lackadaisically used it to clean the lens of his camera. Then he drew his smile back so his teeth showed bright in the sunshine.

'If that's the case, then, really, don't you think . . .' he spoke so quietly that Violet had to step forward to catch his words '. . . really, Aster should come back to Charlecote too? Yes, my children should come home with me, *all* my children. Good work out in the field, however, Lieutenant Fairling. Very much appreciated.'

Jack spun his head slowly to look at Violet and then over at Aster, who was giggling and bubbling away on the back of the wagon, nudging elbows with Harry and little Kate.

Violet cried out in horror and darted over to the wagon. With the lightest of put-on voices, she cried, 'Come on, children, let's get back to the house. Let's go, it's very nearly bedtime.'

'No it's not, Mama,' Aster told her in all seriousness. 'We haven't had our picnic. Not properly.'

'Do as I say, all of you!'

'Auntie Violet,' said earnest Harry, 'bedtime is when the sun is gone.'

She glanced back to see her husband twitching with fury. Weston Penruth looked like he was preening himself, carefully turning back his cuffs and straightening his tie that Jack had ruffled.

He pulled himself up to his full height and squared his shoulders to leer at Jack, 'The baby wasn't early, Lieutenant Fairling, she was right on time.'

Jack lowered his forehead into the palms of his hands and Violet watched helpless as an awful shuddering infested his limbs.

'Think about it, Fairling,' Weston persisted. 'Have you checked the dates? Think about when you got married, and when the baby was born.'

Violet pulled the children one by one off the back of the wagon and tried to herd them towards the gate. She wanted to stay and fight for her and Jack, but could not let the children, could not let Aster hear these awful lies.

Then she cried out in delighted shock as her mother suddenly appeared at the gate with a basket over her arm and a huge hat and veil to keep insects off.

She blurted, 'Oh Mother, thank goodness!' She had never been so relieved to see her.

'Yoo-hoo, just brought some more sustenance for the workers!' May cried out, tottering over the new stubble. 'George said I ought, so here I am. How are we all doing?'

Violet leapt on her, 'Mother, can you take the children home, please? They're getting rather overheated. They need their afternoon nap.'

'Ah yes, hello, Mr Penruth, so lovely to see you. And how are you, Jack? Oh, are you all right?'

'Too much sun,' muttered Violet in her mother's ear.

May then began her inevitable fuss over the children, playing grandmother and gathering them up. 'What a lovely time you've had,' she sang to them, throwing Violet a quizzical look but being surprisingly compliant. 'Now, come back home with Grannie.'

As the little troop of children and grandmother eased themselves at an excruciating leisurely pace out of the field, Violet realised that Weston was still goading Jack. 'Did you take in what I just said, old fellow? Have you checked the dates? I heard that when Aster was born she had my hair.'

'Why are you doing this?' Violet screamed at him. 'She's Jack's child. How *dare* you!'

Weston did not relent. 'If I were you, mate, I'd get yourself a Blighty so you can take better care of your wife.'

Jack was crumbling, his head shaking, his stare fixed on his feet. He began to mutter, 'I can't remember. I simply can't remember . . . dates . . . ? When she was born . . . ?' Violet put her arms around him, to pull him away as he stuttered, not making sense: 'This is worse . . . this is worse than ever . . .'

She saw a hollowness in his eyes; as if his soul had been erased.

With sudden fury, goaded to absolute primitive loyalty, Violet lunged at Weston, her fist flailing. Her aim was true as her knuckles smacked into his jaw. Weston laughed, and touched his face as if he had a mild itch.

'Believe me, Violet, we were meant to be together.' His face was close enough for her to smell the brandy fumes on his breath, his eyes entreating her in a way that made her stomach flip sourly. 'And believe me, Jack,' he looked over her shoulder to direct his final salvo at her husband, 'Aster is mine.'

Violet turned in horror to wrap herself around Jack, to put herself between him and Weston's dreadful verbal assault, but Jack was suddenly no longer behind her.

He was heading towards the edge of the field, his fists clenched by his sides, his neck elongated in blind fury.

Violet's breath seared her chest. She was helpless, stupefied. She saw Jack return, with the speed of a man with dreadful purpose, holding something in his hand. He moved with blinkered intent, as if he had no weight in his body. Whatever he was carrying glinted merrily in the sun. Her eyes burnt as she squinted through the dusty dull gold of the wheatfield to see that her husband was holding a sickle that one of the workers had left behind. In the corner of her eye, one of the elderly men began to hobble back through the wheat, waving and calling out with increasing alarm. Something appalling was about to happen.

She sprinted towards Jack, to try to put herself in the way of the harm that he was intent on, but he refused to look at her, did not see her, pushed right past her. He marched straight up to Weston and with one mighty fist knocked him to the ground.

Violet screamed, long and hard, her voice tearing and breaking in her throat as Weston, flat on his back, began to struggle, to kick and push himself, reversing through the stubble. His smirking face dissolved into terror. Jack swung the crescent blade of the sickle high. Violet saw the sun sparkle on it for a brief, poised second amid an eerie, massive balloon of silence before he swung his arm down and sank the weapon into Weston's thigh.

Violet heard a sickening crunch, an intake of breath, during which she heard Jack mutter, 'There you are. There's *your* Blighty.' There was a strange crushed stillness before Weston's screams swung violently across the broken wheat stubble and high up into the bright, clear air.

Chapter Twenty-Four

In the language of flowers:
Sweet pea, departure

They sat huddled together in the lea of the dune, sand shifting around them in the strong breeze and the hundred voices of the wind in the rattling marram grasses. Time seemed to be expanding generously through the afternoon, bestowing more moments on them as the sun melted across the sky; moments in which Violet could comfort Jack, prescribe him little measures of solace, if only he would allow her to.

She kept watch over him, supported him as he leant against her on the sand. She saw near-hysteria march over his face, heard his chattering teeth. She held him through long shuddering sighs. He scratched himself, imagining lice in his clothes; constantly rubbing at the stubble on his face.

'When will this end?' he asked, his trembling fingers plucking at the cigarette at the corner of his mouth. Weston's blood was on his shirt. Glancing down, he said, 'If he's dead, then it will be over. At least I will be spared the front again.'

Violet wanted to protest, to tell him no, but she knew the struggle was over; her ability to reason with him was dissolved. She made him lean against her, his head on her shoulder. What else could she do?

A bitter laugh suddenly broke from him. 'You can kill all you like over there. Kill the men that have done no wrong, just happen to have been born in Dusseldorf or Berlin. Born your enemy. Innocents. Boys, some of them. But here at home, to finish someone off, someone as malicious and as foul as he is . . . it's the noose for me, isn't it?'

Violet could say nothing. She rested her face on the top of his head and let her hot tears soak his hair.

Dr Prideaux found them there, with Jess leading him to them. The little traitor, Violet thought in anger, in the depths of distress.

Her father took one look at Jack and declared officiously, 'This man needs a sedative.' He rested his doctor's bag on the sand and began to rummage in it.

'I don't need anything,' Jack said, trying to sit up.

George noticed the blood on his shirt.

'It's all right, Father,' she said. 'He's not hurt. Not physically.'

'I'll be right as rain,' Jack uttered, slipping another cigarette between his lips.

With her mouth thick with fear Violet asked, 'How is Weston?'

'Bad shape,' said Dr Prideaux. 'Tendons slashed. The wound in his thigh is gaping. Need to keep an eye on gangrene. He'll live.'

She uttered an immense groan of relief and went to pull Jack closer, but he shuffled away.

'Where the hell are the police? I thought I'd be in cuffs by now.'

'He's not pressed charges. Not yet. In no fit state.' Violet's father looked at her. 'He is, of course, being cared for at Charlecote. Ironically, he is at home with a whole host of doctors and nurses to tend to his needs.'

'He doesn't deserve that. Or any of their care,' Violet snapped, thinking of Morgan and Cartwright and how they'd come to be there. 'He is a narcissist, a sadist, too. He is monstrous.'

Her father was unnervingly calm. 'That's as may be, but this is serious, Jack. When your commanding officer finds out . . .'

'I'm leaving at first light. Back into the thick of it. I'll deal with it then. Most of them have a lot more on their minds than a bit of common assault.'

Violet's father sat down on a hillock of sand and grass. 'Your behaviour might have repercussions for all of us,' he told Jack. 'Penruth is our landlord. After the engagement was broken, he made serious threats to throw us out of Old Trellick. Something made him change his mind, however. What that was, we'll never know. But this time round . . .'

'Oh, he won't do that,' Jack crowed, staring hard at Violet. 'He wouldn't cast out his own child. And he loves Violet.'

In despair, Violet cried out, 'Oh, where is Aster?'

Her father told her that Aster was fine, back home with her grandmother and great aunt, slipping in that Mr Penruth had ordered a car to be sent to Old Trellick to pick up Harry and Kate and all their belongings.

'So it's over between you,' Jack stated blandly, and turned to stare at the sparkling sea horizon.

'It's always been over,' Violet said weakly, her thoughts

chattering and complicated. How the consequence of her father's one act of kindness towards Weston all those years ago damaged her life, changed her and destroyed the girl she was.

But, she remembered, Jack had brought her round, from the moment she walked across Regent's Park not knowing he was watching her, capturing her. Her memory found it for her and a light of happiness flashed in her head. She was walking with Muriel's parasol, the light was glorious, the rose garden ahead of her a blur of colour. She trod over daisies in the grass and a sieve of sunlight through the willow leaves speckled her, bathed her. His first painting of that perfect moment was tucked away in the garret. We should bring it out, she decided, it should be framed and on display for everyone to see.

As she walked unknowingly across the park, in her mind they had already met, had been in love for years. She knew him then, at once. And Jack was her first, in all reality. Jack, sitting locked in his black world beside her, his soul wrecked by the war. Always Jack.

She realised he was speaking quietly to her.

'And yet still, Violet, he'll want to spare you. He won't throw you out,' he said. 'He still loves you. And Aster? Why would he *think* that about Aster?'

Dr Prideaux stood up abruptly and picked up his bag, telling them he was heading home. He took Jess by the lead and walked away across the sand.

Violet watched until her father merged with the dunes, heading back up the path, and then took a long ragged breath. She turned to her husband. 'There is nothing to tell you about Aster. She is your daughter. Just look at her.'

'But why would he even *say* it? That man knows you. He has known you . . .' Jack paused and she saw his eyes vivid with a desire for the truth and a wish never to hear it. 'When you came to my studio and I showed you *Violet in the Daytime* for the first time, you cried. And you have never really told me why. When I look at the painting I did of you on our wedding night, there is something there that you are holding back. I can see it in your face. I can feel it, in the way you are looking at me, straight out of the canvas. Am I right?'

Violet tore her hands together, feeling the sweat on them slip through her fingers. The ice in her veins stopped her blood.

'Truth is, I don't want to tell you,' she said at last. 'For if I do, I believe you *will* kill him.'

'Well, you know,' he said, the gravity in his voice incompatible with the flippancy of his words, 'I can give it a bloody good go.'

She paused. Tangible fear crackled between them, snapping around their heads as they both stared at each other, waiting for the truth.

'He forced himself . . . he made me . . . he would not stop.' Her words broke under the burden of the blunt facts. 'We were engaged. It was our party. My parents, they were just outside. No one knew, no one was there. Just him, in that hellish place. That's why I came to London. I ran away. I needed time . . . to get away. It was over. It never began.'

As he listened, Jack's face stretched apart and she saw an understanding behind his eyes which momentarily erased the struggle inside him.

He reached his hand towards her. 'He did that to you . . . ?'

'I've never told anyone.'

'He did *that*?'

Jack was ready to spring, his fists coiling, his jaw rigid.

'Please, no more anger,' she began to speak quickly. 'We'll

move away. We shouldn't be here in Cornwall. We'll go and live in Camden with Mrs Ellis. I'm sure Auntie Muriel will return to London when the war is over. When it's over . . . It will be over.'

'It is never over,' he said in all simplicity, sinking back. His anger dissolved like a wave receding, leaving familiar despair behind.

Jack shuffled wearily around and lay his head on her lap. She rested her hand behind his ear and gently stroked his hairline. Part of Violet wanted him to spring up and race to Charlecote and attack Weston again. But another part was weeping with relief. There was to be no more anger.

'It won't be over until I can sleep,' he said. 'And I can't sleep.'

He confessed that he dreaded the night, and what he saw when he closed his eyes. He assured her he would not desert, would not be a coward. 'What can a man like me do, but go on with his sickening fate?'

He reminded her of the newspapers, how word came back from the front. The casualty figures printed in columns. He saw those men beside him, he told her, in a long, long line.

Shifting a little to catch her eye, he said, 'I told you about Welstead, didn't I?'

Violet reminded him, 'But you have never told me much more.'

'Do you really want me to?' Her silence gave him her affirmative answer and she waited.

Eventually she pressed him: when did Welstead die? Two or more years ago? Three?

'That was just the start. To speak of it makes it sound like so much time has passed, but it is all still so present. All

252

of it,' Jack said, his voice trailing through memory, his face flinching at the tableau inside his head. 'Thought it would not get any worse than Loos. But what happened two years ago out in Picardy, on the Somme, that's what I see now when I close my eyes. It never leaves me. Keeps replaying . . .'

Jack winced. 'We were the boys who had trained together. Pals, we called each other. We were ready for this, my God, we were ready. This is what everything since 1914 has been about. This is what we came for. We were skilled, trained in the way of war. Civilian life had become a foreign country, do you understand? This was our purpose, our reason. I remember thinking this as we crawled along in darkness on our bellies among the barley, standing tall and untended because the farmer – his house was just over there on the hill – had to leave it to the weeds. Perfect cover for us. We crawl in and wait for the dawn. But not wanting it, even though this was our *purpose*. Never wanting it. The hour.'

Violet held her breath, her skin turning cold. The answer to the question she had wanted to ask him, had yearned for that very morning as she stood at the kitchen door, was playing out for her now, was being presented as a picture by her husband, the artist: dawn on the Somme.

'There's a signal, a whistle, somewhere along the line,' he said. 'Hundreds of us, identical in drill and dress rise up out of the crop, but each one of us separate, a distinct life. If you could hear what was in our heads, instead of this silence of dawn, you'd hear a clamouring storm. Our memories and thoughts clattering together. We are all men, we all have our lives, our ways, our homes. We stand, emerge out of the barley, being born. Hundreds upon hundreds. We want to apologise to the farmer, wherever he is, for ruining his crop. And yet still it stands, it's grown so tall, shoulder height. We have the advantage, the element of surprise. An adventure story. We'll win, of course. They told us we will win. We emerge, we stand, armed and ready. The ground is dry and stony, birds fly. Yes, there are birds there, still there, feasting on the seeds, taking their fill. But they're soon gone when the noise starts. It comes from nowhere: metallic, mechanical, persistent hacking. Men to my left fall to their knees, rifles still brandished, useless. Men to my right bow, a strange salutation to the pristine light of the morning. And they keep falling, some in silence, their lives cut before they hit the ground, harvested, falling. Some screaming like children. Over in the copse, the little knoll of trees we did not notice, did not reckon with, the machine gun nest keeps up its sickening strafe. No matter how many of us fall, it keeps going. And I hear it. The swell of screams, swearing, cursing God. I hear chaos. This is what death sounds like. I hear them cry, *"Why, why, why?"* We lose our humanity, dying like cattle. Shrapnel turns the sky silver. They're sending in the shells. Great clods of thick, lethal smoke. We have no means of protection against this . . . this. Let me tell you about the noise, Violet. The sound of men dying like this is not human. It is a revolting momentum, a revolting inevitability. They got it wrong. Got it so wrong.'

Violet leant forward and pressed her face to his, to hear her husband whisper, 'How is it I am still alive?'

They stayed like that, with the cradling motion of the sun-sparkled sea before them. Violet found no comfort in it, and she knew Jack was beyond any solace when he moaned into her skirts, 'And that man, that man taunts me about my most precious things. My Violet and my Aster. The things I stayed alive for.'

* * *

254

As they walked slowly back up the pathway from the cove towards Old Trellick, the afternoon shifted into the long golden light of evening, the very light that she had no way of imagining, all those hours ago standing that morning at the kitchen doorway.

Jack insisted he did not want to go inside for a while and asked her to sit with him in the garden. From their bench by the high brick wall, she could see that the drawing-room French windows were open. Through the tied-back curtains, she spotted her mother and auntie sitting at the little polished table, snapping cards over its surface. They were identical to her – coiffured grey hair, ramrod backs in their old-fashioned S-bend corsets – so alike, they were, and yet each offered her such a diverse kind of affection.

And there was Aster, curled up in the wing armchair, her little head sleepily lolling, fighting her tiredness. She traced her finger lazily over the half-finished newspaper crossword that Jack had started before breakfast and left on the arm of the chair. From the hallway sounded the chimes of the little clock and the birds' chorus in the garden rang on a different key. Dusk was settling like a soft cloak and the stock in her father's flowerbed began to breathe out its heady scent in the half-darkness. It was way past Aster's bedtime.

'She should be in bed,' Violet observed as Jack lit another cigarette. 'It's seven o'clock.'

He looked at Violet, put his hands on her shoulders and turned her to face him.

'I cannot do this to you any more. I can't put you through this. You need happiness, stability. He can give it to you. Not me. No, no, look at me.' Jack lowered his face and peered up at Violet. 'Go to him.'

'Jack, I don't want to,' she whispered, exhausted. 'Don't say such things. I hate him, don't you understand? He is nothing to me. You are upset.'

'*Upset?*' he laughed a little, his face carved with desolation.

Panic boiled in Violet's mind. Her memories raced back to the time she met Jack, her time in London, their wedding night. The secret she kept from him then. The way Aster slipped out into the world, tiny. She *looked* premature. Her little life was a battle for the first few months. Her father had called in a specialist. But was it possible that she was a full-term baby and simply just malnourished and sickly? Could she be Weston's child?

Jack scrutinised her face, 'See how his blood is up when he talks to you, sees you together with Aster. There is something there. And you wanted to marry him, once. How can any of us be sure?'

'The man raped me!' Violet pushed him aside, stood up and walked away, throwing back at him, 'Even if she is his child, what does it matter?'

She stalked across the lawn through the trailing fragrance of night-scented stock and her father's sweet peas, breathing hard, tears soaking her face. Jack's suspicion made the ground under her feet crumble. Made her question her existence, made her believe it was true. She stumbled and halted at the French windows, leaning against the doorway.

Her mother, sitting at the polished table, was watching avidly while Muriel laid out the Tarot. A strangely calm thought rose to the surface of Violet's mind. Oh, I wish they wouldn't. Such silliness, always wrong; only ever what you want to read into it. Not tonight, of all nights. *After all*, she remembered, *when I first arrived in London, Muriel did a reading, told me I was to marry* – Violet caught her breath. The turn of the cards, back in the salon on Montagu Square, had been true.

Now, she fixed her eyes on her aunt as she laid the last card with a flourish: 'So what have we here,' she announced. 'The Final Outcome, let's see . . . Good Lord, it's *that* card, May. He's not coming back!'

Violet pressed her hand over her mouth: *They cannot mean it. Surely, they cannot!*

Both ladies looked up at the same time to see she was standing at the doorway. Her mother sank back with guilt, turned on Aster still curled up in the armchair and began to berate her, telling her she ought to be in bed.

Violet walked quietly in and knelt by Aster's chair, watching her little girl sleepily struggle with her yawns. Noticing her suddenly, her daughter opened her eyes wide in surprise and reached up to touch Violet's wet cheek.

'Mama . . . ?' she murmured.

'And it is high time Auntie put the cards away,' Violet said smoothly, despite the hole of pain opening wide in her chest.

Muriel hastily gathered the cards together, swearing she'd never use them again.

Slowly, step by careful step Violet took Aster by the hand and walked her up to bed. She tucked her in and promised her that her dad would be in to say goodnight. Aster wondered briefly where Kate and Harry were, and Violet told her gently that they had gone home. Sleepily Aster reminded her of the Flower Book, and of her promise that they would look through it together tomorrow. Violet repeated her promise and Aster made her cross her heart. They argued just a little about the fact that the sky was still light outside, that the birds were still singing and that the long summer's day was holding on. By the time Violet had reached the door, her little girl was asleep.

She passed her mother and father on the stairs.

'Muriel's already retired. She feels dreadful about the cards, she's thrown them away. She's terribly sorry.'

Violet muttered, tired to her bones, 'A silly, dangerous game to play . . .'

'We're all going up to bed, leaving you in peace,' said May, and Violet looked down in surprise as her mother rested a gentle hand on her arm.

'Take care of him tonight,' her father said to her. 'We don't seem to be able to get through to him any more. We're so sorry.'

'Goodnight, both of you,' Violet said, false brightness in her smile. 'Sleep well.'

She found Jack standing in the drawing room, splashing brandy into a glass.

'Do you want one?'

'I hate brandy,' she said.

He looked at her, mindful that he should never have asked. 'I know.'

She slumped down in the armchair as an immense tide of fatigue dragged through her body. Gazing out through the open French windows, she noticed the light was at last beginning to fade. The day that had begun with such promise that morning was finally giving up the ghost.

Jack walked over and handed her a folded piece of Charlecote-headed notepaper. 'This arrived for your father while you were upstairs. He's not going to press charges. He's not going to throw you all out of Old Trellick. See, here, it's in black and white.'

Violet screwed it up and tossed it to the floor, not wishing to see Weston's handwriting, to touch anything he might have held, unable to find comfort in its contents. All she wanted was for Jack not to leave, for Jack to come back to her. He sat in the chair opposite and the room darkened around them. As the night stole in to fill the spaces with shadow upon shadow, his features and his body faded into the gloom. He was disappearing before her eyes and a swell of panic inside ballooned and blossomed like a stain of ink over a page.

'Remember Regent's Park,' he said eventually, the glow of his cigarette a tiny red dot in the darkness. 'The rose garden.'

'Always,' she replied as tears rolled silently down her cheeks.

'I wish you had told me all about it when we were first married. I love you. But . . .'

'*But?*' she repeated.

There came a great empty pause, a hard silence in which Violet was devoured by fear.

'You need to go to him.' She heard Jack reach down and fumble for something in the darkness. She heard the crackling of the letter as he began to unfold it. 'He's just a stupid hot-headed brute, certainly not a gentleman. But if Old Trellick is safe, Aster will always have a home. That's for the good, isn't it? A future for you both.'

'Jack, please don't . . .'

'What am I?' Jack said, his voice like a bell tolling. 'I could walk out one morning next week, and have my head blown off. Turn around and I am gone. Just a pile of something in the corner. I've seen it far too many times. If he has half as much feeling inside him for you as I do . . .'

His voice was broken off by the sound of Aster above

them, crying out suddenly, harshly in her darkened room, screaming in fear for her dad.

Jack stubbed out his cigarette and hauled himself up from his chair.

'Sounds like she's having a bad dream. I'll go to her,' he said. In the dark he walked past her. Violet closed her eyes and breathed in the scent of him as he rested the back of his hand lightly against her cheek.

The night grew quiet, whispering with its own voices as Violet's sleepy eyes adjusted to the gloom. Curled up in her armchair, she watched the shape of the furniture in the drawing room emerge and the sky lighten a degree through the open French windows. The perfume of the night-scented stock thickened the air. A nightjar called from the trees at the bottom of the garden and another creature, a vixen or a screech owl, intoxicated by the lightness of the night, responded from the woods or the valley or the green bridleway. Her ears opened and below all of these fleeting sounds she heard the sea murmuring, its sighs reaching her up the path from the cove, across the cow meadow and along the lane. She jolted, astonished by it. So it was true: the sea could be heard from Old Trellick. She was comforted by it as it crept towards her, hypnotic and soothing, proving everyone wrong. Visiting her like a wonderful old friend. Wrapping Muriel's shawl around her shoulders against the chilly air, she listened to the sound of the waves, just as she heard them when she pressed a shell to her ear, and drifted with its indistinct lullaby.

The room was grey with light when she opened her eyes. Jack stood in front of her, no longer her Jack. He was buttoned up in his khaki-brown uniform. Belt tight, puttees laced, cap pulled firmly over his eyes. He was shaved and smart. He was remote, his chin tilted up with dignified pride. The discipline of the officer's uniform seemed to increase his height, straighten his shoulders. The wrecked man who was with her yesterday, who she had tried her best to help, was gone.

'You were sleeping,' he said. 'I did not know if I should wake you.'

Violet drew the back of her hand over her face to dash away the tears that were stealing out of her eyes. Her longing for him made her mute; all her strength fixed on keeping herself from screaming his name.

Jack said blandly, 'When I said goodbye to Aster earlier, in the middle of the night, I didn't promise I'd come back. I couldn't do it.'

'You *must*,' she whispered.

But his face was solid, unreadable. She did not see the fight in him any more. Just a man, another man in a long, long line, dressed the same as all the others, going back to war.

Then, peeling through the quiet, still air came the throb and rumble of a motor car. Jack flinched when he heard it, then glanced at the screwed-up note which still rested innocuously on the carpet.

'Be happy and live your life,' he said and walked out to the hallway to pick up his pack, hoist it onto his shoulder.

He can't go. He can't be gone, she thought. *I simply won't let him. Not to that place he calls hell.*

'Wait, oh wait!' Violet cried out, her limbs suddenly alive and burning with the desire to move, to sprint to his side.

With a desperate pounding in her chest, she hurried to the hallway to catch a glimpse of him closing the front door behind him. She raced up the stairs and flew into her bedroom. She pressed a hand to her side, groaning with panic. Disabled by the frenzy in her head, her hope lay in tatters, fell away, turned her body to straw. But lying there on her table, the Flower Book waited.

Why didn't I think of this before, why did I never explain properly to him? She frantically leafed through the pages, turning them with a snap, her pressed flowers crackling in protest.

She found the page of pressed tansy with a cry of joy and took hold of it, ripping it from the spine as dried leaves and petals scattered to the floor. She snatched up an envelope and stuffed the page into it.

He was saluting his subaltern driver and turned at the sound of her footsteps ringing out along the slate front path as she hurtled towards him. She stopped a few feet from him, her heartbeat blazing in her throat, her body taut with desire for him, for him to understand. He dropped his pack to the ground with a thud and stood still, retaining infuriating discipline in front of the driver, who tactfully slipped into the car to wait.

Motionless, her blood thundering, Violet knew that he was already a world away from her. She stared at him with an intensity that made her shudder. She reached out her hand that clutched the envelope, as if she was crossing a void, gesturing that he should take it from her.

'This is my only proof,' she whispered to him, her hand, her arm trembling. 'This is all I have. Trust me. Forgive me. And come back.'

Jack looked at the sky, at the ground, the tall trees, but never at her. He took the envelope and put it in his pocket.

'Believe me,' she whispered, never sure if he ever heard her.

Chapter Twenty-Five

In the language of flowers:
Wild daisy, I will always think of it

The air was close and still in the green-tunnel bridleway, scented with privet blossom and musk mallow. Dappled sunlight winked at Violet through the canopy of leaves, flecking her hands and sleeves. She stopped to listen. So this, she thought, was what peace sounded like. The warm, heady afternoon had silenced the birds and bees drowsily knocking into one another among the pale-pink blackberry blossom. She noticed this new patch of brambles scrambling up the earth-and-stone bank. Oh, Claudia would have made a beeline for them, thought Violet, come blackberry time.

Through a gap in the high bank she caught sight of the new wavering crop in the field beyond. Blood-red poppies were scattered through it, punctuating the blades of wheat, startling and raw against the sea of silvery green. She'd read the newspaper reports of how, this summer, poppies had spread themselves over the churned-up filth of the now silent battlefields. How quickly and swiftly nature swooped in to disguise devastation, she thought, dress it up as if it never happened, to show us that life moved on, with us or without us.

And indeed it had done, right here at Old Trellick. Since the telegram from Jack's commanding officer last October, Aster had grown another inch, had learnt cat's cradle and hopscotch. She had developed a good eye for picking out willow herb and cow parsley for the Flower Book, and daisies were now her speciality. How appropriately she was named, Violet smiled. She could even do the seven-times table, with a little prompting from Gran or Auntie Muriel.

Last week, they'd waved Muriel off on the train. It was time to go back to London, back to normal, she'd said. Smithson was willing to return, at a price. She'd demanded all sorts of new labour-saving devices that she'd seen advertised in the *Evening Mail*. And a pay rise. Violet missed Muriel and her generous laughter, her no-nonsense manner. She knew that Aster pined for her too but London called Muriel home. She had her friends there. Her society was gathering itself back into Fitzrovia and around the park, most of them in shock, most of them bereaved, but thanking God they'd made it through. And that's how I should behave, thought Violet. I should slap on a smile and face the world. There was a life, as always, that went on without Jack. And she'd have to find beauty in it. He'd not have wanted her to suffer and fade away, as tempting as it was to hide herself from everything in the pinewoods, in the lanes and at the cove. He had told her on that last, dreadful night, to *be happy and live your life*. But the telegram had sliced through her, snuffing her out. She didn't dare to hope, for hope was futile. *Missing presumed dead*: the three words haunted her. It was as if he'd known. As if Muriel had seen it coming.

Her fears over four long years of war had come to reality, to cling to her back in a shroud of bewildering grief. She thought of Mrs Davey and of Lady Welstead and what they had endured and what they were still enduring. On the surface, these women's lives and situations could not be more different, but, beneath it all, they were both, they were all, devastatingly the same.

And yet today, on this serene and precious afternoon as Violet brushed past silky grasses and walked through clouds of tiny white butterflies in the green twilight of the bridleway, she knew she must carry on, for Aster. She must fix her smile, for without it, everything was intolerable.

Violet breathed in the sweet air around her, trying to seek its comfort, believing she had lost Jack long before the telegram arrived. For joining up at the beginning had begun the protracted erosion of his soul. The more she loved him, and longed for him through those months and years, the more he drew away from her. The war changed him, took him away from her and yet her loved endured. For what else was there?

She stooped then to inspect a luscious Canterbury bell, as blue as the midday sky, through a smudged veil of tears, and felt the earth vibrating before she heard the clopping of the horse's hooves. Weston Penruth was riding towards her, ducking under branches, leaning along his horse's neck as dense foliage of the bridleway ruffled and caught his hair. Since the incident at the harvest last year, despite his note, the very sight of their landlord's approach sent everyone at Old Trellick into a spinning fear of a renewed threat of eviction.

'Good afternoon, Violet,' he called. 'I was just coming your way. But you have saved me the trouble.'

She said nothing, simply stepping to one side to allow him to pass. Their paths were bound to cross within these tight, rolling hills, and the rare occasions that they met were to be endured. As weary of him as she was, she had to keep the peace and keep a roof over all of their heads.

He pulled in his horse and dismounted with a rattle of bridle and stirrup. Violet averted her eyes from his leg as he hobbled and stumbled a little on the uneven ground. In her mind, she heard the crunch as Jack's sickle met with bone.

He noticed her smile. 'Ah, is that for me?' he asked.

'Never for you,' she replied but her words rolled off him with irritating ease.

'Come now. I just wanted to drop by Old Trellick to give you this.' He handed her an envelope. 'Just one small gesture in my grand plan to endeavour to make you like me again.'

She took the envelope without interest and put it in her bag.

'Still clipping away at the wayside flowers, I see,' he blundered on. He was standing close to her, his large frame casting a shadow.

As well as being unafraid, she was equally determined not to be angry, but the sorrowful, expectant expression on Weston's face, his wilful imperceptions of what he did to her, sparked the rage that she tried to keep so quiet and mild.

'Weston, I will never like you again,' she snapped at him. 'I believe that I never did. But for my parents' sake and for my daughter's sake, I can never tell you what is really on my mind.'

His face softened and became even more ludicrous.

'Come now. Think of the time you cared for my children. That was a huge undertaking for which I am very grateful. They remember their Auntie Violet fondly. Well, Harry does. Kate was far too young.'

She looked over his shoulder, wondering which way she could escape. 'I did it for Claudia, and for the children.'

He reached out his hand to touch her sleeve. 'That's why you are still so cherished by me. Claudia was a beauty, so gentle and pure, and yet you, Violet. We could have been . . .'

She dared to glance at his face and inwardly shuddered. And then she looked beyond him, right through him.

'Don't ever speak to me again.'

She turned and hurried away, breaking into a run as soon as she rounded the corner in the bridleway. She heard him call her name, just once, but she was soon enveloped and safe back in her own world of green flickering sunlight.

It wasn't until she reached Old Trellick and was walking up the front path that she remembered the envelope. She fished it out of her bag and opened it, drawing out a photograph. Within the sepia image three children sat lined up on the back of the harvest wagon, their faces plump and baby-like. She and Jack were ghostly figures captured in the blurred background like insects in amber. Her memory made an about-turn, taking her straight back there. The day she last saw Jack was captured here on film and her heart was pierced with agony. The pain gave way to the insult. It isn't even a very good photograph, she thought in distaste, why did Weston bother?

Suddenly, a rumble of thunder rolling down the valley startled her with childlike fear and made her scamper indoors. She walked straight up the double set of stairs to the garret and without a second thought, flung the photograph in a drawer. She sat down at the table by the window, out of breath and fuming. She did not need to look at a blurred photograph of her husband, for his face was already branded onto her mind. Staring out at the garden below, sultry in the July late afternoon, her hatred for Weston drained away, replaced by a dreadful longing for Jack, her sorrow dripping to form a stagnant pool in the centre of her head.

The air was warm and muggy. She felt it tight on her chest. Jess, down in the garden, was whining and irritable, glancing up at the sky, sensing, as she knew only animals can, the static in the air. The storm was approaching, the heavy, slaty sky folded itself down over their little valley, stifling and shutting out any air that was benign and breathable. Violet took her handkerchief and rubbed it around her neck under her collar as the first beacon of lightning lit up the trees at the bottom of the garden, blinking for the briefest second like the flare of a match.

At that moment, as the first crack of thunder dropped down from the sky, she heard the doorbell ring, faintly and so normally, below.

'That blessed man!' she cried, leaping to her feet. 'Why can't he just leave me alone?'

But it was not Weston Penruth. The postman stood there, a grin on his face, his cheeks pink with exertion.

'Was hoping I'll get home before it breaks,' he said. 'But I had to deliver this one. Might just make it back to Lansallos with a dry behind. But then I might not. Good day to you, Mrs Fairling.'

Violet took the telegram and walked in a daze into the drawing room. Her parents were out in the wagonette, taking Aster into Looe for a treat, and Old Trellick was quiet. Corners were shadowy, familiar spaces dark, the furniture bulky and brooding as the daylight outside faded under the storm. Despite the heat, Violet shivered as she sat down in her armchair and pulled the chit of paper from its envelope.

She was still holding it in her frozen hand when her father's car pulled up amid a torrent of rain, as new and cold and vital as the first ever rain to fall to earth, turning the old, tired air into cool balm.

Her mother came into the drawing room, her face a picture of indignity, her macintosh dripping puddles on the parquet. Aster squeezed in past her and ran to Violet. She climbed on her knee and pressed on her the events of the day.

'Mama, we walked around the harbour. I had an ice cream. And picked some daisies.'

'Go and fetch a towel for your Gran,' Violet muttered, not hearing her, pushing her away.

Aster recoiled as if sensing the change in her mother, her different, upside-down expression. But she did as she was told and skipped off upstairs to the bathroom.

Silence settled in the room, the view of the rain through the French windows was a blur of saturated grey.

May offered tentatively, 'Violet, you look like you've seen a ghost. Has the thunder scared you? It gave us a mighty fright, I can tell you, as we drove home. Your father's parking the car in a filthy mood. He's concerned the rain will ruin his delphiniums. Violet?'

'He's back,' she said, slumped in her chair. 'Muriel says . . .'

Violet held up the telegram, unable to form any more words, words she'd longed to speak for months, so many months.

'Jack?' May blurted.

She walked over to Violet and took the telegram from her, disbelief making her face crooked.

JACK HOME IN CAMDEN STOP VISITED ME YESTERDAY STOP PLEASE COME STOP NOT AS IT SEEMS STOP MURIEL

'I'm going to take the night train,' said Violet. 'I've thought it all through. I will be in London by the morning.'

'But what does Muriel mean by "not as it seems"?' May blurted.

'I don't care what she means,' said Violet, her body weak with shock. 'I just need to get up to town as soon as possible. I need to go. But don't say anything to Aster. I don't want her troubled or worried, or overexcited just yet . . . I just want to bring her daddy back home to her.'

George Prideaux slammed the front door and came into the room, wet around the collar and his turn-ups soggy.

'Well, I'll be blowed,' he grumbled. 'Did you hear that thunder? It's like all hell has been let loose out there.'

'No, Papa,' cried Violet, laughing suddenly, leaping up and dashing over to him to surprise him with a peck on the cheek. 'Not hell. Not hell at all. For look what I have here. Read this, just read this!'

A mere hour later, Violet stood in the hall to say goodbye to Aster. She knelt down so she was level with her daughter's face.

'Be good for Gran and Grandpa,' she said, unable to wipe the smile from her face. 'For I won't be long.'

Aster asked her where she was going. Could she come too?

'No, my dear. I'm just popping up to London to see Auntie Muriel.'

'Will you be gone one night or two nights?' Aster persisted. 'I didn't tell you about my ice cream. Mama, it was clotted cream and 'nilla. And look, I picked daises from the verge where Grandpa parked the wagonette.'

The little girl reached in her pocket and drew out a little tangle of limp, sorry-looking flowers.

Violet dipped at them with her finger. 'Press them for the Flower Book,' she said. 'When I get home, we'll put them in. And write the date, remember the date . . .'

Violet grasped her daughter, crushing her close to her so that she would not see the tears of joy erupting from her eyes. She whispered goodbye again and again.

Aster wriggled free. 'We should have brought you an ice cream, Mama. And more daisies.'

'Next time,' said Violet. She put on her hat and left the house.

Chapter Twenty-Six

In the language of flowers:
White roses, I am worthy of you

The night train from Exeter was delayed and Violet did not reached Montagu Square until mid morning. She had expected to arrive early with the milk cart and the baker's van, but the day in the street had already begun with whistling window cleaners and the sweep who was just setting up next door. Violet nodded a greeting two or three times as she paid her taxi driver and walked up the steps to Muriel's quietly elegant house.

The door was duly answered and opened a fraction. Violet glanced curiously around it to see Smithson standing back in the shadows of the hallway, a linen mask over her nose and mouth.

'Good morning Mrs Fairling. Best you don't come in.'

'Whatever's the matter?' Violet pushed the door wider and stepped into the vestibule.

'Madam is very ill. She has the influenza. Came back from the post office yesterday, when she sent your telegram, shivering with cold despite it being such a hot day. Went straight to her bed. Doctor's been once. Says he can't come back 'til tomorrow. Too many people coming down with it . . . A new strain or something . . .'

Violet looked at the housemaid's bright and frightened eyes protruding above the mask.

'How are you feeling, Smithson?' she asked.

'I am well. I will do what I can for madam. She's delirious . . . I've never seen anything like it. She's so cold. It's hardly her any more. She's so very ill. Her face is . . . *purple.*'

Violet hesitated, took another step forward. 'I will call the doctor back, this is ridiculous.'

'No, Mrs Fairling!' Smithson's shout stopped her. 'You have a young child. I don't think you should come into this house.'

Violet put her small valise down by the plant pots. 'May I just leave this, for now? You see, I need to go . . .'

'Of course.' Smithson's voice was edged with fatigue but her eyes above the mask were unusually empathetic. 'Here, take this. It's another sunny day, and madam would not want you to be out in the sunshine.'

Violet took the parasol offered by the housemaid, said goodbye and hurried back down the steps.

'Jack may know a better doctor,' she thought as she glanced quickly around the square looking for a taxi cab. There were none to be had, so she began to walk, her steps hastening, towards Baker Street. Amid the jostle of omnibuses and cars, there were certainly cabs, but none were free.

'Oh, poor dear Muriel,' she thought as she turned north, spying the verdant park beyond the busy thoroughfare. 'I must get to Jack. I must see him. He will know what to do.'

As she crossed into the Inner Circle, she became immersed into the tranquil beauty of Regent's Park. How I've missed this place, she thought. It feels like a whole lifetime ago that I was here with Jack. People were strolling, taking the air, forgetting the war, forgetting the scourge of Spanish flu that had pounced on a vulnerable nation at such a weak and hopeless time. But Violet could not help but smile when she saw a young couple driving their sporting buggy pulled by a black pony around the Inner Circle. They have survived, she thought, as we have. There *is* hope, such hope for Jack and I and Aster.

She glanced again idly at the black pony and thought it looked untrained, rather frisky and spooked. But she didn't ponder too long on it, for her mind drifted with fatigue. It was hard to describe the night train as the 'sleeper' for she had not had a wink. A dog barked suddenly and she glanced in horror as the pony rose in its harness and dramatically pummelled the air. But the young man was strong and capable and brought him back in hand, congratulated by his adoring sweetheart. How happy they looked together, Violet mused. And we will be, she resolved. Just as soon as I get myself to him. We can start again, right from the beginning.

But what could Muriel have meant in her telegram *not as it seems*? She took it out of her bag and read it again. Was she worried that Jack might have the flu? So many soldiers came home with it. Ah, but he is home. He is just over there, beyond the rose gardens and across the stretch of green. If she hurried on, soon she would be passing Cumberland Terrace where Lady Welstead sat, no doubt in all her finery, still mourning her son. Then she would be crossing the bridge over the railway and rushing up Parkway. And there, just there, past the pharmacist, and round the corner, she will be knocking on the little shabby door.

Violet stopped for a moment, rather out of breath. Oh, this is where we met, she realised, her joy making her eyes smart. The garden was filled with white roses, like drifts of snow in summer. Oh, where have all the other colours gone? she wondered. But never mind, for white roses were always my favourite. And this is where he was sitting, unbeknown to me, watching me . . . oh my goodness, she thought with a laugh of delight, I am not used to feeling this happy.

As she came out from under the willow trees, the sun was suddenly sharp in her eye and she raised Muriel's parasol. Her happiness formed a blissful bubble around her and her footsteps bounced over the springy grass that was lush and green and spangled with daisies. Oh, the daisies that Aster found. We can press them together when I bring Jack home to Old Trellick. Perhaps we can get the night train home, if he can bear it. This is where he saw me, this is where he painted me, she giggled with delight. This is *Violet in the Daytime.*

I am moving through the park, she whispered to herself, *under the dappled silvery shadow of willow trees; star-like daisies bright at my feet. My face is half in profile. My parasol is the colour of luminous water, protecting me, keeping me separated in my own world. My eyes, even in shadow, are lucid sea green. As I walk, I am not aware of the artist as he sees me; just of the light that comes from below me, reflected from his direction, to illuminate me and set me apart.*

Violet lifted her hand quickly to shield her eyes, as the ringing noise of a horse thundering down on her startled her, forced the breath out of her. The young couple, who a few moments before had been laughing and kissing, were now screaming and clinging to each other, rocking from side to side on the buggy seat in the most absurd manner. Violet glanced at them and her limbs turned to dust. Her mouth opened, silently screaming. In her mind, she stepped neatly to the side as the horse and carriage bore down on her, as the screams intensified and the thrashing hooves kicked out. But there was no moment in which to think of saving herself, for there was no time, no time left at all.

She lay motionless, crumpled on the grass, as people ran from all directions towards her. The telegram, still clutched in her hand, was released and lifted suddenly by a breeze and, along with the parasol, was blown away across the daisy-spangled grass.

Her eyes, still so lucid and sea green, stared up at a sky that was no longer there.

Part Two

Aster
Cornwall, the previous year

Chapter Twenty-Seven

The clock struck seven times and they still hadn't told her to go to bed. This was, Aster decided, because her dad was home. Outside, the sky glowed with summer evening light; inside, the drawing room was soft and luminous. She heard the chimes vibrating from the hallway and shuffled further back into the armchair, cradled in deep velvet scented by his dark tobacco. His newspaper was folded on the arm with a half-filled-in crossword and sleepily she traced his scribblings with her finger.

Aster gave an eye-stinging yawn and peered around the wing of the chair to watch Gran at the card table with Great Auntie Muriel. Both had their backs to her, their identical grey wavy-hair heads poised, their spines in their long, smooth gowns as straight as rods. Aster was fascinated by Muriel as she deftly shuffled her cards, flicking them out across the melted-toffee surface into a cross formation. The old ladies must have forgotten that she was in the room, curled up there in the deep armchair, for if they'd remembered, then they would have certainly sent her straight to bed. She stayed frozen, hardly daring to take one breath.

The sinking sun intensified another degree, pouring gold across the parquet. Aster could hear her mother talking quietly out in the garden, her voice drifting through the open French windows. A comforting whiff of her dad's cigarette wafted with it. She heard his quiet response, his rumbling words. They tickled Aster, seemed to settle inside her. Jess the dog lay in a furry pool beneath her feet, guarding her and sighing with the responsibility.

With a wink of excitement she was drawn back to Muriel and the cards emerging over the table, flipping from fingers. Some cards were familiar to Aster, some she'd never seen before. But all were a peculiar magic, of things buried in her imagination; things she recognised but did not know. They revealed the stuff of fleeting dreams. She saw Temperance's iridescent rainbow linking Heaven and Earth, the cold steel of the Ten of Swords and the inevitable turning Wheel of Fortune. Gran watched the cards, too, drinking her steaming tea, pursing her lips. A glance at Muriel and a hesitant shaking of her head. Muriel lay down the last one with a flourish and declared, suddenly, her voice fracturing the air: 'The Final Outcome, let's see . . . Good Lord, it's *that* card, May. He's not coming back!'

Gran turned sharply from her sister, suddenly remembering, to stare at Aster. In quick, cringing self-reproach, Muriel mixed the cards over the surface and clawed them back together, whispering, 'We shouldn't be doing this now. We really shouldn't.'

'You're not still up, are you?' Gran's voice was pitched at Aster just below anger. 'It's getting late. Time that little girls were in bed.'

'But the garden is still light,' Aster protested, sinking back into her chair. 'The birds are still talking. And Dad is here.'

'Gran is right. Time for bed.' This voice was velvet deep in her ear. Aster turned in surprise. Mama had come back into the room as quietly as a phantom and was kneeling at the side of the chair. Her hair was rolled in a great smooth puff over her forehead, curls escaping to touch her ears. Aster loved the russet depths of it. Her mother's green eyes were cloudy, as if she was hiding. Tears streaked her apple-round cheeks. She flicked something from her eye and declared, 'And high time Auntie Muriel put the cards away.'

'Where's Dad?' Aster asked.

'He's just taking a stroll. He will come up and tuck you in,' Mama replied. There was a graininess in her voice. 'He won't be long.'

Gran said, 'You spoil that child. She should have been asleep an hour ago.'

'Today is different, Mother, you know that.'

Mama was weary and Gran's scowl was too severe to do battle with. With grave obedience, Aster shuffled out of the chair, planted a kiss first on Great Auntie Muriel's powdered cheek, and then on Gran's, which was tilted so far she had to go on tiptoes. She took Mama's hand and crossed the ocean of parquet, crossed the cool stone-paved hallway and began the long climb. Mama smelt of the sea, of fresh air and lily of the valley. Aster wanted to bury her face in the smooth cream skirt that clinched her tiny waist and the blouse that puffed lace over her shoulders and arms.

'Hotch in, that's it.' Mama pulled down the sheet. 'It's too hot for blankets tonight.' Aster thought her mama looked broken. 'Didn't you have a lovely time at the harvest? You and Harry, riding in the back of the wagon. Singing all those songs. Such a lovely time.' Her words were broken and tired. She pulled Aster's bedroom curtains and shut out the balmy dusk, snuffing out the lingering memories of the day.

But Aster clung on to them. She could still feel the sun on her arms, the scratchy straw between her toes. She still sat with Harry and Kate in the back of the wagon, birds still sang in the corners of the fields where she'd gathered the wild flowers and took them to Mama. But Harry was gone. A car had arrived earlier, around teatime, when Mama and Dad were out. The car from the big house took Harry and Kate away.

Her legs twitched with unbearable tiredness, her head thick and drowsy. She could not form the words to ask her mother why her playmates had left. The house was appallingly quiet, the sheet cool and heavy, a scent of the linen cupboard; the candlewick bedspread a wide expanse of dusty pink. She was rocked by a warm wave of rebellious sleep.

'Soon be morning,' soothed her Mama, her face a pale oval in the half-light.

Harry and the harvest and the wagon disappeared.

'But Dad,' Aster barked, rudely, deep in her throat.

'Be patient, darling, he won't be long.'

Aster fought it, wriggled against it, but a thump of dead-weight slumber smothered her.

When she woke, briefly, peering through a crack in a dream, she sensed that night had moved on. It was dark, so very dark, the air cooler in her nostrils. Unbelievably, in the silence, she heard the sea. Waves hissing in over shingle half a mile away, beyond the garden, beyond the woods. Was she dreaming? She strained to listen, wondering how it was she could hear the sea, thinking how it always took an age to get to the cove, down the ferny path, with Grandpa slashing at undergrowth with his stick, Jess racing ahead and Gran dawdling behind with Mama. How well she knew that long sloping path that merged into the dunes, breaking open to the sea. Dad was never with them. He was never there. In the darkness, he wasn't there.

She called out for him. She wanted to stand, to run, to find him. She sat upright in the pitch black and her hand touched a wall where one should not have been. She reached again to the other side. Another wall, hard and impossible, imprisoning her in blank darkness.

'Dad!'

She screamed. The door opened behind her, letting in a triangle of lamplight where she had not expected it to be.

'Oh, what now? You've turned round in bed. You're all of a tussle.' Her dad was close to her, with his fresh tobacco smell and his strong arms hauling her up and plonking her the right way round.

'Are you really going and not coming back?' Aster asked as he pulled the sheet over her shoulders. 'Auntie Muriel said.'

'Hush. Sleep tight. I'm here now.' A kiss on her forehead but she could not see his face. 'Look after Mama for me.'

Her head sank into the cool puff of the pillow. She was cradled by his voice and could fight sleep no longer. He shut the bedroom door behind him.

She woke in cool intangible grey light and heard the strange noise of an engine pulsing on the front lane outside her window. A stranger's greeting. She ran barefoot to pull aside the curtain. With her nose against the pane, she saw a peculiar vehicle parked: dirty green and brown. There was a strange man in uniform with a cap on his head, waiting.

Dad came out of the house through the front door beneath her window. He was wearing his cap and his brown uniform, his awful scratchy brown uniform, and he carried a huge stuffed pack on his shoulder. The stranger drew to attention, saluted Dad and got into the car.

In the strange peeling radiance of daybreak, Aster saw Mama run out after him along the slate front path and through the gate. Dad's pack hit the ground with a thud and he stood facing her, still and stiff, on duty.

Mama was motionless, standing puzzlingly apart from him and staring at him with such intensity that her head quivered.

But Dad looked at the sky, at the slate path, the tall trees, never at her.

Aster heard her mother speak, two urgent words. 'Believe me.'

Her mama took a step forward and reached her hands out as if she was stretching across a fire. She pressed an envelope into Dad's hands, then stepped back, wiping tears from her cheeks.

Dad turned and walked to the car, opened the passenger door and got in. The engine was revved, a slip of tyres on the stony lane. It was gone, leaving her mother, leaving both of them.

Moment followed empty moment. The silence was unbearable as the light increased on another summer day and chased the darkness from under the trees. And yet, her mother stood there, alone and stunned as if she had been planted into the ground.

He'd said in the darkness, *I'm here, now, Aster, I'm here now. Look after Mama for me.*

He did not promise to come back.

Part Three

Aster
Cornwall, 1936

Chapter Twenty-Eight

The memory snared Aster as she kicked her pony on and ducked beneath the branches of the bridleway. Gripping Starbright's wiry mane with iced and trembling fingers, she wondered, as she often did, which part of the night her father left was imagined, made up over the years to become the legend. And which part was the sore, unhappy truth?

The bridleway lured her into dappled sunlight under a ceiling of new leaves. Earth-and-stone walls rose either side to enclose her in a tunnel of green. Ferns sprouted among ancient roots, interspersed with the happy faces of columbine and musk mallow. Aster slumped in her saddle, dazed and swimming through grief. She let the reins hang loose, let Starbright make her own way. The pony's hooves rang on chunks of flint. The rhythm of it seemed to clang in her mind, chiming her loss: first my father, and then my mother, all before I was five.

Instinctively she squeezed her knees to encourage her horse through the giggling ford to the pinewood beyond. She breathed in the green, clean spruce and sat up straight again, forcing her grinding thoughts away. The fleeting scent, the candy sweetness of woodland flowers dissolved the sadness. The familiar surroundings were a balm: straight, naked trunks cushioned by a haze of ferns and punctuated by spikes of extravagant-pink foxglove. Far, far below her, below the absolute silence of the pines, came the trickle of the stream in the crook of the valley. There it went, invisible, on its way to the sea.

Aster lifted her chin to take in the tender air and noticed Starbright falter, prick her ears.

Way along the path, merging with the fabric of the wood, she saw two riders, identically straight-backed and strong-armed. Of course, she allowed herself to smile: Harry Penruth had said that he and his father had recently taken to riding out this way. She pulled Starbright up and waited as Harry kicked on across the soft carpet of pine, followed somewhat hesitantly by his father.

Harry was by her side in moments, their horses greeting each other with snuffles and snorts. He doffed his cap with humorous ceremony, laughter mapping his eyes.

'So we meet again, Miss Fairling. What a glorious spring morning. Aren't we lucky? We have just spotted a kestrel out on the top field, and a kingfisher down by the stream. Everything is coming out at last to greet us. But it's far too good for riding out alone. I say all this glory needs sharing.'

'Sharing it? But I like to be alone,' Aster said, half joking, her humour returning. 'Everyone knows that.'

'In that case, we'll ride on by. We'll keep our own company.'

He gave her an exaggerated shrug, making ready to kick Sparrow on. But his smile told her he understood.

'Good morning, Miss Fairling,' Weston Penruth stopped his horse a polite distance away. He took off his hat and nodded in her direction, but tilted his face from her, his eyes not meeting hers. His profile, rugged and weathered handsomely, was detached, his mouth set in a grim line. Aster had certainly heard of Weston Penruth's surly aloofness. He was well known in the county for it and, as her grandparents inferred, best left to his own devices. But his son, Harry, could not be more different.

After being strangers for many years, since he, and his sister also, disappeared from her life, Aster had recently become reacquainted with Harry. And on the handful of times they'd met, felt a lightness and ease talking with him, a pleasant settling of her spirit.

'You're not going until you've told me all your news, Harry,' she said. 'I have nothing to tell you, of course, and that is quite normal for it is always so quiet over at Old Trellick. But you, you must have something to tell me. How is everything over at Charlecote? How is Kate? Is she enjoying school? Mr Penruth, I heard you had a poorly lamb? What about the red barn roof? Can you see daylight through it yet?'

'All fine, all fine. Kate is fine,' said Weston, his charm forced, distracted by the loud scolding of a blackbird in the pines.

Harry said, 'My little sister will be home soon for Easter. There is nothing else to report, to someone who shuns our company, who shuts herself away. It has to be a fair exchange. You told me it was your birthday the other week.

We were expecting a little tea party, if nothing else. And until you have something exciting to tell me, then I will also stay quiet and mysterious.'

With that, he reached out and patted Starbright's grey neck.

'Doing well, aren't you, old girl?' he told the horse.

Aster watched Harry's peaceful face as he concentrated on rubbing her horse's neck. She observed the fine cloth of his jacket and admired the fine cut of his fair hair glimpsed under his cap. She relented, giving into his passive charm. It was hard for her to believe that he and his little sister Kate had lived at Old Trellick for nearly a year when they had all been very young. This had been, her gran had told her, because Mr Penruth could not cope when his wife died. But after they were taken back home, so abruptly to Charlecote, all ties were severed.

The family homes were mere country miles apart, along the valley and through the pinewoods, and yet their lives had travelled in completely separate orbits. Only last year, when Harry came down from Cambridge, she met him on this very bridleway, for the first time as grown-ups. And yet, Aster thought, it was as if no time or distance had ever come between them.

'All right, then, how about this,' she laughed. 'I warn you, it's not exactly groundbreaking. Gran dug out an old recipe for saffron buns, my mother's favourite, apparently. She told me my mother would make them once a month as a treat, when there was saffron to be had. Gran was putting a batch in the oven as I rode out this morning.'

Harry sat upright, gathered his reins, adjusted his seat. 'Buns? Saffron buns? You'll have to do better than that, Aster Fairling.'

'Come to tea, and try them for yourself. Call it a belated birthday celebration. And you, Mr Penruth,' she added shyly, 'of course.'

'Oh no, oh no, no.' Weston looked startled. 'And I'd rather you came back with me, Harry. We need to sort out that paperwork.'

'Surely, Father, that can wait one afternoon.'

Weston's brows lowered like a sullen storm, his eyes staring at his hands resting on the saddle. Aster and Harry waited in uncomfortable silence for the man to speak.

'If you must,' he muttered. 'I'll see you at home.'

'As you like, Father,' Harry said, as Weston abruptly turned his horse away.

They rode their mounts in companionable silence back the way Aster had come. Side by side, they eventually exited the green half-light tunnel of the bridleway and followed the track that skirted the side of the hill. Exhilarating folds of wooded valley lay before them, and beyond the hills, where the sea was hiding, the sky widened in a watery arch. Emerging from a dip in the quilt of fields and copses stood the granite stone of Old Trellick, Aster's home. The house was squat and topped with a lichened slate roof, centuries old and recorded in the Domesday Book. Her home, the woods, the sea: her security, the constants in her life, Aster thought, and glanced at Harry.

'Do you remember much of living with us at Old Trellick?' she asked. 'Memories can be so sketchy. I remember my father leaving, and you and Kate were gone too. All so suddenly . . .'

Her words were snatched by a sudden hard wind that came down the valley, lifted the horses' manes, tugged at Aster's hat, churned the trees.

'Christ, where has that come from?' Harry said, pulling back on Sparrow's rein. 'I think it's such a shame we lost touch. I've asked Father about it, but he won't be drawn. Like he is with so many things,' he glanced at Aster. 'But I'm mighty glad I was riding out this way last year . . .'

'You know,' said Aster, bashful. 'I don't think I've ever seen your father without his horse.'

'He hates walking anywhere. His leg gives him trouble. It was injured during the war. It gets worse in the winter, and these days he would rather ride. Takes the pressure off.'

'He always seems so preoccupied,' she ventured.

'Oh, that's normal. "Cantankerous" is the word.'

'Well then, that's perfect, isn't it?' Aster mused. 'Everything is normal, and thank goodness for that. What quiet, peaceful lives we do lead.'

In Harry's new and delightful company her dark, unsettling memory vanished, blown away by the breeze. As she kicked Starbright on and rode home to Old Trellick through the freshening wind, she could hear Sparrow's hooves ringing out over the pathway behind her and Harry laughing, catching her up.

Chapter Twenty-Nine

'Look who I've brought home for tea,' announced Aster breezily as she walked into the drawing room.

Gran got up from her armchair but instead of walking over to greet Harry, she went to the French windows to open them, pulling back the drawing-room curtains as far as they would go.

'Thought it was just about to storm, with that fret just then off the sea. But it's settled again. Smell that air. How lovely.' She seemed flustered, fussing with the way the curtains hung, glancing constantly at Harry. 'First time this year we've had these open. Well, good afternoon, Mr Penruth. I must say. What a surprise . . . I'll put the kettle on. We have saffron buns, you know.'

'It's all right, Gran,' said Aster, wondering briefly why her grandmother was bothering with the French windows. 'I've filled Harry in on your morning of baking.'

Aster watched her grandmother, noting her still firm frame and well-cut shoulders. Her once grey hair was now as white as moonlight. There was an unprecedented scattering of dust in her hair. Aster thought she really shouldn't say, but did she not realise that she had a cobweb in her hair?

'I shall pretend I did know.' May Prideaux forced out a laugh and patted at her parting with a handkerchief, her eyes blazing in embarrassment. 'Is it gone now? Good. Apart from baking, we were both up in the garret this morning having a clear-out. Having a good old rummage. Place is sixes and sevens now. Perhaps that's what wore Grandpa out.'

Aster thought of the rather romantic name her grandparents gave the shambles of a room upstairs under the eaves packed with all manner of junk squirrelled away in the belief that one day they'd need it again.

'Where is he?' she asked.

'Having his constitutional nap. Though he should stir when he hears the kettle whistle.'

Harry asked after Doctor Prideaux.

'Always under my feet now he has retired,' said Gran, throwing a look at Harry that bristled with hostility, as if she wished he'd not spoken at all and would kindly go away. 'He's always finding things to tidy and fix up.'

Harry politely observed that it does everyone good to have a clear-out and Aster felt grateful to him, for he was steadfastly ignoring her grandmother's rudeness.

'Shall we have that tea, Gran?' she asked pointedly.

Her grandmother left the room and came back with a tray of tea and the fabled saffron buns. With it, her mood had lightened. Either that, or she was making a monumental effort to be civil, Aster decided.

'Ah, now listen,' Gran said on a more pleasant vein. 'This is what they call a coincidence. I found this old photograph up there this morning.' She put her hand in the pocket of her cardigan. 'It says "Harvest, 1918" on the back. But that's not my handwriting or Grandpa's. Never seen this before, but isn't that the top field over at Charlecote, Mr Penruth?'

Aster peered at the photograph: three little children – a girl in a smock, a boy in a tunic and short trousers and a smaller baby girl in a bonnet squashed between – sat on the back of an old-fashioned farm wagon. The older two were the same size, the same age, and both tilting their heads to the side as the shutter clicked.

'Look at that,' Aster said. 'Oh, look how I'm squinting in the sun.'

'It was a blazing hot summer, as I remember,' said Gran. 'Last year of the war. A good harvest, if I remember, over at Charlecote . . . Oh, but of course—' She stopped speaking and stared hard at the handwriting on the back of the photograph, her eyes roaming along memories she appeared not to relish.

Harry took the photograph. 'Well I never. Yes, I think I remember the harvest, how scratchy the straw was on my feet, the smell of it filling the air. Or perhaps I am remembering later years. Sometimes I can't distinguish the occasion of one memory from another.'

Aster said, 'Looks like you were in breeches by then. So we were how old?' He handed her the photograph and she turned it over to check the date once more. 'Can't have been more than four. And Kate must have been a year or so younger. Oh, look at her!'

The moment returned: the image blinded her, like the

burning, sinking sun out in the wheatfields of Weston Penruth's farm. Her dad laughing, sitting with her at the back of the wagon, his trousers rolled up, blue braces against a baggy white shirt. He was a handsome man, with a roll-up in the corner of his mouth. His fair hair, straight and thick, in a floppy arc over his forehead.

She stared into the photograph until Harry took it from her. 'Who's that standing in the background?' he asked. 'Is that your parents, Aster?'

'I hadn't noticed *that*,' Gran snatched the photograph from Harry and slipped on her spectacles. She peered closely, tilting her chin. 'Well, I'll be blowed.'

Aster glanced fearfully at her grandmother, expecting to see her in distress. Instead she looked annoyed, her face cold and secretive.

Harry politely took the picture from Gran and handed it back to Aster. In the blurred, unfocused, spectral background of the photograph behind the wagon where she sat with Harry and Kate, there indeed was a young woman in a loose linen dress, her face half-shielded by a huge sun bonnet, looking away from whoever was holding the camera and up into the face of her husband beside her. Violet her mother, and her father Jack, caught unknowingly in a moment one summer afternoon. Aster stared as shock and sadness collided inside her.

'I had no idea we had this photograph. I've never seen them . . . together,' she said.

Gran pressed a china plate with a saffron bun on it into Harry's hands, saying brightly, 'You'll want a dab of butter, young man, no doubt.'

Aster saw Harry glance at her, his features pulsing with

anxiety as he concentrated on holding the delicate plate in the centre of his palm. He drank his tea and then began to laboriously slice the bun in half and slaver it with butter. Aster sank back, mute and bewildered.

After far too long, Gran breezed, 'Well, Mr Penruth, and how is your family?'

'Much the same – very well, in fact. My sister Kate is due home from boarding school.'

Rousing herself to pick up her cup and saucer, Aster thought of how her grandfather had explained why her dad was no longer there. She was a child, sitting on his knee, when he told her: *Telegram from his commanding officer at Plugstreet, missing in action presumed killed, last month of the war, terrible, terrible shame.* She thought of the wastelands, the battlegrounds, the notorious mud. Flickering brown footage in documentaries at the cinema as the regiments go jerkily over the top, stumbling into oblivion. Slaughter on an imperial scale. Sitting there, taking tea, Aster remembered how the war lived on all around her, even now, twenty years later. It continued with the men that she saw in the towns and villages: the wheelchairs, the wooden legs, the burnt faces, the sightless eyes and empty sleeves pinned by a medal. The degradation of her father's generation was compounded by the ranks of unmarried women who had lost sweethearts, or who would never find them.

And what about Mama? was always her next, trembling question. And Grandpa would say, 'You know, young lady, we have told you before. She died in London when you were a very little girl.'

She was an orphan, her parents both gone before she was

able to form any reasoning as to how and why. And now, having just turned twenty-one, she was still nowhere near any understanding. She glanced tearfully across the tea tray in question at Gran, whose sharp dark eyes and the minute shake of her head were a caution to be quiet, for they had company.

'Ah, now I *do* have some news,' Harry said, making Aster jump.

'Goodness,' she said, laughing rather too abundantly. 'You are a rotten tease.'

His cheeks flushed as he drew himself up in his chair, squaring his shoulders. 'I have bought a new motor car.'

'So, you will be tearing up half the countryside, then?' Gran asked, stiff-faced.

'Well, if I do, it will be with Aster by my side in the passenger seat.'

'Well if you do, it will be you on your own,' she retorted, but gave him an encouraging smile, hoping he had not seen her wet eyes. 'What is it? I mean what type of motor car? Is it very big? You must show Grandpa. Take him for a spin.'

'Oh, don't encourage him,' Gran said, the tension in her cheeks at last sliding into some sort of smile. 'His motoring days are over. That old wagonette he had before the war is now crumbling away in the barn making a fine home for the mice.'

Presently, Aster saw Harry to the door, and handed him his crop and cap.

'Are you quite well?' he asked her, his hand firmly on her arm. 'It was a shock to see that photograph, wasn't it?'

She nodded, inhaling rogue tears, and giving him her best, bright smile. 'You in your breeches.'

Harry tightened his grip on her arm, his fingers moving over her sleeve. His face was open, his eyes wide.

'Talk to me, if you like, any time. You know where I am.'

Aster fought the strange urge to touch his collar. She said, 'And the saffron buns? Were they as good as any you'd find in Cornwall? What shall you be telling your father? Marks out of ten?'

'You know what he's like. He only cares about things with four legs.'

'You mean tables and chairs?' She made him laugh.

'Your tea treats, Aster Fairling, will not even register.'

Chapter Thirty

She woke to the chattering of fighting robins in the rose bush under her window. The sunlight was clear and pure, finding its way around her curtains. Her first thought was of Harry and their trip to Bodmin Moor. She would sketch, she decided, and they would take a picnic. How wonderful to be up there, in all this fine spring weather. She was smiling to herself, sitting up in bed, as Gran came in with a morning tray.

'Ah, so you are awake. Thought I'd treat you to breakfast in bed. This arrived this morning for you.' She set the tray over Aster's lap. Propped behind the teapot was a letter. 'Now I must get back upstairs. We're tackling the garret again today. If you feel inclined, perhaps you'll give us a hand.'

'Have you forgotten Harry is coming by? We're going for a drive.'

'Ah yes.'

Gran walked to the window and drew the curtains. Her straight back, turned towards Aster, was tense and forbidding.

'Mr Penruth is a super fellow,' she said, fingering a loose thread on the edge of the curtain.

'He is.' Aster tipped a splash of milk into her teacup.

Gran turned. With the light behind her, her face was a shadow, her expression indiscernible. 'He is rather keen on you.'

'Really!' Aster found herself laughing. 'We do get on very well. Even though we only met up again about a year ago, it's as if we've always known each other. And, of course, he and Kate lived here that time when we were all very young, but we both don't remember much about it . . . how funny.'

Gran began to fold a cardigan that Aster had left on the chair. 'Was wondering if he's too keen, and that perhaps he should not be so.'

Aster frowned. 'How do you mean?'

'I think – Grandpa and I think – you should set your sights a little further afield, my dear. Cast your net wider.'

Her words were absurd.

'We're not *courting*, if that's what you mean.'

'You say you're good friends.'

Aster assured her that, indeed, they were friends.

'Perhaps that's how it should stay, then.'

Gran left the room, leaving Aster to pour her tea and butter her toast. Baffled, she shook her head and licked crumbs off her fingertips. The birds outside the window were setting up a racket, distracting her as she sipped her tea, musing on what to wear since the weather was so fine. Ah yes, she had some post. She picked up the envelope. It was expensive heavy-grade paper, postmarked London. With a start, she noticed that it was addressed to *Miss Elizabeth Fairling*. No one called her this. When she was born, there had been a great turmoil. She had been a very tiny baby. Her mother had been quite unwell. Her grandparents, they told her, suggested a traditional name for a swift christening and Elizabeth was chosen in haste. But she had always been Aster because, apparently, her mother had loved the flower. She hadn't a paperknife so she wiped her butter knife on her napkin and deftly slit the envelope.

The solicitor's heading, address in Cavendish Square, W1, confirmed that it was as suspected, a rather official letter. Why on earth would a London solicitor be writing to her? She read, quickly, the succinct and formal contents and then cried out, covering her mouth with her hand. Prickling ice formed a cap over her scalp, tighter and tighter. She tried and failed to rationalise the words that rushed through her mind. And she read the letter again, her eyes growing wide in horror, cold nausea raking her guts.

From upstairs in the second floor garret, Gran's footsteps resounded across the ceiling. Aster sensed the sick memory returning: the summer evening long ago when she watched Great Aunt Muriel lay out the Tarot cards, her uneasy proclamation. The Final Outcome, according to the cards. The memories collided – could it all have *really* happened on just one day? The harvest, Harry and the wagon, the snapped photograph, the short night before her dad left to go back to the war. Her queasy sleepiness and her seasickness of confusion in the darkness, the voice of the far away waves rocking gently. Her calling for her father and the grasping out in the pitch-black room. Her hands pressed against the blank imprisoning wall.

She pressed her palms to her face. Her fingers were cold and damp. She pushed the tray aside, heedless of spilling her tea, her legs shaking. The letter was crushed in her sweating hand. Her flesh trembled as the shock of the news kicked her, and kicked her again.

'They have got it wrong, utterly wrong,' she spluttered, fumbling for her dressing gown. 'How dare they *do* this to me? I will sue. I will find out who they are and sue. How *could* they? How could they lie to me and say that my dad is alive?'

Aster stood barefoot at the threshold of the garret and pushed the door ajar. A trestle table that should have long been firewood had been moved out from the corner and a battered, stained cardboard box stood on it, spewing old jigsaws, a threadbare quilt and a stringless tennis racket. Stacks of crumbling books, their backs broken, were ready for the bonfire. Tarnished candlesticks, thick with wax, a jar of broken nibs, and Aster's old doll's house had been assigned to a corner. Balls of dust collated and spun across the floor.

Aster watched her grandparents. They were unaware of her, so engrossed in the dusting, filing, putting away of things. Grandpa had lit a cigar and forgotten about it and it lay on its ashtray with a stream of blue smoke rising to the low, sloping ceiling. Gran was tickling a framed picture with a feather duster, pronouncing how much she loved it, and why wasn't it on the wall downstairs? 'That's only fit for the scullery,' said Grandpa, glancing at it with distaste.

All this chattering, this industry excluded Aster, made her unwelcome. Suddenly she did not know these people.

'Ah, there you are. Good morning.' Grandpa glanced at her. 'Still in your dressing gown, I see. Never mind, roll up your sleeves and get stuck in. Rag-and-bone man will have a field day with this lot.' He stooped to lug a drawer open. Whatever was inside it made him swear under his breath.

'Oh Aster, I'd rather you got dressed first,' her grandmother told her, barely glancing up.

'Do you know that my father is still alive?' Aster raised her voice amid the clattering. 'Do either of you know? Of course you do. How silly of me. You *must* know.'

As she spoke they turned startled faces towards her. In the taut silence, the noise of their flurrying exclamations and denial rose suddenly like dust from the floor.

'What have you there?' asked Grandpa, straightening up, his face unyielding.

'It's just a letter,' said Aster, waving it frivolously. 'From a Messrs Baldwin and Son of Cavendish Square.' She tried hard to restrain the anger boiling in her head. 'It appears that on the occasion of my twenty-first birthday just past, I am to be bequeathed a series of paintings by Mr Jack Fairling. Works that he has accomplished over the past twenty or so years and that are being exhibited in London at the . . . let's see, the Portland Gallery.'

'What on earth . . . ?' uttered Gran, taking hurried steps towards Aster.

'Oh yes, astonishing, isn't it, the way that he has been able to produce, let's see, fifty-odd paintings, when he died years ago in the trenches. But he did not die, according to these people. Except you, you and Grandpa, told me he did.'

'Missing,' interjected Grandpa. 'Missing in action.'

Aster regarded him with distaste. She spoke with a clarity that chilled her blood. 'According to Messrs Baldwin and Son, he is alive and well and living in Camden, and looking forward to the retrospective of his life's work. But why didn't I know? This isn't what I . . . who I . . . how any of this can be . . .'

Grandpa had her by the elbow and propelled her to the old chair in the corner. 'Sit, sit. That's it.'

'But what *is* this?' Aster's legs were straw. The letter dropped from her hand, fell to the floor. Her tongue stiffened, she could not speak.

'Brandy,' she heard Gran say. 'I will fetch the brandy.'

'Well, I'll be blowed,' said Grandpa, picking up the letter. He read it through, then turned it over as if more clues would appear on its blank reverse.

Aster looked up at his silence in horror, staring through chaos. She clung to his arm, in the hope that he would say something to save her, something to right this, set her world back on its axis.

He simply tutted, shaking his head as if he had come across a bad case of hives.

'Jack Fairling should have warned us about this,' said Gran, returning with the brandy. 'He should have told us there'd be a letter.'

Grandpa glanced at his wife in fury and Aster saw remorse flicker over her face.

'Warned you?' Aster fired back as the crystal tumbler grazed her teeth. She drank on the fiery alcohol, her body reacting to it with a twitchy spasm. 'Why should you or any of us be *warned*? I should have *known*.' Her voice was yelping now. 'I don't understand. I just don't understand why you would keep this from me.'

Grandpa knelt by the chair, his knees cracking like gunfire. He took her hands. 'To all intents and purposes, dear Aster, Jack Fairling was dead to us.'

Aster took the letter from him and glanced again at its cold formality. She latched on to Grandpa's *to all intents and purposes*. Meaningless words, they spun, rocking her insides with nausea. She pressed her icy fingertips to her brow, screwing up her eyes. 'But he was my dad,' she whispered desperately. 'And he is *alive*?'

'I think we may have handled this entirely the wrong way,' Gran said, blandly. 'When your mother died, that was the end of it for us. We blamed him for her death. The telegram, which we showed you, said he was missing, remember, missing. We didn't actually lie. After all, how many of them ever come back?'

Aster stared at her with an astonishing spasm of anger. 'But I would have tried to find him.' She set the brandy glass down and wiped at her mouth with the back of her hand. 'And why did he not contact me? Why did he not come home and find me? Why has he ignored me all this time?' Her face was cold with tears.

'Looks like he has just written his will,' said Grandpa. 'Handed the possession of his paintings to you. It sounds like a very generous gesture. Don't you agree, May? An olive branch?'

'I don't need an olive branch.' Aster let out a hard laugh, 'I just needed my dad.'

Chapter Thirty-One

Harry parked the brand-new little blue Morris on the gravel and parped the horn. Aster buttoned her jacket in front of the hall mirror. Grandpa told her again how sorry they were. Then Gran reminded her, rolling her hands together, that they thought they were doing the right thing. That all they were thinking of was her.

'Fact is,' said Gran, bristling in defence, 'If your mother hadn't gone to London that day—'

'It's all so terribly complicated . . .' Grandpa said, stepping forward. 'So much you will never understand.'

'Please don't talk to me,' Aster snapped. 'Because everything you say to me sounds like a lie.'

She set her little hat with the perky brim firmly on her head and gave her grandparents a devastated look. She slammed the front door behind her and hurried out to the car.

'Oh, steady, there's no rush. We have all day,' Harry said as she slammed the passenger door. 'Oh, whatever's the matter?'

'Just drive. Please,' she said. She could not look at him.

In astonished silence he drove, trundling along the tight lanes between high hedges from where little birds darted out quite recklessly. Every now and then Aster caught glimpses of sublime views through farm gates, suddenly a portion of blue water. All of this was her home and her life. Had been her home, her life. The new leather interior of the Morris was scented and cushiony but she was pinned and trapped. She wound down the window, breathing a sudden balmy whiff of the sea.

'Stop the car! Stop!'

Harry slammed on the brakes, jolting them forward. Aster opened the door and fled. She raced along the lane and ducked down the steep footpath that led to the cove, her mouth open, a sob clotting her throat. Her grandparents' voices rattled in her head: *We blamed him. If she hadn't gone to London that day.*

She made it to the sand, stumbling over its shifting folds and sat, numb, her insides stretched with loneliness. The sea was moving, rocking, as familiar as an old trusted friend. Her mother used to come here with Harry's mother. They had been great friends once, so long ago, so the Flower Book told her. A glacial cloak of disbelief folded round her as seagulls called and wheeled over flickering currents of air.

Harry found her. He sat by her side, out of breath and red in the face.

'I have had some shocking news,' she stated, faltering on her words.

And, after a while, she told him about the letter. He did not speak. His profile, Aster noticed, was rigid with distress. He reached across and held her hand. Tears stung her eyes. She glanced sideways at him and saw the depth of concern. He was trying to smile at her but it was not enough to comfort her.

Presently, he drew out his large handkerchief and handed it to her. She dabbed the tears that coursed silently down her cheeks.

'Such a filthy huge shock,' he said at last. 'But we will dig out the truth one way or another. I will do whatever you want me to. I will talk to you, or I will shut up. I will stay by your side. I will go away, if you like.'

She looked at him and his kindness swamped her. She could give him no response. There was a steel rod through her core.

'You know, Aster,' Harry went on, 'there is no need for me to get to know you again. Somewhere, deep down, you're part of me. There's something about that time we had together as children, a shared memory . . . yes, we grew up apart. I blame boarding schools, university. I haven't been here. But now I'm back . . .'

He moved closer, put his arm around her shoulder. The warmth of his body shielded her from the fresh sea air but, inside, she wriggled with discomfort.

'You're so very nice to me,' she said. 'But you must understand how I . . . Until this morning, I thought I was an orphan. Now, I don't know who I am.'

'You are Aster to me.' He turned her so that she would look at him. His face, firm and determined, was bright in the sunlight. 'You'll always be—'

She stopped him with a hard look. 'We're friends only, Harry. Please don't say anything else.'

The afternoon was fading into evening when he dropped her back at Old Trellick. Aster walked into an empty house. A note on the telephone table in the hallway told her that her grandparents had had to attend a long-standing arrangement, a bridge party at Looe town hall. They hoped they'd not be too late. They hoped she'd had a nice day with Harry.

They had left a lamp burning for her in the drawing room and a plate of sandwiches covered up in the larder.

Aster sat in the kitchen to eat. Until now shock had delayed her hunger, made her nauseous, but now she was ravenous. She chewed, barely tasting her food, then put the kettle on the range to make a pot of tea.

While it was brewing she went into the library. She slid the book carefully from its tight resting place on the shelf furthest from the door. She returned to the kitchen, cradling it. She treasured it, almost couldn't bear to touch it. It was small, but thick with pages; the spine a little cracked, and the corners a little worn. The dark-green of the leather cover reminded Aster of the most secret corners of the pine wood. Inside the front flyleaf, her mother had written: *Violet Prideaux, aged 10, her book*. A pressed violet – perhaps the first she'd ever gathered – its purple colour faded, transparent, was her mother's emblem pasted down proudly next to her name. In a sentence below it, underlined for emphasis, young Violet had warned: *So long as the leaves are not picked or too much trampled*.

Aster closed her eyes and imagined her mother: thick auburn hair in Victorian ringlets, dressed in bloomers and buckles, studiously recording the flowers she had gathered – violets, and heather and lady's smock and periwinkles – along with her thoughts and her dreams. The Flower Book was the only real way Aster could know her mother.

As the kettle sang merrily on the hob, Aster turned the pages. Her mother's handwriting was looped and faded, precisely documenting the flowers of the wayside as and when she found them. Her handwriting improved as the years slid by, as page after page was turned. Aster took her time to browse the familiar pages, feeling their solace like a balm seeping into her blood. There was an abundance of wild flowers preserved here: round-faced daisies, cow parsley's fairy-like fronds, the innocent blue of the forget-me-not, and the yellow marigold. The pages were crinkled, stiffened and aged. Violet's legacy lay here, all of her passion and wisdom, Aster thought, passed down in silence. Sitting at the kitchen table, her head bowed into her hands, she shook with longing.

'I really never knew you,' she whispered, her voice edged with wonder at the amount of pain she felt, 'but you left me your legacy. Here in your book, the buds and blooms you collected ever since you were a little girl speak to me now. Our very own language of flowers.'

Dazed and exhausted, Aster fingered the edge of one torn-out page that must have once been ragged but was now worn smooth by years of handling. It was in the section towards the end of the book. Aster often wondered what had been written on the vanished page, what flower had been mounted there. Or had it simply been torn out to make a shopping list?

Aster alighted on a familiar snippet: *Sea Holly*, her mother had written, and under it a delicate specimen, plucked from a crook in the dunes, rather dried out and rather bent. *A day on the beach with Jack and Aster. We took a picnic. Claudia was there, expecting her second, and Aster met Harry. She found some seaweed and we brought it home for pressing, but sadly lost*, she'd written. *Jack has to go back to France soon. May, 1916.*

Dad must have been on leave then and I was just over a year

old, Aster pondered and then whispered, suddenly, 'Oh Mother, why did you go up to London on *that* day? Why not another day, any other day? You'd be here now. We'd all be here now.'

Her craving for lucidity became physical. She could not sit still. She shut the Flower Book, returned it safely to its shelf and went upstairs, taking the lamp with her. Grandpa had not yet put electricity into the upper floors of Old Trellick and so shadows danced behind her, gliding above her on the gloomy staircase. She took the second set of stairs and opened the door to the garret, noticing that it was rather tidier than it had been that morning.

Aster set the lamp down on the trestle table. The cool dusk was settling outside and deep shadows sank into the corners of the room. She turned to the cupboard in the slender alcove by the fireplace. Years before Grandpa had asked her if she wanted to keep her father's portfolio, but her young mind had not quite understood. She had never linked the man, her dad, who resided only in her memory, to the drawings and paintings in this dusty attic. She hoped with everything she could muster that her grandparents had not taken it upon themselves to throw it out, either today, or any day in the years that stretched back into the past.

Her relief was visceral as she laid her fingertips on it. It was still there, right at the back, its cardboard cover stained, the corners crumpled from the confined space where it had lain alongside a pair of cracked riding boots and a mildewed eiderdown. She pulled the portfolio out amid a puff of musty dust that covered it. His name was written at the corner: Jack P. Fairling. She carried it over to the trestle table and spread it open in the lamplight. Night birds were beginning to call outside in the garden and she breathed, then, in a short flare

312

of memory, on the odour of his cigarette. There were a dozen loose pages of cartridge paper inside. Sketches, pastels and one or two oils. That was all. *His life's work*, Grandpa had told her, when he'd shown her it many years before.

How wrong he was.

She shook her head, shaking until there was no more space for rage inside her skull.

She turned over the first painting, on paper stiff, textured and curling, and that had long ago lost its frame, and drew breath. It was an oil painting of her mother. Gazing hard at the soft daubs of muted colour, fluid and intense and still so alive, Aster pulled out of her memory the time she first saw this picture. Grandpa had shown it to her and, at thirteen years old, she had been detached, cross and embarrassed. Probably longing to flee. But now she took her time, looked on it with more mature eyes.

Her father had captured her mother fleetingly, a stranger in Regent's Park. It was his first glimpse of her, on that long-past day, apparently, and the start of everything that was to follow. In the corner was his signature and the title. He'd called it *Violet in the Daytime*.

In the painting, Violet is moving through the park under the dappled silvery shadow of willow trees; star-like daisies bright at her feet. Her face is half in profile, the line of her cheek exquisite. Her parasol is the colour of luminous water, protecting her, keeping her separated in her own world. Her eyes, even in shadow, are lucid sea green. As she walks, she isn't aware of the artist as he sees her; just of the light that comes from below her, reflected from his direction, to illuminate her and set her apart. She lifts her pale hand quickly to shield her eyes.

Chapter Thirty-Two

In her bedroom at Old Trellick, Aster's small suitcase sat on the bed stuffed with two or three blouses, a skirt and a handful of knickers. She stood by the window for a rare spell of calm, wondering what she might have forgotten, what she might desperately need for London, which at the moment had completely slipped her mind. Keeping an ear cocked for Harry's car, she pulled out the latest letter from the solicitor which had arrived the day before. It was a short note this time, attached to an invitation on which some beautifully scrolled wording said simply: *Jack Fairling: A Retrospective, The Portland Gallery, W1.* A neat parameter of dates declared that her father's paintings would be on display for two months only.

She placed it on top of her sponge bag, alongside the old photograph of the harvest wrapped carefully in her silk petticoat. She'd found a spare frame for it in a drawer somewhere and it had fitted surprisingly well. The photograph needed its protection for it had been neglected for years, stuffed in a drawer up in the garret and hidden away for such a long time, she thought with a shudder, just like the truth in this damn house.

'Ah, nearly forgot you,' she muttered and plucked a bottle-green cloche and matching leather gloves from the drawer. Going to her father's exhibition, with the possibility of actually coming face to face with him, Aster required the boost that these rather glamorous accessories provided. After all, it was as if she was visiting the dead, and for that, she thought with misery, she needed her best hat and gloves. And, of course, Harry. She slipped the Flower Book into the safe nest of her bundled stockings and snapped the case shut.

As she walked downstairs she heard her grandparents stir in the drawing room, a folding of newspapers, a drawing of breath. The air was still clogged and static with yesterday's wretched attempts at persuasion. Aster popped her head round the door and her gran threw her a particularly bitter look.

Ignoring her, Aster said brightly, 'Just saying goodbye, now.'

Grandpa cleared his throat. 'And how long do you think you'll be away?'

Aster answered in all honesty, 'I have no idea.'

He began, 'Look, if we could have handled this better—'

Gran interrupted, 'It's like she's eloping with him!'

'If you say so,' Aster muttered and went out to the hall to put on her coat.

Since the first letter had arrived, propped so innocuously on her breakfast tray, Aster's world had crumbled and her compass had ceased to work. And Harry had endeavoured to set it right. He'd arranged everything without her having to ask – the train tickets, the hotel suites, one each of

315

course – and she had relished telling her grandparents his involvement during one particularly fraught exchange.

But eloping? She allowed herself a smile as she buttoned her coat and heard the little Morris pulling up outside. She had far more important things on her mind.

As she opened the front door, the glory of the June morning embraced her. The garden was dripping with honeysuckle and tangled with jasmine, and butterflies bounced through the air. A breeze from the hills brought to her the perfume of clover fields and grass meadows. Catching her breath, she quickly stepped along the path, waving at Harry waiting earnestly behind the wheel of the car, then glanced back at the house as it sat there as benignly as ever, the granite soft in the new sunshine.

Her grandparents hurried out to the hallway. Grandpa called out doggedly that she must keep in touch, that she must telephone if necessary, if there was anything she needed.

Gran was standing beside him, her face grey and bewildered, her anger fading. She raised a hand and uttered, 'Aster, I—'

'I have to get away from here,' Aster called back. 'I have to do this. I hope you understand.'

Gran shook her head, her mouth compressed on whatever it was she wanted to say.

Aster turned so that they would not see the tears in her eyes. As she brushed past Grandpa's prized lavender cushioning the gate, the pure scent of it made her want to reach down and pluck a handful to take with her. With a crushing feeling of fatality, she realised she had no idea which season would see her return.

She woke next morning in a boudoir of gilded elegance, still tired and with her inside fragile with uncertainty. The strange and opulent trappings of the Langham Hotel made the feeling worse and she turned to the night stand where, last night, she had set her mother's Flower Book and next to it the framed photograph. Gazing at them in the half-light of the shuttered room, she searched for comfort, wishing she could turn a corner in her mind and suddenly feel no longer lost.

Opening the shutters, Aster gazed at the view down the fine straight avenue of Portland Place. All was busy and unfamiliar, and in that way, strangely reassuring. The cars and buses and hurrying folk in their smart working clothes distracted her for some moments while she waited for the deep bath to fill in her adjoining bathroom.

On the dot of eight-thirty, as arranged, came a knock on the door and in walked a waiter wheeling a trolley stacked with breakfast. Once he'd left, Aster unlocked the connecting door and shouted through to Harry. He had suggested they'd need a good spread before heading off to the Portland Gallery and, by golly, they were going to have one.

'How are you this morning?' he asked, settling down at the table in Aster's suite.

She confessed that she did not really know.

It didn't fail to strike her how bizarre this whole set up was – she and Harry Penruth staying in adjoining rooms within all the finery and elegance of the Langham Hotel. But the ritual of shaking out napkins and stirring the teapot and the lifting of silvered domes to marvel at what cooked delights lay underneath became a welcome formality in which they both knew how to behave.

'What have we here?' Harry asked conversationally. 'Ah, the menu says it's Cornish butter. It'll remind us of home.'

'I don't want to be reminded,' said Aster, her words sounding braver than she felt.

'I suppose all this doesn't help,' said Harry, looking around the sumptuous room. 'Your grandparents must think you've run off with me.'

Aster glanced at him, noticing he looked hopeful.

She took a deep breath. 'I'm twenty-one years old, Harry, and it's 1936. Lots of girls come up to London to be secretaries and live in flats with other girls. Yes, it feels like I've left home, so maybe that's what I'll do – earn my keep, find my own way . . .' She trailed off, wondering if that was the answer: to leave Old Trellick once and for all. She almost laughed and blurted, 'Gran did warn me off you, you know.'

Harry looked up from his fried bacon and begged her pardon.

'Just something she said,' Aster faltered, immediately regretting speaking of it.

'I noticed she was giving me rather sharp looks when I dropped in for tea the other week, but that was before you received the letter,' he said. 'I think she's cross with me because I am on your side.'

She glanced up, suddenly cherishing him.

'Don't you think it's strange,' she mused, stirring her tea with a pleasing absence of mind, 'that you and Kate came to stay at Old Trellick when we were very young? And then we disappeared out of each other's lives.'

'I can barely remember it, do you?'

'Just a vague picture in my head of a little boy to play with and a baby sleeping down the landing, crying in the night. And of course, the harvest. That seems to sit like a bright light amongst it all. You only stayed for a year, and for children, that is an eternity. And yet . . . it seems as quickly as I would have got used to having you around, part of the furniture, you were gone again.'

'We left soon after the harvest, so my father tells me,' said Harry.

Aster glanced over at the photograph on her night stand. Yes, there they were, she and Harry, two plump children perched on the wagon, their heads tilting the same way as the shutter was closed, with little Kate between them. But it was the shadowy background that drew her in, made her scrutinise.

'Do you know, when I look at them,' she said, indicating her parents caught unawares as the picture was taken, 'far from relishing an idyllic moment in the sunshine during a brief lull in the war, it looks as though they're having a first-class argument.'

And then she was back at Old Trellick, waking in her pitch-black bedroom with her father coming to find her, to rescue her from her strange nightmare prison.

Aster put her cup down, her hand trembling. The last time she'd ever seen him had been in the strange thin dawn that followed. And now, today, tomorrow, as her new future unravelled in London, she would possibly see him again.

'I still can't understand why we were strangers all these years,' she said, forcing herself to smile at Harry's keen and compassionate face. 'Up until that day we met on the bridleway – what is it, a year ago now? And to think all that time you only lived the other side of the woods. If our families had been friends then, what on earth happened?'

'You can't blame your grandparents for everything,' said Harry, reasonably. 'I expect it was also my father's doing. He has always been a recluse. I think he lost his mind when my mother died. He carted us up to Scotland then, but I was too young to remember that at all. Kate has been no comfort to him – she is too much like our mother, that's her curse – and I'm no use.' Harry looked away from her, his face rigid. He

319

took a breath, 'We have a lot in common, you and I. We both lost our mothers when we were very young. And the awful thing is that I cannot remember her. I've tried, God knows.'

Aster got up from the table and walked over to fetch the Flower Book. She handed it to Harry.

'Your mother's in here, have a look. Turn to March 1914, "the gorse that tore Claudia's dress", and then to two years later – May 1916 – when my father found the sea holly and I found the seaweed. Our mothers became friends again that day right there on the beach. It's all in there. But I don't understand why they fell out in the first place. There's a gap of two years when she isn't mentioned.'

Aster drew her chair around the table and they sat side by side, leafing through the book together. She glanced sideways and noticed Harry's eyes were watering and his cheeks reddening as he read Violet's snappy and humorous entries and struggled to find Claudia somewhere in his memory. He smiled broadly when his birth was mentioned: *Heard today in the village that Claudia's little boy delivered safely. An August baby, born in the heyday of the year.*

'Of course,' said Harry. 'Our mothers were estranged when I was born.'

Turning back a few pages, they paused at a garish pressed peony, dated March 1914.

'This always bothers me, this one,' said Aster.

Harry wondered why.

'I'm no expert but, really, a peony in spring. It's horrible. Looks like a bloodstain spreading across the page,' she said. 'I read somewhere, that in the language of flowers, "peony" means *shame*. It's horrible, isn't it? It's my least-favourite flower. Seems like it was Mama's too. She obviously wasn't keen on it.'

'How can you tell?'

'She didn't write anything about it.'

'Ah, but here's pressed honeysuckle from her wedding bouquet,' observed Harry, turning some pages.

'Oh, we must find the church,' Aster said. 'It can't be far from here.'

'And what a shame this page has been ripped out.' Harry chanced upon the torn ragged edge near the end of the book.

'The worst of it is,' said Aster, 'it makes me think it was something really important, the clue to all of this mess. Some wild secret that nobody will ever find out. When really, it might have been that Mama needed to write a quick note for the milkman.'

Harry leant towards her, suddenly embracing her, holding her close.

Aster surprised herself by allowing herself to relax into his arms.

'You're being so very brave about all of this,' he said, resting his head against hers. 'It makes me admire you even more, you know, which is very dangerous.'

She laughed lightly, feeling his love begin to permeate through to her, making her feel courageous, that she could face anything with him by her side.

'Do you know what my grandfather said to me, the day the letter arrived?' she asked, suddenly pulling away from him and sensing her own anger rise again. 'He said that to all intents and purposes, my father was dead to them. They blamed him for Mama's death. But what did he do that was so wrong?'

Harry looked dumbfounded. 'You've seen what the war did to people, what the war has done,' he began tentatively. 'Did he have shell shock? So many of them did. Perhaps he went into a mental hospital. A lot of them were put there, you know. They removed them from society because their minds were shot to pieces. They were often an embarrassment. Maybe your grandparents were only trying to protect you.'

'He still managed to paint, though, didn't he?' she mumbled petulantly, fighting a childish desire to kick the table leg. 'You know, when I was a little girl,' she went on, 'Gran told me all about the Unknown Soldier. How his body was taken from the battlefield and brought to England. How the coffin was draped in a Union Jack and born on a gun carriage drawn by six horses along the streets of London, past immense crowds. They buried him in Westminster Abbey. I was only five when this happened but I remember it . . . a picture in the newspaper, the stunned and weary crowds. I was convinced that the soldier was my dad.'

She faltered and covered her face with her hands. Through a blur of tears, she saw Harry rummage in his top pocket for his handkerchief and hand it to her. He stood up and walked to the large window and pulled aside the gold-braided curtain.

'Will you look at that sky,' he said, wiping the back of his hand over his eyes. 'We're going to get drenched.'

And Harry was right. As they walked down the Langham's steps an enormous murky black cloud slipped over the London streets and they were caught, suddenly, amid a torrential downpour. The rain splashed like mercury and the tarmac gleamed. Taxi lights glowed in the sudden green half-darkness and buses rumbled with an enormous swoosh as they glided up Regent Street. Within a moment, Aster's stockings were splattered, her shoes soaked and her umbrella dripped a steady stream onto her shoulder.

But still, she wanted to walk to the gallery. After all,

Harry told her, it was only on the other side of Cavendish Square and she could do with the fresh air. Again, how right he was. She certainly needed to clear her head. Harry was kind, Harry was wonderful, but, suddenly, she craved privacy: wanted to do this on her own.

'How are you doing?' he wondered, struggling with his umbrella, hunched under the downpour. 'I can see you're nervous.'

'There's no need to ask, then, is there?' she snapped.

'We could dart back to the hotel. Ask the doorman to order us a taxi.'

'No, I want to *walk*.'

She stalked off down the street, clutching her umbrella, head down. The rain fell in long silver strings around her and she felt her life, everything she knew, peeling away from her in great painful layers. In her handbag was the formal invitation to the exhibition of her father's paintings. *Which daughter on earth receives this sort of thing via a solicitor?* She pounded along the pavement, her fury festering and aimed at her grandparents and the false, empty world they had built around her. As beautiful and as sacred as Old Trellick was, tucked away in Cornwall, it was only half of her life. The other half was one huge secret.

A car drove past sending a scoop of water over the kerb towards Aster's feet. She very nearly laughed. Surely, she could not get any colder and wetter. Her best green cloche was sopping. So much for looking smart and well turned out. Harry tried his best to keep up with her, chattering, throwing well-meaning phrases at her. But they landed, ignored, at her feet.

'I think it's this way,' he said, and 'Oops mind that puddle,' and occasionally, 'Blessed weather.'

They stood for some moments in the vestibule of the

323

gallery, resting from the shock of the rain, holding dripping umbrellas away from their bodies, relishing the dry, the quiet and the warm air. Aster's face was wet, her hair in tatters. Harry eased her coat off her shoulders and prised the umbrella out of her hands, passing them to the cloakroom girl. He gave Aster her cloakroom ticket, which became soggy and crumpled even before she put it in her pocket.

Aster remained where she stood, making a puddle on the marble floor of the vestibule, her gaze fixed on the poster on the wall. She squinted at it, feeling a strange coldness trickling down inside. Beneath the title *Jack Fairling: A Retrospective* was the reproduction of a sketch in brown ink, dashed off hurriedly, she guessed, between roll call and stand-to. At the bottom of the sketch, very nearly sliced off by the limited size of the poster, was his signature and one simple word, *Hope*.

A shaking began inside her chest. She reached for Harry and held onto his hand. Through it, his strength came into her once more, the warmth returned. He was no longer bothersome or irritating. He was simply Harry. The dashing of the rain on the skylight above them ceased like the abrupt turning off of a tap, and the sun emerged as benign watery-yellow light glancing down from the ceiling. The sudden warmth sent a shiver of shock through Aster's bones. There was an aching seriousness to the hush in the room beyond where, she guessed, her father's paintings must be hung. Aster stepped forward still holding Harry's hand tightly in her own. She kept her eyes focused ahead of her, away from the poster, away from the inked sketch, for she could not take it in. *I am Hope*, she thought. *My name means Hope*. The drawing was a portrait of a little girl, barely three years old.

Chapter Thirty-Three

According to the brochure for which Harry paid thruppence, Jack Fairling's paintings had been divided into three periods and, subsequently, three rooms of the gallery, to trace his growth and development as a painter. Visitors were encouraged to start in the first chamber, with the *Camden Series*, to be able to witness the fascinating evolution of such an underrated and little-known artist.

Drying off now from being caught in the rain, and feeling a little stronger, Aster walked by Harry's side into the spacious and rather stuffy first gallery. Skylights beamed down, illuminating a dozen works executed with the characteristic daubs of paint that she'd seen in the portfolio left hidden in the garret at home. The small painting of her mother, *Violet in the Daytime*, that had been left behind at Old Trellick, had been sunlit and dappled in the dreamy midst of a fairy tale. Yet these works were altogether different. Here, her father depicted the city of London in a stark and brutal yet plainly beautiful way: pavements and railways shimmered with rain, the oily canal glided past the rickety stables at Camden Lock, terraces of houses were aligned in smooth blocks of colour, and smoking chimneys belched their emissions over crowds of bent and hurrying people.

While she waited for a couple, the only other people in this room, to move away from the last of the paintings, the tail of her eye caught the back view of another man in a coal-black suit pondering the room as a whole, his hand scratching his chin. Her stomach leapt with furious curiosity and she stepped backwards, treading on Harry's toe.

'It might be him,' she hissed in his ear.

Harry, ever keen to please, asked, 'Do you want me to find out?'

A bubble of absurdity broke from her mouth with a giggle. 'For goodness' sake, he's got a brochure in his hand and he's got dark hair. My father had fair hair. And he might not have any left by now . . . Who knows? He might be bald, he might have a beard. How will I know him? I won't, will I? I won't know my own father.'

Without a word, Harry took her hand and encouraged her around the corner into the next room. Here, the frames were tiny, compared to the confidently generous Camden paintings; the works were the size of pages torn from a pocket sketchbook, snaking around the walls at eye level. There must have been fifty of them: identically dark, charcoaled and scribbled, hard to make out until Aster stepped forward. It was only then that she could see how intricate and unique they were; she stared at each one in turn, absorbed it and moved on to the next, her horror expanding with each step and each ragged breath she took.

With bald and intimate strokes of his blunt pencil, Jack Fairling had depicted soldiers in their trenches wearing tin hats, their grins breaking dirty faces. In these miniature sketches, they fixed their bayonets, cooked over fires, gathered around braziers, ate from metal plates, were fed their rum ration off a spoon, burnt lice off their seams with matches, marched around unburied bodies being devoured by rats, stepped over skulls blown up out of the ground, were blinded by flares, witnessed guts hanging from between tunic buttons, saw screaming agony on faces close up, grinning this time in agony, cut their pals from the wire, drowned in mud, drowned in gas, begged to die.

A notice to her right informed Aster that it was a miracle any of the charcoal sketches of the *Trenches Series* had survived, stowed away as they were for many wretched months in Lieutenant Fairling's kit and very nearly lost. Some were creased and torn and soiled, others more pristine, but each one depicting a darker kind of hell.

Aster felt herself dragged closer, compelled to stare, unable to look away. She wanted to know, to feel what her father her lived through, what he had seen, images that he surely would never be able to erase. Mesmerised, she came to a stop in front of the last picture. It was enormous, a hundred times larger than all the others and it forced her to step back, lift her face and stare upwards until her neck began to ache. It was a huge painting, obviously a studio work done in oils, not crouched and cowering in a sodden trench. The painting glistened, illuminated by the skylight, and became alive as she turned her head, flicking her eyes from top to bottom and side to side, unable to take it all in in one glance. A lone tree, simple and stark, stood out against a sunny blue sky. A peculiar relief washed over Aster and a smile stretched her face for it was a blessed relief, so easy on the eye compared to the confined abyss of the little trench sketches. And then she shook her head, closed her eyes, took another step back and stared again, raising her palm to cover her mouth. Cold sweat coated her throat and her stomach caved in. The tree was naked, obviously long dead but somehow still standing in the blown wasteland of battle, and its stretching jagged branches, like contorted arms, were hung not with fruit or leaves but with rags, flesh, torn limbs, parts of men, shapeless festoons of what was once human, what had once been a son, a brother, a father.

She felt Harry's arm around her shoulder and she longed to turn her face away. But she could not peel her eyes from the painting, for the horror was addictive. It became physical, visceral, stiffening her flesh. Swaying on her feet, her knees ready to buckle, Aster leant forward to read what her father had written in the corner: his signature, then *Somme, July 1916*.

And, according to the little typewritten sign tacked to the wall beside it, he'd given the painting one simple word as a title: *Monument*.

Chapter Thirty-Four

Aster walked with Harry, leaving the room of the little charcoal drawings and the grotesque tree, and finding herself in the next gallery. There was a murmur of busy voices as a small group of people drew away towards the exit, dispersing and flicking over the pages of their brochures. Aster fumbled with her own copy, her blood running as ice as she tried to eradicate the images that her father had created, the hell that her father had lived in, twenty years before. But they were burnt like a photographic negative onto the hard surface of her memory. She stood still and pressed her fingers over her eyes, wishing for it to go away, waiting for a quiet blessing of strength to help her face the room and carry on. She hid her face, realising the tears had only just started.

Harry's hand was on her shoulder, his voice in her ear,

assuring her that they could do whatever she wanted. 'Do you want to go home now? Go back to the hotel? I'll order a cab.'

She shook her head, her voice a wet whisper. 'No, I want to see them, see them all.'

Accepting his handkerchief, she took his arm, and he guided her forward, distracting her with an observation about the dark-haired man in the coal-black suit they'd seen in the previous room, supposing he was from the press.

'He's still here, Aster, over by the door, talking to that couple. I expect he's doing an interview, look.'

Aster glanced over to see the man in the suit flipping the pages of a notebook at the same time as listening intently to a well-dressed older man, in a mackintosh coat and trilby, who was speaking softly, his attractive consort, a handsome woman of a certain age, nodding attentively.

Watching the little animated group for a moment or two cleared Aster's mind. She glanced at Harry and her soul settled a little, found a place of serenity.

'I didn't realise how much I need him,' she thought and turned to the new set of paintings, wiping her eyes discreetly as her mother's face pulled into focus.

Aster paused with her blood thumping absurdly around her head. There she was . . . Violet, sheltering under a parasol which she cradled delicately in her hands, her complexion lit by unearthly tranquil light. Aster knew this light, she knew this painting so very well for another version, very much smaller than this, languished in the garret of Old Trellick. But now here, the deep layered daubs of oiled colours were shifting constantly, breathing and glimmering before her. In a painting taller than *Monument* and wider still, her mother was alive, walking through the park *under the dappled silvery shadow of willow trees; star-like daisies bright at her feet. Her face is half in profile, the line of her cheek exquisite. Her parasol is the colour of luminous water, protecting her, keeping her separated in her own world. Her eyes, even in shadow, are lucid sea green. As she walks, she isn't aware of the artist as he sees her; just of the light that comes from below her, reflected from his direction, to illuminate her and set her apart. She lifts her pale hand quickly to shield her eyes.*

'Seriously, Aster, are you all right?' Harry stepped forward, breaking the spell.

But Aster did not mind, for she knew that she'd easily find the magic again.

'I'm fine, I'm more than fine,' she said. 'This is wonderful. Can't you see? This is more than I have ever had in my whole life. You see, I have the Flower Book, and a few grainy old photos. But she is a ghost there, so fleeting. And my mother wrote in riddles. I expect she wanted to be clever. She was clever. It seems she was a curious, secretive little girl and a rebellious young lady. I try to understand her, understand what she means by swarms of bees in July, and April showers. I try to understand because that helps me believe I know her. She wrote down all the days and all the seasons and all her years, but what did it really all mean? It is beautiful but what was she trying to say? And now, just look. You can see her. My father knew her, understood her, and it shows. Can't you see? This is she. This is Violet.'

Aster's voice rose high to a sing-song pitch and a tiny echo responded from the ceiling. Suddenly conscious of her outburst she stopped with an involuntary hand over her mouth. Out of the corner of her eye she noticed the well-dressed couple glance politely in her direction. But then they were gone. She turned back to the painting and her vision was filled once more with light.

Harry's calm manner recounted what the brochure said, that there were just three paintings in this last series, all executed in Jack Fairling's studio in Camden during the early-to-mid 1920s. All three were the same immense size, each given their own wall here; they lit the room with colour and with a deep beauty that was beyond what Aster could actually see.

Harry was speaking but Aster did not want or need to listen to him.

'She's life-size,' she uttered with breathless incredulity. 'Violet is life-size.'

A clean light shone in her head, a purity of understanding. She remained still and clear-headed, the lucidity inside her immobilising her as she stared at her mother. Then, after many minutes, she pulled herself with reluctance from *Daytime* and walked with Harry to the next painting.

The window had no curtains, just an architrave peeling with paint. Through it lay a London skyscape, a tumble of chimney pots and grey slate roofs. Little globes of dust bowled along the bare floorboards under the chaise beneath this window. A gas lamp in the corner spilt a tentative light over naked green walls and onto the sleeping form of Violet, curled on the cushions, oblivious to her effect on the observer, any observer.

'How safe she looks, so safe and happy,' Aster said in a voice trailing in wonder.

Harry, his words a flat drone in comparison, read from the brochure: '*Violet in the Evening*, completed in oils 1923. Taken from an original sketch in pastels, 1914.'

'Even asleep, she looks happy. So they were happy, weren't they? They were.'

Harry's arm around her waist pressed firmly, supporting her. He rested his face against hers and they gazed together, drinking in the peaceful scene of twenty-year-old twilight in a dusty Camden studio.

'We can be happy,' he said quietly into her hair. 'We can be too.'

She found his hand at her hip and bound her fingers around his. 'Yes. I know it,' she said, with a bravery that almost floored her.

Who else but Harry? Who else would bring her here, would stand by her side while her world fell away to smithereens and then brought itself together again in such irregular, misshapen pieces?

The memory of him as a very little boy, living at Old Trellick, bobbed up to the surface and she seemed to swim below it, not quite seeing him through murky water. But the recollection was there, like a snatch of a tune, the odour in a long-closed cupboard. She stared up at him while her thoughts settled surprisingly neatly into place. While she was getting used to this new, sensible way of thinking, she realised Harry was speaking quietly, earnestly to her. He was asking her to marry him.

Struck suddenly by something her gran said about Harry – *you're friends, perhaps that's how it should stay* – she felt neither angry nor defiant. She was a long, long way from that morning in her bedroom at Old Trellick when she opened the solicitor's letter and was hit by the shock of her alternative life. Aster looked up to Harry's troubled, hopeful face and simply said *yes*.

* * *

The third and final painting made Harry blush, and Aster laughed gently with him, feeling her own cheeks smoulder as they both gazed up at *Violet in the Night-time*.

'Stop giggling,' Harry teased her. 'You're spoiling it.'

'Did you know that when you blush your ears also go red?'

'Well, the tip of your nose has gone all shiny.'

She laughed out loud. She couldn't help herself. In the space of a few moments, they'd made their decision and their lives together were resolved. A whole new chapter was unravelling luxuriously before them, just as it had for Violet and Jack some twenty years before. And she welcomed it, wanted to run right into it with open arms.

'I say, this is rather risqué,' Harry uttered. 'Perhaps we better stand a few feet apart while we look at this one.'

'I don't know where to look,' Aster told him.

But she was lying, for she was staring directly at the adoration on her mother's face as she relaxed on a window seat, with her body reclined luxuriously against a pile of cushions, the hinting glow of street lamps through a gap in the heavy draped curtains. Jack had used caressing paint strokes to capture the light and shadow over her skin, the silk of her grey dress that had slipped artlessly from her shoulders, the fascinated flicker of her smile, a dot of mischief around the lucidity of her eyes. At first glance, Violet's face was open and innocent but Aster spied a dab of mystery in the deep green of her eyes that engaged her, made her look again. Was it that her mother was holding something back, and that Jack could see it?

'. . . completed at the Camden studio in 1925. First time it has ever been exhibited in public . . .' Harry was saying.

'From a sketch executed at the St Pancras Hotel. On their wedding night. Goodness, it is rather something, isn't it? Far too racy for wall space at Old Trellick, don't you think?'

A laugh bubbled from Aster, a strange sound in the staid, confined gallery. Trust Harry to lighten the tone exactly when she needed him to. She grabbed his hand and kissed it. 'This is why I will marry you,' she said.

Some people had approached them without them realising. Aster turned to see the older gentleman and his companion suddenly at her shoulder. He was doffing his hat, dipping his head in a greeting of old-world courtesy. The lady by his side was noticeably younger than him with lots of black hair, piled up precariously under her hat. Threads of silver added to its wild beauty and her eyes were a shooting emerald. She patted the man's arm gently.

'You must say it now, Bertie, or it will drive you mad.'

'We couldn't help ourselves, you see,' he began, engaging Aster and Harry as if they had been party to their previous conversation. Aster stared at the man, at his fair-grey hair, and sparse neat moustache. A familiarity came to her, some sort of inherited wisdom, a feeling of knowing her own kind.

'But when I heard you mention Old Trellick,' the elderly gentleman went on, rambling somewhat, 'I just had to come over. We had to. This is my wife, Cecelia, and I am Bertie Fairling.'

Harry lurched to grab Aster as she swayed backwards as if hit by a blast of hot air.

'Fairling, you say?' Harry asked, and Aster, shuddering to her bones, felt his arm like a dead weight around her shoulders.

'Yes. That's right, the artist's father. We were on a little trip around Europe, Venice, Florence, you know, when the exhibition opened, so thought we'd better catch it or we won't hear the end of it. Of course, we've seen the paintings before but to view them here . . . This is a grand space, isn't it? Not too large or overpowering. Perfect size for what Jack wanted. But I must say, my dear, are you quite all right?'

'Of course she's not,' Cecelia Fairling dipped in and held Aster's arm. 'It's as if you've seen a ghost, isn't my dear? We need to take her outside. Look at her face. White as a sheet.'

Aster felt herself helplessly propelled forward by a kindly throng, bolstered by kindly voices assuring her that this was the best thing, to leave this place, get some fresh air. Kindly hands rummaged for smelling salts and instead proffered a slim silver flask of something a little stronger. And suddenly she was stepping over a rain-washed pavement, with the smells of tar and rain combining as puddles dried in the sun, hearing Harry assuring her that he had her coat and hat, and hearing the older man's benevolent tones informing them that there was a good tea room just around the corner.

'Strike that,' said his wife with a snort. 'We'll go to the Crescent Moon across the road.'

As the party of four ducked into the public house, Aster retrieved her voice, recovered her senses and the words that were spinning in her head.

'Excuse me,' she said, tugging on the gentleman's sleeve, 'but are you not my grandfather?'

Chapter Thirty-Five

Four brandies were set out on the glossy round table. All four people sat and stared at the tumblers in collective shock. One by one, they picked up the tumblers and took thoughtful sips. Aster gripped hers, knocked it to the back of her throat and squeezed her eyes tight as the alcohol scorched her inside.

Harry said, 'You have to understand what a blow all of this is to Aster. Up until a month or so ago, she thought her father had died in the trenches. Her *other* grandparents have been less than truthful with her, I'm afraid.'

Bertie Fairling ventured, 'Were they ashamed, perhaps? So many soldiers went doolally, were shut away in asylums. People just didn't talk of such things. Was that their fear? You see, Aster, your father was terribly injured in the last weeks of the war. We'd given up hope. We also thought he was dead. He was *missing presumed dead*. The telegram would have been sent to your mother at Old Trellick. She would have known as much as we did. God knows what that did to her. And when he came back, by golly, it was as if the dead *had* returned.'

Aster planted her tumbler firmly in the centre of the table, with a snap of irritation.

'Please tell me what happened, for I am going out of my mind.'

Her grandfather, taking a ludicrous amount of time to gather his thoughts, eventually said, 'Jack was taken prisoner just before the Armistice. Got him back eventually, thanks to the Red Cross, by summer 1919, back on English soil. He returned to his studio in Camden. But he couldn't stay there. He couldn't be left alone. He was in a bad way. We put him in a hospital in Sidcup for a year.'

Aster blurted, 'But why did he not come and find me when . . . Why did he forget about me . . . ?' A blunt shaft of pain stopped her speaking. She wanted another brandy.

'Years passed,' explained Bertie. 'It was a great shock for all of us, the war. Such a great silence followed. Oh, the bright young things all got roaring drunk and danced the nights away. Those were the people who were too young to know, or chose not to know. But the ones who came back, well, they didn't want to speak about it. And the ones who had to deal with that, like us . . . we kept our heads down and ploughed on. I was not part of any of it, really, although we heard the guns, oh yes, didn't we, Cecelia, from our house in Kent? Did you know that, my dear? The roar of the guns like distant thunder, across the Channel, but never moving on as storms do. But we never heard from Violet.

338

We wondered if she might write to us . . . ? The silence became normal.'

Cecelia was gazing broodingly at Aster, her emerald eyes blazing. 'You are the image of your mother, you know. I met her before they married. She came to his studio. I called her "the girl in the painting". You are just like her.'

'People do say that,' Aster was struggling. Her composure remained with her by the thinnest of threads. She wanted to scream and fight. Only Harry's hand in hers kept her planted in her seat, ensured she didn't leap up, tip the table over and escape. She was utterly beaten and could only sit and stare in a languid daze.

Bertie glanced at Aster, and realising she had ceased to converse, he turned to Harry. 'We are very sorry for all of this. How poor Aster has suffered. How it ended up like this. But you see, the war did terrible things to so many people, my Jack included. He was a changed man. He felt it was for the best. But we've supported him, haven't we Cecelia, in everything he wanted to do?'

'I was his landlady in Camden,' his wife chipped in. 'I saw him struggle as a young artist. I suppose I was his patron. When he met your mother a huge flood of creativity opened. He was crazy, passionate, as you can see from his work. And with this retrospective, of course he wanted you to have the paintings, as a peace offering. A way of saying sorry.'

'He always hoped you'd forgive what has happened. And that he should no longer be estranged,' Bertie continued. 'We have always supported him, of course, since he lost your mother. But by golly, what a stroke of luck that we happened to be at the Portland at the same time. We weren't even going to come today, because of the rain.'

Aster flinched, imagining the brief and captivating happiness her parents must have had together before the war started and spread like fire, separating them and taking them away from each other.

Harry, forever scrutinising, piped up, 'Mr Fairling, earlier, just now, you said that Jack felt it was for the best . . . what was for the best?'

Bertie said, 'That perhaps they went their separate ways. Perhaps they were happier that way. Who can tell? When Violet left him, you see, Jack went downhill. Couldn't paint for years. It's a miracle we have these wonderful paintings at all . . .'

'She didn't leave him!' Aster cried, aghast, her flailing hand knocking a tumbler over with a crack against the table.

Her grandfather lowered his voice, his hand reaching across the table to press hers. 'Perhaps this was your grandparents' way of protecting you from the shame of it all. You see, dear, when the war was over she left him.'

Aster violently shook her head, her voice for a moment lost inside confusion. 'No, you don't know!' she cried. 'No she didn't.'

Bertie looked from Aster's gaping face to Harry and back again. 'We understood she left him, she left Jack for a local Cornish landlord. One Weston Penruth.'

Harry's laugh was a short sharp bark. 'That's my father! And she certainly did not! This is ridiculous. This is an insult. How can you draw that conclusion?'

It was Aster's turn to calm Harry, to reach out and link his arm.

'You see, what you don't understand . . .' she said, quietly watching Bertie's face stretch wide and flat with astonishment. 'Do you not know? Does my father not know?'

Cecelia leant forward, her face gawking unattractively. 'Oh my dear, *what*?'

'Violet is dead,' Aster said simply, her own calmness now worrying her. 'My mother died in an accident in London, the year after the war ended.'

Bertie and Cecelia sat back, as if slapped, and turned to stare hard at each other.

Aster went on lamely, her voice trailing, 'It was the summer, after the war. Summer 1919. Of course I was still very young, I . . .'

Cecelia spoke first, for Bertie was gulping, bewildered.

'Jack *doesn't* know,' Cecelia whispered. 'He *never* knew. He . . . he thought Violet left him for Penruth. That Violet didn't want to be with him. He was terribly injured you see . . . he thought she . . .'

'. . . didn't want a man maimed like him. Half a man, he said,' Bertie spluttered, his voice as thin as a reed. 'He thought Violet didn't want such a man as he.'

Chapter Thirty-Six

The street was thronging with motor cars, squeezing over the bridge that spanned the railway into Euston, tooting quite comically as they jostled for space. Pedestrians hurried along the pavements, going about their everyday business, stopping for a chat to pass the time of day, or walking on by. They were all so assured in their individual little industries, with matters no more pressing, thought Aster, than purchasing a loaf of bread or a yard of muslin.

The scene was commonplace, flickering before her like a newsreel compiled to show how any ordinary day should look. And it was a strange comfort that all this normal activity should carry on while her own world continued to spin and crash. Only yesterday she'd been at the Portland gallery, gazing at her father's paintings as they unfolded her parents' story; paintings that had been bequeathed to her in such a manner that was almost brutal. As she got out of the taxi cab on busy Parkway, she stepped into this new present-time, another life.

She waited outside the pharmacy that her grandfather Bertie had told her to look out for, while Harry paid the driver. Peering through the shop window, she tried to distract herself from the momentous crushing noise in her head. The little store looked like it had not changed in years, and yet she herself had changed with the simple opening of an envelope.

'The last time I saw my father,' Aster reminded Harry after he'd tipped the driver, 'was out of my bedroom window at dawn, the day he left for the front. He asked me to look after Mama.'

'That's a great deal to put on a little girl's shoulder,' Harry said, his arm about her as he led her to the entrance tucked around the corner, just off the main thoroughfare.

'And of course I couldn't. No one could.' Aster's words stumbled. 'Violet was a free spirit. No one could catch her. I know that much.'

'You must take after her,' said Harry playfully, trying, Aster knew, to lighten her mood.

Aster pondered, 'At least he did not promise to come back.'

She remembered in the darkness of that strange night of nightmares amid the soft whispering of the sea, her father saying: *I'm here, now, Aster, I'm here now.* Tears washed her eyes, blinding her. 'After all that, he did come back. I just never knew about it.'

They stood in the porch and Harry put his hands on her shoulders, holding her steady.

'I can't stop trembling,' she admitted. 'Is this so unbearably silly? I shouldn't be like this, brimming with dread. I should be ecstatic. But I'm scared, Harry, I am very scared.'

He spoke low and calmly to her, reminding her that he was with her now, would always be.

'Are you ready?' he asked her. She nodded, unable to speak.

Cecelia opened the front door to them, ushered them inside. Aster could barely take in the narrow panelled hallway and the steep stairs, for her eyes were blinkered and staring ahead into the unimaginable moments to come. She was aware, vaguely, of the smell of paint, of artist's chemicals. Bertie met them on the first landing, his face stiff with nerves, and ushered them into a front parlour.

'Ah, good to see you again, so glad you could come,' he said, as he quietly closed the door, his voice unreasonably chipper. 'My, my,' he stalled, glancing at Cecelia who gave him a disappointed look, and then back at Aster and Harry. They stood stiffly in excruciating anticipation, Harry steadying her trembling hand.

'Oh, I see you're wearing Violet's ring,' said Bertie far too brightly. 'It belonged to my first wife, I'm sure you know.' He blustered on, 'She died giving birth to Jack. He was premature. That's what probably—'

Cecelia chipped in, 'For goodness' sake, Bertie. Aster doesn't need to hear all of this now!'

'So sorry,' muttered her grandfather. 'Wittering on as usual, but you see, Aster, we had a bit of a to-do yesterday,' Bertie's voice fell to an urgent whisper. 'We came straight home from the gallery to tell Jack that we'd met you, and to tell him the most dreadful news about Violet. But before we

344

could even begin . . . we got as far as saying we'd bumped into you, when he stormed out of the house. He must have been very distressed. He was gone all night. Has only just got back. God knows where he's been.'

Cecelia explained, 'Jack has these spells occasionally. When things get too much for him. He disappears for hours. Then he locked himself away in his studio. Played his gramophone at top volume. Will not talk to us.'

Aster said, 'He's not playing it now . . .'

'And I heard him unlock the door a few moments ago,' surmised Cecelia.

'He must be very distressed,' said Harry reasonably. 'But the way I see it, he wanted to bequeath the paintings to Aster. It was his idea to contact her via solicitors. It's no surprise that this moment would come.'

'The thing is,' Bertie gave Aster a dark look, 'he doesn't know yet. He doesn't know about Violet.'

'You haven't told him!' Aster felt her knees buckle.

'We couldn't exactly shout it through the studio door.'

Aster fumbled for a handkerchief to wipe the sweat from her palms. 'Dear God,' she uttered.

Harry stood by her side. 'I'm coming in with you,' he declared.

She looked up at Harry's concerned face as his eyes searched her for clues to her state of mind.

Bertie stepped forward. 'You must also remember, dear, that your father was severely injured in the war. Prepare yourself.'

Prepare? Aster thought wildly. I've longed to see my dad since that strange grey morning. For such a long time I knew him to be dead. And he still doesn't know my mother passed away so many years ago. How can I possibly prepare for this?

'I'll be with you,' Harry reassured her.

As she looked from her grandfather to his wife, from one anxious face to another, a black cloud lifted from her mind. Her reason to be here, right now at her father's home, became suddenly mortifyingly clear. She had to be the one to tell him about Violet. This was why she was here. It had to be her. It simply had to.

'No,' she said. 'This is something that I must do on my own.'

'You're braver than the lot of us,' muttered Cecelia.

'Darling, I—' Harry began, but Aster's look silenced him.

Chapter Thirty-Seven

She knocked once and twisted the door handle, walking alone into a bright, wide room. It stretched the full length of the building with a window at either end, offering escalating views over the rooftops of Camden. Immediately she recognised the window overlooking the street at the front. *Violet in the Evening*, she said in her head, and the words became a little repeated chant as her gaze travelled around the room, over canvases, pots of paint, fans of brushes, the detritus of art. She became aware of the figure sitting in the armchair behind a screen by the old-fashioned hearth and the reality of who he was scorched through her bones.

He was sitting in the shadow of the screen, looking deep into the embers in the grate and so she was able to study the back of his head at length and at liberty. *Did he not hear me come in?* she wondered briefly. Perhaps he had lost his hearing in the war? She took in the fair hair, flecked with grey. He'd kept it short, just as she remembered, and she wondered about the floppy wave of it that he used to have falling jauntily over his forehead. Her curiosity about the minutiae in her memory distracted her from the enormity of where she was and who she was in the presence of. At last, through the years of craving, here she was. She felt as if she was waking from a long, long sleep.

'Dad?' Her voice was small and plaintive, like a child's.

Jack turned incredibly slowly and she realised that he was holding a handkerchief to his face. As he swivelled in his chair, he kept it pressed in place over the left side and Aster immediately grew worried that the brightness of his eyes – oh, those laughing eyes in the wagon on the way to the harvest, his rolled up sleeves, the cigarette cocked at the side of his mouth – meant that he was crying.

He moved the handkerchief down and stood up, his right hand offered out in greeting. His stride was surprisingly energetic as he moved towards her out of the shadow of the screen, his demeanour a far cry from the devastated and crippled man that her grandfather Bertie had suggested or that Aster had built in her mind. He was wearing a collar and tie, his trousers loosely gathered in the baggy fashion that Harry and so many men were wearing nowadays.

Aster Violet fixed her eyes on the collar, glanced at his tie, which was a pleasing shade of blue, and then back to his collar. The sparkle in his eyes increasing as he took her in, girding himself – she decided – for the shock of seeing her for the first time as a grown woman and not the little girl he remembered. He was bathed, suddenly, in the full light from the large windows.

'Oh Dad,' she uttered again and drew in her breath in a long excruciating gasp.

'You are just like her,' he said and Aster was immediately startled that he was able to speak at all. 'And I am so glad she has never seen me like this for I could not bear to see that look on her face. The look you're giving me . . .'

Above his smart collar and tie was not the person Aster recalled during lonely, orphaned nights. For on the lower plains of the ghost of a once-handsome face lay a hollow of scarred flesh and oddly protruding bone where Jack's jaw and chin would once have been. As he smiled, his mouth, a mere hole began to widen in a grimace of welcome.

Aster's mind emptied of all her memory. Rudely, and finally, her father's looks, his smile disappeared and was replaced by this shattered mask that was now half a face. *Half the man she remembered.*

The floppy lock of hair was gone; a jagged, brutal scar ran along his hairline. The skin on the damaged left side was an odd yellow shade, taut and crumbled like parchment. And yet still his eyes gleamed like stars in a storm.

'So this is what he meant?' Aster blurted, her thoughts spilling from her mouth, her voice rising to a wail. 'This is what Bertie meant! That Mama left you after the war, because of *this*. Because in her eyes you were half a man. But it's not true. She never knew. She did not know what happened to you. But you and grandfather thought that she was capable of leaving you for Weston Penruth? No. If you read her words, here, then you'll know . . .' Breathless, Aster sank into an armchair by the hearth and slumped down. She plunged her hand into her bag and drew out the Flower Book. She lay it on her lap and gazed down at it, rogue tears splashing its worn deep-green cover at random intervals. 'What she wrote in here meant that she loved you, she loved you. But she didn't know . . .' Aster's voice tore in her throat. She looked up at her father, who stood still, waiting, perplexed. She gazed at him full and unflinching in the face. 'It wasn't her fault, you know. How could she help it? She died.'

Her father cringed and a dreadful silence sealed the room. From the space where Jack's mouth once had been rose an inhuman howl. Out came a voice that was embryonic, struggling to react, struggling to understand what he had just heard her say.

Aster waited, her blood frozen. Time slowed, drifted.

'No,' he cried at last. 'No, she's not dead. Violet's not dead.'

He jerked his shoulders to fight it, disbelief breaking his face in two. He lurched for his own chair, reaching for it blindly. He slumped down, as if run through with a sword.

'She cannot be dead. Why didn't they tell me?'

'This I don't know,' said Aster, surprised at how calm she sounded. '*They* also didn't tell me you were still alive.'

Jack stared at her and breathed out. 'You didn't know? You didn't know I made it back?' He shook his head, running a hand over his face. 'I thought she'd *left* me,' he stuttered. 'I thought she didn't want to know me, after this!'

Aster, her energy spent, could only whisper. 'There is so much I don't understand. Why have we been strangers all these years?'

Jack put his hands over his face and rested with his head

bowed. His breathing shuddered, animal-like groans issuing like the dull intermittent toll of a bell. Aster sat still, running her fingertip over the smooth cover of the Flower Book, her anger towards her grandparents at Old Trellick resurfacing. If only they could see what their half-truths had done to this man, and to her.

Eventually, Jack got up and knelt by her side, drawing his handkerchief out to shield her from his disfigurement.

'Violet's parents never approved of me. I was a poor artist scraping a living and there was this fellow, Weston Penruth. He was a powerful, eligible landowner. I was jealous of him. I think your grandparents preferred him, rubbed their hands with glee when I went off to war. After all, what was my life expectancy?' His voice broke. 'On my last night, before I went back to the front, I was monstrous to your mother. I was a cold, strange man. That's what the war did to me. I told her to go to this Penruth. I wanted you both to be safe, with a roof over your head. I believed then that she did just that, when she found out about my injuries. I thought she was happy and living her life . . . just like I told her to.'

Perhaps that's what he was saying to her, thought Aster, standing outside Old Trellick in that strange grey dawn.

'I've just realised,' she said. 'The last time I ever saw you, was also the last time Mama ever . . .'

Jack looked down, could not meet her unswerving gaze. 'I feel so guilty. I didn't even try to get in contact, but when I look in a mirror . . . You know, they didn't allow mirrors at the hospital . . .' He glanced up at her. 'Offering you my paintings when you reached twenty-one was my peace offering, I suppose, to you both. To you and your mother.

All the years,' he uttered. 'All that time. Wasted. But how can she be dead, when she's been alive in my mind, alive all this time?'

Aster gently reached out her hand and pushed her father's handkerchief away and down, then watched in breathless silence as tears spilt out of his brilliant eyes and ran in strange and unfamiliar channels towards his ruined chin.

'She is still alive,' she tapped the Flower Book. 'In here.'

Chapter Thirty-Eight

They sat quietly for some minutes facing each other on the shabby Louis-style chairs by the little old-fashioned stove. Light shimmered around the studio courtesy of the generous windows, streaming through the jars of paint, highlighting flecks of dust and the chipped corners of Jack's workbench. Outside a vague hum of traffic and day-to-day voices kept Aster's nerves remarkably steady. Cecelia tapped on the door with some tea and brandy.

As soon as they were alone again, Aster poured out the cups, ignoring her own but adding a tot of brandy to his.

'Ah, just like your mother,' he said. 'She hated brandy. But I don't mind if I do . . .'

Aster watched his private pain creep slowly over his features, altering them as each fresh reality gripped him.

He stirred his cup three times, tapped his spoon twice on

the rim. 'I must take you to the Pavilion in Regent's Park. Let's go there tomorrow.'

'Is that where you met?'

'Nearby . . .' He drifted on, thoughts puzzling his expression. On reflex, he lifted his handkerchief to his face.

'What happened to you?' Aster asked.

His eyes moved past hers and into a brutal memory where he paused for some moments, gathering his thoughts.

'A shell passing overhead emits a whistling sound,' he said. 'If you hear it, the reckoning is that you're safe. That it has passed overhead. Of course . . .' he cocked his head and gestured, 'I didn't hear this one coming.'

Aster watched his hands tremble as he lifted his cup. 'And when shrapnel hits bone, it's like me smashing a jam jar of water into my porcelain sink over there.'

She waited, unable to comment. All she could do was sit and sip her tea.

He had not known what had hit him, he went on. It was during a fiercely relentless shell attack during the last battle of Ypres at Plugstreet.

'That was October 1918,' he said, dryly, 'if you want a history lesson. I was captured and interred in a prisoner of war camp near Berlin,' he elaborated, 'with half of my lower face missing.'

The German surgeons were unfeeling but generally efficient, he said. But the one assigned to his case botched it badly.

'Of course, a month later, I was still too busy drowning in the depths of morphine to know that peace had been declared. It took months for me to be returned to England by the Red Cross. Early the next summer, I think. I came straight here to London. Didn't give my home in Kent, where my father and Cecelia were now living, a second thought. I went straight to Camden, dropped my suitcase, then headed for Montagu Square.'

'Great Auntie Muriel's?' Aster asked.

'Knocked on her door. I seem to remember the particularly prickly housemaid Smithson being struck mute, staring at me. She wouldn't let me in at first. I was off the morphine and disorientated by pain. I must have looked like a madman, a terrible spectre. My scarf must have slipped, I must have frightened her. Then Muriel thundered down the stairs, took one look at me and ushered me inside. We sat in her upstairs drawing room. She had just returned from Cornwall. Was unpacking her Meissen, she said. I remember, we laughed at her love of German porcelain and made a joke about it making it through the war intact. Unlike some of us. She told me she had found one of my pastel sketches in her cellar. It was my first version of *Violet in the Night-time*. She loved it, she said, thought it "scandalously beautiful". I'll never forget that expression. She wondered that if Violet did not want it, could she keep it?

'I was frustrated, impatient. I wanted Violet. I longed for Violet. But I knew what I had become. Muriel understood. She is a great fixer, Muriel. She said that she would send a telegram that day to Old Trellick, and tell Violet that I had made it back and was here in Camden. That she should come to London straight away. Muriel said that she would warn Violet as best she could and as gently as she could, about the state of me. I didn't doubt her for a moment. I thought it would be all fine by the end of the week. That Violet and I would be together. We'd all live together, you,

355

she and I in Camden or Kent or Cornwall, it did not matter to me. We could start again. Rebuild our lives. Have the time together we deserved.'

'With the war over, it sounded like you had so much hope,' observed Aster, quietly wiping her eyes.

'I felt we could do anything. Cast all our troubles aside once and for all. Perhaps it was the morphine talking, still coursing through my veins. But I believed it.'

Aster said, 'Mama did come up to London. I know that much. That's when the accident happened.'

Jack set his cup down and turned away from her. He stared for some moments out of the window, covering his face with his handkerchief.

'You may not know, Dad,' Aster continued, 'that Auntie Muriel caught Spanish flu around that time. She passed away. Their funerals were within a week of each other. Poor Gran . . .'

Jack remained perfectly still. 'Muriel had spirit. Both sisters did, and do, I suppose. You say she became ill around the same time? Perhaps she never sent the telegram?'

Aster reminded him that she must have done, for that's why her mother had come to London, summoned by it. She poured some more tea, and a separate nip of brandy for her father who took it without a word.

'But, Dad,' she pondered, 'why all this talk of Mr Penruth? You see, grandfather Bertie mentioned him yesterday and, well, Harry . . .'

Her father felt with his fingertips into his pocket and pulled out a battered old envelope stained by time and creased like geriatric skin.

'Never mind him, look at this, Aster,' he said. 'This is

what your mother gave me when I left, that very last time for the front. I'm ashamed to say I lost my reason during that last leave. I was ready for the loony bin. The thought of going back stripped me of humanity. I attacked Penruth at the harvest, but that's another story. I did not even open the envelope for a month or so – must have done so in my dugout at Plugstreet. But I didn't look at what was inside properly until at least a year later when I was recovering. I remember, I was in hospital in Sidcup, lying on a bath chair, thinking: what the devil is this? Her handwriting slayed me, still does. Can you tell me . . . can you help me . . . ?'

Aster opened the envelope and pulled out the folded piece of paper that was tucked inside. She knew immediately that it was the missing page from the Flower Book. Particles of crumbling decades-old pressed flowers fluttered and fell like dust through her fingers.

Her mother had written on the page in her neat, sloping handwriting in her beautifully familiar brown ink:

20th June 1914. Found by the Regent's Canal, London.
Tansy flower (also known as bitter buttons, or cow buttons).
Flowering time: June to September, grows in hedgerows and wasteland. Highly aromatic. Used by old wives to bring on a birth or menstruation in women. Soaked to skin when I found it, walked back across the park to see the rose garden, roses battered by rain, petals over grass, like a watercolour painting left out in the rain. Perhaps the artist will paint them like this one day?

Aster rubbed her finger along the ragged edge of the torn-out page, tracing the marks where the pressed tansy once lay. All that remained was a ghostly outline of the plant and a faded stain of glue.

She glanced at her father who was tense with expectation, and saw the younger man riding along in the back of the harvest wagon, singing with the workers, the sun in his eyes. She saw her mother sitting on her picnic rug in the field of wheat, calling out for her to mind the nettles. She saw her mother sifting through the offering of wild flowers that she'd plucked from the tall grass along the hedgerow.

'A poison,' Aster said, her thoughts walking through a closed door in her mind. 'I found this plant once and Mama told me to throw it away. She let me save some of the others: cornflowers, mayweed, mint, I think.' Aster quickly turned the pages of the Flower Book. 'Here is our entry all about that: 28th August 1918, the day of the harvest.'

'The next day, I left,' Jack said. 'You say it's a poison? Is that why she gave the page to me? Did she mean that if it all got too much for me that I should seek out this flower in Flanders and do myself in?'

'Of course not, Dad,' Aster scolded him. She stared at the creased page in her hand. 'She meant something else. Does the flower have a meaning? Remembrance? Eternal love?'

Jack sighed. 'We're clutching at straws. We will never know. As far as I can see, tansy is an insignificant weed, but then your mother liked to fox me sometimes . . . Can you paste the page back into the book?' he asked her. 'It's where it belongs.'

Aster placed the envelope inside her mother's book and put it back in her bag, the little yellow buttons of the plant still flickering in her imagination.

She asked, 'What did you do, then, once you'd visited Muriel?'

'Another month passed. This place was empty as Cecelia

358

had married my father and they lived at our home near Canterbury. I stayed here until they insisted I travel to Kent, to be admitted to a specialist hospital in Sidcup. There I met the kindest, most thoughtful surgeon who listened, really listened to me. He repaired my face as best he could. He made me a mask from galvanised tin, can you believe it? And all the time I kept thinking, any moment, Violet will appear at my bedside, or surprise me as I walked the grounds. She'd have got Muriel's telegram and will have made her way to London, found out where I was. I left a forwarding address with the pharmacist next door and posted one to Muriel at Montagu Square. Of course, I know now that poor Muriel died. Should I wear the mask or should I let her see me? Some days, my courage was better than others, you understand. And still, Violet did not come. And then I decided. That she must have gone to Weston.'

Aster grew irritated at the mention of that man's name. 'But how would you even *think* that of her?'

Jack sighed like a man dying. 'So many reasons.'

Aster only ever considered Mr Penruth as Harry and Kate's father; a rather aloof, moody man with a pronounced limp and odd demeanour. Someone she was a little bit scared of, if she was honest. But she knew she must get over all of that, for the man was soon to become her father-in-law.

Jack said, 'I convinced myself that she would have gone to him. That it was for the best. I didn't want her pity. I wanted her to be happy. I was bitter, oh so angry. And in a strange way, a very selfish way, I am now pleased to learn that she did not leave me for him.'

Her father got up quickly, hiding the expression on his face from her and told her to come and look at something, beckoning her over to a sideboard. He opened a drawer and drew out a box, lifting the lid to reveal the mask still nestled in cotton wool. It followed the curves of his now shattered cheeks and once firm jaw, a facsimile of the man he once was. Rather a pathetic and poor imitation, thought Aster harshly. It was eerily immobile, like an effigy of the dead.

'This was to spare the nightmares of such people as Smithson,' he said. 'I never wore it. Go ahead, touch it.'

Aster reached out a finger and lightly brushed the edge. It was smooth and cold. She realised with a jolt how a mask such as this would have given so many young men new hope, a new life.

'Thank God my nose is still intact,' her father said, wryly. 'Got a good Fairling nose.'

Aster laughed briefly and began to cry. Her father led her back to her fireside seat, glancing at her intently.

'Now listen, I take it you're sweet on this Harry Penruth,' he said, 'but—'

'Oh,' she said, brightening and wiping her eyes. 'We're engaged! I haven't had a moment to tell you. In all of this . . . finding you, meeting you, I realise I haven't had a chance to tell you our news.'

'He's asked you to marry him?'

Aster blossomed, celebrating her joy. 'Why, yes, of course – we're going to be married.'

'Well, you can't.'

'Whatever do you mean . . . ?'

Jack began to speak, rushing, his words falling around her like missiles, making her wince.

'Don't you see?' he said. 'One of the reasons I was convinced that Violet did not want me, when she knew I was back from the war, was that she had always been in love with Weston Penruth. They were engaged once. Did you not know that? Oh God, no you didn't.'

Aster pressed her hand to her throat, trying to keep breathing.

'Your Prideaux grandparents were ecstatic, as you can well imagine, for it was the match of the county, fulfilling their dreams,' he went on. 'But she ran away. And that's how I met her in London. We married very quickly. I loved her. Never wanted to let her go. But the way things worked out. How can I put this delicately . . . ?'

He stopped then, as if he'd said too much. And now that the words had spilt out, they could never be taken back. Aster saw sadness turning his eyes opaque. She decided to be brave. 'Dad, what are you saying . . . ?'

'You see, after all of this time, after all of this dreadful upset, and you coming here, us meeting again . . . You see, we thought you were premature when you were born, but . . .'

He swallowed hard.

'Please . . .' she whispered.

'I'm not your father.'

Aster's teacup smashed on the floor.

She gaped at him as a sheet of ice sliced through her middle. When she could look no more on his stricken, mutilated face, she glanced over at the mask lying there in its box. *Not my father?* Her mind plummeted. *He's not my father?*

'You're *not?*'

Jack took a longer shuddering breath. 'I am convinced it's him. Weston Penruth. That man is your father.'

Chapter Thirty-Nine

Harry tried his best, with comforting words and trays of tea, but Aster was sick of tea, couldn't swallow another mouthful. Pacing the hotel room, she plucked the meagre clothes she'd brought with her from the drawers, refolded them and then squashed them back in. She ran a bath and let it go cold, rang the bell for some sandwiches and they now sat curling and dry, uneaten on the table.

'How are you feeling?' Harry asked from the armchair by the window, in a tone that told Aster he already knew the answer.

'Look at me, I think I'm better off on my own.'

'If you're sure, I'll only be next door . . .'

He gave her a warm and tired smile. But as he rose to go, Aster experienced a surge of stupid cold fear.

'No, stay!' she cried. 'You must stay.'

He suggested that she get ready for bed, have a lie down and try to sleep.

'I'm not undressing,' she said, 'I haven't the energy.'

She curled herself up on the bed, resting herself against the luxurious hotel pillows and Harry tucked the silky eiderdown around her waist, planting a kiss chastely on her forehead.

'Thank you.' She tried to smile. 'I don't know what I'd do without you. Switch the lamp off,' she said sleepily, and then in an instant, 'No, turn it back on!'

Harry returned to his armchair by the window, ready, it seemed to Aster, to settle in for the night.

'I'm rather scared of the dark, you see,' she said quite sheepishly. 'I had a nightmare when I was a child. I was trapped in my room in pitch blackness. I thought I was in a prison, in my grave, locked away. But Dad came up to sort me out. It was a silly thing, really. Apparently, I had turned around in bed and was facing the wall. I thought there were four walls all around my bed.'

'You see,' said Harry, 'you still call him "Dad". Nothing can change that, Aster, nothing.'

'And it isn't going to,' she announced defiantly. 'Do you know, that night – it was the night he left – I heard the sea. The waves reached me right up there in my bedroom. It had never happened before, has never happened since. Gran and Grandpa always said it was ridiculous, that the sea could not be heard from Old Trellick. But that night, there was something on the air . . . something there. I heard it.'

'We'll go back to the cove,' Harry assured her. 'That will make you feel better. Get out of the city. So we can breathe again. Get back to Cornwall and sort this mess out once and for all.'

'But how can anything make me feel better?' she snapped. 'And I don't think I ever want to lay eyes on Old Trellick again.'

Harry checked his watch and got up to draw the brocaded gold curtains and shut out the London street lamps. He looked white with fatigue, his spark extinguished.

'It's nearly midnight,' he told her.

'Twelve hours ago I was in Camden, meeting my father, which was traumatic enough,' she said. 'But then, then he said that most awful thing . . . the poor man. He felt terrible. And it still does not make sense. None of it does.' Aster's voice meandered. 'There was something he said about me when I was born . . .' She drew her hand out from under the eiderdown to gesticulate and make her point. She counted on her fingers. 'They married in early September, I was born in late March. Something about me being premature, but then grandfather Bertie mentioned something too about when Dad was born and his mother died. She died, you know. God my head is a muddle, it's spinning so fast I feel sick.'

'Try to sleep, you must sleep,' said Harry.

'You go if you want to,' she said, her weary mind latching on to one fine and inextinguishable point: that Jack Fairling brought her up for four years. She *felt* she was his daughter. But Weston Penruth, with his limping gait and surly demeanour, invaded her thoughts again. She looked at Harry and his open, concerned face and she knew that she loved him. And then wondered how such a man as Weston could produce such a son.

'I don't deserve you,' she whispered.

'Utter rot!'

She blurted, 'But I can't marry my half-brother, can I?'

Harry came over and sat by her on the bed, despairingly, unable to counter her argument.

'You must sleep, my love.'

'But all I hear are voices, everyone's voices telling me things I don't want to hear.'

'You must stay strong. You're still going to meet your father tomorrow?' he asked. 'In Regent's Park?'

'Of course I am. Just try to stop me! You mean Jack, don't you?' Aster tried to laugh and reached for Harry on reflex. 'This is our beginning, Harry. We're not going to let all of this ruin it for us.'

'I will speak to my father,' he said. 'It's the only way to get to the bottom of this. I can't lose you, Aster, to a nasty rumour from years ago that no one seems to remember. I don't want to.'

He lay beside her and embraced her; his warm body enveloped her in a cradling, rocking motion. She held him close and her worries washed away from her, and tears of joy prickled her eyes. But as he kissed her neck, she suddenly cried out and pushed him away.

'Stop it. What will everyone say? This can't happen! You must go. Just go.'

Harry sat up, his face ghostly in the lamplight, visibly stung.

'I will be next door,' he said, resigned and slow with fatigue. 'I don't know what else to say to you. Goodnight.'

Aster lay back down in the lamplit room, her hands on her stomach, unmoving and stiff as if she was in her tomb, her face as dry as stone. She listened out for the odd late omnibus sweeping along the street outside. No tears came and the uneasy, fearful small hours began to creep painfully by.

Chapter Forty

Next morning, the rush-hour traffic was building along Regent Street. Aster lay on top of her bed, still dressed in the same clothes from yesterday. Although her body was cold, aching with shock, her mind was numb and mercifully empty. The voices had gone away.

She saw that Harry had not drawn the curtains fully and the morning light outside was dull and grey, a typical London skyline threatening rain.

'He's right,' she decided, whispering out loud to the silent gilded room. 'We simply can't lose each other to everyone's supposition and sketchy memories. I can't lose him to half-truths and people not being able to talk about things. It's just not good enough. Jack is my father. I know it. Something is telling me—'

With a startling surge of energy, she sat up abruptly and

reached for the Flower Book on the night stand. Kneeling up on the bed, with a sharp giggle of excitement, she pulled out the envelope that her father had given her and leafed through the book to find where the page had been ripped out: 20th June, 1914. She pulled the page from the envelope, scattering the last dust from the pressed bitter buttons and slotted the ragged torn edges together just as the telephone rang shrill and urgent, scolding her.

'Good morning, miss. This is the concierge. There are two visitors for you downstairs. A gentleman and a lady. I shall show them into the Rotunda Room.'

'My father?' she asked, but the concierge had put the telephone down.

He's very early, thought Aster. We were going to meet for morning coffee at the Pavilion, and we said eleven o'clock. Something must be wrong. And why would Cecelia be with him? Maybe grandfather Bertie has been taken ill? Or perhaps it is Bertie himself downstairs with Cecelia. Perhaps something is wrong with Dad . . .

She leapt up and dashed into her bathroom to wash her face and spray on cologne. She brushed her hair and left her room, clutching the Flower Book, not wishing to let it out of her sight. It was her talisman, her comfort. Her mother's voice.

Thank goodness I am already dressed, she thought with a wry smile, and knocked on Harry's door. Cocking her head to listen, she thought she could hear the shower. Darting back into her room, she quickly dashed off a note on Langham-headed paper to tell him that she had gone downstairs to meet her father if he'd like to join them.

The Rotunda Room was to her right as she exited the

lifts, its enormous curved bay window protruding at the side of the hotel onto Regent Street where the traffic rattled past. But here inside the room, all was peaceful and quiet, with a tinkling of china and a murmur of soft conversation. There was a bar, staffed by darting smart waiters in black, at present serving breakfast and morning coffee. A number of high-backed brocaded booths lined the resplendently panelled walls beneath an enormous twinkling chandelier. The thick carpet muffled Aster's footsteps and so the people who were expecting her did not hear her approach.

She stopped in the centre of the room. Weston Penruth, the country squire, was wearing brown. Doesn't he know the rules? she thought in irritation. Beside him, sipping delicately at a china cup, sat Kate, looking as fair and fragile as ever in her best cloche hat and velvet stole.

Aster was no longer scared of him. She was aware that she had paused, just for a fraction of a second, on her way across the Rotunda carpet, but she continued now, her blood rising along with a strange feeling of fatality, straight towards the booth.

Mr Penruth looked up and gave her a guarded look, his intense eyes edged with alarm that she was approaching at such a fierce pace.

He stood up and the china on the table rattled.

'Good morning Mr Penruth, good morning Kate,' clipped Aster, her cheeks burning but her voice steady and strong. Her hand, holding the Flower Book, was no longer shaking.

Kate said hello, her sweet smile showing lovely white teeth. Her corn-coloured hair looked like it had been newly bobbed. She was quite the grown-up young lady. At least she knew not to wear a tweed suit in town.

'Enough of the pleasantries, Miss Fairling,' Weston said, indicating that she should sit down.

Aster looked straight at him as she did so, not letting her outward poise slip for a second.

Weston began to speak before she had even settled in her seat. 'I've come here to stop this nonsense. Harry sent a wire, saying that you were engaged. Well, I'm here today to drag Harry back to Charlecote and put him in the navy. Anything to keep you two apart. This is not going to happen, so don't imagine for one minute that it will. I suggest you, Miss Fairling, stay here in London and wait for it all to blow over. I take it you have separate suites upstairs? I damn well hope so.'

Kate's cup landed hard in her saucer. 'Father, really! I thought we were coming here to celebrate their engagement and take Harry and Aster out for a lovely luncheon.' She turned her pale-blue eyes on Aster. 'I'm so sorry, I have no idea what my father is talking about.'

'Don't worry, Kate, Harry is not going into the navy, or anywhere,' Aster said evenly. 'Yes, indeed, Mr Penruth, we are engaged and we have come to London to visit with my father. In fact,' she glanced at her watch and shook her head, 'if I talk here with you for very much longer, I will be in danger of being late meeting him. And I wouldn't want to do that.'

'Your *father*? You mean Jack Fairling?' Weston puffed his chest out, his brown suit stretching a little at the buttons. 'You misunderstand, Miss Fairling. There is something I need to tell you. You and Harry must not marry . . .' He glanced around at the room, lowering his voice, his stern features collapsing suddenly with a beseeching look. 'Which is why I am here.'

Aster glanced at Kate, who sat immobile with confusion, her eyes darting aghast from her father and back again.

'Mr Penruth,' Aster insisted, 'I ask you not to go any further. Please, do not.'

'But this has to be made public. It's the only way to stop you two—'

Aster flinched as Kate suddenly cried out in desperation, 'Ah, here is Harry! I hope he can explain what on earth is going on.'

Harry approached the table gingerly, his face moving with confusion. From her note, she realised, he was expecting Jack Fairling to be sat with her in the Rotunda. The fact his own father was now glaring across the room at him made Harry wince. He joined them.

'Good morning, Father. This is very unexpected.'

Harry sat next to Aster and leant towards her. In a concerned whisper, he prompted, '*Your father?*'

She nearly laughed and whispered back, 'No, no, I know that's what I wrote in the note, but I didn't know our visitor was your father. Don't worry, I don't think he is my father.'

'This is all very lovely,' piped up Kate, clearly confused. 'But can someone please tell me what's going on?'

Weston growled, leaning his broad frame forward onto the table. 'This is something that should have been sorted out years ago before any of this got out of hand.' His finger stabbed the air in Aster and Harry's direction.

Acutely conscious of the trappings of polite society surrounding them, Aster kept her voice low and precise. 'I'd like to speak with Mr Penruth alone, please.'

'No, my children have to know the truth,' Weston snapped back. '*All* my children.'

Aster looked at Kate's innocent and trusting face and sighed, 'Very well; you see . . .'

Before she could catch her breath to continue, Weston once more launched his vitriol.

'Harry, son, you are to stop all this rot and return now with me. *Without* Miss Fairling.'

'Look here, Father,' he retorted. 'I am not leaving her side for a moment. Aster has been through a terrible, traumatic few days, and we need some peace and calm so we can gather our thoughts. And may I remind you we are in a public place.'

Weston glanced about, with a sarcastic grin. 'Very nice too. And may I remind you that you cannot marry your half-sister.'

Kate gasped and dipped her head in shock.

Aster put her hand on Kate's arm and turned to Weston, her thoughts turning over with such clear conviction as the truth settled and revealed itself to her.

'Weston, you are wrong.'

He turned his menacing face towards her in disbelief and she realised it was the first time she'd called him, rather preposterously, by his first name. Aster pushed the Flower Book across the table. It sat there in the centre and everyone stared at it, as if it was about to say something.

'I have it all here,' Aster said. 'This is my mother's journal. In it she tells me her secrets and her dreams from when she was a little girl. Right up to the moment she died.'

'What, her silly Flower Book? With all its country lore and fanciful rhymes. Such amateur poppycock. I told her as much.'

Aster ignored him. 'And you, Weston, were certainly not

371

her dream, and one of her secrets, written in here, around June 1914, explains that I am most certainly Jack's child. Nothing to do with you.'

'But don't you see,' Weston thundered, his face brick red and his eyes wide with affront. 'Violet and I were engaged, we . . . had relations.'

Aster did not flinch. She tapped her fingertips on the deep-green cover. 'That may be so. My mother is not here to confirm or deny. But, let me see . . . did you give her a crimson peony once, in March 1914?'

'Perhaps I did, perhaps I didn't. How am I supposed to remember that?' he blustered. 'Ah, yes, the peony amongst a bunch of hothouse beauties. She loved it.'

'No she didn't. The book says it all, or rather it doesn't. She pasted it in but she did not comment on it. It was ugly and inappropriate. She didn't love you. She loved my father. It's all in here.' Aster was tempted then to pick up the book and turn to the page, but stopped herself. It was her mother's book, her mother's privacy. She went on, 'There is also a humble little tansy plant she found by the Regent's Canal and that's all the evidence I need to convince me that you are not my father. I'm not going to say anything more about it, out of respect for her.'

'A tansy plant?' Weston was incredulous. 'That silly little weed?'

Aster went on regardless, 'Now, if you will excuse me, Harry and I are going to Regent's Park to meet my father. Good day to you both.'

Weston groaned and put his hands over his face. 'But you don't understand. I *did* love her.' His voice was thick, surrendering. 'I told her how sorry I was.'

The three of them waited in silence while Weston Penruth wept into his hands, choking back sobs and muffling his mouth. He ran his fingers through his thick hair, which was now as silvery as a badger's pelt, until at last collecting himself. After some moments, Harry passed him his handkerchief.

'Do you have something in your eye, Father?' he asked with irony.

'Come on, Father, you're being ridiculous,' said Kate briskly, ignoring the incredible sight of her father crumbling before her. 'If we get a move on we can catch the eleven oh nine and be back at Charlecote in time for tea.'

'I'll say goodbye, then,' said Weston, finally composed. He glanced down at the Flower Book still lying in the centre of the table and Aster watched a terrible sadness alter his face. The anger had disappeared, the fierce look in his eyes extinguished. Had he finally given up?

Aster watched him walk away across the thick carpet, his head bowed, the limp caused by his injured leg pronounced.

'How did he hurt his leg?' Aster asked.

Harry supposed that it had been during the war.

'But he didn't go to war, did he?' she hazarded.

'It must have happened somewhere on the farm, then.'

'Ah, something Dad said, about attacking him during the harvest . . .' Aster pondered. 'Would you stall them for me?' she said to Harry. 'I will be five minutes.'

She hurried out of the Rotunda Room and across the vestibule. Thankfully, the lift was there and the pageboy could take her straight up to her floor. In her room, she grabbed the grainy old photograph, snapped it out of its frame and raced back down the stairs.

Harry was standing in the marble-floored reception with Kate, who was heroically calm and staid in the face of it all.

'Where is he?' Aster asked, a little out of breath.

'Waiting outside in the cab. I've never seen him so beaten,' said Harry.

'You're the lucky one,' Kate observed to Harry. 'I have to travel all the way back to Cornwall with him in that condition.'

Harry said, 'I was just telling Kate about Jack's exhibition. It really should not be missed. But perhaps another time.'

Aster agreed. 'Yes, perhaps.' She handed the photograph to Kate. 'Please give this to your father.'

Kate glanced down, puzzled. 'Oh, it's us. Three little children on the harvest wagon. Well I never!'

'He can take it home with him,' said Aster. 'I think it is something he desperately needs. He just does not realise it yet.'

Chapter Forty-One

The gloomy morning rain had blown itself away and left London basking under a benign summer sky. Along the Outer Circle, the white mansions were resplendent in the sunshine, positively sparkling with elegance and discreet wealth, and the huge trees in the park were vigorous and green, showering captured drops of rain into the air.

Aster and Harry walked among them, heading for Queen Mary's Rose Garden. Beyond was the Pavilion where her father would be waiting.

'Let's take a short cut through the roses,' said Harry. 'Look, I've picked up an early copy of the newspaper. The review is in here.'

'Oh, let me see.' Aster stopped among the flowerbeds and Harry found the page for her.

'The reporter – remember him? – in the black suit,' he

said. 'He must have spoken to Bertie and Cecelia. Got a very nice quote from them. Here it is.'

The rain had intensified the scent of the roses and it lifted like a stupefying vapour around them. The headline was under the paper's 'Saturday Review' banner. Aster read: '*Jack P. Fairling: A Retrospective*. A message of love from the trenches.'

'How wonderful . . .' she uttered, her eyes darting passionately over the typeset columns. The picture they'd used was the sketch of her as a three-year-old child. Her own eyes gazed solemnly out of the page at her. 'How serious I look,' she said, her words choking her. 'Oh, I can't read it now. Let Dad read it first. After all, it's all about him.'

Her father was waiting outside the Pavilion, wearing a particularly perky trilby and a peacock blue silk scarf around his chin,

'I can be as flamboyant as I like with these scarves,' he said, greeting them with his crooked smile. 'I have a whole wardrobe of them.'

As Harry and Jack shook hands, Aster peered into the tea room. 'It's rather busy in there. We'll never get a table.'

'Then let's take a stroll first,' said Jack. 'The roses are looking exceptionally beautiful today.'

'Well, we have had a lot of rain,' observed Harry rather blandly, and they laughed.

They walked back to the rose garden. The seat under the bower was empty. Exhaling a lonely sigh, Jack sat down amid the colony of wild roses, their wide pretty faces populated by bees in the sunshine.

'This is where she was sitting, under this canopy,' he remembered, rearranging his scarf. 'I was over there. I first saw her walking over the grass. She looked so angry and bewildered and beautiful. She came and rested here – just for a moment or two – and I didn't miss my chance. She was done in a matter of minutes. Perfect.' He paused and looked up at the sky. 'I thought I'd never see her again.'

'And that became *Violet in the Daytime*?' Aster asked.

'The start of it all,' said Jack.

'Hotch up a bit, Dad.' She sat down next to him, opened her bag and drew out the Flower Book. 'You know that in the last few months or so, I've been walking through a storm. Finding out about you, coming to London with Harry. Meeting you. Was it really only yesterday? But this has been my talisman,' she tapped the book. 'It's like she's speaking to me.'

Her father's gaze was fixed steadfastly on the roses that gathered all around them in every colour imaginable.

'We both wanted to tell you, together,' Aster went on. 'Harry and I, we can be married. It's all in here. Somehow, in her mystifying and playful way, Mama has revealed her secret.'

'Are you sure?'

'Yes. Mama was sure.'

'And this means that you and I, that you're my . . . ?'

Aster looked at her father and could not speak. She nodded, her face beaming, tears pooling on her cheeks.

'I'm sorry I ever doubted it,' Jack said, his voice a whisper. 'You see my reason was gone, my mind tricking me. I was lost. Coming out of the war . . .'

'You've no need to explain. Mama explains it. Find the missing page, I've fitted it in the right place. It will make sense, after a fashion.' Aster glanced up at Harry. 'We're going to go now, leave you to it. We'll see you tomorrow?'

She leant down and kissed her father on his hollowed-out ruined cheek.

Jack held the book in trembling hands. He turned it over, stared at the back, caressing the tight, battered green leather and ran his fingers across the pages. He opened it.

'Dad, you're supposed to start at the beginning of the book,' said Aster, laughing.

'I'm curious about the last entry. You see, I want to know what she was thinking right up to the end when . . . Ah, I see.'

'That was me,' said Aster. 'I pasted in those rather limp and sorry-looking daisies on the last page. I've dated it July 1919. It's my rather bad four-year-old handwriting, look. But I'm so sorry, I simply don't remember doing it.'

Jack's face brightened with emotion. 'She never let me read her Flower Book, ever,' he muttered. 'She was so damn secretive sometimes. There were times I could not read her. All I should have done was sneak a look now and again,' he laughed. 'If she could see me now with it, she'd be so cross!'

'We'll see you tomorrow, Dad,' said Aster.

She linked arms with Harry and they said their goodbyes, making their way along the snug pathways through the roses. Their steps were light and their pace was swift, the start of a journey.

'The daisies at the back, so that was you?' remarked Harry. 'That reminds me – the title of that sketch of you as a little girl on your father's exhibition poster. *Hope*. That's what aster means, doesn't it? Asters, or daisies, stand for hope.'

Aster tightened her grip on Harry's arm as her mind

sparked with a strange sense of a circle turning, completing itself inside her. Her future with him opened before her, beckoning her on.

'We need to transport Starbright and Sparrow to Kent as soon as possible,' she said, looking up at Harry as they fell into step. 'We can't possibly leave them behind. They'll love it down there, won't they? I'm so glad we'll still be near the sea. I'm going to write to Gran and Grandpa Prideaux tonight, to ask if they can make all the arrangements.'

'I jolly well hope they will make the effort and sort it all out,' said Harry, amused. 'After all the trouble they've caused you it's the least they can do.'

Aster's giggle chimed with Harry's laughter and she caught the lightest, sweetest breath of the roses as she brushed past them. She glanced back to see her father sitting quite still at the centre of it all, surrounded by cascading colour that shifted and blurred as the breeze blew. He unwrapped the scarf from his ravaged face so that he, too, could breathe more deeply on the scented air.

She watched him open the Flower Book, turn to the first page and begin.

Epilogue

One year later
Kent, 1937

Aster watched from the upstairs window as cloud shadows chased across hop gardens and orchards, patchworked in gold and green. Starbright and Sparrow shook their manes in the sunshine, wading through the emerald pasture, pricking their ears to Harry's whistle as he worked out in the garden. Such a different land, such a different world here, Aster thought, compared to the miniature wildness of Cornwall. So ordered, serene and secluded. There was an exquisite peace in the air, with only the occasional little plane buzzing out of the airfield at Manston on the far horizon. And beyond there, of course, the sea.

The breeze through the window ruffled the letter in her hand. Her father's despair, his nightmares, ebbed and flowed with crushing inevitability, he wrote. Sometimes, he struggled to contemplate the unthinkable: that Violet had been dead for almost twenty years. But her enduring spirit, his muse, remained in his darkness. He wrote: *I paint and I paint!*

Aster and Harry must promise to travel to London to view his new exhibition, he said. He also welcomed their own exciting news and would come down to Kent to visit before the summer was out. But that wasn't all . . .

Aster reached back inside the envelope and pulled out another piece of paper. It was the drawing, her father explained, that he'd chanced upon recently in an old sketchbook, dashed off, he said, towards the end of war in a Flanders trench.

On the paper, soft with age, tatty and stained, was the drawing of a single crimson flower, clinging precariously in the mud, gasping and vulnerable, its petals still blood-red despite time having faded the lines and shading. And beside it, so many years before, he had written:

Darling Violet, Here I am hemmed in by wasteland, walking with death at my shoulder, but I found this flower growing, living, one bright moment in hell and it reminded me of you – for the thought of you conquers my fear of dying . . . and I will get through this. I, too, will live.

Jack did not send the drawing to Violet, for the next day his jaw was blown off by a German shell.

Aster stood by the window, staring at the sketch as it first swam out of focus and then re-emerged as her tears fell and soaked it.

A memory nudged her: lying in her bed at Old Trellick. It was a late-summer night and, incredibly, she could hear the whispering of the sea. Suddenly, again, even though it had been impossible then and was impossible now, the sound of waves filled the room, swaying her gently, moving in a cradling embrace.

Aster reached for the Flower Book on its shelf and slipped her father's sketch inside the back cover. It will become, she decided, the beginning of a new Flower Book.

As she slid the journal onto its shelf, the silent child inside her kicked her twice and she smiled, soothing it, telling it to hush, stroking her fingertips over her stomach.

'If you are a boy,' she told the baby, 'I will call you Edward. Because a long time ago, your daddy's mama once loved a man called Eddie.'

Aster glanced again out of the window at the sublime peace of the Garden of England.

'And if you are a girl, I will call you Poppy.'

Acknowledgements

A walk across Regent's Park, a stroll down Parkway in Camden, and getting lost in the woods at Lanwarnick, near Polperro, Cornwall, have all contributed to the writing of this novel.

The Imperial War Museum provided me, as always, with the facts and the background to this traumatic time, and military historian Iain McHenry put it all into vivid reality on a battlefield tour of Ypres and the Somme. I found inspiration at two particularly memorable places: Sanctuary Wood Museum Hill 62, near Ypres, Belgium, and Museum Historial de la Grande Guerre, Péronne, France. Also from the books: *Forgotten Voices of the Great War* by Max Arthur, *The Great Silence* by Juliet Nicolson and *Testament of Youth* by Vera Brittain.

Thank you to my father Gerry for lending me his Book of Wild Flowers and for passing on to me his love, knowledge and appreciation of the countryside.

And to James: thank you for the epilogue.